KU-142-480

Other Novels and Novellas

Many of these titles are also available as abridged and unabridged audiobooks.
Order the full range of Horus Heresy novels and audiobooks from
blacklibrary.com

THE HORUS HERESY®

James Swallow

THE BURIED DAGGER

Doom of the Death Guard

BLACK LIBRARY

A BLACK LIBRARY PUBLICATION

Hardback edition published in 2019.
This edition published in Great Britain in 2019.
Black Library,
Games Workshop Ltd.,
Willow Road,
Nottingham,
NG7 2WS, UK.

10 9 8 7 6 5 4 3 2 1

Produced by Games Workshop in Nottingham.
Cover illustration by Neil Roberts.

A CIP record for this book is available from the British Library.

ISBN 13: 978-1-78193-970-3

See Black Library on the internet at
blacklibrary.com

Find out more about Games Workshop
and the worlds of Warhammer 40,000 at
games-workshop.com

Printed and bound by CPI Group (UK) Ltd, Croydon, CR0 4YY

For Lindsey and Marc, with thanks.

THE HORUS HERESY®

It is a time of legend.

The galaxy is in flames. The Emperor's glorious vision for humanity is in ruins. His favoured son, Horus, has turned from his father's light and embraced Chaos.

His armies, the mighty and redoubtable Space Marines, are locked in a brutal civil war. Once, these ultimate warriors fought side by side as brothers, protecting the galaxy and bringing mankind back into the Emperor's light.
Now they are divided.

Some remain loyal to the Emperor, whilst others have sided with the Warmaster. Pre-eminent amongst them, the leaders of their thousands-strong Legions are the primarchs. Magnificent, superhuman beings, they are the crowning achievement of the Emperor's genetic science. Thrust into battle against one another, victory is uncertain for either side.

Worlds are burning. At Isstvan V, Horus dealt a vicious blow and three loyal Legions were all but destroyed. War was begun, a conflict that will engulf all mankind in fire. Treachery and betrayal have usurped honour and nobility. Assassins lurk in every shadow. Armies are gathering.
All must choose a side or die.

Horus musters his armada, Terra itself the object of his wrath. Seated upon the Golden Throne, the Emperor waits for his wayward son to return. But his true enemy is Chaos, a primordial force that seeks to enslave mankind to its capricious whims.

The screams of the innocent, the pleas of the righteous resound to the cruel laughter of Dark Gods. Suffering and damnation await all should the Emperor fail
and the war be lost.

The age of knowledge and enlightenment has ended.
The Age of Darkness has begun.

~ DRAMATIS PERSONAE ~

The XIV Legion, 'Death Guard'

MORTARION	Primarch
CAIPHA MORARG	Equerry to the primarch
CALAS TYPHON	First Captain, commander of the *Terminus Est*
HADRABULUS VIOSS	Grave Warden
GREMUS KALGARO	Captain, commander of the *Endurance*
SEROB KARGUL	Captain, commander of the *Malefic*
GIDEOUS KRALL	Captain, commander of the *Ceaseless Advance*
MALEK VOS	Captain, commander of the *Balefire*
ZADAL CROSIUS	Apothecary
RAHEB ZURRIEQ	Lieutenant
HUNDA SKORVALL	'The Bitterblood', warrior and legionary
DURAL RASK	Master of Ordnance
KAHGOR LOTHSUL	Warrior and legionary
MORGAX MURNAU	Warrior and legionary
JASUN HAZNIR	Warrior and legionary
THOMEN AHRAX	Warrior

Knights-Errant

NATHANIEL GARRO	Agentia Primus, former battle-captain of the Death Guard

TYLOS RUBIO	Former Codicier and legionary of the Ultramarines
VARDAS ISON	Former Codicier and legionary of the Blood Angels
GARVIEL LOKEN	Former captain of the Luna Wolves
MACER VARREN	Former captain of the World Eaters
HELIG GALLOR	Former legionary of the Death Guard

Those Who Serve the Will of the Imperium

MALCADOR	Sigillite and Regent of Terra
AEL WYNTOR	Confidante of the Sigillite
MALIDA JYDASIAN	Witchseeker, Thunder Vane cadre
TELEDION BRELL	Scientician, Chosen of Malcador

The Nine Who Are Named

KOIOS	[++*identity redacted*++]
SATRE	[++*identity redacted*++]
IANIUS	[++*identity redacted*++]
YOTUN	[++*identity redacted*++]
IAPTO	[++*identity redacted*++]
OGEN	[++*identity redacted*++]
KHYRON	[++*identity redacted*++]
EPITHEMIUS	[++*identity redacted*++]
CRIUS	[++*identity redacted*++]

Others

| EUPHRATI KEELER | Saint |

'This is where the end begins.'

– *We Have Always Hated*
(Insurrectionist propaganda leaflet, author unknown)
[M31]

'After walking among titans, I am all the more humble for it. But I have seen the true faces of those who claim purchase on their souls, and it leaves me enraged.'

– attributed to the remembrancer Ignace Karkasy
[M31]

INTERVAL I

Ante Mortem

[The planet Ynyx; now]

THE REAPER OF Men had grown weary of the screaming.

The cries from a million throats, the ceaseless cacophony of it, now fatigued him. He had long since become jaded with the pleas of those he killed, be they babbling streams of words as the doomed begged for pity, the foolish and furious curses of the fatally enraged or the endless, irritating wail of those who wept brokenly.

There was, at least, a small mercy to be had here on the surface of Ynyx. The monstrously poisonous atmosphere of the manufactory planet meant that every soul who toiled upon the world had no mouth with which to cry out. From the instant of their birth, the machines of the magos biologis sealed shut the apertures upon the faces of the human populace, organo-printing protective membrane masks over lips and nostrils. The workers were implanted with grilles and nutrient intakes, along with countless chem shunts and protective grafts, these enhancements and alterations sufficient to make them immune to the toxic fog that belched continuously from the core of the mineral-rich world. The people of Ynyx could only communicate via vox transmission, their voices muted in all other senses, and so it was that the Reaper of Men could walk in silence among them if he simply tuned them out.

The only sound was the rumble of the planet's breath, forcing its way up through geothermal vents in the black landscape all around him, that and the steady crunch of brittle glass beneath his heavy plasteel boots. Scattered all over the battlefield, more numerous than the ragged remnants of dead bodies from the pre-invasion shelling, were endless numbers of empty cylindrical vials. Drug ampoules by the thousand, discarded by the Ynyxian defenders. Whatever effect they had brought – blissful oblivion, docility or merely resistance against the swirling churn of atmospheric contaminants – it counted for nothing. This world's populace would be dead by nightfall, and it would not matter.

The cold ember of his familiar, obdurate resentment pushed him forward, one heavy and echoing step after the other, over the oily ebon sand towards the great citadel that was his objective. At the edges of his supremely genhanced vision, the Reaper of Men was aware of his praetorians marching in lockstep with him, each at a distance of seven by seven paces, all carrying their weapons across their chests in a blank mirror of his own aspect.

Held at rest against one of his shoulders was a skeletal scythe that was sooty with dried blood and tainted fluids. His other gauntleted hand wandered often to the heavy, drum-like shape of a unique, master-crafted energy gun hanging at his hip. Like the warrior himself, everything about his weapons was beyond human scale, built for the grasp of giants and demigods. Even his chosen guard, huge as they were, could not match his scale. Only two beings had ever stood taller than the Reaper of Men; the first had died at the hands of the second. *As to the fate of the second...*

In time, that question would be answered. The old, bitter ember stirred anew at the thought, but the giant stifled it before it could grow. Such things were a distraction. His mind was supposed to be here, at the march through Ynyx's polluted dusk, not picking at this deep-rooted, forever unhealed wound. There would be time enough to nurse his lingering hate in the days ahead.

He cast a glance over his shoulder plates. Out past his hooded bodyguards, marching in lines behind them, came the body of his war band. Battle-captains and commanders, the striding forms of Dreadnoughts and Terminators, and rank after rank of legionaries in grimy, slate-coloured armour. He advanced with them at his heels, for they would never dare to march into battle without him at their head, even on as pitiful a killing ground as this one.

His Legion. His Death Guard. His unbroken blades.

They were all that occupied him now. His sons were the only thing he saw clearly, as the haze of the great insurrection led by his brother seemed to coil ever thicker around every deed, every thought in mind of the Reaper of Men. With his warriors, in battle, he came closest to *clarity* – or something like it.

He marched on, into the twilight and towards the great shadow cast by the citadel. The tallest structure for kilometres in every direction, it protruded from a great axial canyon that ringed the upper hemisphere of Ynyx. Thousands of such depthless chasms fractured the planet's surface, vanishing into hellish pits kilometres deep where toxic smoke exhaled from the roiling core. The ashen matter vomited up from below was the source of the world's fortune, laden with rare and precious heavy metallic elements that the manufactora of the Imperium sucked in and reprocessed. The refinery engines – lumbering city-sized arachnids of tarnished brass and grey iron – sat atop the richest of the vents for decades at a time, draining them dry before moving on to fresh pastures.

Few places on Ynyx had any permanence except the great citadel, built on the ancient site of the planet's first colony landing. Formed of sapphire-dark stone dragged up from the abyssal depths, it was both palace and monument. The blocky, brutalist architecture of its design was as stark as a grave marker, its mere presence acting as a statement to the universe beyond. *We have built in this unliveable place and ripped out the riches at its heart,* said the citadel. *We have done this in the name of the Emperor and Terra.*

The Reaper of Men had his orders to cast it down, of course, but Mortarion would do so more because he *wanted* to. Because to do so would be to destroy one more possession belonging to his absent father, and in the act, find a few grains of satisfaction.

Movement at the edge of his helm's auto-senses brought the primarch of the XIV Legion back to the moment, and he looked in the direction of the alert icon. Curious, he stepped off the line and wandered towards an impact crater blasted into the dense, clumped basalt sand. Behind him, he heard the clatter of a thousand troops halting, but he paid it no mind.

In the crater there were three humans who against all odds were still alive. Ynyxians, and not soldiers but civilians. Their physical alterations meant it was difficult for Mortarion to tell which of the genders they fell into or how old they were. Each wore the hood and eye-mask typical of their people, the feed tubules of their sealed mouths coiled in bunches against spoiled nutri-feed packs they carried around their necks.

They were so very afraid of him. He imagined that he could taste the odour of it in the ashen air. Mortarion had deliberately left his breath filters open wide so that he could drink in the noxious atmosphere of the spoiled world, and now he took in a great gale of it, feeling the subtle burn of the pollutants as they attempted to scar his mighty lungs. Unprotected, the weak bodily tissues of these humans would have melted to slurry before they could fully inhale, but for the Reaper of Men, the lethal air of Ynyx was no distraction.

He watched them, looking through the lenses of his helm, searching their faces for an understanding that would never emerge. It was a fruitless endeavour; these pitiful creatures were no different from the others. No matter how many he found on whatever planets, none of them could see past the fear. That same terror, buoyed up by the same hate simmering away just below it. They would never know him. They could not.

In those desperate, beseeching faces, he saw something familiar – the stirrings of a memory recalled by similarity. The Reaper of Men quickly smothered the moment, irritated by the conceit of it.

Mortarion moved, letting the action happen of its own accord. His free hand drew the heavy energy weapon from its holster, and the device reacted, powering up the moment its gene-lock registered his touch. The *Lantern*, as the gun had been named, turned towards the figures cowering in the pit. They reacted, silently raising their hands in a gesture of warding. If they were screaming, he did not hear it.

A brief pulse of searing white light erased them from existence, their bodies becoming a faint trace of vapour in the moment of discharge. The *Lantern*'s shrieking power atomised the survivors and turned the surface layer of the crater into a bowl of fused fulgurite. He turned and marched away, leaving the newly formed glass crackling and hissing as it cooled.

What he had done for them was a mercy, a quick death. He knew all the kinds of dying, and to end by the *Lantern*'s flame was a better way than many. Mortarion had given them a gift.

He forgot the humans as he marched on, the image of them slipping away as his thoughts returned to more martial matters. The primarch allowed his gaze to rise along the line of the darkened, windowless citadel, and the questions that had been nagging at him since the Death Guard arrived on Ynyx returned.

Why did Horus send me here?

Mortarion drew in another deep, tainted breath. There was little of tactical value to the manufactory world and the storehouse moons that orbited it, and less still to the other spheres of rock that circled the watery white light of Ynyx's sun. The Death Guard had found the chem-loaded combat helots who defended the planet to be a perfunctory and unchallenging foe, rolling over their positions with the Legion's signature tactic of inexorable advance. Tearing this planet from the control of the Imperium and denying it to the Emperor was a task that could have been accomplished by a handful of battle cruisers and lesser companies. The vast force and numbers that the Warmaster had bid Mortarion to bring to Ynyx was nothing short of overkill.

It vexed the Reaper of Men to be ignorant of Horus' true reasoning, and in the void where answers ran out, he was wont to fill the gap with suspicion.

Mortarion knew of Horus' dalliances with the beings of the warp, the things that called themselves the Ruinous Powers. These monstrous intelligences craved gifts of death and bloodletting, and while Mortarion did not speak openly of it, he was aware that among his rebellious brothers there were some who were all too eager to appease them. Worlds burned in mass sacrifices, and arcane horrors were committed as if such acts could court the favour of these... *things*.

He wondered, had Horus sent the Death Guard to exterminate the population of Ynyx as part of such a bargain?

Am I simply his tool in this?

Behind his breath mask, Mortarion's pallid lips twisted in a grimace. Once, it would have been nigh-impossible for the primarch to think ill of Horus Lupercal. Now, his corrosive distrust had eaten away at that certainty. And perhaps that was fated. Over countless years and hard-won, bitter experience, the Reaper of Men had learned that in the end, he could only completely trust his own counsel.

The more he dwelt on the possibility, the more it seemed to grow to fit the facts. Mortarion himself had dared to peer into the lore of these warp-beings, the creatures that some named *daemons*.

In the skies above the ruins of glorious Terathalion, he had looked into the face of such a monster for the first time, named it and interrogated it, for what little that had been worth. That had been the turning point, he reflected, the moment when he could no longer dismiss these aberrations out of hand.

The primarch's long-dead foster father – the corrupted and callous being who had named him, the one he thought of when that notion came to mind – had taught him many lessons as he grew to adulthood, not least of which was the value of knowledge as well as endurance.

If you know the truth of something, then you can destroy it, his foster father had said. *And that is all you need to hold true power.*

Mortarion was learning a new truth, page by page, step by step, scroll by scroll. The witchery and sorcerous cankers he hated so much were widespread in this new and changed war, employed openly by Horus, that arrogant braggart Magnus and the rest of them. He detested the psykers and the warp-things with such an inchoate fury that it was impossible for him to find words to encompass the emotion, and he loathed his brother primarchs for lowering themselves to have congress with such creatures.

But Mortarion was a child of blighted Barbarus, and no sons and daughters of that death world lived long enough to walk erect if they were not pragmatists. Hate was all well and good, but it could not outdo obstinate reality. Hate alone did not make walls fall. And so, in the space between his repugnance for things tainted by the immaterium's gelid hand and his need to win the war inside his own soul, Mortarion had grudgingly found a place to accommodate these horrors.

One of them, in particular, that wore the face of an old friend.

Mortarion paused once again as he entered the remains of a rubble-strewn plaza before the citadel, and his thoughts returned to his grand shuttle, moored a few kilometres away in the blasted landing zone where the Legion's invasion force had made planetfall. The vessel, a war-barge named *Greenheart*, was a segment of his flagship that could operate as an autonomous command-and-control nexus if the mission required it. It could be parked in orbit and set to direct bombardments or pacifications, hard-landed in target zones or, as in this day's circumstances, used to light the way towards a decapitation strike.

Greenheart carried cannons more powerful than most ships its size, volkite tech and displacer guns that could batter cities, but Mortarion rarely used them. His thoughts held not on the potential of those devices, but on the power of the weapon chained up in a stasis-null cage on the barge's lower decks.

Even now, the primarch was uncertain that he had made the right

call in bringing the caged beast with him, wondering if it would have
been more prudent to leave the thing in the dungeons of his flagship,
the *Endurance*.

It had *begged*, in the end. Begged him to take it along, begged Mortarion to drop it from the sky and let it eat all life it found on Ynyx,
just as it had done so well during the battle for Molech.

'*Let me serve you,*' it said, in a grotesque parody of the warrior-son
Mortarion had once known. '*Let me kill them for you, gene-father.*'

He refused, of course. That would have been too easy. What value
would there have been to bring his Legion here, only to let the daemon with the face of Ignatius Grulgor do the deed for them?

Was that part of the plan? A manoeuvre to push Mortarion closer to
the path laid out by the Ruinous Powers?

The creature, twice dead and resurrected by his primarch's own hand,
was a weapon unlike any the Death Guard had ever employed, even
at the height of their powers in toxin warfare. Wherever it walked, life
turned to blackened ruin and disease. *A tempting dagger to wield*, Mortarion told himself. *Far too tempting.*

Perhaps, when this day was done, he might abandon the daemon
with Grulgor's face on this cracked and broken world. Perhaps he
might gather the papers and scrolls, every pict-slate and data crystal
containing the lore of these warp-things, and pour them into the abyss
of Ynyx's deepest chasm. Be rid of the ideal of them and fight on to
Terra as he was meant to.

We could return to the purity of warfare, he told himself. *As the inexorable, unstoppable force that makes the galaxy tremble to hear our approach.*

But even as the possibility crossed his thoughts, Mortarion knew it
was already being betrayed. Pragmatism did not flinch from using the
most horrific of tools, even if the abhorrence of such works was great.
The ends justified the means, and there would eventually come a day
when such tools were no longer needed.

Then, they would not merely be *discarded*. They would be expunged
from existence.

'My lord?' The voice did not come over the vox-network, but was instead carried by the thick, foetid air.

The Reaper of Men turned and with a nod from his tarnished helm, his Deathshroud praetorians parted to allow a lone figure in battle-plate to approach him.

The primarch's equerry inclined his head as a wary salute and paused, eyeing the citadel tower.

'Speak,' rasped Mortarion.

'The enemy appear in no rush to meet us.' Caipha Morarg gestured towards the great obelisk. 'Auspex readings show no visible entrances around the lower level of the citadel, and no signs of enemy activity. I would ask, lord, how you would have us proceed.'

'You are mistaken,' he told the legionary. 'They are here. They are watching us.' As the hoarse words left his mouth, Mortarion took a step further into the empty plaza, and deliberately triggered the ambush he knew was waiting for them.

All around, the fractured flagstones and the clogged black sand ranging beyond them trembled and shook underfoot. Clawed fingers sheathed in polycarbonate burst forth like the shoots of obscene plants seeking sunlight, and human bodies shelled by carapace armour and deep-pressure mining rigs erupted from where they had been buried. The last battalions of Ynyx's defenders had willingly allowed themselves to be interred beneath the metallic sands so that they might spring this trap upon the Death Guard.

What foolish ideal do they cling to? Mortarion gave a grave shake of the head. *Did they actually believe I would not intuit their plans? Do they think they have a chance?*

He had no need to give the order to fire. His legionaries were already killing, the rancid air vibrating with the smacking concussion of bolter fire. At his side, Morarg used his pistol to behead a human in a mining exo-frame, blasting flesh and skull into crimson slurry through the heavy rad-plates of the machine the attacker wore like an over-suit. Spinning drills and whirling cutters buzzed and clattered as the mechanism stumbled on a few more steps, sporadic neural impulses from the dead man within still pushing it forward.

Mortarion gave it a desultory backhand blow with the flat of *Silence*'s blade, his towering scythe flashing briefly in the bleak daylight. The exo-frame cannoned away under the force of the impact, ricocheting off the high outer wall of the citadel. It sank to the flagstones in a sizzling heap, leaving inky marks on the rock.

He ignored the storm of bolter fire and clashing metal at his back and marched on, meeting nothing he considered to be resistance as he crossed the last few metres to the wall. Surrounding him, his Death-shroud wove shapes in the air as their blades cleaved any of the Ynyxian troopers who dared to stray into range. Emerald-hued lances of fire rippled from flame projectors mounted on their gauntlets, as power-ful chem-munitions discharged into the mass of the enemy ambushers and melted them where they stood.

Morarg trailed at the primarch's heels, his helmet bobbing as he looked to and fro. They reached the foot of the impregnable citadel, and if there had ever been an entrance to the tower here, it had been sealed away so cleanly that the rock appeared to be carved from a sin-gle gigantic piece of obsidian.

'There is no way in...' muttered the equerry.

'Patience, Caipha,' admonished Mortarion, reaching up to detach a handful of globe-like censers from a bandolier that hung across the brass-and-steel expanse of his chest-plate. Each of the orbs was drilled with thousands of holes, and within alchemical philtres and fluids of great potency nestled in permeable sacs.

Mortarion brought the cluster of globes up to the breath mask that covered the lower part of his gaunt, pallid features, and rolled them in his long fingers, stirring the volatiles within. Wisps of thin white smoke issued from the pits in their surfaces, and he inhaled them, savour-ing the lethal bite of the chemicals. Then, with a flick of his wrist, the Reaper of Men hurled the orbs at the wall of the citadel and watched them shatter against the stone.

The hyperacidic fluids within spattered across the black rock, instantly softening the surface into something waxy and frangible. Mortarion counted silently to seven and struck the weakened wall with the heavy pommel at the base of *Silence*'s shaft. The stone cracked like glass. He hit it again and again, until the blow had torn open a ragged gash large enough for two Dreadnoughts to walk through abreast.

'Follow,' growled Mortarion, and he advanced once more, his pace as careful and as steady as it had been during the march from the landing zone.

MORARG KNEW WELL enough to stay clear of the arc of *Silence*'s wicked reach, remaining near to his primarch but beyond the singing silver streaks of Mortarion's murderous scythe. They plunged through the mass of common troopers crammed into the main atrium of the citadel and the Reaper of Men moved among them with an almost machine-like action, cutting them down in their hundreds with each back-and-forth sweep of the mighty sickle blade.

Morarg busied himself with killing any who survived the kiss of *Silence*'s edge, but he had sparse trade. Such was Mortarion's unflinching aim and dogged advance that barely a handful of souls did not immediately die from contact with him, and those that endured the first blow did not live long. Meanwhile, the equerry and the Deathshroud mopped up whatever forces tried to flank them from the echoing arcades along the sides of the atrium, blasting them apart against the spindly, fluted columns that held up the vaulted roof far above.

Pulses of laser fire spat down in a crimson rain from balconies and glassed-in galleries hundreds of metres overhead, drawing his attention. Morarg fired back, then barked out orders to the Death Guard line legionaries pouring in through the breach their liege lord had made. He blink-clicked target icons to the vision blocks of the squad commanders and they answered by ranging their guns up. A screaming salvo of concentrated firepower obliterated the platforms where the

Ynyx las-sniper battalion was concealed, and the bodies of the sharp-
shooters came raining down around him to crack against the marble
floor, along with shattered bricks and shards of crystalflex.

The *Lantern*'s distinctive song keened its banshee wail, and Morarg
picked his way through the dead to where Mortarion stood. The Reaper
of Men used the energy weapon to burn off the thick hinges of a huge
brass hatch set in a raised dais. As the metal turned molten and drooled
away, the door slumped and slid back to reveal a descending passage.
Searing, fume-laden air gushed out.

'We go down,' said the primarch. 'The day's work ends below.'

Morarg nodded, and turned back to the warriors behind him. 'Secure
the building and terminate all remaining targets!' He paused, then
turned back to Mortarion. 'My lord, do you wish to–?'

But the Reaper of Men had not waited, and was already descending. His seven Deathshroud fell into formation behind and followed.
Morarg nodded to himself, then went on.

'Keep me apprised of any developments,' he said into the vox-net,
knowing that his orders would be relayed to *Greenheart* and from there
to the Death Guard fleet in orbit. 'Lord Mortarion wishes to conclude
the battle by his own hand.'

Morarg took a moment to reload the sickle magazine in his bolter
and jogged down the wide stairwell in the wake of the primarch's praetorians. He suspected his presence would not be needed in the fight to
come, but he had been in this circumstance before, reduced to standing back and acting as witness to the unchained maelstrom that was
Mortarion's cold wrath. If that was to be his function today, then so
be it. He would take pride in the deed.

Caipha Morarg was a Pale Son, a Death Guard born of stock from
the Legion's home world of Barbarus and not, as some were, sired
by tribes from Terra. For many among the brotherhood there would
always be a schism, a rivalry in place between the 'original' warriors
of the XIV Legion – the ones who had been known as the Dusk Raid-
ers, who had come to Barbarus when the Emperor arrived there to find

His lost son – and the common men whom Mortarion had uplifted from his ragged Death Guard into the Legion's number, and in whose honour it had been renamed.

The memories of that auspicious day were hazy but they still existed in the equerry's distant recall. He cut off the recollection, lest he lose his focus in a moment of reverie, and kept his attention on the descent.

Ahead, gunfire and screaming sounded off the curved walls of the wide stairwell as Mortarion and his personal guard dispatched all those who were too slow to flee the reach of their manreapers. Their pace did not slow as they went.

The unspeaking Deathshroud mimicked the primarch in some aspects, not just with the design of their modified Terminator armour and the war-scythes they wielded, but with their shadowed reaper's hoods, dark cloaks and the heavy plasteel helmets that covered their faces and aped the impassive aspect of Mortarion's own portcullis mask. The Deathshroud never uttered a word, communicating only through battle-sign or audial break codes on the rare occasions they were required to transmit a message via vox. There were always seven of them at the primarch's hand, never straying more than seven by seven paces from his side at all times. The repeated number was said to be an auspicious one, an old belief dating back to before the seeding of human colonies on Barbarus, but it had lost its superstitious taint over the years and was now seen as a simple tactical nicety.

Morarg had never given it much thought, at least not until recent times. Some of the warriors he conversed with in the Davinite Lodges talked about the number with reverence; they spoke of the power of such symbols and how they could affect things in the real world. The equerry found these notions intriguing, but little more. He was, and always had been, a man of uncomplicated paths. The numinous and the uncanny were anathema to him, an ingrained reaction born of a taught hate for the creatures who embodied such ideas. He had lived to kill such things, back on Barbarus, back when he had been just a man. But like the tale of the numbers and their powers, the longer Morarg lived, the more that too seemed like a story he had once been told and not something he had actually experienced.

One of the Deathshroud glanced back towards him, then away. It was difficult to tell them apart at the best of times. Morarg had no idea what faces were concealed behind those sealed masks. The Reaper of Men himself personally chose the legionaries who were granted the shroud and told no other of his selections. When one of Mortarion's praetorians fell in battle, the armour was said to consume the body within. The warrior then picked to replace the lost would himself be declared dead on the field of battle, and entered into the lists as if he had fallen to enemy action – but in reality, he would strip himself of all identity and become Deathshroud, there to carry the honour of standing at Mortarion's side, as close as any Death Guard could ever come to being considered a confidante of their liege lord.

Would I ever be worthy of such a tribute? Morarg entertained the thought briefly, then shook it off. He already carried a high accolade of his own. The primarch had plucked him from his posting in the Breachers and made him his factotum.

His witness, Morarg amended. There had never been any lore keepers or remembrancers in the Death Guard, only those like him – battle-brothers with keen memories and sharp eyes. *If I am to document all that befalls my Legion and my master, then so be it. That is as good a calling as any.*

Ahead, the stairwell widened still further to deposit them in a chamber dominated by two semicircular doors in the far wall. The sheer amount of visible opulence, from the rich carpets and thick tapestries adorning the support columns to the gilded objects and artworks in every alcove, spoke of this place as the domain of an aggrandised ruler. Morarg's trigger finger twitched. He saw the lavish, self-indulgent affluence of it all and immediately wanted to destroy it.

Pillars of toxin-laced steam and damp, oppressive heat climbed through ventilation grilles in the floor, and a sullen orange illumination channelled up along vast light traps gave everything an infernal glow. Morarg heard a strange echo behind the march of his boots and tensed. The chamber had the feel of an arena, despite all attempts to make it seem otherwise.

The Deathshroud appeared to sense the same portent, and they moved into a protective formation around Mortarion's flanks. Only the Reaper of Men was unmoved by the air of ready threat in the chamber. He gave *Silence* a shake, flicking off the blood of those it had cut down, and kneaded the haft.

Morarg heard the clacking of great metal claws on the marble then, a scraping and clashing noise like a hundred swords being dragged across the tiles. His auto-senses picked out two hulking forms as they burst through searing walls of steam, man-shaped things that stormed across the floor towards Mortarion, each bearing an orchard of blades and buzzing beam emitters where they should have had arms. A jangling disharmony of bell tones sounded from thousands of rattling injector ampoules jammed into the bare flesh of their torsos and thighs. The hulking forms were some kind of altered human, ogre-like with their chemically forced gigantism. It struck the Death Guard that they were what someone inexpert might have created had they tried to duplicate a warrior of the Legiones Astartes. Twinned freaks powered by cocktails of metatropic drugs, set loose to act as gate guardians for whoever waited in the chamber beyond this one.

The first strike came in a flash of quick moves. Mortarion raised a hand, a simple order to the Deathshroud to stand back and not intervene, and then with a pivot so quick that Morarg barely registered it happening, the Reaper of Men spun *Silence* around to invert the great scythe and kiss the head of the blade across the marble floor. White sparks flew where the scythe touched the ground, and the primarch thundered forward to meet the leading guardian-creature. He closed the distance in the blink of an eye, and *Silence* rose in a spinning arc.

Morarg smiled behind his helmet as the curved blade opened the first of the guardians from crotch to throat. Momentum kept the chem-altered mutant stumbling forward as its body opened like an overripe fruit, belching ropes of intestine and organ matter onto the marble in a red gush. *Silence* was still moving, coming around, and the Death Guard heard the air sing as the blade cut again before the guardian could register that it had already been killed. The scythe took the creature's head off at the neck, and it tumbled through the air to land with a wet thud.

The second guardian fired a sheeting wave of energy beams across the chamber, burning blue rods that melted stone where they touched and boiled off the grubby patina of the primarch's battleplate.

Mortarion didn't attempt to dodge the attack. With an arm across his face to protect himself from the beam-fire, he planted *Silence* in the ground, ramming it into the marble with enough force to keep it upright. Then he advanced directly into the assault, snatching at his own energy weapon. The *Lantern* almost leapt into his grip, and the primarch lit the gun, drawing a black trench down the distance to his attacker as the beam from the giant pistol melted marble and metal before finally reaching the guardian. He carved off a leg and an arm from the creature before releasing the trigger.

Morarg inhaled the stench of burned, spoiled meat, and his smile grew. It was always an education to watch the Reaper of Men at his art.

Mortarion went to the second guardian – it was still alive, but not for long – holstering the *Lantern* as he walked. He gathered a great knot of the fleshy wattles around the mutant's throat and hauled it off the ground where it had fallen. With a grunt of sour disdain, the primarch pitched the creature into the sealed doors at the far end of the chamber. The collision was of such force that it shattered the guardian's body and rammed open the doors to reveal the throne room beyond.

'Who pretends to rule here?' growled Mortarion, pitching the question into the ill-lit space ahead of them. 'Present yourself.' He retrieved *Silence* from where he had left it, made another small motion with his hand, and immediately the Deathshroud were moving again, coming up to trail him through the broken doors.

Morarg took a step forward, then hesitated as a data-feed spooled past his eyes, a line of text projected on the inside of his helmet's lenses. It was an alert message, a high-priority code routed to him from an officer on board *Greenheart*. Several ships had been detected approaching Ynyx, angling to make orbit. But no arrivals were expected at this time, and to confuse the matter, the new craft were sporting the Death Guard's aura-identifier pennants.

How is that possible? The whereabouts of all the Legion's ships are known... The equerry stopped himself. *Well, that isn't exactly true. Not* all *our ships.* Morarg didn't dare to consider what the alternative might mean, but he did his duty and called out to his master, relaying the message.

For a moment, Morarg thought that the Reaper of Men had not heard him speak, but then his primarch gave him a sideways look. 'One matter at a time.'

THE THRONE ROOM was a bowl of reinforced crystalflex built into the roof of a cavern, and far below it churned a shimmering lake of fire. Jets of steam spat from the turbulent magma field, and an observer could have picked out hundreds of machine-slave diggers in their protective suits, still working at drills or syphons in their endless labours to gather Ynyx's mineral bounty.

That sight slipped past Mortarion's gaze without register. It was the throne that brought him up short.

Placed in the centre of the room, at the bowl's lowest point, the throne of the governor of Ynyx was a scaled-down representation of a great seat that Mortarion had once glimpsed before, in the days when his father had taken him back to Terra to see His Palace and look upon the works within it.

'Such arrogance,' he breathed, as much to those in the chamber with him as to that faded memory of the Emperor's studied magnificence. Mortarion peered into the shadows of the chamber, sensing other beings in there with the Death Guard, but nothing that appeared to be a threat. 'Do not make me ask again. Where is your ruler?'

'Here.' The voice was artificial, broadcast from a vocoder module. It emanated from a cylindrical tank floating just above the seat of the ersatz throne. The object was the size of a man, made of faceted crystal framed in gold, inlaid with precious gemstones. It swayed gently on a throbbing suspensor module, held up by contra-gravity technology. 'I will not surrender to you, rebel,' it added.

Mortarion stood and watched as the tank drifted away from the throne, becoming better defined by the orange light thrown by the magma fires. Inside the tank was a bubbling potion of thick, clear oil. At its centre there was a clump of whorled grey matter adorned with delicate circuitry and feeder implants. Wires came at it from every angle, connecting the blob of organic material to the systems of the floating container.

'I am Magister Greaterex Nalthusian the Forty-Fifth,' it went on, in stentorian tones. 'I own this system by order of the Emperor of Mankind–'

'You are a few kilos of stale meat in a jar,' Mortarion interrupted, a faint note of disgust entering his voice. 'And your existence... such as it is... is forfeit.' He rocked off his heels and strode forward. His irritation at this useless, waste of time of a mission bubbled to the surface, and the Reaper of Men reached out a hand. He would crush this thing and be done–

–Something there?

A wall of hurricane-hard force struck him from out of the darkness. Mortarion was lifted off his feet and blasted, along with the Deathshroud and his equerry, into the crystalflex panels of the throne room.

Mortarion reacted, using the crook of *Silence*'s blade to snag a support pillar, arresting his motion. Morarg and the seven Deathshroud were scattered about the chamber. Two of the praetorians took the brunt of the phantom blow and were blasted clear through the crystalflex, both of them spinning silently away to vanish into the magma lake below.

He scrambled back to his feet, and tasted a greasy, acidic tang in the air. *Witchery.* Mortarion knew that hated odour only too well.

A piece of the shadows behind the throne detached and a skein of darkness fell away, revealing a hollow-eyed youth whose face was half hidden behind a mess of long white hair. He grinned behind his bio-mask, unafraid of the legionaries or the primarch.

Somehow, the psyker had concealed himself from all of them, but now he was revealed, Mortarion sensed the raw power crackling around his form. It was a pressure in his head, the feeling of a storm about to break. The Reaper of Men had faced this kind of kinetipath many times before, in the Overlord Wars on Barbarus and later in the battles of the Great Crusade.

He knew enough to be wary. Physically, the psyker was a skinny wretch, weak enough that Mortarion would have been able to break him in two without an iota of effort. But psionically, the youth was as dangerous as a melta bomb, a raw elemental power barely contained.

The witchkin called upon that vitality, conjuring a torrent of force that gathered up loose fragments of metal and crystalflex, throwing them at the Death Guard in a storm of shrapnel.

Mortarion grimaced and set himself in slow progress, one foot in front of the other, pushing against the barrage flooding from the youth's outstretched hands. Frost formed around the psyker as he desperately drew in energy to oppose the primarch's steps, growing more frantic by the moment as the Reaper of Men drew closer. The ripping, tearing wind burned at Mortarion's armour.

He ignored everything else. They were in the teeth of the psycho-kinetic hurricane, witch and witch-killer, psyker and posthuman, enemy and enemy.

I have killed a hundred thousand of you. Mortarion let the declaration shine at the forefront of his thoughts. If the youth could read his mind, then he would hear this. *You will perish at the hands of the Death Guard.* He leaned forward, step after punishing step, almost close enough to strike. *The hate I have for you is greater than any other.*

'That is not so.'

The ghostly reply was almost lost in the wind, and Mortarion hesitated for an instant, uncertain if he had truly heard it or if it was a trick of the mind. Then the moment broke as an emerald flash illuminated the throne room from the far side of the chamber.

When the light faded, shapes in heavy Cataphractii battleplate were suddenly there, moving lightning-fast, and the psyker was distracted. The ethereal wind faltered, and it was enough for the closest warrior to sweep in and take the kill that was the primarch's due.

A manreaper blade – a sibling weapon to those held by his Death-shroud – cut the psyker in half with a diagonal downward stroke. Bloody segments tumbled to the floor, the brief enclosed storm dying as suddenly as its creator.

Mortarion glowered at the new arrivals, feeling the still-fading crackle of a teleport effect in the close, dense air of the chamber. He instinctively knew whose face he would see before the lead figure stepped into the light. 'Calas.'

Typhon, First Captain of the Death Guard, saluted with his bloody scythe and bowed as well as he could in his heavy armour. 'My Lord Mortarion. Well met.'

Mortarion refused to answer the ritual hail. 'Those are your ships up there.' He walked over to the reproduction throne, not waiting for a confirmation. The floating tank and the brain of the planetary governor within it was babbling a stream of panicked words, as Morarg and the Deathshroud set about executing any retainers in the chamber who were still alive. Without halting to listen to what was being said, Mortarion punched through the tank and crushed the organ inside to paste, before angrily tossing the remains away. 'You chose this moment to show your face again.'

'It was opportune,' Typhon offered, nodding at the dead psyker.

'The psyker didn't see you coming.'

'No.' The First Captain smiled slightly, and Mortarion saw his teeth had yellowed, his skin drawn; as if he had been recent victim to a powerful malaise. 'You know I have gifts. Stealth is one of them.'

The primarch scowled at the suggestion behind those words. The witchery he so detested ran strong in Typhon's blood, a legacy that his

First Captain had refused to completely eschew, much to Mortarion's displeasure. 'Why return to us now? You broke away from the Legion, took your own fleet to seek... What? Answers?'

'You have sought me, have you not?' Typhon took a step closer, deflecting the question with one of his own. 'And it is time, my lord. It is time for the Death Guard to be united in full once more. The final day is almost upon us, and we must be ready.'

Mortarion's irritation deepened. He had no patience for those who spoke in vagaries, and would not tolerate it among his commanders. 'Speak plainly or not at all,' he demanded. 'Why did you come back?'

'I have the answers I want,' Typhon replied. 'I would have come back, even without the orders.'

'What orders?' The primarch eyed him.

Typhon gave a nod, the smile widening, his voice dropping to a whisper. 'The Warmaster calls us to the greatest battle, my lord. The invasion of Terra will soon begin.'

TYPHON FELT THE citadel's end rumble through the black ground beneath his feet, and watched the fortress crumble with a jaundiced eye. The great construct's sad destruction put him in mind of a dying man, slumping and collapsing in on itself as the earth it stood on gave way.

Geoformer charges left behind by Legion Tactical Support squads fired in concussive sequence, blasting apart the supporting structures that had held up the citadel for thousands of years. The tower sank into a roiling stir of heavy dust, disappearing through the thick mantle to fall into the magmatic underground lake beneath it. The final act was the ejection of a column of dark ash and superheated steam – the last, fading grave marker for the rulers of Ynyx.

A sombre wind brought him the sound of distant thrusters. Looking up, Typhon spotted the metallic darts of Stormbirds racing away before vanishing into the low, foul clouds. Mortarion had dispatched search teams to conduct a final sweep over the planet's surface, just to be certain all life upon it had been expunged. But Typhon felt the certainty in his dark and tainted blood. Nothing lived on this world but the forces of the XIV Legion. Every settlement and city was a mouldering heap of corpses, the dead discarded and decaying.

A perfect garden of death from which new things will be born, he told himself. Typhon turned his gauntlet over, absently studying the pattern of the plates across his palm and his fingers. A tiny speck emerged from one of the knuckle joints – a black-silver fly with an oily body – and he watched it take flight and buzz away.

Behind him, heavy boots crunched on the ebon sand, and he turned, half bowing as his primarch approached.

Mortarion gave him a dismissive, irritable gesture. 'Stop. Do not bow and scrape.' Unhooded now, his gaunt aspect remained set in its accustomed scowl. 'I seek truth, not obeisance.'

Typhon was aware of the Deathshroud standing at their full permitted distance of forty-nine paces, away on the rise of the black basalt dunes. Mortarion would have ordered them to stay back, he guessed, so as to keep what was spoken of between the primarch and the First Captain private.

'Much has changed since we parted ways, brother.' Typhon dared to be informal with his Legion master, knowing that to do so would summon memories of their shared past. 'I tell you with all honesty that when the Warmaster declared his insurrection, I was uncertain of the path I should take.' He saw Mortarion's eyebrow rise questioningly, and headed off his primarch's train of thought before he could voice it. 'I do not speak of holding Terra's banner. I mean *my* path.' Typhon beat a fist against his chest-plate, above the site of his primary heart. 'I broke away because I needed that distance to see clearly.'

At the edges of his vision, Typhon glimpsed the now familiar black-silver flicker of insect wings, and in the deep registers of his hearing he sensed the drone of invisible flies. His primarch remained oblivious to them, but they comforted Typhon, in their own way. He held back a smile. There was so much he wanted to share with Mortarion, so many things he needed to say.

I was right all along. I promised you, and I was right.

But it was too soon. He needed only to study the face of his liege lord to know that the time was not at hand. The moment was close, though, closer than it had ever been before. The embrace would come when due. Nothing could stop that from happening.

Mortarion's gaze suddenly flicked up, as if he had seen something hidden to all other observers. His eyes narrowed.

Does he sense it? Typhon pulled at the question. *Can he hear it too? The coming change…*

Perhaps he did, even if he could not articulate it. Typhon could taste the psychic stain in the air around the primarch, the spoor left behind by his deliberate contact with the warp. For all Mortarion's hatred of the immaterium and the forces that swam in its depths, he had willingly exposed himself to such powers. Typhon had talked to chattering messenger-monsters in ghostly unplaces, heard them speak of how the Reaper of Men had defied his own revulsion to satiate his desire for knowledge.

Horus Lupercal's bloody schism had changed so much in its wake, from the great to the small. Typhon wondered if Mortarion would ever have dared to walk in the shallows of the Formless Seas, if his brother had not first broken the unbreakable faith of the Legions in so shattering a manner.

Mortarion was on the cusp, ready to be guided over the edge, even if he was not aware of it. Typhon knew of the primarch's fateful conversation with Lermenta, the mantis-crone the Death Guard had taken on Terathalion, and his wild success binding the daemon-tied essence of that braggart Ignatius Grulgor.

The latter was a challenge that few would have been able to accomplish with such scant experience, and yet Typhon's liege lord had managed it with the barest knowledge of the ways of witchery. Given the mercurial and wicked manners of the Ruinous Powers, Typhon had to wonder if they had eased the path for Grulgor's capture, deliberately pitching the act against Mortarion's hatred of them.

The more he loathes them, the sweeter his assimilation will taste, thought

Typhon. But the path to the fall was not flowing as it should have. *He should have used the Eater of Life on this wretched ball of dust. It was the ideal weapon.*

Erebus had told him as much. Speaking through his ruin of a face, the Word Bearers legionary had promised it. Erebus told Typhon that he would return to his Legion and find them willing and ready to take the Cups. To drink deep of the new way.

But Mortarion – stubborn and unyielding in all things – resisted the inevitable, as he always did.

'And now you come back,' the primarch was saying, 'and all is forgiven?'

'I will submit myself to any censure you deem fit,' Typhon replied, inclining his head. 'I only ask that you delay such judgement until we can regroup for the mission ahead.'

'Yes.' Mortarion glanced away again, towards the rest of his forces mustering in the blasted wasteland. 'The mission. Morarg brought me word from the *Endurance* that confirms what you said. The Warmaster wishes us to unite for the final invasion.' He paused, his frown deepening. 'His twisted equerry, Maloghurst, told me that we would be the first to attack the walls of the Imperial Palace. My brother, it seems, was unwilling to give me that command in person.' Typhon sensed irritation in his words. 'Did you speak to him?'

Typhon shook his head, again seeing Erebus' torn aspect in his recollection. 'No, only an emissary.' The First Captain did not mention what else the Word Bearers legionary had given him – a velvet bag of hololithic diamonds encoded with dense fields of encrypted data. One of the gemstones was in an equipment pouch on his hip, and his hand strayed towards it. The others were already in the process of being secretly distributed throughout the command ships of the Death Guard flotilla. They were, in their own way, utterly priceless.

'The home world…' said Mortarion, pausing again to frame his words. 'Barbarus. You are aware?'

Typhon nodded. 'It is no more.' He had been thinking on this moment ever since Erebus had told him of the planet's destruction, and now it was here, the First Captain did not know what face to wear before his commander. Should he be morose over the loss of that blighted sphere? Furious? Or coldly dismissive? He was unsure which expression would be best suited to mimic Mortarion's thoughts.

'The Dark Angels destroyed it to punish us,' Mortarion went on. 'I should hate them all the more for this deed but I cannot.' He shook his head slowly. 'I have always detested the Sons of Caliban. The chasm of my enmity is as deep as it ever was.' His tone was level, distant. 'They will pay along with the others.'

Typhon decided to keep his own counsel with regard to his recent contact with factions of the Lion's Legion on Zaramund. If he spoke of it now, it would only cloud matters, and the First Captain's Grave Wardens knew better than to volunteer the information. 'Barbarus was our cradle, brother,' offered Typhon. 'Aye, the Death Guard were born there, but we were always meant to abandon it.' He let his gaze drop, to appear sorrowful. 'We passed beyond it long ago. We left behind our errant fathers and eclipsed them.'

The primarch nodded once. 'This is truth. You have always cut to the core of things, Typhon. But there are many among my sons who do not share your... clarity.'

'Of course.' He had no doubt that amid the rank and file, there were Barbarun-born legionaries whose rage was stoked high by the thought of that hell-world cracking beneath a bombardment of planet-killers. There would be the need for revenge against the First Legion, and calls both private and public to find the Dark Angels and punish them. Once, Typhon reflected, he would have been shouting loudest among those voices, but not any more. On Zaramund, he had finally found the perspective that had been beyond him for so long.

The mission before Typhon was far more important than the fate of one toxic cloud-wreathed world and its populace of primitive mud farmers. The future of the Death Guard, and their role in the galaxy's savage destiny was at stake. The two things were so unlike in significance that they could not even share the same scale.

'I say this,' Typhon went on. 'If it is bloody vengeance that is required, then there is one certain place where we will have it. *Terra.*'

Mortarion gave a grunt of reluctant agreement. 'The Lion's whelps will be there, if they do not hold their honour cheap. We shall trample them upon my father's doorstep. It will be a fitting end for the First.'

Typhon smiled slightly. 'When he has the Golden Throne, we can bid Horus to give us Caliban... and then take our payment from it, over centuries if we see fit.'

'Yes.' The primarch's head bobbed. That was the kind of justice that appealed to Mortarion, the kind that only someone who had been hated and rejected could espouse. Typhon knew this truth because he shared it. Not for the first time, he reflected on how alike the two of them were. *Shared pain, shared hate*, he thought. *In that, we both spring from the same dark well.*

He had to restrain the smile on his lips from growing any wider. It was going to work – it was *all* going to work, and Typhon would be at the centre of it.

ONE

A Path Denied
Lost Soul
The Battle of the Walking City

THE FROSTS ALWAYS came in the dead of night, despite the best efforts of the Imperial Palace's weather management systems. They were gone by dawn, so few but those who patrolled the Eagle's Highway would ever have seen the way the thin patina of ice shone on the dark antipode marble, as it caught the light of ships passing along the sky-corridors above. In the past, many who came to the Emperor's earthly domain observed the highway from a distance and thought it to be a purely ornamental feature. It stood so far up above the Precinct and the great towers of the Inner Palace that it seemed to float there, a ribbon of stone drifting in low clouds, defying crude gravity by the sheer beauty and wonder of its existence. It was a minor glory among the magnificence of the Terran capital, but a glory nevertheless.

Wyntor imagined that such thoughts had never even occurred to the Praetorian, before he began demolishing the path. Dorn, in one of the endless diktats of defensive measure he had issued since returning to Terra, labelled the Eagle's Highway as both a military weakness and a waste of resources. Large sections of it had been deconstructed and the marble repurposed for ugly, battlefield uses. Talking to a wine-seller of his acquaintance on the Avenue of Sacrifice, Wyntor learned that the stone was now a series of gargantuan tank traps out on the Katabatic Slopes, and at the time the news had been enough to make him weep.

That seemed like such a terrible thing. An act of martial, uncultured barbarity in the name of a war yet to arrive, a hard-souled soldier taking a chisel to a thing of transcendent splendour in order to carve himself another graceless redoubt. But now that ignominy seemed utterly trivial.

Pretty marble meant nothing. Beauty meant nothing. Not when ranged against the horrors of what Wyntor knew *now*. The secrets he had been told had unseated his reason. A lesser man might have gone mad to know them. Perhaps, in some subtle way, *he had*.

Wyntor's thoughts inexorably slipped back towards the revelations and the dark realities lurking in the back of his mind, and the giddy, terrifying rush they brought up threatened to overwhelm him. It was as if he were being stalked by the medusae out of ancient Hellenik myth. To look directly into the eyes of this truth would petrify his flesh and bone.

His flimsy leather shoes, over-elaborate and made for soft, carpeted domiciles, slapped on the frosty stone. Wyntor skidded to a halt to catch his breath, hiding in the lee of a carved griffon. The cold marble burned at the soles of his feet, and the icy air at this great altitude was hard and heavy in his lungs.

Rake-thin and taller than most men, on other days he would have been more graceful than his gangly form suggested. Beneath the hooded robes he wore, his colouring was that of deep sand, and above an elegant chin and a regal face, his violet-hued eyes flitted back and forth on the verge of panic. A learned observer who knew human cultures might have guessed he was of Yndonesic extraction, and they would have been gravely mistaken.

His heart hammered against the inside of his chest. It had taken him several days to store up enough courage to make the escape attempt, and now he was fully committed to it. Wyntor did not look back the way he had come, for fear of seeing the towers and minarets of the Palace. He wanted to remember them as the beautiful and unsullied things that had greeted him on his first arrival here a decade ago. He was afraid that if he gazed at them now, he would only see the lies they stood upon, and the awful reality kept hidden from the Imperium at large.

If only they knew, he thought, looking away towards the lights of the Petitioner's City thousands of metres below. *What would the people say if they knew what I do? If they could see the truth behind the insurrection?*

But those were questions he could not even begin to fathom a reply for. All that mattered in this moment was *flight*. He had to flee the Palace, put as much distance between himself and the truth, get as far away as he possibly could from *him*.

The sound of his voice. The cadence of his footfalls. The rasp of his robes, that faint but ever-present scent of amasec in his chambers.

Wyntor felt this collection of elements forming into a recollection of the man and he stamped down on them, dispelling the moment before a name took shape in his mind. If he were to think fully of that face, it would be too late.

'He will know,' Wyntor said aloud, sucking in a deep breath to steel himself. 'I won't go back.'

He dashed out from behind the statue and ran as quickly as he dared, keeping his head bowed, one hand fishing in a deep pocket for the stolen cypher key that would allow him to use one of the Palace's transit flyers. The little craft would be able to get him to the plains. If he was quick, if this could be done before an alert was posted, he could escape.

To his credit, anyone else would have been caught already. But then there were few who knew the byways of the Imperial Palace as well as Wyntor did. The study and documentation of its architecture and construction had been his sole duty for the longest time. He knew how the Guardsmen patrolled, and in which sectors the Custodes held their vigils. It was said it would take a lifetime of study to know the dominions of the Emperor's bastion, but that was the dedication of Wyntor's existence.

Or at least it had been, until the conversations began. If he could have gone back to that first day, to that chance meeting in the gardens, he would have refused the offer. The glass of fine Venusian wine. The pieces assembled on a regicide board, awaiting a match.

'*I have so few opponents…*'

'No.' He spat out the word. *Too close.* He almost thought of the name. *Be careful.*

Wyntor was so deep in his fear that he almost stumbled over the temporary barrier that had been erected across the access ramp to the pad. He flinched away and a breath of wind caught his hood, pulling it back to let the long, jet streaks of his hair fall loose. He gripped the cypher key so tightly that it cut into the palm of his hand.

The landing stage was gone.

Blinking, he cast around, momentarily afraid that he had made a mistake and set off on the wrong path along the Eagle's Highway; but no, he knew for certain that was not so. The griffon statue confirmed it. He was in the right place.

But the flyer pad was not where it should be. *How could it be gone?* He inched forward, pushing at the barrier, and looked down at the sheer drop where before there had been a marble platform ringed with auto-servicers for transit craft, aeronefs and civilian ornithopters.

Then he understood. The stone had been cut with the harsh mathematics of a laser, with nubs of reinforcing flex-steel protruding here and there where the framework had been forcibly removed by combat engineers. It was another of Dorn's works, something else the Praetorian had carved off the Palace to repurpose to his military whim.

I should have known that, Wyntor told himself, frustration rising to the fore. *Why did I come up here? Why did I think this path would take me away?*

A troubling possibility occurred to him. Perhaps *he* had made Wyntor follow this route from the very start. That would be like him, to build an elaborate scheme just so he could prove a point, rather than merely speak the words and be done with it.

The panic Wyntor had been holding in broke the banks of his self-control, and he felt himself tremble as he turned back.

Blocking his path was a legionary in full battle armour of the Corvus iteration, his war-plate cast in the unadorned slate-grey of the Chosen. A Knight-Errant.

'Stay where you are,' said the warrior. He almost sounded uncertain.

'I won't go!' called out the man, jerking backwards in shock. Humans were often surprised at the stealth with which a legionary could move, and this combined with the shock effect of seeing a transhuman at close quarters could terrify even the hardiest of them.

This one did not seem robust by any measure, as he opened his long-fingered hands in a gesture of not-quite-surrender. A datum card dropped to the stonework at his feet and the wind pushed it away, out of reach.

'That choice is not yours to make,' said Tylos Rubio, keeping his tone level as he removed his helmet. He hoped that looking the man in the eye might make this easier.

The alert vox had said little about the fugitive, concentrating more on a wide-band message to all stations that the man was to be arrested on sight and detained for questioning. He did not seem dangerous – but the psyker had too much experience of the commonplace becoming the uncanny to relax his guard, even for an instant. Rubio had chosen to delay his imminent departure from the Palace in order to join the search, compelled to do so by an impulse that he could not directly identify.

His bolt pistol hung holstered at his belt, and his free hand rested on the gold Ultima forged at the hilt of his force sword, the weapon quiet for the moment in its scabbard. Rubio's stance communicated a warning to any who looked upon him. He was a scion of the Legiones Astartes, and as such danger was inherent in everything he did.

Once, Rubio had served with pride in the XIII Legion, the Ultramarines. First as a psyker-warrior of the Librarius, and then after the

Edict of Nikaea had forbidden the use of his powers, as a line Space Marine. But that felt like a lifetime ago. Here and now, his allegiance was turned towards a more clandestine end, as were his more ephemeral abilities.

Rubio was not just a legionary – although the genhanced warrior-kind of any Legion were never 'just' anything; he was a gifted fighter on the battlefield of the metaphysical as well as the material. A psychic hood, a complex device of crystalline matrices and psi-tuned alloys, rose up behind his head, glowing with a soft inner light. The hood had been at rest during his ascent to the Eagle's Highway, but now he was close to this human, it awoke of its own accord and pushed new awareness into his mind.

Or rather, it showed him the *lack* of something. Rubio's eyes narrowed as he reached out with a subtle telepathic probe, reading the ebb and flow of energy around the thin man in the robes.

Nothing.

Where the colours of a human psyche should have coiled and drifted like living smoke, there was a void without depth. Rubio's psionic senses recoiled from him, repulsed by the literal anti-form to his own powers.

'You are a pariah,' he said.

Those of a more fanciful bent than the former Ultramarine would have said the man was without a soul, but Rubio did not believe in such ephemera. Rather, he saw clearly that the fugitive was of the rare, one-in-ten-million breed whose psionic trace was diametrically inverted. Where others left an imprint on the invisible tides of the empyrean, this unfortunate had only nothingness within him. In some cases, such a being could be disturbing to the equilibrium of a psyker, even metaphysically dangerous. Rubio did not sense that threat here, however.

In point of fact, the man was unlike any of the psychic nulls he had encountered before. It was impossible to grasp even the smallest sense of the alien shape of his essence.

'What do you mean by that?' The figure in the robes shook his head. 'My name is Ael Wyntor. I have committed no crime! I am a sanctioned historicist in the Emperor's service. You cannot hold me against my will!'

'Your recovery has been ordered by the highest authority.' As the words left Rubio's lips, the man sagged and the colour drained from his face. 'Don't make this difficult.' Rubio extended a hand. 'Come with me. You won't be harmed.'

'That is not so!' Wyntor shook his head and backed away a step. His voice rose into a half-shout, half-whimper. 'I cannot go back to him, do you understand that? I can't hear any more!' He buried his face in his hands, and pressed those long fingers to his ears. 'I can't, I can't, I can't...'

Rubio prepared to move. It would only take a quick motion, but he was fast enough to cross the short distance between them in half a second. He plotted the action in his thoughts: take him by the arm, apply gentle pressure. He would need to be careful. Humans were fragile things. 'Don't resist,' he warned.

'No!' Wyntor bellowed the word at him, full of fear and last-ditch defiance. 'You don't know what he tells me! The things he shows me! The truth that cannot be denied...' The man abruptly trailed off and fixed Rubio with a firm gaze. A change came over his face, a sudden recognition. 'No... I'm wrong. You *do* know.' He raised a hand and pointed at Rubio's face. 'Yes. I see it in your eyes, Knight. Clear as daybreak. You've seen what lurks out there, haven't you? The horrors that are coming.' He whispered the last like a shared secret.

The legionary was momentarily lost for a reply. The man was right. Rubio had seen horror of a kind that he lacked the words to describe, things that chilled him to his core and sickened his heart. Those monstrous things had almost been the death of him, out in the void aboard the *Vengeful Spirit*, the dread flagship of the Warmaster. And now, even though he was freshly healed and returned to battle duty, the inner scars that confrontation had left on him would never fade.

'How do you know of this?' Again, he tried to gain a telepathic appraisal of the man, but Wyntor's strange non-self prevented any psionic reading.

'He's lying to you,' hissed the trembling man. 'They'll be here sooner than you think. Horus is bringing the end. A sky black with carrion flies and the stench of death.'

Rubio stiffened. The mere mention of the Arch-Traitor was enough to send a cold thrill through his nerves. Across the planet, Terra was poised on the precipice of total war, waiting for the invasion that would soon be upon them. Out in the darkness, the greatest enemy the Imperium had ever faced was coming for the Throneworld and the final reckoning. 'The Warmaster will be defeated,' said the legionary, and he meant every word.

'Yes,' said Wyntor, his panic rising again, 'but you will still lose everything you stand for. And *he* knows that. He knows it!'

'Enough,' Rubio snapped, and Wyntor retreated still further. 'You are bound by law on the order of Malcador, High Regent of Terra. You are one of the Chosen, just as I am. So *obey*. Come with me now, or I will break you and drag you away.'

'You spoke his name. You shouldn't have done that.' Wyntor's eyes filled with tears. 'Please, just let me go. I'm only one person. I don't matter. But I can't hear any more. It's tearing me apart inside.'

'I am… so very sorry, Ael.'

Rubio twisted towards the sound of the new voice, pulling a good measure of his sword from its scabbard before he caught himself. His psychic hood sizzled with the bleed-off from the sudden metapathic presence that had joined them on the elevated pathway.

His gaze found an old man in robes similar to those worn by Wyntor, but the new arrival supported himself upon a tall staff of black iron, topped by a basket of muttering flames about a carved metal eagle. Malcador, last of the Sigillites, had arrived without hint or indication, and for a moment Rubio experienced the same shock that Wyntor must have felt upon seeing him.

Not for the first time, Rubio wondered if the Sigillite was actually *present* by any measurable means of understanding. Malcador's immense psychic might, second only to that of the Emperor Himself, dwarfed the warrior-Librarian's powers. It was said that he could kill a man with a look, and Rubio believed it.

But in this moment, the expression on the Sigillite's face was only sadness. 'This is always so difficult,' Malcador said quietly. 'This is not what I want.'

'Then why burden me?' Wyntor screamed back the question, accusing him with each word. 'I did not ask to know! I yearn for the days before, when I was ignorant and unnoticed!'

'Yes,' said Malcador, glancing to Rubio, then away again. 'But it was necessary.' He took a long, despondent breath. 'Please, Ael. Return with me. You are needed.'

Rubio had never heard the Sigillite speak to anyone in this tone. The Regent of Terra would cajole, he would influence, he would demand, but he would never make a request, as he did now. His manner was almost *beseeching*.

Wyntor drew himself up, and at length he shook his head. 'That may be so. But I know too much ever to follow you again.' Then, before Rubio could react, the man in the robe let himself fall backwards over the safety rail and into the cold mountain air.

The warrior surged forward, reaching out to snatch at a fold of the fugitive's flapping robes before he was beyond reach, but Malcador spoke again – the single word '*No*' – and Rubio became a statue, unable to move.

He could do nothing but watch Wyntor fall silently away, captured by the gusts and carried towards the ragged minor peaks. The tumbling figure grew smaller and smaller, until it crumpled against the top of a high tower in a blink of crimson.

'I could have saved him,' Rubio said, as control of his body was returned.

'That ship had already sailed.' The Sigillite gave a shake of his head.

Rubio hated the sudden sense of powerlessness that had passed through him. It seemed a pointless waste of human life to let this poor, tormented fool plummet to a bloody death. If his value had been so trivial, then why was Malcador's attention upon him?

The Sigillite pulled the question from the warrior's thoughts. 'A tragic chain of events,' he clarified, but the explanation seemed rote and hollow. The deep and honest sorrow Rubio had seen in Malcador's old eyes dithered there for a moment longer – and then it was gone, melted away like the frost on the marble.

'I do not–'

'You do not *need* to understand, Rubio.' The Sigillite spoke over him. 'You will not speak of this matter again, and you will not question what took place here.' The words resonated with subtle psychic force, embedding themselves in his thoughts.

He found himself saluting, his fist to his chest. 'Your will, Regent.'

Malcador walked away, circling behind him as he gazed off towards the southern sky. 'Don't you have somewhere else to be? Your fellow Knights-Errant have need of you.'

Rubio gave a reluctant nod, and turned again to face the Sigillite, framing a reply, but he was alone.

THE NARROW IRON corridors of the Walking City rang with panic, and all Vardas Ison could hear were the screams of the people and the droning of the things that were consuming them. The mobile tech-nomad settlement sat atop a gigantic, twenty-legged platform that trudged on a looping course towards the equator and back, kicking up huge plumes of stale dust from the parched earth beneath its colossal feet, but today the constant grinding noise of its motion was blotted out by the sound of terror and destruction.

He tried to keep himself in the moment, but it was difficult to stop his thoughts from flitting around, ranging back through the day in some attempt to seek out the precise fulcrum, the exact moment when it had gone awry.

'Get back, damn you!' Varren shouted at the civilians clustering around them, the tallest of the humans barely reaching the height of their elbows. 'Clear my line of fire, or so help me you'll be ash as well!'

His harsh words sent a wash of fear through the people and they shrank back like a retreating tide, their feet ringing on the rolling metal deck as they flowed around the immobile rocks of the two grey-armoured legionaries. Ison could have projected a calm over them if he had wanted to, broadcasting it from the Codicier's psychic hood mounted behind his head – but to do that would rob potential and focus from his combat abilities, and he feared he needed weapons more than the civilians needed comfort.

'Here they come,' Varren hissed, bringing up the twinned volkite serpenta pistols in his hands. The other legionary had taken the Mars-born guns from the weapons locker aboard their Storm Eagle, eschewing the use of the power sword sheathed upon his back in favour of the deflagrating beam weapons. It was true the guns were better suited to the close-combat environs of the Walking City's passageways, but Ison thought it more likely that the former World Eaters legionary chose them because he liked the destruction they wrought.

Ison made no secret of his ill will towards Macer Varren. For all his readiness to break away from his primarch, the bloody-handed traitor Angron, Varren was still very much a son of his violent and hate-fuelled Legion. That the ex-captain kept to his oaths to the Emperor and Terra against the turning of his battle-brothers was laudable, but it didn't change the colour of his heart.

Only recently returned to active duty after emerging from the healing sus-an coma, his fresh suite of scars gave him a permanent snarl that Ison felt revealed the truth of his crude and brutish nature. By his lights, Ison considered Varren a poor fit among the Knights-Errant of Malcador's Chosen.

The dislike went both ways. Varren thought Ison was haughty and inconstant, and reminded him of it at any opportunity. A point of particular contention was the name of Ison's origin Legion. He had not deigned to give it to any of the other Knights, and Varren carved trivial amusement out of his attempts to goad him into a reveal.

'Stay focused, peacock,' Varren demanded. The casual insult was made to suggest Ison might be a son of the Phoenician, and he ignored it.

'That is all I do,' he replied, reaching out with his psychic ability to feel for threats in the web of corridors around them. Burning, indefinite shapes seared his sensorium as they closed in on them.

The attack on the Walking City had begun, as many of these assaults did, in the halls of a makeshift church. Hidden from sight deep in the lower levels of the great ambulatory metropolis, a chapel dedicated to the Cult of the Imperial Truth had flourished. Ordinary people, terrified beyond reason by the threat of the Warmaster's invasion, came together to seek solace and direction – and the preachers of the Truth gave it to them. They told the lost and fearful that the ruler of mankind was, in point of fact, a God-Emperor, a deity who had created Himself. He would lead them to salvation, if they believed... And in these turbulent days, when the end of all things endangered not just Terra but the galaxy beyond, there was no shortage of those who needed a palatable response to all their terrors.

But in recent months, Malcador the Sigillite had dispatched Ison and others of the Knights-Errant and the Chosen to cult sites across the planet, and on each occasion they had encountered incidents of bloodletting and destruction. What they found were the harbingers of unspeakable things that until now had been confined to worlds beyond the light of Sol.

It was happening with greater frequency. With each one of these incidents they put down, two more occurred. What was transpiring here on the Walking City was the worst of it yet, and even with the force of four Knights-Errant and a squad of Malcador's best Chosen armsmen, Ison wondered if they would be up to the challenge.

Some among the group spoke of these events as signs that the long-awaited invasion was almost upon them, the suggestion being that the malign shadow of the Warmaster's influence in the immaterium was pressing hard on the metapsychic barriers erected about Terra by the Emperor Himself. Ison imagined those invisible shields, no longer seamless and perfect, but marred by tiny cracks through which a strain of malevolent power could still squeeze through.

There was always a church at the heart of it. As the Emperor's grand secular revolution had wiped out the old religions of ancient days, He had sown the seeds of the cult that now worshipped Him. Ison wondered how a being of such incomparable power could not have foreseen such a happening – but then the Emperor had never expected His sons to turn against Him either.

Or had He?

The manifestations bloomed in the halls of the Imperial Cult with such potency that the connection could not be ignored. The creatures of the warp were clearly drawn to these pious gatherings, and Ison imagined they could taste the raw *need* of the desperate Terrans, as sharply as selachians might taste blood across kilometres of ocean water.

He had known it the moment they landed on the shifting platform atop the multi-legged frame of the massive mechanical city, felt the piercing sharp pain behind his eyes as a droplet of blood escaped his nostrils.

'*Attackers!*' Varren's battle roar shattered Ison's reverie, and the other legionary opened fire on the mad horde of bloated figures that came falling through the hatches and into the corridor before them.

It was Helig Gallor, with typical Death Guard aplomb, who had named these transformed foot-soldiers 'the flyblown'. Humans bitten and transfigured by exposure to the mutagenic venom of infernal pests, they were mindless killing machines that lived only to destroy or to build their numbers by infecting others. In a closed environment like the Walking City, they were akin to a fast-acting virus. If not burned out, that infection could spread unchecked.

There was no cure, only excision. Varren's volkite guns shrieked white fire and blasted the front rank of the flyblown into ashen gobs of matter, but their fellows stamped their remains into the deck and stumbled on.

The creatures were ugly and misshapen. Something of the people they had once been could be determined by their clothing and the tone of their skin – both now stretched to the point of splitting by the swelling of diseased tissues beneath – but no features were recognisable. Burst human eyes became insectile, turning into grotesque, multifaceted jewels. Tiny flickering wings and mandible parts emerged from boils on bare flesh, quivering and rasping as the mutation took hold.

Ison's bolter barked, the concussion of the shot deafening many of the civilians crowding behind him. He could feel their terror churning like boiling water. The passageway beyond was a dead end, and if the Knights-Errant fell against the mass of the flyblown, the humans would be fodder for the mutants.

The mass-reactive rounds from his gun blasted through the creatures, but each one he killed erupted with quivering new life as buzzing streams of birthing flies swarmed out to sully the air. Varren's ray weapons turned everything they touched to powder, but even he was in danger of being overwhelmed.

'Can't hold these off much longer,' snarled the other warrior. 'Stop pissing around like a tyro and do what you have to!'

The psychic hood at the back of Ison's head glowed at the unvoiced thought in his mind. 'If I use it here, the civilians will be at risk.'

'Forget them!' Varren retorted. 'Just do it!'

Damn him for being right. Ison's jaw set as he let his bolter hang free on its sling, and he brought his hands together in a prayer-like gesture. Tiny jolts of crimson-white fire collected in the crystal matrix of the hood, growing to shimmer down his arms, gathering around his fingers. The flyblown were almost upon them now, and Varren's pistols were sizzling with built-up heat.

Ison closed his eyes and mouthed a mnemonic. *In the Angel's name, I smite thee.* A blinding blaze of red lightning leapt from his hands and washed out across the narrow corridor, sweeping up and through the mass of the flyblown. Backwash from the blast writhed around him, buffeting Varren and striking dead a handful of civilians too close to get away – but the psychic weapon did the deed, atomising the mutants in a single wave, turning them and their insect progeny into black dust. As the blast faded, the dark ash settled to the deck in a deep drift.

VARREN GRANTED THE enemy the only honour they were due, and spat into the mass of their remains. He turned and eyed the young whelp-psyker. 'You're good for something,' admitted the former World Eaters legionary, coming as close as he ever would to anything resembling con-trition. 'I was wrong. You can't be one of Fulgrim's – those braggarts are useless.'

He fell silent as he realised that Ison was taking no notice of him, staring away down the corridor.

'Don't ignore me, boy.'

Ison shook his head. 'Something else is coming,' muttered the psyker. As the warning left his lips, the corridor around them set to a thrum-ming vibration.

The sound was so bass and low that it made Varren's teeth hum in his jaw, and around him he saw many of the civilians clasping at their noses and ears as blood trickled from the orifices. He clamped his mouth shut and triggered the gas vents on the breeches of his ser-pentas, but even as the cool-down cycled he knew he would not have time to dwell.

From around the far corner of the corridor came a colossal, rough-edged shadow that spilled over every surface. Buzzing like chainsword blades, it was a huge, dense swarm of carrion flies. The mass of the insects was great enough to deform metal where it impacted, and it befouled the air with a cancerous corpse-odour.

Only one of Varren's pistols answered the trigger when he squeezed it, both of the guns still radiating great washes of heat that he could feel through the palms of his gauntlets. The single volkite beam bored through the swarm, killing part of it, but the rest of the mass seethed and parted around the blast.

'Got another one in you?' Varren shouted, nodding towards Ison's psychic hood. The younger warrior was already gathering his preternatural power anew, but the glow was weaker than before and Varren suspected it would not save them a second time.

Eaten alive by flies. It was no way for a gladiator son to perish. He had not survived a bitter climb to maturity on Bodt, endured brutal warfare on Susa and Sha'Zik and the breaking of his own oaths just to die unremarked in a plasteel tunnel, surrounded by wailing humans. He would keep firing the guns, then. He decided this as the overload warning icons on their grips flashed crimson. *Yes. Keep firing until the weapons in his hands exploded.* Volkite flame would consume everything.

'It's… all one mind,' Varren heard the psyker mutter. 'A single swarm-consciousness…'

'Then we'll die killing it!' he shouted, and opened fire again.

'*Not today, brother.*' The words came over the vox. '*Look sharp!*'

Across the corridor, where the metal wall became the outermost hull of the Walking City's construction, a shimmering sword blade burst through the steel with a howling screech. Thick yellow sparks flew as the blade cut a molten-edged 'V', and then the weapon withdrew.

Ison was already herding the surviving civilians back towards the rent in the wall, as ceramite-clad fingers wrenched at the glowing cut and pulled the metal back from the outside, as if flaying the pelt from an animal.

A gust of icy cold air blasted in through the tear in the hull and Varren saw a figure silhouetted there – a legionary in grey with a smoking sword in one hand, and about his head, an armour cuirass detailed with a brass Imperial aquila. 'Get them out!' shouted Nathaniel Garro, wrenching a melta bomb from a hook on his belt.

A wild laugh burst from Varren's mouth and he drew back, still firing, ignoring the burning pain through his gauntlets. The swarm wavered, as if the mass of insects sensed what was about to happen. He was the last through the rip in the hull and as he passed Garro, the other Knight-Errant pounded a fist on his shoulder pauldron.

'Gallor is on the grav-platform,' Garro shouted over the roar of the wind and the screaming buzz of the swarm, pointing his sword down-range. 'Regroup! I will be right behind you!'

But Varren slowed his pace. He wanted to watch.

Garro flicked a switch on the melta device and slung it back through the tear in the Walking City's flank. The dull green cylinder vanished into the midst of the carrion fly horde and detonated. Pale yellow fire thundered through the framework and the decking, and later Varren would swear that he heard the insects *scream*.

The Walking City lurched, several of its supporting legs stumbling into the slopes of a steep mountain, and across on the far side of the great moving platform, sheets of ice and dislodged snowpack sloughed off the rock and collided with it.

With the deck shuddering beneath them, Varren and Garro sprinted the last few metres to a floating service platform hovering alongside. Garro, serving as the Sigillite's Agentia Primus among the Knights-Errant, was commander of this mission, and he would have been within his rights to chastise Ison and Varren for almost getting themselves killed – but that wasn't his way. The former Death Guard battle-captain and the Hero of the *Eisenstein* was unlike the warriors Varren had served under in the XII Legion – never quick to his rage, never leading by fury when reason could serve as well. It had taken him a while to get used to it, but in truth there would always be a part of Macer Varren that expected death to meet him. When his primarch and his Legion had broken faith with the Imperium, Varren's refusal to follow had started the pendulum swinging on a clock that counted down his days.

Climbing aboard the sputtering, overloaded grav-platform, he spied Helig Gallor – another Knight-Errant from Garro's old Legion – at the controls and threw him a nod. Did Garro, Ison and Gallor think of their time as Varren did of his? His lips parted in a feral grin. *I'll probably be dead before I ever have the chance to ask them.*

'Go!' called Garro, and the platform shot forward, up and around the Walking City's eastern quarter.

Varren shoved a few whimpering civilians out of his way so he could get a better look at the metropolis. He estimated over a third of the city was on fire, although it was hard to be sure if the black smoke he saw was from conflagration or if it was more of the gargantuan insect swarm. The moving construct had lost one leg on the western side, and it appeared to be stumbling forward on an uncontrolled course. Ahead of it, the walls of a steep-sided valley were narrowing.

'Are we retreating?' Varren asked to the air. He glanced at the handful of civilians. 'This is a pitiful number to count as rescued.'

'We are regrouping,' Garro countered, as Gallor brought the grav-platform up and over the Walking City's spinal boulevard. 'Look there.' Again, he pointed with his power sword, and Varren spied the target at once. A towering column of shimmering darkness that did not move as smoke did.

As he watched, the legionary saw the swarm thicken and solidify. 'It's taking on a shape...'

'Billions of those carrion flies, merging together,' said Ison. 'I have an inkling of the enemy's intention.' He glanced at Garro. 'You won't like it.'

Varren felt a jolt of cold understanding. 'It's going to infest the city's machinery, just like it bred inside the flyblown.'

'The World Eater has it,' agreed Ison.

Gallor frowned. 'Can they do that?'

'We have seen them co-opt organic forms,' Garro said gravely. 'And corrupt the inorganic. I do not doubt these things have the power to do more.' He turned to Gallor. 'Helig! Find somewhere to set us down, then give the controls to one of the civilians.'

Varren kept his eyes on the swarm-form. 'So how do we kill it, then?' He gave his pistols an irritable shake. They were near-useless to him now, so he let them drop and drew his sword.

'In the middle of that is the first victim of the carrion flies, the first human they infected,' said Ison. 'I sense the malignancy in the core, like a blighted beating heart. We kill that one–'

'And that will be the end of it?' Gallor did not sound convinced, and Varren shared his scepticism.

'We will find out,' said Garro, and then he showed a gallows-humour smirk. 'After all, we are still writing the book on this kind of war.'

'I don't want to perish before we reach the last page,' said Ison.

'Ha!' retorted Varren. 'Speak for yourself!'

INTERVAL II

A Pale Horse

[The planet Ynyx; now]

MORTARION MEASURED TYPHON with a hard gaze, as if by will alone he could peer through that sallow face and pull back the layers to find the old friend from his youth. That person was still in there somewhere, obfuscated under years of change and a fathomless distance, but the bond between them seemed blurred now, and hard to grasp.

Do I still trust him? The question lurked in the gloom of the primarch's thoughts. *Is it conviction, or just the inertia of the kinship we once had, back then?*

He had no answer. All he could be certain of was that Typhon had changed while he was gone. Something had tested him, physically as well as mentally, that much was clear by the gauntness of his aspect and the moments when he failed to hide the haunted flickers in his gaze.

There was no other warrior, living or dead, whom Mortarion would have wanted by his side for the invasion of Terra. Bitter memory cut through him as he recalled the last time he had tried to attack the house of one he called 'father', and he vowed that shameful failure would never be repeated. With the Death Guard whole and reunited, with clever Typhon at his right hand, it would be done *right* this time.

It will be done! He had to hold back the impulse to snarl the words.

Mortarion drew in a slow breath, momentarily surprised by the potency of his own emotions. Such reactions ran deep and low in him, and it was a rare thing in these days for them to rise so close to the surface. He became aware of his hand gripping the haft of *Silence* tightly, as if the weapon were straining to be let free.

Typhon advanced and made the old gesture of salute, one mailed fist to his chest. 'My lord, would you grant me a request? I ask this of you as your comrade and your brother in battle.'

'Name it.' Mortarion's eyebrow rose. This was unexpected.

'Your command barge, *Greenheart*. When we quit this world, you would return aboard it to the *Endurance*, to dock with the flagship and lead the fleet from there.'

'That was my intention.'

'I suggest that you do not. Instead, I ask that you bring *Greenheart* to my warship and give me the privilege of carrying your banner to Terra.' He bowed his head, despite Mortarion's earlier disapproval of the action. 'It would say much for sealing any rifts that may have grown between those of my splinter fleet and the rest of our armada. It would reaffirm our unity of purpose.'

The primarch's first instinct was to deny the First Captain's entreaty. It would be a break from protocol for the Reaper of Men to command from another officer's ship, even as fine and mighty a vessel as Typhon's *Terminus Est*. But his brother's words held merit. In the time while the splinter fleet had been gone, Mortarion had heard the grumblings among his warriors and seen the seeds of division being planted. He wanted none of that, especially at this critical juncture.

The rumours of breaks within the Legions themselves were rarely spoken of, but known. There was talk of warriors on both sides of the rebel and loyalist divide breaking faith with their commanders and seeking to ally with their opposite numbers. The mingled rage and regret

Mortarion still felt over the betrayal of Battle-Captain Garro of the Seventh Great Company, and his men aboard the starship *Eisenstein*, had never gone away.

Unity was needed here, and Typhon's unconventional suggestion had merit. *Protocol be damned, then*, Mortarion told himself. *Better to send a message.*

'Agreed,' said the Reaper of Men. 'You and I will stand side by side as we break Terra's barricades and bring my father's defenders to heel. As dusk falls, their fears will rise.'

Typhon looked up, and his eyes were bright. 'So shall it be.'

BY DAY'S END, the work of killing a world was declared complete.

Ynyx was reduced to a barren grave. The command had been to raze it for daring to defy the Warmaster, and now that deed was done.

But perhaps, on their way back to the great flotilla of battle cruisers and warships in high orbit, the last few Death Guard scouts sent out to make final judgement might have seen something stir, if they had cared to look closely enough.

Not survivors, of course. Perish the thought. Everyone down there was dead.

No, something *else*. Something borne out of the festering mass of rotting corpses, something that animated the decayed remains, consuming even as it exerted its own grotesque parody of life. Silver-black and swarming. Crawling and mewling.

These things went unseen.

Above the clouded nightside of the planet, above the haze backlit by the ceaseless fiery ejecta of a thousand volcanic eruptions, the Death Guard's ships moved into deployment formation. They gathered their Stormbirds and Thunderhawks to them, pulled in the close-range system boats that had been used to blast away Ynyx's lunar defence batteries, one by one orienting themselves to leave the murdered world in their wakes.

The exhausts of huge plasmatic drives were lit and the ships made space for the closest Mandeville point, high up above the plane of the ecliptic where they would be beyond the effect of the system's mass shadow, and free to enter the warp.

Greenheart powered along with the fleet, steering through the mass of them with its landing wings unfurled. This was the closest Mortarion would ever come to the gaudy displays of battle pennants, laser glyphs and high honours that bedecked the command barges of his brother primarchs. Such things were irrelevant, foolish indulgences and beneath the dour martial character of the Death Guard. The appearance of the ship itself, and the knowledge of who was aboard it, would be enough to stir the spirit of this Legion.

Greenheart passed over the bow of the *Endurance* and her helmsman made a salute of sorts, dipping the solar wings as it vectored away from the craft's usual berth at the rear of the warship's great operations tower. The vessel flew on, allowing the crews of all the other great ships to witness the passage. The *Indomitable Will*, the *Spectre of Death* and the *Undying*, the *Reaper's Scythe* and the *Stalwart*, all of them ceremonially raised the cannons of their turrets and bared the lenses of their mega-laser batteries – each action a signal of their readiness for war.

And then Mortarion's war-barge approached the *Terminus Est*. The match in size and raw combat potency for the primarch's battleship, First Captain Typhon's vessel was a terror to behold. A capital ship of unique design, it radiated lethality from its great forked prow to the complex structures of its heavy gun tiers. The fearsome vessel's decks opened to accept *Greenheart*'s arrival like a supplicant's embrace.

The primarch's first footfall within the battleship's massive primary landing bay echoed and rang across the cavernous space. In return, a thunderous report of fists against chest-plates answered Mortarion's arrival, as countless ranks of legionaries saluted him. Typhon's elite warriors, the Grave Wardens, were there to greet the Reaper of Men and the First Captain.

He saw Hadrabulus Vioss, Typhon's trusted second, at the head of the formation. Like their commander, Vioss and the others were ashen and drawn, but only if one observed them in a certain light.

Mortarion gave no speeches, he made no entreaty to be broadcast across the flotilla. Aware that images of his arrival were being seen on all the ships, he only paused to give the landing bay a considering gaze and then a nod, as if to say *this will do, this will be enough.*

On the bridge of the *Terminus Est*, Typhon gave the command to ready the ship for the warp, but held back on the final word. He extended a hand to his liege lord and nodded towards the blackness of the interstellar void, out past the great armoured glass of the dome above their heads.

'By your will,' he said. 'Speak the words, and the Legion will follow.'

Silence clanged against the deck as Mortarion struck the metal with the hilt of the massive scythe. He pointed with his free hand, into the blackness. 'We go to the war,' he rasped.

'And there we will be renewed,' Typhon said quietly, as the battle-ship's reality-distorting drives spun up to critical momentum, keening their song.

Barriers sprang up to cover the viewports across the bridge, physical baffles as well as the non-corporeal shields of the vessel's Geller fields that would serve to conceal the shattering lunacy of the raw imma-terium. It was said that no living being could stand to look into the madness of that other realm for more than an instant, lest their mind be forever petrified by what they saw there.

But Mortarion had seen the face of the daemons that writhed and howled in that place – indeed, he had one of them trapped in fetters that he had forged with his own hands – and the black fear of their origins did not intimidate him. Mortarion reached out to touch a con-trol and held open the last shutter with a press of his thumb, ignoring the chiming clockwork trills of alarm bells and the rush of dismay from Typhon's crew serfs.

The warp opened up to them in a raw-edged, bleeding orifice, a wound in the surface of space-time. It grew into an abyssal, laugh-ing maw that engulfed them as the *Terminus Est* was first to cross the boundary into the unreal. Mortarion held the shutter open for long seconds, ignoring the weeping and babbling of human helots and the crack of their necks as they were silenced by the Grave Wardens for their disgrace. He stared directly into the empyrean, almost *daring* it to show him something.

They carved through the wispy membranes of reality and, at last, the Reaper of Men released the switch and let the shutter slam closed. Something close to a smile began to form on his pallid lips.

But the next breath he took was a mouthful of ashes.

His mighty lungs twitched in reflex, the multi-lobed organs tightening within his ribcage. Pain lanced through him. Impossibly, he was *choking*.

Mortarion's hand went to his throat. The muscles there went into spasm as his flesh refused to obey. Breath was suddenly a memory. He was struck voiceless, unable to emit even the slightest gasp.

How was this possible?

He was one of the most powerful posthumans in existence, a demigod of war capable of incredible feats of prowess. Nothing could stop him. Nothing could *choke* him.

The primarch turned to see every figure on the bridge suffering the same sudden, impossible malaise. Morarg, clawing at the neck guard of his armour; his Deathshroud, rigid and uncomprehending; and close at hand, crew serfs whose faces turned cyanosis-blue as they suffocated. Only Typhon seemed unaffected, the First Captain staring away into nothing.

With all the strength he could muster, Mortarion tried to force a sound from his mouth, but there was only the rough, stifling sensation of cinders filling his gullet, packing his lungs–

Then a memory exploded in his thoughts.

I know this...

Mortarion had experienced this horror once before, deep in his past, forgotten and buried until this moment brought it back to brutal life.

His vision fogged, shading with nauseating hues of bruised emerald. He glared back at the closed shutter and the hidden horrors beyond.

It was the warp. An undeniable instinct, that bone-deep hatred he held for the ways of the witch, made him certain of it. Something out there was doing this.

Making him *remember*.

[The planet Barbarus; before]

THE OVERLORD THAT called himself Hethemre had earned the displeasure of the Barbarun Elect by taking lands that did not belong to him, and then refusing to return them to the rightful tithe-owner. In a fit of screaming, murderous pique, Hethemre had decided that rather than retreat back to his own territory, he would kill every servile and chattel in the region and burn the sodden, muddy land in revenge.

It was one more hateful act in an epoch of small, pointless skirmishes that seemed to have no end. The Barbarun Elect were the uncontested masters of this blighted world, with no threats from below or above to challenge that dominion. And without such outside concerns to occupy their venial and combative manners, their innate cruelty turned poisonous if not given opportunity to be vented.

They would regularly turn upon one another for the thinnest of reasons – an imagined slight, the resurgence of an old grudge, or just out of sheer desperation against the monotony – and take a perverse joy in visiting their malice upon each other.

But it was said that the Overlord-kin could not easily be killed, at least not by means that men understood, and the scars they gave one another in rare moments of face-to-face battle were few and far between. More often than not, they would inflict damage not through direct conflict, but through the destruction of holdings and the ceaseless brutality they inflicted on the humans that were unfortunate enough to serve them.

This was the life of a 'lesser' on Barbarus. To be human on this mist-wreathed world was to be born knowing only fear, to be beneath consideration, to live with the expectation that the reaper's blade would fall with each new dawn. To know that creatures ancient and horrific held your life in their clawed hands, apt to ruin it or end it on a whim. To dare to hope that these ghoul-like intelligences would consider your existence so far beneath them as to ignore it, and through that disinterest let you live for another day.

What fear there was on Barbarus. What dread there was to know one's life was valued less than a pawn upon a regicide board.

In the newly ruined wasteland created by Hethemre, stretching from the flaming remains of the Roadscar Mill and clear across the Hadea Winds Moor, there was only ash and cinders. The furious Overlord had called up green witchfire from beneath the dull earth, great tumbling jags of it that exploded out of the marshes to set even the damp mosses and knife-grasses alight. Thick, cloying smoke hugged the ground and the fires spread in loping bounds, burning everything. No one escaped the inferno at the mill, as it moved like a living thing to surround the settlement's walls and then drew tight to smother it. Elsewhere, caravans on the dyke roads were caught in the open by falls of acid that came from flocks of fattened blight harriers – one of Hethemre's favourite killing methods. Bodies fell there, moisture drawn from them until they became brittle husks and masses of powdery remains.

Hethemre had no tactics in mind, and there was no great military plan afoot to gather power or land. This was simply an act of petulant retaliation, to salt the land and destroy what had never belonged to the Overlord in the first place. The crowning action of his viciousness was to unleash a great pack of revenants and creatures stitched together in the dank confines of an experimentum chamber. The horde of things jabbered and roamed the burned lands, looking for any lessers who had not been lucky enough to die from fire or acid-fall.

All this destructive spite might have been tolerated if it had ended there. But Hethemre was a bellicose fool and not given to consideration of much beyond the next moment, the next caprice. The minor Overlord's forces were so desperate to make murder that they chased the survivors into the foothills of the great grey mountains, the lowest ranges of the peaks atop which many of Hethemre's ghastly rivals had their fortresses and holdfasts. They dared to encroach upon territory that the other Overlords actually *valued*.

This is where Mortarion came upon Hethemre's monsters, as they concluded their killing of a survivor group that had been discovered hiding in a shallow cavern. The lessers had gone to ground there, not just in hope of avoiding death from the roving creatures but also to seek escape from the noxious fogs that swirled endlessly around the low slopes.

They had unwittingly trapped themselves. To go downhill would take them into the teeth of the monsters, but to venture upward would force the humans into the higher reaches where the atmosphere's toxicity grew denser with each rise.

The lessers were mostly dead by the time Mortarion arrived, but he heard enough screams to know that the remainder would keep the pack interested, long enough for him to get close.

His own cadre of golem-soldiers – if such a name could ever really be given to these once-men – muttered and whispered to themselves in their ranks behind him, as he observed the scene from the cover of a ridge. Beings of high savagery and low intellect, the golems that had survived long enough had learned to obey the sharp, grunted commands of the tall and gangly youth, who stood a head higher than the largest of them.

While he was pale like bleached bone, his consumptive aspect and black leather armour hid the truth of a wiry and whipcord-strong body. Dark eyes the colour of soured blood peered out from beneath an unkempt fall of lank, black hair. Never at rest, his searching gaze flitted from place to place, constantly looking for the next threat.

Hands with long and skeletal fingers clutched at the haft of a heavy cleaver falchion with a rusted blade, rocking it back and forth. The weapon was a battlefield find, fit to be used until broken, and like all his swords before it, it had never felt right in Mortarion's grip.

He sucked in a breath of heavy, turned air. The strongest of any lesser would find nothing but poison in the foetor of the mists, but the toxins at this altitude were meaningless to Mortarion. His constitution worked on a different scale to those of the ordinary humans. It was just one more of the secrets about his existence that had never been explained, and not for the first time, the youth wondered what the air would taste like down there in the valleys, where the lessers lived out their miserable existences.

His father had forbidden him to find out, of course. Mortarion's back bore the scars from where he had been whipped to bare the bone, as punishment for once daring to venture too far beyond his master's sight. He had been a child then, but that time still seemed close to the youth, set in recent memory.

It was difficult to reckon the passage of months, even years on Barbarus. What could be thought of as a 'day' was only a few hours of feeble, directionless sunlight in each cycle, the faint glow piss-yellow and sickly. Nights were long and damp. There were no true seasons to speak of, only a bruised grey pallor in the sky that would wax and wane, sometimes bringing vicious storms that wept black, greasy tears.

'Help us!' The scream echoed up from the hollow, breaking through Mortarion's reverie. A man, wailing in desperation, repeated his entreaty over and over, as he lost all reason in the vain hope that some deliverance would come, if only he asked for it.

What a fool, thought the youth. *Who does he think is listening? Who does he think cares?*

The golems grunted and shifted on their thin legs, stirred by the frantic note of panic in the man's voice, and Mortarion's own question echoed back at him through the canyons of his mind.

He dismissed it with a grimace and drew the black-powder repeater pistol holstered at his hip, shaking the iron gun to spin up the chemical trigger batteries in the grip. The golem-soldiers knew that noise and their agitation grew. They knew it was the precursor to the kill command.

Mortarion gave Hethemre's monsters a last look, listening to the man's cries die as they ate him alive. This would be a close-hand and needlessly messy engagement, he knew that from experience. Had his father seen fit to grant him use of just one of the Overlord's warclads, it would have been over in moments. A single iron stalker-tank would have quickly destroyed the rival's revenants with gel-fire projectors or shot cannonades. But his father knew that full well, and as with every other thing in Mortarion's life, this battle was a test for him to pass. If he did not win by brutality alone, if he was not strong enough for that... then he was *lesser*, and would be treated as such.

The thought burned in his mind and it pushed him up, over the ridge, and into a sprinting advance. The golems howled in pleasure and spilled across the muddy ground behind him, spitting and brandishing their pikes. Mortarion's repeater sparked and bellowed as he fired into the closest of the nondead and the patchwork horrors unleashed by Hethemre's resentment.

Festering meat blew apart as the gun's fat bullets impacted upon their targets. The heads of the rounds were filled with an incendiary-explosive compound of Mortarion's own creation, something he had invented in idle hours spent in the hollows of the bastion tower his father had built for him. Bodies were still falling as the gun's magazine clicked empty and he entered blade's range, setting to work with the cleaver falchion. He chopped ragged limbs from torsos, stamping still-twitching hands into the ashy slurry. He used the heavy pepperbox cluster of the repeater's barrels as a cudgel to cleave in skulls. Spurts of thick, congealed blood and stringy greenish ichor spattered over his armour as he advanced, step by step.

The revenants possessed enough instinct to know where the greatest threat lay, and a clump of them attacked him in unison, even as their fellows were being run through and battered down by Mortarion's golem pikemen.

The youth was suddenly swarmed before he could pause to reload the repeater and it was knocked from his grip, clattering as it was trampled into the cinders, dragging a length of safety chain from his holster along with it. Mortarion ignored the loss of the gun and grabbed the throat of the nearest nondead, using it as a shield. The falchion in his other hand was already labouring to cut the cankerous meat of the creatures, growing blunt with each successive blow he landed.

The melee became hack-work now, a punishing butchery that was art-less and grisly. Talons raked over Mortarion's body, claws cutting in a hundred different places, and the sheer weight of the attackers slowed his advance to a crawl.

His boot crunched on something wet and breakable, and the youth caught a glimpse of the still-warm corpse he had stumbled over. He saw the torn face of the screaming man, frozen in death, wisps of steam rising from the myriad bites and slashes that had ended him.

The moment of hesitation allowed the nondead to knock Mortar-ion off balance, and he cursed as his footing slipped away. A colossal heap of vile, stinking flesh heaped upon him, attempting to crush the youth beneath their weight. Snapping at him, blackened teeth in grin-ning mouths crowded on all sides, beneath milky eyes that seeped oily tears. The dry decay of papery skin filled his nostrils, along with the bitter metallic stink of pus oozing from buboes in livid triad clusters.

Mortarion released a murmuring growl and drew in, his muscles bunching as he found his centre, planting himself firmly against the despoiled earth. With a savage, violent explosion of force, he slammed back against the mass of the revenants and threw them off, sending bro-ken bodies flying, cleaving with the scarred and cracked sword blade. Dozens were crushed to paste from the concussion of the blow, torn apart for daring to meet this dark champion in close combat.

But even as the youth staggered free of the clutch, a new and greater foe came loping out of the toxic haze. As big as one of the Elect's steam-crawlers, the kill-beast was an agglomerate, a patchwork thing made up of human and animal pieces. Maddened by pain, it hooted through double sets of phlegm-drooling nostrils cut and stitched from what had once been a pair of herd grox. A distorted, bulbous body bal-anced on seven muscular legs, some transplanted from humans, others not, and there was a cluster of eyes in a clump across one quivering sheaf of muscle tissue. It resembled an insane child's sketch of a spider, a misshapen creature made of nothing but deformity.

It belched a jet of bile, and where the thick, glutinous matter landed the ashen earth melted into vaporous pools. Several of Mortarion's golems were caught in the fluid and they burst open at its touch.

He threw corpses at the agglomerate and dodged the next noxious ejection, striking for a knee joint in the nearest leg. The falchion cut through skin and muscle, but when it met gristle and bone it stopped dead, the impact force jerking Mortarion's arm and causing the kill-beast to hoot in agony.

The youth attempted to dislodge the blade, but it bent in his grip and finally broke clean in two. He staggered back, holding the stub of the sword, just in time to meet the agglomerate's wild counter-attack. Another giant's limb, this one ending in a broad tripartite hand, slammed him into the ground, clutched him, and then did it again and again. Mortarion's head rang and he lost focus. He jammed the broken remnant of the falchion into the limb but then the weapon was gone. He flailed around, trying to catch the spinning links of the chain to which his repeater pistol was still attached, but the kill-beast flung him about with such mad frenzy it was impossible to grab it.

The next blow was struck with enough force that it distorted his armour and broke bone. Mortarion's head was rammed into the earth, filling his mouth and throat with the powdery ashes of Hethemre's fires.

Mortarion was strong, *yes*, stronger than any lesser and more than a match for any champion the Barbarun Elect could field – but he was not invincible. The cinders were choking him, suffocating the air from his powerful lungs. A strain of potent emotion shocked through him, a rare and fleeting grasp of what had to be *fear*.

He was not a stranger to it. In the darkest hours, his perfect memories would draw up a sip of it, gathered from moments that he could barely comprehend, recollection from before his birth, from some kind of womb-space. Fear lurked there, the not-knowing and the not-understanding. The lack of self and the missing purpose. The awful, crushing certainty of abandonment.

Mortarion did what he always did, and used that fuel to stoke the will to survive. He would not die. He would not perish. There were too many questions to be answered, too much about his origins left unknown. The shadow of death was not here to take him, but to be his guardian.

Struggling against the monstrous pressure of the kill-beast's claw, Mortarion fought to find one last breath, to hold on one more moment.

And then he saw light. Golden light, captured in the blade of a massive scimitar. Burning brighter than truth.

The sword cut through the air with a shriek of thunder and he knew he was wrong. The glorious, perfect hue faded away and the towering weapon became something rust-caked and damned. Mortarion's heart sank as he realised that this would be the failure of today's particular test.

The blade severed the limb holding him down and all pressure ceased immediately. The youth scrambled to his feet, coughing out the ashes that had almost suffocated him, and he saw the weapon make another brutal cut.

This time, the scimitar cut open the agglomerate and vented its innards to the misty day. The kill-beast's death cry was a pathetic, childlike wail that rang away to echo off the mountainside. As it fell, so chugs of fire flew in on arcs of black smoke thrown from the turrets of stalker-tanks rising from the ridgeline. The remnants of the Overlord Hethemre's killing parties were blasted apart as they ran, and several of Mortarion's golems suffered the same fate by being too slow to flee the target zone.

He turned, knowing who he would see standing over him. The rank odour of his foster father's midnight robes stung the air.

'Boy,' said Necare, greatest of the Barbarun Elect and Highest of Overlords. 'You disappoint me.' The words dripped with contempt.

Tall enough that he could look down upon Mortarion's rangy form, the Overlord was a burned-bone charcoal sketch upon diseased pages. He was garbed in a hooded mantle of sailcloth so dark it seemed to eat the light around it, and what could be seen of Necare's corpse-flesh face and hands was nightmarish and alien. If his kind had ever shared any kinship with humans, that history had been seared away and forgotten. Now, like all of the Overlords, Necare was a horror, as if the universe had decided to express the fullness of the word *cruelty* in a living, breathing being.

The huge sword that had cut the agglomerate in two vanished into the folds of his robe, even as it seemed impossible to sheathe a weapon of such size beneath it. The Overlord took a step forward, appearing to glide over the burned lands without the actual effort of walking. Even that simple act was beneath him.

'How many more times must I preserve your life?' Necare never tired of posing this question to Mortarion. He had asked it after throwing the boy into a pit of starved canids, before he could walk upright. Asked it when he stripped Mortarion naked and left him to scale the sheerest cliffs during a torrential acid-storm. Asked it when he had forced him to slay barehanded a legion of golems and then a legion more. Always in judgement, often in mockery. Never satisfied with the reply.

'I needed no help,' said Mortarion, spitting on the ground. 'I can kill well enough alone.'

Necare arched as he bent closer, and the youth sensed the turn of the page towards the next step in this performance. 'You have not earned that right, boy. You are never out of my sight, remember that. You live at my pleasure.'

'I know.' Mortarion bowed his head, not because he felt gratitude, but because he knew it was expected of him. He had long since grown to hate his foster father's reasoning for keeping him alive, and there were some bleak days when he wished the Overlord had simply murdered him as a foundling.

The tale of his beginning on Barbarus was known to the youth, partially from his confused memories of the events and partially from what

Necare had told him in order to secure his gratefulness – or when he beat him for his wilful nature.

The High One had a reputation for brutality that made even his fellow Overlords pause, but he was also a capricious being. There had come a day when he had bathed the bleak summits in the blood of a rival, and in the wake of the massacre, Necare had gone to gloat over the dead. His enemy had been concealing something, a prize that the Overlord's slaves had told him fell from the sky. Necare decided he would possess it, out of spite and raw jealousy.

The prize was not what he had expected. Among the fields of the dead cast across the mountainside, a newborn's cries broke the silence of the mouldering corpses. The Overlord hesitated to kill the youngling, intrigued by its uncanny resilience. It looked like a lesser, a human. It should have been dead. *And yet...*

Necare delighted in ridiculing the young Mortarion with the story, declaring he suspected him to be an aberrant mutant of some stripe. At other times, he would relay the tale differently, claiming the foundling story to be a lie he concocted out of cold amusement, and the truth being that the boy was a failed experiment the Overlord himself had created from raw genetic matter and abducted lesser chattels.

Wherever his origins lay, the child was claimed by Necare and given his name – a word in the Barbarun dialect of High Gothic that meant 'born out of death'. And in his twisted, inhuman way, the Overlord groomed Mortarion as his heir. He tested Mortarion's limits, learning how great a concentration of toxins the child could survive and used that knowledge to determine exactly where to erect a walled domicile along the rise of the mountain range. High enough that the poisoned atmosphere kept a rein on the fast-growing boy, distant from the lessers in the valleys below and far from Necare's own dark castle in the upper reaches, where the youth could not venture.

There was nothing approaching affection in that association, however. It was a harshly transactional relationship, weighted completely in favour of the foster father.

The boy became the youth, the youth became the Overlord's tool. *Perhaps*, Mortarion wondered, *that had been his aim all along.*

To forge me into a weapon filled with nothing but hate and anger.

'You are loyal to me, my son,' intoned Necare, making the statement solid and real with his declaration. 'But you have much to learn, and far to go.' He gave a shake of the head. 'This is the last time. Show me weakness again and I will give you to the cutters to toy with.'

The Overlord drifted away, fading towards a humming steam-crawler bedecked with ornate decorations and his majestic chains of sworn fealty.

Mortarion watched in silence as the craft clattered away, picking up speed as it headed into the mists and up towards the flank of the tallest peak. There, where venomous snows coated the dead rock and the air itself was so poisonous that even he could not walk, stood the black manse of Mortarion's adoptive father.

And like the warmth and the peace that the youth would never know, it would forever be beyond his reach.

[The warp; now]

An undeniable instinct, that bone-deep hatred he held for all the ways of the witch, made him certain of it. Something out there was doing this.

'My lord!' Caipha Morarg's voice was as close to dread as a Death Guard's might be, and his dim shape hove near to Mortarion, one of the equerry's hands coming up to touch his vambrace. 'Do you hear me?'

Mortarion angrily batted away his gauntlet, and he spat black fluid on the deck to clear his throat of the fading constriction. 'Step away.' Bad enough that this unexpected assault had actually affected him, it was worse that the primarch had been forced to weather it in front of his men. It annoyed him to think that he might have shown even the smallest iota of weakness before them, and Morarg's concern deepened that sense all the more. 'I am unharmed.'

He cast around the bridge of the *Terminus Est*. Stricken legionaries were climbing to their feet, some wiping dark purple blood from their nostrils and the corners of their eyes. Other listed as they recovered their senses, gasping in breaths of air like men who had nearly drowned.

Many of the human helot crew were not so fortunate. Dozens of uniformed serf-officers lay dead, some slumped over their consoles, others in tormented, stricken poses on the deck. Mortarion saw a helmsman whose face was nothing but red rags, clawed to ruin by his bony fingers, and a gunnery controller who appeared to have deliberately broken her own neck against a support pillar. A grim-faced Legion Apothecary crouched and prodded the dead woman, scanning her corpse with an auspex reader.

He felt an unexpected flash of anger. *Humans are so pathetic.* The primarch rejected the thought and strode to the middle of the command deck. 'Who will explain this to me?' he demanded. 'What happened here?'

'We are still within the grasp of the empyrean,' said Typhon, scanning an oil-lens projector screen in front of him. He nodded towards the shuttered portals, and the sinister glow that seeped in around the edges of the sealed panels. 'During the fleet's transition, the scry-sensors registered an unexpected discharge of energies.'

'Sabotage?' said Morarg, in a low, warning tone. 'Or a malfunction?'

'Too soon to know,' said the First Captain.

'Status of the other vessels.' Mortarion made it a command, and Typhon echoed it with a nod. His second, the Grave Warden Vioss, moved to a vox-console and spoke to the operator.

'Reports coming in from other decks,' continued Typhon, watching trains of text unfurl across the projector. 'Many casualties among the human serfs, numbering in the thousands. The majority appear to be self-inflicted. Some of the lower tiers were vented to space by crewmembers who opened airlocks.' He paused, showing little more than passing concern. 'A notation here... Some forced executions have been required.'

'What say you, Crosius?' Morarg asked the Apothecary, looking askance at the crewman with the ruined face.

'They are void-cursed.' The Apothecary scowled at the cooling corpse and gave a sage nod. 'I have seen it before. The touch of the immaterium turned their minds, drove them insane.'

'And yet our Geller fields are intact.' Mortarion glared at the ticking brass console from which the protective energy barriers were controlled. The dials were all set at full potentiality. 'How then can witchery invade the *Terminus Est*?' He eyed Typhon over the mask of his breather. Some touch of the psyker had always been a part of his old comrade, and it had never – *it would never* – sit well with the Reaper of Men.

Typhon knew what was unsaid there, knew the suggestion of blame that was not made solid, but he did not rise to the bait. 'The equerry may be right. This could be a weapon our enemies deployed against us. But it could also be some peculiarity of the warp, my lord. The non-space we pass through does not follow the rules of the material universe – it is a capricious and changeable sea. Its effects can never be fully predicted, nor prepared for.'

Mortarion shook his head. He was well aware of the strange anomalies that could occur during a warp transit. Peculiar shifts in time that could mean a ship arriving weeks before it set sail, journeys that took the blink of an eye while a century passed in real space, the incidence of ghosts and visions and other phenomena.

But a phantom malaise that could strike at the indomitable constitution of the Death Guard? That was something he would not accept. 'This is not a psi-tempest, or some artefact of the Ruinstorm. Find me the answer, captain. We have a rendezvous to keep. This Legion's appointment with eternity will suffer no delay – I will not allow it!'

Typhon hesitated, and in that moment Vioss spoke. 'My lord. We have made contact with several other ships in the flotilla. They report similar circumstances. Thousands of humans dead, and legionaries briefly brought low.'

'I will address their commanders.' Mortarion turned, and as he did a handful of shimmering figures emerged out of the air. Fully dimensional images of a dozen other Death Guard officers formed from sculpted laser light that fell from hololithic projectors in the ceiling. The phantoms flickered and juddered, broken by random transmission artefacts, but they were clear enough for the primarch to recognise familiar faces and armour heraldry.

He addressed the first of them directly. 'Kalgaro. Do you hear me?'

'*Lord Mortarion, aye.*' Marshal Gremus Kalgaro's eyes glittered in the artificial light. '*We are still recovering. There has been some damage aboard the* Endurance. *An armed confrontation on the engine decks.*'

'A confrontation with what?' Morarg broke protocol by asking the question, but the primarch let the moment slip by unremarked.

'*Unclear,*' said Kalgaro. '*First reports suggest an outbreak of mass hysteria among the deck-swabs. They've been put down.*' Mortarion's Master of Ordnance looked troubled. During the absence of Typhon and his splinter fleet forces, Kalgaro had served as the primarch's second-in-command, but the stoic officer was ill-equipped to captain a starship, even a battle-barge as mighty as the flagship *Endurance*.

'*The same occurred here,*' said the image standing alongside Kalgaro's. Serob Kargul was senior legionary aboard the battle cruiser *Malefic*, another of Mortarion's chosen elite officers. '*A great number of deaths. There was a moment when all aboard the ship... All of us, lord, and the Legion included...*' Kargul's hand reflexively went to his throat.

'Yes,' said Mortarion, cutting him off. 'We felt it here too.'

The other commanders – among them Malek Vos aboard the cruiser *Balefire* and Gideous Krall, on the bridge of the *Ceaseless Advance* – nodded in weary unison.

'*Our sensors registered the loss of three ships in the forward task element,*' said Krall. '*Two destroyers and a strike cruiser. Weapons fire was not exchanged. It appears to be the result of a self-destruct or critical system failure.*'

'Some maddened soul ended themselves and took others with them,' Morarg offered.

'I'll warrant this ill-effect touched every craft in our fleet,' said Typhon. 'No mere malfunction could have caused it. This was deliberate.'

'If the Reaper permits,' Kargul added, 'I would suggest we attempt to de-translate from the empyrean and regroup. If there is a threat here with us in this tormented realm, then better we remove ourselves from it.'

'Is that wise?' Vos' lined brow furrowed. 'If this is the effect of a weapon deployed against us, another transition may trigger it once again.'

'We'll be ready this time,' countered the other Death Guard.

Mortarion's instinct sounded as Kargul's did. His immediate desire was to put as much distance as possible between his fleet and this daemon-infested space, but he also saw that Vos' reticence had merit. A cold, forbidding sense of threat drifted on the horizon of his thoughts, and although he could not articulate it, the primarch knew there was a greater danger lurking.

'For what it is worth, I concur with Captain Vos,' offered Typhon. 'We are Death Guard, are we not? We have never been known to retreat, even in the face of an unknown threat.'

The primarch left the comment where it lay. 'We will do nothing without first understanding,' Mortarion intoned, after a long moment. He looked towards Typhon's second. 'Vioss. Send word to every ship in the fleet to close ranks. If needed, have the larger vessels extend the perimeter of their Geller fields to ensure the others are fully protected. For the moment, we will proceed apace and gather ourselves.' It was very much a Death Guard tactic, to draw in and advance with armour raised against the dangers beyond. The primarch glanced back at Kalgaro and the other holographic images. 'See to your ships and your crews, my sons. Gather what data you can on this assault. We will not attempt another transition until I am certain it poses no further threat.'

'With respect, lord, that could take days of subjective time.' Krall folded his thick arms in front of him. 'Will the Warmaster delay for us at Terra's gates if we do not arrive when expected?'

'My brother cannot begin the invasion without me,' snapped Mortarion, unwilling to look too hard at his own statement. 'Do as I say.' He slashed the blade of his hand through the air, ordering Vioss to cut the hololithic connections.

'Lord,' said Typhon, stepping forward. He spoke with quiet intensity. 'The quicker we find the source of this attack, the better. I have a suggestion.'

'I will not like it,' he replied. Once, long ago, this exchange had brought cold humour to both their faces. But not today, and not here.

Undaunted, the First Captain continued. 'I will take some of my men, some... *specialists*... out into the fleet.'

Mortarion eyed him. He knew exactly what that meant, and his jaw hardened. *Psykers. Witch-kindred.* Those touched by the very thing he had fought his whole life to eradicate, that even now was attacking them.

He looked into Typhon's steady gaze, and once again considered a question that had plagued him for a very long time. *This man is my brother in battle. My first friend and fellow outcast. But in him lies the poison I loathe so. The weapon I abhor to wield.*

Would the Reaper of Men look away now, as he had so many times before? Would he take the meagre ease of knowing that this was a matter of expedience over scruples?

'If there is something irregular in this, I will know,' Typhon went on. 'I will find it. Grant me your trust, Mortarion. You let me carry your banner – now let me do this.'

'Go,' he said, at length. 'But bring me an answer that I can grip in my hands.'

Typhon showed a cold smile and bowed. 'Your will.'

The First Captain strode away and Mortarion walked to the back of the command arena, dwelling on the order he had just given. None of the Death Guard had spoken of it in the aftershock of the transition, but he knew, as only a gene-father could, that every single one of his warriors had suffered that same terrible moment of dread he had experienced. The suffocating, choking paralysis that no warrior of the Legiones Astartes, no primarch-born should ever have known.

It felt as brief as the blink of an eye, but the duration was unimportant. In that impossible instant, Mortarion had been *weak*. His memory had dragged him back to a past moment when that same dire sense had filled him, and he could only wonder if his sons had shared the same terror.

But to speak of it would be to give it form and power. To admit it. *Better*, he thought, *to deny and dismiss, to excise it as if it had never happened*. The alternative was to open a door towards a possibility he did not care to face.

'Lord Mortarion?' His equerry was at his side. Morarg was no fool. He saw the new distance in his master's mien. 'What would you have me do?'

'Give Captain Typhon whatever he requires,' said the Reaper of Men, opening a hatch to the shuttered dome of the warship's observatorium. 'And for now, give me my solitude.'

TWO

You Know Me
Silence Broken
Fragments

THEIR ARMOUR SEALED tight against the droning onslaught, Garro and
the Knights-Errant stormed into the swarm cloud with their weapons
charged and burning. The whirring morass of insect bodies bombarded
them with clustered, hammer-blow impacts upon their battleplate, each
hit like the punch of a Dreadnought.

It was impossible for Garro to see more than a hand's span in front
of him, as all around the black-and-silver glitter of the billion-strong
throng raged. Just as the psyker Ison had warned, the carrion flies
moved with a singular intelligence, working to separate the Knights-
Errant from one another as they forged deeper into the swarm.

Garro blink-clicked an icon on the inner surface of his armour's controls and the eye-lenses of his helmet shifted into a thermographic
mode, rendering the space in front of him in shades of heat-colour.
Dark dots writhed everywhere, and he picked out the cold blue of the
decking beneath him. In the middle distance, he glimpsed ill-defined
shapes in pale green – the ceramite-clad forms of Gallor, Varren and
Ison, each of them engaged in their own struggle to advance.

Garro left his Paragon bolter holstered for the moment, instead

carving his way forward with the blazing edge of his power sword.
The weapon known as *Libertas* had been his constant companion for
so many years that it was almost a part of him, and he wielded it
with deadly grace. He led with the blade, slashing through the thickening mass of the swarm, in figure-of-eight sweeps that destroyed
great clumps of carrion flies caught in the lightning aura around the
weapon's length.

His only compass was a digital marker glyph that Ison had communicated to the team, the most likely location of the core of the swarm.
Garro moved steadily in that direction, never faltering.

Fighting through the deafening tempest of the insect horde was like
battling a hurricane, and each carrion fly rattled against his armour
with a tinny clatter, as if they were stones hurled at him through the
winds. Monitor outputs projected directly into Garro's retinas warned
that the exhaust vents on his backpack power module were already
clogged by a paste of pestilent bodies – a threat that could lead to a
critical overheat if left unaddressed for too long – and seething masses
of the venom-jawed pests were at work chewing on exposed cabling
and flex-joints. The swarm would eventually erode his protection and
eat through to the meat and bone of him if he tarried. Garro had
seen what these creatures left behind them, in piles of crumbling,
acid-burned bone. He had no desire to let this mission go on any
longer than it needed to.

'One hundred metres,' he reported, over the general vox-channel.
'Bearing thirty-seven degrees relative.'

'*It knows you are close,*' Varren told him, through gritted teeth. '*It is…
Ach, it is keeping the rest of us back!*'

'*Aye,*' agreed Ison. '*Garro, be wary. The host is drawing you in.*'

'I will be careful.' His jaw set, Garro pressed on, but a moment later
an icon blinked before him, indicating a transmission on a private
channel from Gallor. He frowned and opened the link. 'Speak, Helig.'

'*Do you hear that, battle-captain?*' Gallor had once been a Death Guard
of the line in the Seventh Great Company, the fighting force that Garro

had commanded, and he used the old honorific to address him. '*A voice. Out there. I think it spoke my name.*'

'Ignore it, brother,' he told him. 'Focus your will.'

But no sooner had Garro closed the channel than he heard it.

'*Nathaniel. I see you.*' The voice was made from the rattle of mandibles and rush of glittering, metallic wings over one another. '*Do you remember me?*'

The distance was down to thirty metres now, and the swarm was so dense that the light of the day falling across the upper platform of the Walking City was almost totally occluded. Through the thermographic scan of his visor, Garro saw a humanoid form coalesce ahead of him. It wasn't quite solid, and it wavered and danced like a flame. But he found recognition in it.

A whirling, screaming mass of claws and green-black armour. A face malformed into something arachnid and loathsome, raising an arm in a gesture that was almost a greeting. The arm ended in deformed talons spiked with oily hairs.

'Decius?'

'*The same.*' The shape cocked its head. '*Or not. Not quite. I am not quite there yet, Nathaniel. But soon. Very soon.*' It drew out the last word into a crackling chuckle, and Garro realised the voice was being transmitted to him through the sympathetic buzzing of thousands of flies, echoing through direct contact with his armour.

Once, Solun Decius had been the youngest warrior in Garro's command squad, a lifetime ago before the insurrection of the Warmaster had set the galaxy on fire. Once, the unwavering and bright-eyed legionary had stood with him as he defied their primarch Mortarion and vowed, at any cost, to take word of the great insurrection to Terra. Once, Decius had fought the plagued monstrosities that the warp had made of his brother Death Guard, and there he had fallen to a grievous wound from a corrupted knife.

Whatever abhorrent venom lay on that blade had broken the young warrior and granted him the same atrocious rebirth. Garro was forced to kill him twice, once on the airless surface of Luna, and again when he pitched Decius' defiled remains into the Sun.

'*How is Meric?*' The question came at him through the roar of the swarm. '*Did he embrace the Gift, at the end?*'

Garro's gauntlet tightened around the hilt of *Libertas*. 'Meric Voyen wanted to save you, did you know that? The Apothecary thought he could bring you back.'

'*He was always an idealist. A poor trait for a Death Guard.*'

'Agreed,' Garro allowed. 'But better that than a weakling, a turncoat!' He rushed forward, swinging the blade at the figure.

It flickered away, briefly becoming insubstantial, then reforming. Garro caught a glimpse of a shambling, bloated corpse in the heart of the mass – the first host of this manifestation, the one that Ison had spoken of, wearing the aspect of his enemy.

'*Do not fear the truth,*' it hissed. '*We are all weak. We all eventually turn. The lie is to believe that we will not. The truth is to accept it... and take the Gift that comes next.*'

There was that phrase again, the speaking of 'a gift'. Each time Garro had faced such a horror, that offer had been there. It was not enough for the dread powers of the immaterium to simply destroy – they had to possess.

'*You cannot kill that which will never die,*' came the whisper. '*You can only submit to the inevitable.*'

'I won't let you take this city,' spat Garro, carving a sparking course through the swarm, into blade's range of the shimmering figure.

'*It is already ours, Nathaniel,*' admonished the creature. '*You have lost, and you will lose again and again until you understand.*'

Garro struck out and cut through the mass of the clustered form, destroying a great swath of it with one sweeping blow.

But the strike seemed to have no effect. '*I am only a pathfinder,*' said the Decius-voice. '*The means of your death will come soon enough. You will know his face as you know mine.*'

'You will not be there to see it,' Garro snarled, and then spoke into a secondary vox-channel. 'Strike element, the objective is before me. Target my location and fire all weapons!'

'*Strike element confirms,*' came the reply. '*Commencing attack run.*'

THE STORM EAGLE pilot had been orbiting the Walking City for some time, tracking the massive moving platform as it stumbled out of control through the snowy valley. The huge circular paws at the end of its multiple legs crushed the trunks of hardy trees below and pounded them into pieces as it passed, and as the valley narrowed, the far-side motive limbs skidded off the steepening slopes.

The platform was a huge target, wreathed in clouds of vapour from outgassing exhaust chimneys mixed with a strange black haze that moved against the path of the wind over the hills. Banking sharply, the pilot turned the Storm Eagle's blunt nose towards the midline of the Walking City and a locator icon blinked into being on her head-up display. The combination gunship-transport was heavy on the stick, much different from the Viento-class atmospheric attack fighters she had trained on, but it was tough in the fight and far more durable. Sucking in metallic, reprocessed air through the mask over her nose and mouth, she switched the fire selector from *safe* to *arm* and readied to release the Storm Eagle's missile load into the target point.

Before she had become one of Malcador's Chosen, there might have been a part of her that would have baulked at the idea of dropping her entire war-shot on the same coordinates as the warrior giving her that order. Not now, though. She had learned. The Knights-Errant were not suicidal. They were certain.

Garro had given her an order like this once before, when she had shuttled him out to the Azovik Litters, on a termination sortie against a band of treacherous agitators and propagandists who called themselves 'the Enborn'. After the barrage that followed had turned them and their pitiful hideout into ash, Garro had walked out of the bomb-smoke without a scratch on him.

The pilot knew then that she was serving in the company of war angels, and all the old tales her mother had told of the divinity of the Emperor and His progeny snapped into hard focus. So now she obeyed without hesitation, bringing the Storm Eagle down in a screaming power dive towards her designated target.

Ready lights blinked on her console, and her gloved finger hesitated over the firing stud on her flight yoke. Out past the Storm Eagle's nose, she could see a writhing tower of darkness that moved and danced in unnatural ways. She had seen many strange and disturbing things since joining the Chosen, and so it did not panic her when the darkness briefly took on the contours of a screaming human face. If anything, the strange sight strengthened her resolve.

Her trigger finger tightened. 'Missiles away now, now, n–'

She never completed the act. Faster than her eye could register, a great tendril of swarming carrion flies broke off from the twisting shadow and rose up to strike the nose of the Storm Eagle head-on.

The impact threw her back against her acceleration rig with enough kinetic force to break bone, and dimly she heard the shriek of tearing metal as the aircraft shed one of its wings. The pilot tried desperately to mash the firing stud, but it was already too late. The cockpit's armoured canopy splintered and a torrent of buzzing insects poured in, filling the cramped space. They chewed through her oxygen pipe and flooded her mask, suffocating her.

The pilot's hands left the flight yoke, and the wounded Storm Eagle spun down out of control, until it collided with another of the Walking City's legs. The resultant concussion blew apart the massive steel limb at the knee, forcing the great platform to lurch to a halt, grinding it into the ice and rock of the mountainside.

'Was that your plan?' Gallor called, across the static-choked vox-channel, as the Walking City trembled and shuddered. The sound of the interference was the harsh, contemptuous laughter of the swarm-mind.

Garro cursed the spear of fire that marked the Storm Eagle's destruction, and took a brief moment to whisper something in the lost pilot's name. 'God-Emperor, mark her sacrifice…'

'*Say again?*' asked Ison. '*Did not copy your last transmission.*'

Garro thought of words in red ink printed on battered and torn pages, of the guidance that the book of the *Lectitio Divinitatus* sometimes offered him. In this moment, the inspirational text seemed disconnected and far away from the battle before him. Here was another death, as rote as the last. Another noble soul, doused like a candle's flame. Bitterness rose in him as he cleaved his way through the swarm, striking at the formless figure of the Decius-thing, the host.

The muttering non-voice buzzed through the steel of Garro's helm, mocking him. '***You will lose again and again until you understand.***'

'*Battle-captain.*' Gallor's urgent call cut through the sound. '*Above us, I spy another aircraft at high altitude. Moving very fast.*'

Garro drew back, turning his gaze skyward, but the dank mass of the swarm made it impossible to see more than a few metres.

'*It has ejected something,*' Gallor went on, watching from his vantage point at the edge of the insect mass. '*Falling now. Towards us.*'

A ripple of involuntary motion moved through the swarm, as if an electric charge had gone through it, and in the wake of the effect Garro swore he could sense something too. He was no psyker, and by the Emperor's Grace that accursed talent would never be part of him – but still he knew enough to recognise the acidic crackle of psionic energy in the atmosphere. Through the swarm's shrilling shadows, he glimpsed distant flashes, like blue aurorae.

'Ison,' he called, addressing the legionary-Librarian. 'Do you feel that?'

When Ison replied, it was with a smile in his voice. '*I do. It seems our kinsman has come to join us. And he is bringing the storm with him.*'

'Rubio…?' Garro could not articulate how he knew it was the former Ultramarine; the fact of it simply seemed right. And now he knew what to do.

He turned back to the host. It was losing coherence as he watched, the ghostly black shade resembling Decius' mutant form coming apart.

His enemy was withdrawing its essence, leaving the predators it had unleashed and the flyblown victims to perish.

'What are you afraid of?' he shouted. 'Where are your riddles now, Decius?'

'The Lord of Flies ate Solun Decius,' it told him. *'And in time you will be consumed too. But not here. Not today–'*

Garro grimaced, weary of the creature's verbosity, and made riposte with a sudden, two-handed stab of his power sword. Caught off guard, this time the proxy did not escape the blade penetrating the dense insect horde clumped around the host body, and the entire swarm shrieked in sympathetic agony. Pushing the sword deeper, Garro ran the creature through and pinned it to the decking. It squirmed and cursed him as a million tiny fangs spat venom.

'We may not be able to kill you today,' he said, as daggers of electricity sparked down through the swarm from up above, connecting to the deck, turning clusters of flies into burning ash. 'But we will take your victory from you.' Garro looked up, and through the thrashing of the collapsing swarm a figure in grey ceramite descended, buoyed by the heavy turbine drums of a flaring thruster pack. His head and hands were wreathed in captured lightning.

'Well met, Nathaniel,' called Rubio. 'How may I assist you?'

Garro released his grip on *Libertas* and stepped back, nodding towards the pinned creature. 'Finish this for me.'

'With pleasure.' The eyes of Rubio's helmet flashed with actinic colour and the blaze of psychic force he had been holding in check was now released. 'Ison? Make sure none escape.'

'*Done,*' said the other psyker, and Garro felt the air tremble. The two brothers of the Librarius worked as one, with Ison corralling the swarm and Rubio exterminating them.

Garro raised his gauntlets to shield the lenses of his helm as the killing aurorae raged all about him, atomising every tainted thing it touched, but leaving the Knights-Errant unharmed.

When the searing light finally faded, he reached up and removed his headgear, finding Rubio standing ankle-deep in a black drift of burnt flies. As the psyker shrugged off his spent flight pack, Garro trudged back to where he had left *Libertas*. The sword stood upright, a heap of unidentifiable cinders piled around it. Retrieving his weapon, he brushed it clean.

With the abrupt absence of the swarm's droning chorus, the quiet seemed almost oppressive. Save for the distant creaking of the Walking City's stalled engines, the only other sound was the faint susurration of dead insects falling around them like black snow.

'As ever, Tylos, you have an aptitude for being in the right place at the right time,' said Garro.

'You may thank the Sigillite for that,' came the reply. 'It seems he was right to dispatch me.' Rubio peered up into the sky, finding the glittering contrail of the shuttle that he had dropped from.

'Should have sent you with us in the first instance, then,' Varren called out as he approached with Ison and Gallor following behind, their boots crunching on the ash-fall. 'But then Malcador does like to stir up his little dramas, doesn't he?' Like Garro and Rubio, the others had also unhooded.

'The Sigillite is nigh-immortal,' noted Ison, wiping a patina of sweat from his brow, despite the cold. 'I imagine when you get to be that old, you have to find your amusement where you can.'

'Mind what you say,' Gallor warned. 'He could be watching.'

'He is *always* watching,' said Garro.

Varren shot him a look. 'What now? If the infestation is dealt with, then we go, aye? Let the civilians deal with the mess.'

'Not yet,' Rubio said, drawing himself up. 'Malcador left one more command for me. He said we need to search the site.'

'For what?' Varren bristled. He didn't like idea of such a duty. His forte was creating destruction, not wading through its aftermath.

'He didn't tell me,' said Rubio, moving away to survey the wreckage. 'But I'll warrant we will know it when we find it.'

✠ ✠ ✠

THE KNIGHTS-ERRANT SPREAD out into a standard sweep-and-clear pattern, moving through the wrecked spaces of the platform's upper deck, and Rubio allowed his preternatural senses to guide him.

He would not have spoken of this to Garro or the others, but there was a part of him that only felt *whole* when he allowed his psionic abilities to come to the fore. To admit that openly was almost unseemly for a son of Macragge, against the martial culture of stoicism and resigned fortitude that was the character of the Ultramarines, and the manner in which he had been trained. But, as he reminded himself, he was not of the XIII Legion any more. He was not part of *any* Legion now.

At first that reality had angered and dismayed him, and he held tight to the only symbol of his old life he had been allowed to retain after accepting Malcador's mark – the gladius force sword he had wielded as a Codicier. But slowly, he had adapted, little by little coming to understand that his new role granted him a greater agency to fight in the Imperium's defence. A freedom, he realised, that he would never have known as an Ultramarine.

Perhaps it had been his near miss with death aboard the *Vengeful Spirit* that had finally cemented that understanding. A possibility was forming in his thoughts. Soon the Warmaster's invasion would be at hand, and when that moment came, Malcador would need all his forces to defeat Horus Lupercal... and Tylos Rubio would be in the front rank among them.

'I wondered where you had been.' Garro's voice interrupted his musings. The older warrior picked his way through the debris behind him, the sharp eyes in his scarred and patrician face studying the psyker's expression. 'We have not spoken in some time.'

'Not since the incident at Manatan,' he agreed. Rubio and Garro's last shared mission had been on the island hive city-turned-mega-prison, where they had put down an incident among the convict population. 'I was recalled to the Imperial Palace. Tasked with a recovery mission.'

Garro raised an eyebrow. 'That seems a rather limited use of your skills, kinsman.'

'Perhaps. My quarry was a... unique one.' He decided to say nothing else. How would Garro have reacted if he told him the truth? The man the Sigillite ordered Rubio to track down in the sinks of old Albia had worn the colours of the Night Lords, revealing himself as a dream-eater of that turncoat Legion's Librarius. Garro would want to know more, and he would press Rubio to answer questions that he himself had no answer to.

The Night Lord had been delivered to Malcador's presence for judgement, as instructed, but he was not the only one. Rubio was aware of other new faces taking the storm-cloud grey of the Chosen's armour, warriors whose auras he did not recognise – and some that he did, as enemies rather than allies.

He sighed. 'There are strange matters at hand, and I confess I have no measure to put to them.'

Garro was perceptive, and he must have heard the reluctance in Rubio's voice. 'You and I have not always seen eye to eye. But after what happened to you aboard the Warmaster's ship, I hoped you might have re-examined your perspectives. To meet me halfway.' The battle-captain took a weary breath. 'I respect your honesty, Rubio. So I ask, what troubles you?'

Rubio pushed aside his concern about the Night Lord and the other new arrivals, and instead concentrated on something more recent – but no less disturbing. 'Something happened today, upon the Eagle's Highway.'

'I know of it. But Dorn struck that down, did he not?'

'Not yet.' Rubio paused in his search through the wreckage and told Garro what he had witnessed with the fugitive named Wyntor, the man's deliberate choice of suicide over surrender, and of Malcador's uncommon manner through it all. 'When it was over, the Sigillite vanished, along with any explanation,' he concluded.

Garro gave a brief, humourless smile. 'He does that. It is irksome.'

As he dwelt on it, Rubio's frustration finally found a shape. 'What are we doing, Garro? These missions that Malcador sends us on, back and forth across the face of Terra – what are they accomplishing? I can intuit no greater design or military objective at hand. The Warmaster has broken through at Beta-Garmon. The insurrection that we glimpsed on Calth and elsewhere is almost raging at Terra's walls, but what are *we* doing?' He gestured around. 'We should be on the offensive, but instead we plug the gaps in an ethereal barricade and terminate fifth column insurrectionists. And for each one we expunge, two more arise. This does not feel like waging a war. It feels like marking time.'

'Aye.' Garro's wan smile faded and he became grave again. 'But that time is running out. The people of the Throneworld know it as well as we do. Panic and fear hang over every human settlement on this planet.' He nodded towards the pitiful state of the Walking City, as if to make it the exemplar of his words. 'The Imperium's influence can only hold so much before it falters. And these... incidents that we have put down do not escape greater notice. The chapels of the Imperial Cult are widespread, perhaps more than even Malcador suspects, and they carry the news within their own network of contacts. And yet, even as they give succour to the fearful, I am afraid they may also entice the darkness towards us.'

There was something beneath the older warrior's words that Rubio wanted to read. *A belief*, he thought, *a truth that Garro holds closer than any other.* Skimming the surface of the other Knight-Errant's psyche, he glimpsed fleeting images of a book with red text and a tarnished golden aquila hanging from a broken chain, things he had seen more than once in the battle-captain's mind. But then Garro gave him a sharp look and he withdrew.

'Forces are converging. It is known to me that the Sisters of Silence have quit the Somnus Citadel and returned to Terra to regroup,' Garro went on. 'They would not leave their base on Luna without good cause.'

'And the Seventy? What of them?' Rubio referred to a small group of Death Guard loyalists, who had originally accompanied Garro on his desperate mission to Terra aboard the starship *Eisenstein*. Since their

Legion had been declared *Excommunicate Traitoris*, those warriors had been held in abeyance with their future still undecided.

'Their numbers are far less than that now,' Garro admitted. 'The Sigillite gave me no answer as to their fate when I demanded it of him, save to tell me that they live. I suspect they are somewhere on Terra.' He looked away. 'This war has taken everything they knew from them.'

Rubio sensed that Garro was speaking as much of himself as he was of his former cohorts. *He is hiding something.* The psyker was certain. *From the moment we first met on Calth's blasted landscape, I've known it.*

Rubio reached inside himself, fashioning the most subtle of psychic probes. Perhaps the mysteries guarded by Malcador were beyond his ability, but for all his strength of will Nathaniel Garro was not.

But when Rubio reached out, his telepathic power ebbed away, drawn from his target by a subtle, abyssal darkness that dragged it in like matter towards a black hole. Rubio halted, the colour draining from his face. For the second time in less than a day, he sensed a negative shadow in the warp, close enough for his psyche to touch it.

'Rubio? Speak!' Garro saw the shift in his expression, and the battle-captain pulled his bolt pistol from its dusty holster, expecting the worst. 'What is it? Another psyker?'

'No...' The null-void in the unseen psionic current around him became clearer. 'The very opposite, in point of fact. There is a pariah...' Rubio turned and found the source of the effect. 'Here.'

He pointed towards a collapsed section of the platform, a collection of damaged frames and support panels that had once been part of a habitat module. A metal hatch was visible beneath a pile of wreckage, and Rubio moved towards it. The closer he got, the greater the suffocating negative sensation became. This felt very different to the odd, atonal psionic emptiness he had experienced with Wyntor, closer to the horribly familiar, soulless, sickly cold Rubio knew from previous engagements with a blank. He held his breath, letting his weight settle on the broken decking. A faint sound reached him from within the hab-module. *A voice?* He could not be certain.

Garro heard it too. 'I will follow your lead,' he said.

Rubio nodded and moved to the rim of the hatch, grabbing at the latches holding it shut. The crystals of his psychic hood emitted tiny, high-pitched crackles as their delicate structures reacted to the presence of the null. Being this close to the deadening effect repulsed him, and instinct screamed at Rubio to fall back, out of range. He gritted his teeth and held firm. 'Ready?'

Garro nodded, and Rubio gave the latches a savage twist, snapping both off with a squeak of breaking metal. Pulled open by gravity, the hatch swung wide and slammed against the frame with a concussive bang. Garro was already stepping inside, leading with his bolter.

'IN THE EMPEROR'S name, show yourself!' Garro swept left and right, peering into the dimness. His genhanced vision adjusted instantly, bringing the jumbled interior of the broken compartment into sharp relief. Amid piles of wreckage, he saw an amber-skinned woman garbed in rags, her wrists and ankles bound by heavy manacles. Chains pooled around her where she crouched on the floor. Despite her dirty and dishevelled appearance, the woman had the spare, muscular build of a warrior, and Garro noted a broad scar across her chin that could only have come from a sword blade. Her scalp was bare but for a fuzz of coppery hair, and she bore wounds along the visible skin of her arms that looked freshly self-inflicted.

She did not seem to notice him. Instead, the woman stared blankly at the walls and muttered to herself, rocking slowly backwards and forwards.

Garro's aim did not falter. The woman appeared to be no threat to him, but in the war of lies and rebellion he was fighting, it was hard not to suspect everything as a falsehood on first sight. He closed in, aware of Rubio waiting at the door. The psyker was reticent to come any nearer.

The air inside the compartment was heavy with dust and the odour of sweat. Garro suspected that the woman had been a prisoner in here for some time – but for what reason, and to what end? 'Identify yourself,' he said, taking care to measure his voice. 'What are you doing here?'

Still she ignored his presence. At length, Garro frowned and returned his pistol to its holster, dropping to one knee so that he could look the woman in the eye. He was close enough now to hear what she was saying.

'Schism. Broken, sundered.' They were the same words, repeating at the interval of every other breath she took. 'Schism. Broken, sundered.'

'I do not understand,' he said, trying once more to engage her. Gently, Garro reached out and touched her face, but she did not react. He saw something on her neck, the lines of raised scarification in a defined shape – a crimson eagle, wings spread and talons bared.

The symbol was familiar to him, and suddenly things made sense. The woman was an Untouchable, a psychic blank, but with a warrior's aspect to her. Carefully, Garro reached up to her throat, and opened the grimy tunic she wore to reveal the skin above her right collarbone. There, laser-tattooed in stark black ink was a string of numerals and text in High Gothic. A name, a rank and a serial code.

'Malida Jydasian.' Garro read her name back to her, and there was the briefest of flickers in the woman's eyes. But the moment passed, and she returned to her rhythm of repeated speech. He sighed, and guided her to her feet, pausing only to snap off the chains holding her in place. Applying steady pressure to her back, Garro impelled Jydasian to take one step, and then another, guiding her to the hatchway and out into the cold light of day.

Rubio backed away as the two of them emerged. 'Do you know her?'

Garro shook his head. 'I know what she is.' He indicated the eagle scar. 'This woman is a Null Maiden of the Silent Sisterhood.'

'But she speaks. Their kind are oath-sworn never to utter a sound.' The other warrior narrowed his eyes. 'What is she doing here? And in such a state?'

'I do not know,' Garro admitted. In their missions to hunt down the rogue psykers who threatened the safety of the Imperium, the Sisters of Silence rarely operated alone, with their preferred tactic being the deployment of a huntress team numbering six or more. But if there were more within the Walking City's environs, Rubio would doubtless have sensed them. The most logical explanation was that Jydasian had been captured by some insurrectionist faction operating on the platform, but even that seemed hard to accept. Garro had fought alongside the Silent Sisterhood, against the jorgall at Iota Horologii, and their fortitude and martial prowess had greatly impressed him. Among humans, there were few warriors who had earned that praise, and he imagined that none of the Sisters would submit easily to captivity. The distant, hollow look in Jydasian's eyes and her toneless manner suggested that it was not only her physical form that had been maltreated, but also her mind as well. 'We need to get her to safety,' Garro concluded.

'Indeed,' said Malcador.

Garro and Rubio stiffened as the Sigillite made his way down the slope of a fallen wall, measuring out each step with a thud from his towering staff upon the metal.

'Always watching,' Rubio said quietly, throwing Garro a sideways look.

Garro's lip curled, and he eyed the figure in the hooded robes. He knew he was looking at an illusion, cast telepathically across the planet to this location, but still it was hard not to feel daunted in its presence. He chose to mask that with acerbity. 'Lord Regent. Can you not simply use a vox-channel, like anyone else?'

'Quicker this way,' Malcador replied. 'More direct. And less chance of my commands being creatively interpreted.' He halted at the bottom of the fallen wall, and seemed to become insubstantial for a moment, before the image reasserted its solidity.

Garro glanced at the woman. The pariah's null effect was strong enough that it could affect the Sigillite's ghostly presence.

'This woman is dead,' Malcador pronounced, examining the freed prisoner. 'Or so her sisters believe. She was a Witchseeker of the Thunder Vane cadre, but the rolls list her as missing, presumed killed in action during a pogrom on one of the Mercury orbitals. That was over six months ago.'

'Did you know we would find her here?' asked Rubio.

'No.' Malcador shook his head, and there was genuine concern in his tone. 'It's rare that I encounter the unexpected. I hadn't anticipated coming across another so soon...'

'Another?' Garro seized on the word.

Beneath his hood, the Sigillite's brow furrowed, as if he had allowed something to be said that was better left hidden. Garro knew him better than that, however. Malcador never uttered a word without first weighing every possible import of it. 'There have been others, discovered in similar condition.'

'How many?'

Malcador went on as if he had not heard Rubio's question. 'This is a delicate time. It is important that the attention of our disparate forces are not split by secondary concerns.' He looked Garro in the eye. 'Nathaniel. You will take the Witchseeker to a place of safety. Coordinates will be transmitted to you on an encrypted data-channel.' Then he glanced at Rubio. 'Ensure the Walking City is secure, then stand down. I will find a new assignment for you and the others in due course.' The Sigillite turned and retraced his steps, back up to the top of the ramp.

'If you are not really here,' Garro called after him, 'then why are you walking away?'

'If I vanish like a mirage...' The hooded figure gave a low chuckle as he reached the crest of the broken wall, passing out of sight. 'Well. Where would the theatre be in that?'

'IRKSOME, INDEED,' RUBIO said, staring after the hooded figure. 'These matters grow more complicated by the day, and as always, he does his best to reveal nothing to us.'

'Malcador is a creature of artifice,' said Garro. 'If you expect anything other than that from him, you will be disappointed.'

A reply began to form on Rubio's lips, but he held it in check. Garro was right, up to a point – but Rubio could not shake the memory of the Sigillite's behaviour up on the Eagle's Highway, before the man Wyntor had chosen to die. He had seen truth then, some tiny fraction of who Malcador really was, and it sat poorly with him.

Garro looked away as Varren and the others approached from the far side of the tumbledown plaza where they stood, and he signalled with a cutting motion. 'We have our orders, then. You will take command of this team.'

'The World Eater won't like that,' said Rubio. 'He outranks me.'

'Not any more.' Garro tapped the ghostly mark etched into his battle armour. 'Do as Malcador said, but be swift about it. I have another task for you.'

'Oh?' Rubio eyed him, while warily observing the woman Jydasian from the corner of his sight.

Garro studied the freed prisoner. 'Why does he not turn this unfortunate over to her fellow Untouchables? I warrant he will not reveal her existence to the Silent Sisterhood.'

'What benefit would that have?' Was Malcador fearful of alarming the Witchseekers, or distracting them from Horus' invasion? Rubio's personal antipathy for blanks aside, the Sisters of Silence were fellow warriors in the Emperor's service and he disliked the idea of misleading them.

The auspex unit on Garro's belt gave a melodic chime and he glanced at it, reading off a string of data. 'As good as his word. A location in the Polar Radwastes... I will need to secure some transport.' He frowned, then fixed Rubio with a hard look. 'Search this location,' he ordered. 'Find some of the survivors, get what information you can from them. Someone must have known about a captive being held here. I want to know how Jydasian came to be in the Walking City. It is a long way from Mercury.'

'Malcador said nothing about investigating,' Rubio noted.

'I know. Do it anyway.' Garro showed a slight smile.

Rubio nodded, accepting his part in this act of disobedience. 'How far do you want us to follow her trail?'

Garro placed a hand on the muttering woman's shoulder and guided her away. 'Until we have illumination. We will know it when we find it, yes?'

INTERVAL III

The Grave Lies

[The planet Barbarus; before]

A THIN LIQUID precipitate drooled from the stonework of the walls, following a black furrow gouged in the heavy grey bricks. The ticking of the drips upon the undecorated floor marked the passage of time.

Mortarion sat in solitude, atop a low bench heaped with the hides of crag-dogs, warmed by an odorous fire of petrochemical tar. The blue-yellow light of the flames illuminated the pages of the book in front of him, and drew shadows from the makeshift nib of the pen he pulled across the acid-bleached paper.

The entry in his journal for that day might have described any number of others. *A battle on the escarpments against a rival of Necare. I killed many. My foster father was displeased with me.* He gripped the pen in his hand and squeezed it until the metal creaked. This was his life, repeated over and over. It seemed there would never come an end to the cycle. He was the High Overlord's champion murder-maker, his battlefield tool, and would never be anything more.

Mortarion let the pen drop and brooded, glaring into the depths of the flames. Other books, similarly bound in scraps of old leather or lesser skins, lay in piles among the shadows. At first, Necare had forbidden the young Mortarion to learn the texts of the Overlords, in an attempt to control his education. But the boy had grown fast, faster he suspected than was normal for a typical human, and with that growth in muscle and mass Mortarion's questing intellect had also blossomed. Eventually, the High One saw the merit in having him taught, and books were brought to Mortarion's citadel, downslope from the master's own impregnable fortress.

Most of them were dry tomes on the tactics of warfare and the many manners in which humans could be killed, or works depicting knowledge gleaned from dissections and grotesque experiments. Others contained scraps of contradictory accountings from the planet's past, of wars between the feuding Overlords and the endless cycle of conflict between these immortals. Some suggested that the Overlords had come from another place and taken up residence on Barbarus, inflicting their callous rule upon the lessers. There were hints they might have once been human – or *humanlike* – until a change had been wrought upon them in the wake of a cataclysmic pact with a monstrous, unknown power. With the reality lost after thousands of years, the full truth was nowhere to be found.

The boy devoured them all, read and reread them time and again, until he retained every word in his memory. This eidetic recall he possessed had been one of the first secrets he kept from his foster father, and when he found he had no need to turn the physical pages any more, Mortarion secretly soaked off the ink upon them. The newly blanked books became a record of his hopes, his fears and his simmering fury.

Perhaps that younger version of Mortarion had believed that by giving form to these things, he would find a measure of peace; but as he looked back over past writings, all he saw served only to confirm his certainty of the bleak inequity of his existence.

Abruptly, the youth stood and stalked away, startling a servile standing in the doorway at the far end of the hall. The patchwork golem retreated out of sight and Mortarion watched it go. Like the pikemen who had marched with him, the servile was a flesh-gathered slave, made out of parts of the dead and animated by the warped magicks conjured by the Overlords. It and all the others in Mortarion's citadel were nominally under his command, but that was a thin veil over the truth. Necare was the master here, and Mortarion knew that the golems watched him at his foster father's behest. Like the citadel, it was a lie meant to pacify him. The stone walls of this place were a prison for the youth, not a domicile.

He wandered to one of the thick armourglass doors in the far wall, the once-transparent panes now grimy and green with slicks of greasy algae. Outside, the mists were running thin on fast winds up from the valley below. The gusts were channelled through a narrow pass that Mortarion's abode overlooked, and on some days, the haze hung in sheets so heavy and cloying that he could barely see ten metres ahead of him, the poison in them making his breathing heavy. At other times, hard squalls would push the clouds towards the high peaks. He remembered hearing sounds, on the rarest of occasions. The crackle of gunfire, perhaps even voices, carried from the distant settlements of the lessers far below.

Barbarus did not often permit such reverie. This feral world was an unforgiving environment, and even in its desolation it did not permit the slightest hint of beauty. All native life upon it was ugly and venomous, from the simplest poison lichens coating the rocky tors to the hook-toothed lamprey serpents that writhed beneath the surface of the murky earth. The very air itself, a smouldering black-orange at the highest reaches, bled toxins into everything. Excited by radiation from a sun seen rarely as a white smudge in the high heavens, the clouded atmosphere of Barbarus wept acidic rain and bred a bestiary of noxious miasmas. The higher one climbed, the denser the poisons became. Up there, nothing natural could live. Only the Overlords survived unaided upon the tallest peaks.

Mortarion peered upward, picking out the jagged, broken teeth of the Scarred Mount, tallest of the Barbarun ranges – and there atop it, barely visible in the shadowed night, the distant watchfires burning against the black monolith of Necare's castle.

How he longed to climb the treacherous, winding path to that place, to stand outside the seared metal of its portcullis and tear it open. To prove to his foster father that he could.

It would be certain death to try, of course. Even the youth's beyond-human constitution was not strong enough to resist the incredible toxicity of the air at that altitude. Necare knew this full well, for whenever the young Mortarion had spoken out of turn to him, or dared to challenge something he said, the High One would laugh and give the same retort.

If you wish to be considered worthy, all you need do is come to my halls and show me you deserve the honour.

Mortarion spat on the flagstones as the memory of that denial burned in him, and his long-fingered hands drew into fists. 'This will be my lot,' he muttered to himself. 'Repeated until I die for him in some pointless skirmish over pride, or murder him myself...'

The heady possibility of that, of grasping Necare's thin neck in his hands and twisting it until it broke, shocked through Mortarion. His pallid skin prickled in the wake of the emotion.

What am I? If only it could be done. If only I could find a way.

The crash of blister-shot reached his ears and pulled him back to the moment. Mortarion pivoted, seeing the flash of clockwork guns ripple-fire in the twilight. He could see a caravan of steam-crawlers on the rising road through the pass, a frequent sight on the pathways that led to the higher crags. Often, the slow machines carried golem packs or kill-beasts out on raiding parties, or else they brought up tribute from the lessers, and captives to fill the works of the Overlord's cutters.

Watching through the armourglass, Mortarion's eyes widened as he witnessed a detonation take place inside one of the crawlers, a large cargo carrier on thick tank-tracks. The machine skidded off the road and into a ditch, bleeding smoke. And then, from out of the torn-open cargo bed came a human, clad in rags, clutching at a breather mask and retching. He was a youth, stocky and fox-faced, his eyes wide with fear.

The smaller escort vehicles in the caravan ground to a halt, and hatches retracted to deploy groups of golems. The patchworks sniffed the thick air and barked at one another, catching the escapee's scent.

Mortarion was fascinated by the scene. Before he was aware of the act, he had wrenched open the door and stormed out onto the battlements around his citadel's shield wall, to get a clearer look.

The youth went back to help other humans, and a tide of them spilled from the wrecked crawler, a mix of males and females of various ages, all of them of similar hardy stock. It was a crop for his foster father's experiments, Mortarion realised, each destined for pain and suffering in one of Necare's skinworks. The humans were panicking. At this altitude, lessers would not survive long in the open air.

The youth with the mask saw the walls of Mortarion's citadel and broke into a loping run towards it. He was leading the others to seek shelter, so desperate that even the ominous grey ramparts of an Overlord-built fortress were more welcoming than the golems at their heels. His frantic gaze raked along the walls of the citadel and found the gaunt figure up there, locking eyes with him across the muddy distance.

A strange moment of shock passed through Mortarion, a formless connection that existed for one brief instant, and then was gone. A cluster of golems were sprinting up the rise to mob the escapees, and the youth turned as the first of them closed in.

Mortarion saw an odd ripple in the air around the youth's hand, like the reflection of light off polished metal, but there was nowhere the glow could have come from. Something fell at his feet, then flickered through the mud, darting towards the nearest hulking golem. Before the patchwork could react, skinny white lampreys burst out of the ground around where the golem stood and savaged its legs, bringing it down in a mewling heap.

Whatever the youth had done, it was taking its toll on him. He pulled a broken shiv of rusty metal from beneath his jerkin, gripping it like a dagger, wheezing with each tainted breath he took. 'What are you?' he cried, managing a half-cry, half-shout. 'Up there, watching? You can see us! You can help us!'

What are you? Mortarion recoiled from the question, as if it were a physical blow, hearing in it the echo of his own thoughts.

More golems came running, surrounding the youth, and others attacked the choking stragglers still trying to extricate themselves from the crashed cargo crawler. On the battlements, Mortarion's own cohort reacted with slow malice, raising their javelins or heavy crossbows to take aim at the humans.

'No!' he bellowed, striding to the nearest of them, knocking the wall guard aside with a backhand blow. 'Stand down!'

On the muddy ground, the youth was fighting for his life, slashing with his dagger, kicking and snarling. If nothing was done, Mortarion would be witness to his death.

What am I?

The question hammered at Mortarion's thoughts. *A tool. A weapon. A disappointment. An error. A fool.*

The youth cried out as claws raked him, and he fell. The golems paused, chattering eagerly. They would rip him limb from limb while he was still conscious.

Perhaps this was another test set by Mortarion's foster father. It was not unlike Necare to do something like this, to set up a scenario that would amuse the Overlord, by tormenting his foundling child under the guise that it would 'strengthen his will' or 'demonstrate his loyalty'. And whatever choice Mortarion made, it would always be incorrect in some fashion, always judged inadequate.

Necare imposed countless rules upon his adopted son, many of them mercurial and conflicting, but all ironclad and inviolate – and chief among them, the commands that he was never to interfere with the High Overlord's harvesting of the lessers, and never to interact with the humans, on pain of death.

A cold-hot rage surged up through Mortarion's body with such force that he trembled. Long-buried and long-denied, raw unspent *defiance* now turned to steel. Deep within him, the links of a chain forged by cruelty, neglect and spite broke away, and suddenly he was snatching at the black-powder gun holstered on his hip.

What am I? He decided he would find out.

The shrieking, murderous reports of the heavy pistol extended into one long howl as Mortarion unloaded the weapon into the golems menacing the stricken youth. Each round blasted the soldier-creatures apart as the shots punched through meat and bone.

Another golem guard on the battlements saw the kills and snarled, instinctively turning its javelin towards him, stepping forward threateningly. Still, it hesitated as pain-induced conditioning warred with its natural desire to attack. Mortarion rushed the creature, grabbing the tip of the javelin and yanking it forward. He pulled the golem into range and broke its neck with an axe-blade blow across the throat, shaking it off the javelin's haft and tossing the weapon away.

Then Mortarion took a breath and leapt off the battlements, committing fully to his act of treason.

[The warp; now]

Give me my solitude.

'Those were his exact words,' said Morarg.

A frown grew on Raheb Zurrieq's scarred face. The legionary was young, at least by the equerry's standards, but he had the manner of an old war-dog, and he reached up to run a hand over his face. 'Captain Kalgaro wanted me to speak directly with the primarch. *Alone.*' Zurrieq gave a half-nod at the walls around them and the crew at their stations on the bridge of the *Terminus Est*.

The inference was clear: Kalgaro did not trust Calas Typhon, and it made him unhappy to have their liege lord aboard the First Captain's ship and not his own. So much so, that he had risked sending his lieutenant by shuttle across the distance between the warp-cast ships in the fleet, to communicate that concern in person.

The better part of a day had passed, and the Reaper of Men had not returned from the shuttered observatorium dome. Morarg knew better than to open the hatch and venture inside, to seek the status of his master without permission. The primarch was given to periods of brooding, inward consideration, and his equerry had learned from experience that such introspection could only be interrupted without censure in matters of the most extreme nature.

But was this not an extreme situation? Morarg's gaze ranged around the bridge, watching the First Captain's helot crew at their stations. Despite the shock deaths that had occurred on translation into the warp, none of them showed any fear that the same thing might happen to them.

'They are quiet,' noted Zurrieq. 'Perhaps Lord Typhon had the capacity for panic beaten out of them.'

Morarg didn't reply. He vaguely remembered being human once, recalling pieces of a before-life on Barbarus that was stained by a ghostly sense of overriding doom. Those days were long lost in his ascension to the Legiones Astartes and the Death Guard, and so he let this observation slide. *How do humans process fear?* He did not, in all truth, remember the ways.

'That kind of emotion is of no use to anyone,' he said, after a while. 'Perhaps I once knew of it, before the Great Change. It's gone now.'

Zurrieq raised an eyebrow. 'I think you kept other things, though. Suspicion, yes? That you still have, equerry. I know you do.'

Morarg allowed him a nod. 'A most mortal trait that even the process of transhumanification cannot dispel. It is so. I have survived this long by distrusting everything put in front of me, from the simplest meal to the most complex conundrum.'

'Which is why the Reaper of Men trusts you.'

'It is simpler to view the universe that way,' Morarg went on. 'If what I see is untrue, then I am right. If what I see is true, then I am pleasantly surprised.'

'And do you trust *this?*' Zurrieq gestured at the air. 'Kalgaro wants to know. If we have been sabotaged by our enemies, or our allies, *we must be sure.* Too much is at stake.'

The equerry's patience grew thin. 'I am well aware of the gravity of the situation, brother. We have been in the fangs of this insurrection for nearly a decade, by the Terran march of time, and now the final act begins only for this mystery to unfurl upon invasion's eve? I could not be more cognisant of the weight of days! Lord Mortarion knows it too. We all do.'

'You haven't answered my question,' said Zurrieq. He shot a look towards Crosius, one of Typhon's high-ranking Apothecaries, who wandered the bridge and monitored the well-being of the crew. Morarg imagined that Crosius had other duties too, not least among them keeping a weather eye on the primarch's entourage from *Greenheart.*

'The Reaper of Men trusts the First Captain,' he said quietly. 'He always has, even when they disagree. There is a bond between them that goes deeper than master and warrior. It is the comradeship of exiles.' Morarg's own thoughts on the matter remained unspoken, but his manner made them apparent.

'We reunited too readily,' muttered Zurrieq. 'We do not know where Typhon has been, or what he has done. You have heard the rumours–' The warrior was going to say more, but then his words choked off and he touched his throat, releasing a dry wheeze.

'Zurrieq?' The equerry gave him a hard look. 'What is it?'

'Nothing.' The other Death Guard gasped.

'Is something amiss?' Crosius appeared behind Morarg and inserted himself into the conversation. He reached for his medicae auspex. 'Are you afflicted in some way?'

'No!' snapped Zurrieq, angrily waving off Crosius. 'The… ill-effect during the translation. It struck me when we broke through into the warp. *Briefly,*' he insisted. 'It is fatigue, nothing more.'

'If you insist.' Crosius stepped back.

The Apothecary did not seem convinced, but he never got the chance to press Zurrieq any further. Without warning, the primary hatch leading into the bridge deck irised open and Captain Typhon strode in.

Stumbling behind him came a cluster of bony figures in robes, their heads covered by black hoods of sackcloth, their wrists and ankles bound in heavy phase-iron manacles. Hadrabulus Vioss and another of Typhon's Grave Wardens herded the prisoners, prodding them forward with the barrels of their bolters.

Typhon twisted off his horned helmet with one hand and mag-clamped it to his armour's thigh-plate, his gaze catching the querulous look in Morarg's eye. 'Where is he?'

Morarg hazarded a look towards the observatorium. 'The primarch left orders not to be disturbed–'

But the First Captain was already marching towards the other door, gesturing for Vioss to follow. 'Bring the collaborators,' he growled. 'Mortarion must witness this himself.'

Morarg went after them, as Typhon opened the hatch and strode into the dimness beyond. Vioss gave him a warning glare, but said nothing.

Following the group in, the equerry got his first good look at the hooded prisoners and recognised the thick, ornately detailed threading on the sleeves of their robes. The braids varied on each of them, some woven with wire, others with velvet or silks. Each pattern of threads represented a secret rank within their complex dynastic hierarchy. As the observatorium hatch slid shut behind them, Morarg knew who it was that Typhon had clapped in irons.

These were the ship's telepathic Navigators, dragged from the sealed sanctuary of their isolation chambers elsewhere aboard the *Terminus Est*. Only their kind were capable of steering starships through the inchoate insanity of warp space, their minds uniquely conformed by gene-manipulation and millennia of selective breeding to blot out the turbulent madness and sense the way between stars.

What illumination there was in the shuttered dome was bleed-through from the warp beyond the great baffles locked in place, thin razors of mutilated light cast through millimetre-thin gaps between the metal barriers and their frames. It gave the atmosphere in the chamber a waxen and unpleasant quality.

'What is the meaning of this?' Morarg directed the question at Vioss, but the Grave Warden ignored him.

Ahead, Typhon sketched a bow as Mortarion turned from the shadows to see who had violated his seclusion. 'My lord. You bid me to find an answer for our predicament.' He swept his hand towards the shackled Navigators. 'Behold the quintessential devils in these matters.'

Vioss reached forward and tore the hood from one of the prisoners. Morarg watched the aged mutant hunch forward, hands raised to cover his face and protect his third eye.

Mortarion rose to his full height and glowered at his officers. 'My equerry asked you a question. Answer him. Explain this.'

'The Navis Nobilite have betrayed us, my lord,' said Typhon, casting his accusation into the air. 'I did not speak of this before, as I was not certain, but during my time in separation from the rest of our forces, I came to suspect that the Navigators on the *Terminus Est* and my other ships were acting in concert. Against my will.'

'Not so!' piped the unmasked man, daring to speak. 'Please, Captain Typhon, my house has served your Legion for decades, we are oath-bound to obey your orders!' Morarg recognised the braids of seniority upon this one, marking him as the ship's Navio Primus.

Like the Navigators aboard every ship in the Death Guard fleet, he was a scion of House Zegenda, who had been bonded in perpetuity to Mortarion's patronage by Imperial fiat as a gift from the Emperor – a bond so strong that not even the rebellion of His sons had severed it.

'In the Paternova's name!' cried the Navigator. 'Blind my Eye, I swear it!'

Typhon ignored the interruption. 'I lost vessels in the warp. A sad reality of interstellar travel across galactic distances, to be sure. But it began to happen with regularity... And now I curse myself to think that I did not act on this suspicion sooner.'

'No!' said the Navigator. 'Any ships lost have been to the predations of the ethereal, not through deliberate acts!' He seemed aghast at the idea. 'No son or daughter of Zegenda would ever deliberately guide a vessel to wreck and ruin! It is unthinkable–'

Vioss stepped forward and clubbed the Navigator to the deck with the butt of his bolter. Morarg heard bones break as he rebounded off the plasteel floor and lay there, panting.

'The Navigators do not take sides,' Mortarion intoned.

'They have now.' Typhon removed something from a pouch on his belt and held it up between the thumb and forefinger of his gauntleted hand. A white gemstone, it glittered and caught the chamber's ill light. A strange haze faded into being around the jewel and defined itself into patterns of arcane symbols.

'Psionic glyphs,' offered Vioss. 'Encoded upon hololithic diamonds.'

Typhon handed the jewel to his commander. 'My specialists found them on every vessel we searched. I received reports from Ussax, Blathlok and a dozen others. The same gems, each time hidden in the Navis Sanctorum. The same words encoded upon them all.'

'What does it say?' Mortarion's words were grave. 'You can decipher this witch-speak, Calas. Tell me!'

Typhon's expression became equally severe. 'It is a communique from your father's regent, Malcador the Sigillite. He tells them that the nobles of House Zegenda have sworn fealty to the Emperor and all her children are so bound. He tells them they are to ignore whatever course the Death Guard give them and take us instead to the Falkurien Maw.'

'The Maw is a killing void,' said Morarg. 'A supermassive black hole surrounded by a molten accretion disc one and a half million kilometres wide.'

'From which we would never escape,' said Typhon. 'Yes. This is what sent the sickening effect through our fleet. It was the metapsychic backwash of a concerted effort to misguide us to our deaths.'

'No, no, no...' whimpered the Navigator. 'We felt the effect, yes, but it did not come from us. It came from the warp itself! Our course is...' He slurred the words. 'Our course is true.'

'A lie.' Typhon glanced down at the figure cowering on the deck. 'Your telepathic spoor is upon the stone. You communed with it.' He looked back at Vioss and gave a nod. 'I will not allow you to keep the Death Guard from its destiny.'

Vioss whispered something into his vox, and then there was a ripping crash of gunfire as the two Grave Wardens blasted the captive Navigators into bloody rags.

The shock of the act struck Morarg silent, and even the Reaper of Men was briefly taken aback. Then he was looming over the First Captain, seething with fury. 'Have you lost all reason? Without them, this ship will be becalmed in this hell! Do you realise what you have done?'

Typhon smiled, and an icy chill washed over the equerry to see it. *Yes, he knows*, thought Morarg. *He knows exactly what he has done.*

'I have saved us,' said Typhon. 'The treacherous Navigators are dead. All of them, my lord. On every ship. Executed, in this instant.'

Mortarion grabbed Typhon by the neck ring of his battleplate, on the cusp of striking his First Captain in open anger. 'Then you have doomed us all!'

'No.' Typhon echoed the tone of the dead Navigator. 'We can still travel onward, my lord, and this time we will go where we need to. *I* will see to it. My men will see to it. Ussax, Blathlok, all of them. We can guide the fleet.' He tapped a finger on his forehead, where a scion of the Navis Nobilite would have their psychic third eye, their manner of seeing into the paths of the infinite. 'My mind is strong enough. The *Terminus Est* will lead the way.'

'What choice do we have but to do so?' Mortarion released him and stepped back, his manner growing cold. 'You should not have acted without my approval. You have been your own master too long, Typhon! You forget yourself.'

'I did only what was necessary,' said the First Captain, keeping his tone neutral. 'If I had delayed, the Navigators would have moved against us. They had to be killed in the same moment, so no alarm could be sent.' He paused. 'I will guide us to our deliverance, Mortarion. I promise you that.'

☩ ☩ ☩

[The planet Barbarus; before]

MORTARION STRUCK THE muddy ground with a thunderous impact, the force of the landing throwing up a shock wave of displaced matter. He lost none of his momentum, rocketing forward as a wave of Necare's golems screamed towards him. A few remained near the convoy of steam-crawlers to harry the escaping prisoners, but the majority turned to attack the tall, gaunt warrior.

The golems were simple-minded but they were vicious with it, and they had an animal's sense for the presence of an apex predator. They would try to overwhelm him. Mortarion had deployed them with that very same tactic himself, in previous skirmishes against the armies of errant Overlords. He knew how it would go, and turned that knowledge to his advantage.

As he ran, Mortarion paid out the long steel chain between the ring on the butt of his pepperbox pistol and the hook on his belt, twisting it into a metal lash. He used it to hack through the first row of golems as they came sprinting into range, ripping open their unripe bodies, the razor-sharp links spilling blood and torn flesh in gushing arcs.

He was barely aware of the lesser youth close by, fighting wildly with a corroded piece of brass repurposed into a heavy knife. In his free hand, that oily flicker of non-light Mortarion had seen from the battlements blurred in the corner of his vision, and more lamprey snakes sputtered out from the dank earth, attacking anything that moved. Usually the snakes were daytime hunters, and patient with it. The youth was calling them to him in some way – a skill that Mortarion had only ever known an Overlord to possess.

He had no time to dwell on the thought, however. The golems swarmed him, knowing that Mortarion was the greatest threat, believing that they might defeat him if they attacked collectively. It was a grave miscalculation on their part.

It became a bloody mess of work. Punching. Tearing. Killing. With the humming flail of the chain and his bare hands, Mortarion gouged into skulls and crushed them; he ripped open quivering bodies and stamped them into sludge; he murdered the golems with a ferocity that left him disconnected from the moment.

He became lost in the mechanism of it, dealing out final deaths to creatures that should have perished long ago. The golems were unnatural things and ending them felt like it was restoring a tiny piece of balance to a crooked and cruel universe.

Black, cloying blood coated Mortarion's hands and forearms as he waded through his kills. Nearby, the youth was losing his battle, taking ragged, panicked gasps of tainted air and struggling to hold his breather mask in place. A golem with a club struck him from behind and the escapee lost his makeshift knife, the other patchwork creatures grinding it underfoot as he reeled back.

Mortarion sprinted across the churned earth and grabbed the two closest golems, smashing them together with enough force to break their spines. The others screeched and lost their will to fight, but he was not about to allow it. The chain made short work of them, leaving nothing but pallid, indefinable chunks of meat that steamed in the cold night air.

The youth shook off his shock and looked up at Mortarion. 'For a moment, I thought you would kill us.' He wheezed as he drew from the mask, hauling himself back to his feet. 'You are his son,' he went on, answering the unspoken question.

'No,' rumbled Mortarion. '*I am not.*' He looked away. The last of the golems had broken ranks and abandoned the caravan of iron crawler vehicles. Now they were running as fast as they could towards the thicker mists higher up the rise of the peaks, where they knew that humans could not follow.

From up there, a hooting war-siren sounded. Mortarion's acute vision picked out shadows in motion and a constellation of bobbing yellow lanterns as they moved through the fog. His blood chilled. The call was Necare's declaration. The High Overlord was descending the peak, and he would bring his vicious disapproval with him.

The lessers knew the sound as well as he did. The few who were still alive – they who had not been clawed to death by the golems or suffocated by the thick, toxic air – found their way to an intact, abandoned crawler and piled aboard the machine. Belching grey vapour, the vehicle lurched backwards and skidded down the stony roadway, in the direction of the valley below.

A heavy sense of the inevitable settled on Mortarion and he felt himself hunch forward, almost shrinking in stature. *I have done this thing and in the deed, thrown away the life I had.* The full weight of his rage-charged choice became crystal clear.

His foster father knew. Mortarion could sense that certainty. Necare knew what he had done and was coming down to punish him for it.

There would be an army with the High Overlord. Kill-beasts and spliced horrors, magicks and wicked weapons in terrible array. Mortarion had broken his adoptive parent's edicts and he would pay the price.

And for what? He could almost hear Necare's acid, denigrating snarl in his ear. *For a handful of worthless humans?*

Suddenly, it seemed as if this moment had always been here, waiting to happen, waiting for the right conditions to be met. Mortarion's soul, this deeply lonely and broken skein of a thing, caught like gossamer on the wind, and one more truth revealed itself to him.

If he had been able to revert time to the moment before he had gone to the window, he would have done *nothing* differently. Years of disparagement and spite heaped upon him, a life that was nothing more than a hollow farce, silently building and building until this defiance exploded out of him. There really had been no other way it could have ended.

'Everything has led to this,' he whispered. 'I will face my father and die.' Mortarion turned to stare into the mists, weighing his empty pistol in his hand. 'You have to go,' he told the youth. 'While you still can.'

'They told me you'd help,' replied the human, as if he could hardly comprehend it. 'I didn't believe. But they were right. Why? Why did you do that?'

'Who told you?' Mortarion looked down at the black blood drying on his fingers, then pressed on, leaving the question behind unanswered. 'I did it... because you asked me to.'

'What?'

A rough, humourless chuckle forced its way up from out of nowhere. 'You offered me a choice,' said Mortarion. 'One I could make for myself.' He shook his head, his lank hair smeared across his pale, searching features. 'No one ever did that before.' He sucked in a deep breath. 'Now *go!* Or Necare will take an eternity to kill you!'

The youth grabbed his sleeve. 'Come with me.'

'No...' The idea was beyond Mortarion's stunted experience, beyond his understanding.

'No law says you must stay here and face that!' The youth jabbed a finger at the monstrous shapes in the fog, growing larger and closer by the moment. 'We can reach the valley floor by sunrise. You don't need to die up here, Mortarion.'

He twisted, shocked at the youth's use of his name. 'You... know my name?'

That earned him a rueful nod. 'Everyone knows you. Necare's attack dog. The hollow-eyed death-dealer. A slave of the Overlords, just like the rest of us. At least until this moment.' The youth stepped back, glancing away. On the roadway, the stolen crawler was picking up speed, leaving them behind. 'Never once has one of their servants listened to human pain with anything other than amusement. But not you. Because you know pain too.' He nodded to himself. 'Yes. I think you hate them as much as we do.'

'*More.*' The word overflowed with immeasurable bitterness.

'Then damn Necare and come with me! Don't give that monster another victory over you.'

The raw possibility of it moved in Mortarion's mind, and he dared to wonder if it might be. *But no.* 'If I flee, they will run me down, and you along with me. All those who broke free will be recaptured. Nothing will be earned but greater pain.' He began to reload the pistol. 'If I stay and face him, I trade blood for time. You may still yet escape.'

'I have another way,' said the youth, rubbing his filthy face. 'They tell me I am sly and not to be trusted. I think that just means I am clever. I see things quicker.' He was already moving towards another stalled crawler, the machine's engine chugging as it idled. The chemical stink of its fuel lingered around it.

Mortarion jogged after him. 'Who are you?'

'My name is Calas,' he said, banging a fist on a sealed hatch. 'Can you open this?'

He was half as tall again as the youth, and while Mortarion seemed lean and drawn for his size, what there was of him comprised only muscle, sinew and iron-hard bone. If he was some manner of human, he was an uncommon one. Mortarion found the latch holding the panel shut and shook it off its mount with a grunt of effort, shoving it open with a shriek of broken hinges. A lone golem burst out through the gap, screaming obscenities in the half-second before Mortarion tore off its head and threw it away. The decapitated corpse stumbled a few metres and then collapsed.

Warily, Calas slipped in through the broken hatch and made short work of a set of feeder lines along the inside of the crawler's main compartment. Fuel gushed from opened overload valves and drenched the deck. 'That's it! You see?' He climbed back out and broke into a limping run. 'Follow! Follow!'

Mortarion gave a slow nod, seeing the youth's plan. He went after Calas, cocking the pistol as he ran, and afforded himself a final look into the mists.

Necare's war siren was very close now, and when he listened, Mortarion could hear his foster father's voice carrying to him on the poisonous breeze.

'Face me, boy, or be renounced in all things!' The hollow scream of the ghoul echoed off the walls of the narrow canyon pass, seeming to come from everywhere at once. 'Do you hear me, whelp? If you run from me now, it will be death drawn across eternity! Forsake me and your life is forfeit!'

'I have no life,' Mortarion said aloud, slowing to a halt, taking aim with the pistol. 'Not until this day.'

He pulled the trigger and the pistol brayed, vomiting shot and flame across the distance and through the open hatch of the stricken crawler. The spilled fuel caught the impact of the incendiary rounds and an explosion turned the vehicle into a brilliant yellow fireball. Chain-fire detonations rippled into the prison transport and the other escorts, claiming them too.

Mortarion watched a surge of flame batter the walls of the narrow pass and claw at the grey stone, pulling down sheets of loose rock to smother the fires and the ruined vehicles. Heavy black dust and coils of thick smoke churned, and the last he saw of his abandoned domicile were the dim lanterns on the battlement and the heap of rubble blocking the pass before it.

With a violent jerk, he snapped the chain that tethered the spent pistol to his belt and let the smoking gun fall into the mud; then he turned his back on all he had ever known and started walking.

With each heavy footstep, the mists around him grew thinner.

[The warp; now]

BORDERED BY THE sharp-edged shafts of hellish light leaking in through the chinks in the barrier plates, the Reaper of Men circled the domed observatorium chamber. The tall, lean figure in smeared armour of brass and steel paced like a confined animal, flexing his fists and grimacing.

At the far edge of the space, the Deathshroud stood in a line, silent and immobile as forms cast out of iron. They waited for their next command, and watched their master seethe. He nursed his annoyance as a man might tease out a guttering flame in the midst of a windstorm, cupping it in his hands, feeding it slowly to greater life.

The scant rays of wayward illumination from the immaterium caressed his face as he passed through them, but they cast no warmth. Mortarion could almost smell the spoor of them, the faint stink of ripe psi-witchery leaking through the protective Geller fields and the adamantium hull of the *Terminus Est*. Out there, in the warp, the inchoate lunacy of something alien and unknowable screamed endlessly back at him. The ocean of madness was seeping in, drop by drop.

Once, in the dim past, Mortarion had passed through that domain with eyes open and soul bared to it. Not aboard a ship as he was now, but naked and afraid. Barely a newborn by the reckoning of men, torn from the warmth and security of a womb-chamber in a catastrophic detonation of reality. The memory was one of the first his eidetic recall could place, a wild jumble of feelings and sensations that his undeveloped mind had been unable to process.

He had been cast through the warp in those moments, cast away to the surface of dour and forbidding Barbarus. Exiled, never knowing the reason why.

Mortarion walked to the curve of the dome and let a fall of hell-light bisect his face with its radiance. If he looked out there, what would he see? The same ever-changing storm he barely remembered from that moment? Or something else?

Something to fear?

Once, many years after the Emperor had found him and their ersatz 'family' had regained another lost son, Mortarion had dared to ask a question that no amount of rumination had ever been able to answer.

Father, he began, when they were alone. *Why did you send me away to that death world?*

He hated how the words made him sound fragile, like the mewling of an abandoned child. But the need to know gnawed at him.

The Emperor had not even met Mortarion's gaze. *It was not by my design, son.*

But you are mighty, he insisted. *What power could undo what you set in motion?* The hint of a challenge lay beneath the reply. If the Emperor of Mankind was so elemental a force, then who had such power that they could ruin His schemes?

There is chaos in all things, his father had said, after a long moment. *And what does not kill you, makes you stronger.*

That hoary old adage was barely an answer, more a distraction and certainly a censure in its own way. Mortarion had never asked the question again, instead taking from it another seed of doubt to add to the garden he already tended.

But perhaps I will make Him tell me, thought the Reaper of Men, entertaining the thought of it for a brief time. *When Horus has unseated our father and He is cast down for all His hubris. Perhaps then I will know the truth.*

With a sudden flash of motion, an act powered by decades of frustration, Mortarion's hand snapped out and grabbed the edge of a flex-steel shutter slat. He ignored the Deathshroud as they reacted to his movement, and with a grunt of effort, the primarch tore the metal leaf away from the inner surface of the observatorium dome.

That gelid, swarming light flooded in through the tear he had made, washing across the metal decking, the glow catching every floating mote of dust in the air. Mortarion stared out into it once more, searching for a sign – but there was only a formless veil of haze, a turning churn that had neither face nor form. The warp miasma was thick and random, and it gave him nothing.

He remembered standing at the armourglass door in his bastion on Barbarus, peering into the impenetrable toxin fogs and wondering. Picking at the scab of an unanswered demand, afraid of revealing the yawning void beneath its truth.

'Where are we going?' A different question swam to the surface of his thoughts, pulling the warrior back from his reverie. The directionless light of the empyrean came from everywhere at once, and were it not for the constant thrum of the warship's mighty engines, Mortarion might have believed they were becalmed and immobile.

How could one navigate a war fleet through *this?* Even for clever Typhon, such a task had to be impossible.

'We must advance…' Mortarion muttered under his breath, chewing

on this sworn doctrine of his Death Guard from their first days in war.
'We *must!*'

He let the anger give him leave to storm away, out and through the
halls of the *Terminus Est*, to seek his First Captain.

ON EVERY INTERSTELLAR starship, the sanctum of the Navigators was a
domain unto itself. Typically designed to resemble a spheroid between
two to ten decks in diameter, the enclosed kingdom of the Navis Nobilite was built into the framework of human-made ships while they
were still in their stardocks. Often, the great orbs were delivered by
the representatives of whichever noble house was oath-sworn to guide
the vessel, wholly finished, ready for interface and untouched by the
hands of common shipwrights.

Indeed, there were stories of some great vessels that had sailed
the void for hundreds of years, and never once had their Navigators
ventured outside their sanctum. Power, communication and utility
conduits would feed the needs of those within, and in return they
would do as they were commanded. With their third eye open, the
Navigators would guide the way from star to star. Without them and
their preternatural psychic gifts, any semblance of a galaxy-spanning
Imperium of Man would be an impossibility.

Mortarion understood the disgusting irony of that. They were tools,
he reminded himself, just like the psyker-choirs of the astropathic com-
municators. Tools, like the monster he kept chained up in the bowels
of his command shuttle.

He dismissed the thought as his gaze found butchered parts of the
Navigators from the *Terminus Est* still lying where Typhon's Grave Wardens had deposited them, before the iris gateway that connected the
ship to the violated sanctum chamber. His thin lips curled. Such a display might have been left behind on some planet requiring compliance
as a warning to others, but here on the First Captain's own flagship it
seemed crass and needless.

The warrior Vioss stood guard outside the interleaved hatch, and his manner stiffened at the primarch's approach. He saluted, but made no immediate move to step aside. 'My lord. Captain Typhon is engaged within the sphere. He bid me to have no others enter.'

Mortarion said nothing and merely gazed levelly at Vioss, until the Grave Warden came to the conclusion that was correct of his own accord. The Reaper of Men was not subject to any such strictures.

Vioss reluctantly stepped away and Mortarion reached for the hatch control, but Typhon's man had something more to add. 'My lord, the Deathshroud should not accompany you inside.'

Mortarion's bodyguards bristled at the words, but the primarch raised his hand to halt them. 'Agreed.' He steeled himself for what would greet him within, fighting back a wave of loathing. 'No more of us need be exposed than necessary.' He did not need to add that his praetorians had standing orders in such circumstances: if Mortarion did not transmit to them a certain tone code on his vox every seven minutes, they would storm the chamber and kill whomever they found within.

The iris hatch parted to allow the primarch inside the sanctum, and he stepped into the same bright, smothering light that had met him from the warp.

The interior of the sanctum orb was a riot of colours and shapes. Guide ropes and bannisters ran around the space in patterns that resembled mathematical fractals, and a false sky filled with hundreds of hololithic panes hung about in the still, refrigerated air. As Mortarion advanced to the middle of the chamber, his boots crunched on patches of rust-red hoar frost and the odour of cold blood reached his nostrils.

He saw a construct holding up numerous heavily upholstered couches, a thing built of brassy armatures, flickering lens hoops and click-ticking clockwork. All the couches save two were unoccupied. The figures reclining on them barely fit on the human-scaled furniture. They were legionaries – a pair of the First Captain's so-called 'specialists' – and Typhon himself stood between them still clad in his Cataphractii war-plate. They had their backs to the primarch, but he could clearly see the arcane rites they were enacting. Waxy, terminal light leached

out of the curved walls in serpentine coils, spiralling down to touch
the warriors upon the brow. Had a Navigator stood in their place, the
psyker's third eye would have been open and burning bright.

Bright enough to drive a soul from the body, so the warnings went.

Mortarion's aversion to the process he was witnessing finally broke its
banks and he bellowed out the First Captain's name. Typhon flinched
and lost his connection to the psychic metaconcert, staggering a step
before he regathered himself.

'You... should not have come in here.' Typhon turned his face away,
and Mortarion thought he saw his old friend wipe something black
and oily from his eyes. 'I have things... in hand...'

'What is this?' Mortarion ached to pull *Silence* from its mag-plate
upon his back and swing the scythe into all this witch-machinery, but
he stamped down on the violent impulse. 'Where are you taking us,
Typhon? What have I agreed to?'

'What I do is for the good of our Legion and the ultimate victory of
the Warmaster,' said the First Captain, stepping down from the elevated
platform. He glanced back at the two warriors still in the depths of their
psionic trance, and gestured. 'I know your enmity for these rites. But it
must be done.' He paused, marshalling himself. Typhon's sallow face
seemed even paler than usual. 'You won't want to hear me say this, but
know the truth of my words. There have always been psykers within
the ranks of the Death Guard, brother. You know it and I know it. Even
before the Edict of Nikaea suspended them from active service in the
Legions, you kept them out of our ranks... Or so it seemed.'

Mortarion bristled, but said nothing. There were some things he had
turned a blind eye to, that was so. Now Typhon spoke openly of them,
breaking the taboo.

'I kept the gifted out of your way. I taught them to hide their talents. A handful, out of a Legion of hundreds of thousands. Surely you
knew? Surely you wondered what they were for?'

'I trusted you to keep such things in check,' snarled the primarch. 'I
assumed your... *affinity*... with the warp would be enough.'

'It is.' Typhon nodded to himself, as if accepting a truth. 'And now they play their part.' He nodded at the psyker-legionaries once again. 'These are brothers of the Librarius in all but name. Now is their time to serve, in our deliverance.'

There was an emphasis on the First Captain's words that troubled Mortarion. 'Speak without artifice, brother,' he demanded. 'My patience grows short, and if you continue to hide things from me, I will kill you for it.' At length, he pulled his war-scythe to his hand. 'Must I do so? Was I wrong to offer you my hand back on Ynyx? Are you still–?'

'*Loyal?*' Typhon spat the word back at him, jaundiced colour rising in his cheeks. 'How can you ask me that, Mortarion? Who has been more loyal to you in all the decades than I?' He shook his head. 'You gave me my life that night in the valley, by throwing away everything you had ever known. How else could I ever repay that but through the greatest dedication to you?' Typhon's eyes shone brightly. 'I do this for you, brother. I do it for all of us.'

'And how does it better our Legion to plunge headlong towards nothingness?' Mortarion aimed the head of *Silence* at the hololith panes, upon them a spiralling, meaningless tide of datum from the warship's addled scry-sensors. 'I put my trust in you when others would not have done so. Tell me how it will be rewarded.'

'With strength.' Typhon climbed down and stood before his liege lord. 'That is the one thing we have always craved, is it not? To be eternally strong, unstoppable, undying. To expunge all trace of weakness from ourselves forever.' Before Mortarion could frame a reply, Typhon went on, with the passion of a zealot. 'We cannot turn back now! We are committed, don't you see? Brother, we are close to the end of the road that you and I started down a long time ago. A pathway from the blighted lands of Barbarus to a great rebirth. It is fated.'

For a moment, the primarch thought he heard the faint buzz of insects beneath the strident snarl of his First Captain's fervent words. 'I do not believe in fates,' he growled in return. 'I have told you before, I hold no stock in the numinous.'

'No?' There was a sudden slyness to the other warrior's tone, as if he had caught the primarch in a lie. 'Oh, you may hate and despise what lives beyond the veil, my old friend, but you cannot claim it does not exist. You have seen it...' Typhon looked down at his gauntlet, flexing the metal. 'Even turned it to your will, for a time. Chained it.'

Mortarion's breath held in his throat. 'What do you know of that?' He recalled the conversation over Terathalion. He could count on the fingers of one hand those who knew of the exchange he'd had with the daemon captured there, and Calas Typhon did not number among them.

'You have looked the warp in the eye,' Typhon offered. 'More than once. And each time, you sought something and did not find it.' He slammed the flat of his hand against his chest-plate. 'I *have* found it!' He nodded towards the hololiths and the curve of the walls beyond them. 'Illumination.'

Mortarion's first impulse was to justify his study of the daemonology as a war-time necessity, but the words soured in his mouth. To speak them, he would only echo what Typhon had said moments before. The thought warred with another, deeper concern. *How far has my brother gone into this miasma?*

Typhon removed something from a pouch on his belt and toyed with two battered metal shapes in the palm of his wide hand – a pair of shallow steel drinking vessels, old and careworn with use. He held them up so Mortarion could see clearly.

The primarch remembered. He had drunk from one of those half-tankards, a lifetime ago, under black-orange skies and acid rains.

'We are facing our greatest test, old friend,' said Typhon. 'Everything else has led us here. Every battle we fought through, every conflict we have survived, every wound made a scar. All that the Death Guard have endured has been to prepare us for this moment. To face the most lethal trial... And these are the cups from which we'll drink.'

For a moment, Mortarion thought he could see an ink-dark and oily fluid swirling in the shadows of the battered tankards.

The tradition of the Cups dated back to the first foundation of the Death Guard, in the days when they had been only men, when their bodies had been hardened against the toxins of Barbarus. Now, there was no venom so powerful that the invincible, ever-hardy legionaries of the Death Guard could not resist it.

Mortarion himself had cemented this custom. He would select a warrior in the aftermath of every battle and share with that man a draught of blended toxins. They would drink and they would live, strengthening the unbreakable power of the Legion they embodied. *Against Death*, they would say, and prove it by their endurance.

'We will survive this poison,' Typhon told him. 'Fate wills it, whether you believe in it or not.'

Mortarion heard the buzzing drone beneath the words again, and despite the primarch's iron self-control, he felt his flesh crawl with sudden ill ease. 'What poison?' he whispered, a sharp sense of dread filling him at the thought of the answer to his question.

THREE

White Mountain
Falsehoods
Chorus

ONCE UPON AN age, the White Mountain might have been known by that name because it was capped by virgin snow, but if so, that era was lost to antiquity. Now, the broad blade-tip peak was grey-silver from the ash fall that settled from the biting polar winds and moved in scudding dunes across the lifeless landscape. The old, dead cinders found their way into anything left beyond the great static-webs shrouding the mountain approaches, and each time Garviel Loken ventured up to the vantages in the highest caves, he would track a dusty line of them back with him on his return.

He let himself get lost in the view from the cavern mouth, his gaze slipping focus until the flatlands beyond became an endless pale forever that he could see without seeing. The radlands were a dreadful place, if one took them literally, a wasteland left behind after a catastrophic eco-cidal war that would have – if it had been left to continue – destroyed all life on Terra, or 'Earth' as it had been known in the Dark Age of Technology. The being who ended that war was not the Emperor of Mankind, or at least, he was not at the time, but his legacy remained in this place. The White Mountain had been the lair of that old war's most brutal champion. She had been dead and dust for thousands of years now, but her fortress-palace had been repurposed for other needs and it still served them in good order.

It was tranquil here, in its own desolate way. Nothing lived outside, and within, every one of the mountain's laser-cut corridors and domed inner chambers was lined with sense-deadening metals. The deeper one ventured inside, the more robust the effect of the phase-iron plates and counter-psionic wards. At the inmost core levels, the stillness was so absolute and unsettling that Loken had been unable to remain there for more than a few hours. It was the absence of everything, from the smallest sound to the most distant whisper of psychic wind.

Down there was a giant metaphasic cage they had built to imprison Magnus the Red, crafted to the Emperor's own designs, but few believed they would ever have the occasion to use it. Like the White Mountain itself, the cage was something forged in spite of the inevitable, a reserve, a backup plan in case other, better schemes failed.

When he first arrived here, Loken wondered why the Sigillite had sent him. Any one of the Knights-Errant could have been tasked with the investigation into the recoveries, as they had come to be known. Was it another test? On some level, he knew it had to be. Malcador, Dorn and others had never truly trusted him since he had been found, gripped by madness, on Isstvan III. And in truth, there was still a part of Loken that agreed with them.

Was it a punishment? He had failed in his last mission to board the *Vengeful Spirit* and terminate his gene-father and primarch, the War-master Horus Lupercal. Good men had perished there, others scarred and barely able to escape with their lives. For Loken, it was a shameful frustration that haunted him. He had squandered his chance at cutting off the serpent's head, and the inner conflict that ran through him in those charged moments still burned like fire. Would that opportunity ever come again? Over and over, he castigated himself with the knowledge that it would not.

But as time passed, he thought of the duty differently. The assignment to the White Mountain was not truly a test, not really a punishment. It was a *gift*.

In the silence of the endless dark halls, where errant thought and turbulent emotion themselves were deadened by arcane anti-psyker mechanisms and contra-telepathic barriers, Loken rediscovered something like peace. It was fleeting, he knew that, but it centred him. The whispers of insanity that had plagued Loken's mind in the past, that manifested in the voices of his former comrade Torgaddon, the ghost of old Iacton or the snarls of his lost self Cerberus... they stayed away. For while Loken's physical injuries from the assault on the *Vengeful Spirit* were nothing compared to those sustained by Macer Varren, Tylos Rubio or poor Ares Voitek, the wounds to his spirit and his will were grave. In the tranquillity of the White Mountain, those things found a place to be healed.

Loken heard footsteps coming up the stairs carved into the rock, but did not turn. He had come to know the distinctive pattern of Teledion Brell's boots across the stone, the way she would sometimes half drag her right leg where its bionic joint shifted slightly out of synch with the rest of the organic limb. She was moving quickly. Something had agitated the scientician, enough that she was willing to break protocol and approach him outside of their normal schedule.

'Brell,' he said, by way of greeting, eschewing any preamble. 'Do you have something new for me?'

'Work proceeds with the intake,' she puffed, coming to a halt at his side. The woman was tall for a human, almost as tall as a Space Marine, but spindle-thin with it. Born of low-grav Hyperionite stock from the Saturnian Satellites, Brell had a bone density so thin that she would collapse under her own weight in a Terran-standard-G environment. Age of Strife tech devices that projected a counteracting field around her body allowed her to move normally on other worlds, but to Loken she seemed like a bird with clipped wings, always on the verge of taking flight but never able. Vapour from her breath coiled in the air as she spoke, the words a rapid-fire chatter more akin to a datum download than a conversation. 'Each day the cogitator engines form new combinations of the words and sound elements. I feel as if we are on the verge of a great insight, if only we could force the recoveries into some sort of coherence.'

'Force them,' he echoed. 'I've told you before how I feel about that. Deliberately inducing pain or other hardships will not be permitted.'

'That may be what is required–' countered Brell, but Loken spoke over her.

'I have not been unclear.' This discussion, or something very much like it, was one he and the scientician had gone through on many occasions, and the Knight-Errant was tired of it. 'Remember who these people are. Respect them.'

'I do, I have, I do,' Brell said quickly, 'but they are not who they once were, Ser Loken. Surely you see that? Your compassion is laudable, but misplaced. Their minds are broken beyond repair.'

'That too was once said of me,' he replied firmly, and the thought occurred that Loken's own voyage into the loss of self and back again might have been behind Malcador's choice of him for this mission.

Brell briefly went quiet, as she was wont to do when she was unwilling to concede a point. Then with an exaggerated shrug, she offered him a look at the data-slate in her long-fingered hands. 'Perhaps the addition of a new information vector will alter our perception of the chorus' purpose.'

The slate showed the approach clearance authorisation for a shuttle-craft, and Loken took it in, before turning back to the view of the wilderness to search the stark skies above.

Yes. There it is. He saw a fast-moving dart streaking in from the south-west, dropping low as it angled towards one of the White Mountain's lower landing maws.

'Another recovery,' Brell explained. 'In good condition and exhibiting encouraging clarity, so it seems.' Loken didn't like the way she seemed almost eager to get her hands on the new arrival. 'I thought you would want to know. But I can deal with the induction and preliminary processing if you are...' She drifted off, then gestured at the desolate view. 'Otherwise engaged.'

'We'll both go,' he said, making it an order.

BY THE TIME they reached the landing maw, the shuttle was already settled and its passengers had disembarked. The new recovery was like all the others, a ragged-clothed woman with a shaven head and the honorific marks of the Sisterhood visible upon her, but she seemed more aware of her surroundings than many of those Loken had seen down in Brell's holding pens.

Medicae servitors and some of the scientician's adjutants were circling the woman, conducting non-invasive scans and examining her for signs of outward trauma. As Loken passed close by, he heard her speaking. Even now, after having seen more than one of these tormented Silent Sisters sundering their oaths with meaningless babble, to hear them give voice was unsettling.

'Worlds. Names. Time.'

'Oh,' said Brell, making the sound with an obvious anticipatory edge. 'Very good. That is interesting. More distinct than the others. Very, very good.'

'Remember what I said.' Loken was firm. 'I will not repeat myself again.'

'Understood.' Brell bowed, but the way she shifted her weight from foot to foot made it abundantly clear that she wanted to be away to her laboratories to begin testing the unfortunate recovery.

'Her name is Malida Jydasian, of the Thunder Vane.' The words were an admonishment, the tone mirroring Loken's. Nathaniel Garro walked out of the shadows beneath the hissing shuttle and gave his comrade a nod of salutation. 'The Sigillite bid me to bring her here.'

'Brother-captain.' Loken offered Garro his hand, and he met the gesture with his own, in the old manner, wrist guards clanking against one another. 'Well met.'

'We can but hope,' Garro replied, watching like a hawk as the scientician led Jydasian away into the gloom. 'I am heartened to see you here, Garviel,' he went on. 'But I have questions.'

'I don't doubt it.' Loken gave a rueful nod. 'So do I.'

'Start by telling me what this place is.' Garro looked up, taking in the cavern. 'The air is dead.'

'The most concise explanation? The White Mountain is a prison...' Loken started walking, and Garro fell in step with him. '...a gaol repurposed from the remains of an ancient fortress.'

'A prison for what?'

'Psykers.' Loken tapped a finger to his brow. 'That muteness you feel around us? It's the ghost-effect of a hundred different dampening systems, all designed to smother the power of the ethereal. If you and I can sense it, imagine how it must be for one of them.'

'Ah.' A flicker of recognition passed over Garro's face. 'I thought it felt familiar. I came across something similar on board the *Phalanx*. Lord Dorn has a chamber of comparable function, within which he keeps the brothers of his Librarius.'

'Of course he does,' said Loken, his lip curling. 'I would expect no less of the Imperial Fists.'

'Is Jydasian a criminal?' Garro studied him. 'Malcador said nothing of the sort. But he spoke of others, found in the same state as she was. Are they here too?' Loken nodded once and he went on. 'More like her? More Silent Sisters?'

'All of them.'

Garro halted. 'How many?'

Loken let out a sigh. His orders had been clear: to pursue the investigation but to speak of it to no other members of the Knights-Errant without Malcador's express permission. And yet, here was Nathaniel Garro, dispatched by the Sigillite. What was he supposed to do? Thank the battle-captain for his diligence and then send him on his way? 'This is not a matter for greater dissemination,' he began. 'We are at a critical juncture, and to split our focus would be a mistake.'

Garro folded his arms across his chest and met Loken's gaze. 'You speak but I hear Malcador's voice. No games, Luna Wolf. No obfuscation. You and I are long past such things.'

The former Death Guard said nothing more, but in the silence an unspoken truth remained. Garviel Loken owed Nathaniel Garro his life, not just for rescuing him from his self-imposed exile among the ruins of the Isstvan massacre, but for having the faith in his spirit – for believing that Loken could come back from the dark madness that had almost broken him.

'You once told me that "the Emperor Protects",' said Loken, after a moment. 'I'm not sure He is protecting these unfortunates.' He nodded towards the shadows and the depths of the complex beyond. 'They began appearing several months ago… Or perhaps it is more correct to say, they began *reappearing*. Each of the recoveries we have made is a Sister of Silence whose name is listed on their order of battle as missing presumed dead.'

'Recoveries,' Garro echoed. 'That is what you are calling them?'

Loken went on. 'In each case, a body was never found. Their cadres marked their losses as honoured casualties of war and moved on.' He frowned, drawing up the facts that had been vexing him since the first day of this assignment. 'There is no logic we have been able to discern as to why certain individuals were taken, or the method by which it was done. Each of them has been found on Terra, regardless of where they were lost in the Solar System. And each in the same state – malnourished, barely responsive, able only to repeat a few tones. Elements of words or fragmentary sentences.'

'They have broken their oath, and speak as Jydasian does?'

He shook his head. 'That is the one factor that differs. No two recoveries utter exactly the same sounds. Brell, the scientician Malcador sent here, she believes there is a pattern to be discerned – not that she's found it yet.'

Garro said nothing, processing what he had heard. At length, he turned to look away. 'Is this cruelty the work of the Warmaster?'

'It would appear so. Every one of the recoveries has been in proximity to insurrectionist sympathisers, an infiltrator group or an aberrant manifestation. All of the abducted Sisters have been mentally traumatised, their minds broken and remade by brute force.'

'How is that possible?' said Garro. 'They are pariahs, untouchables. Not even the things that live in the warp would be able to enter their psyches.'

'Aye, that is so,' agreed Loken, 'but there are other ways to twist a human mind, even that of a null. Sanity may be shattered without recourse to metaphysical means.' His frown deepened. 'I have first-hand experience.'

'And so Malcador sent you to watch over this prison because of that.' Garro gave a nod. 'Because Garviel Loken has passed through such a trauma and emerged on the other side of it.'

'Perhaps. I've given up trying to fathom the Sigillite's motives. It leaves me with a headache.'

Garro opened his hands and gestured around. 'So tell me if you can. What is the end point to all this? Are our aggrieved Sisters in battle fit only to be locked away, forgotten amid the smoke and fury of the coming invasion?' He shook his head gravely. 'I have seen that happen. Dorn's psykers. My own men, confined on Luna on Malcador's orders. Left to rot!' His jaw stiffened as his annoyance grew. 'This is unacceptable. Unless these… recoveries… represent a danger, they should not be treated like cattle. The Silent Sisterhood must be told. Every day their kindred are kept from them is a dishonour.'

Loken shifted, putting himself between Garro and the path leading deeper into the White Mountain. It was a subtle motion, but one with clear martial intent – a veiled warning – behind it. 'The Sigillite has forbidden us to make contact with the Witchseeker cadres. They are to remain ignorant of this.' Before Garro could disagree, Loken went on. 'This may be part of a larger ploy, even a weapon of some kind. Believe me when I tell you, my primarch does everything with an order to it. If Horus' hand is in this phenomena, it is turned towards a greater goal we do not yet see.'

'I repeat my previous question,' Garro said firmly. 'What is the end point? What if Horus arrives before your scientician's answers?'

'There is a contingency in place. A… termination protocol.'

Garro's expression turned to stone. 'You would do so?' He pressed down on his clear anger at the words. 'The Sisterhood have put their lives on the line countless times, in the name of the Imperium and Terra! How can you conscience putting them to death, forgotten and unremarked in this desolate prison?'

'It is not something I relish the thought of,' Loken shot back. 'But the Sigillite left little room for interpretation of the order.' Despite his own antipathy to the command, Loken was resigned towards the deed if it needed to be done, and Garro's annoyance chafed on him, as if the blame for this could all be laid at Loken's feet. 'Not all of us have the freedom to defy Malcador as you have.'

Garro's eyes widened at the accusation in his words. 'In all my years of service to the Emperor, I have never defied a lawful, honourable order,' he said firmly.

'This is not a matter of law,' Loken told him, as a line silently drew itself between them. 'If you had seen this war from the same place as I, you would know so.'

THE DENSITY OF the jungle across the Demerara Downland made it necessary for Rubio and the others to move slower than he would have liked. The thickets of tall, hardy trees required care to navigate, as cutting a path would have not only consumed more time, but also what stealth they had at hand.

Instead, the three Knights-Errant moved with care as toxic rain sluiced down from the canopy far above, the fat yellow droplets spattering off the polymerised cowls of their Falsehoods. Each of them was lost in the shadows of the camouflage cloaks, a trio of identical ceramite-clad forms advancing step by step into the wilds of the acid-rainforest.

Gallor was on point, his bolter at the ready beneath the folds of his cloak, and Varren took up the rear, his head scanning left and right as he turned his hunter's sense to watching for threats. Rubio held the middle ground, but in actuality his body was moving like an automaton while his thoughts were elsewhere. The psyker's mind was detached from his physical form, adrift out on a perimeter hundreds of metres distant, and it wove through the stands of trees, resting here and there as though it were a pollinator flitting from plant to plant.

Life, of a sort, teemed out here, just below the muddy surface of the earth, or in the vast network of deep taproots that fed into the trees. Hardy reptiles and scuttling insects, things with dense skins and tough carapaces that had evolved to survive in the polluted, radiation-scarred outlands of Terra. There were few domains on the Throneworld that could still be considered truly 'wild', but this was one of them. Hundreds of thousands of years before, the Downland had been an abyssal plain below fathoms of ocean water. Those mighty seas had shrunk to shallow ghosts of their former glory, revealing these scarred wastes to the punishing light of a pitiless sun.

For all its miracles and monuments, for all its great works and human accomplishments, Rubio had always been disenchanted with Terra. Outside the hive cities, the greater enclaves and the majesty of the Imperial Palace, the birthplace of mankind was a scarred and bitter sphere. Compared to verdant, glittering Macragge, it seemed ancient and unwelcoming. He frowned at the thought and pushed it away. Rubio wore the cerulean of the XIII no longer. Macragge was not his to remember. He focused instead on the mission at hand. They were here following a lead gathered from the survivors of the Walking City, a clue that might reveal more of the mystery shrouding the broken Sister of Silence.

He drew back to himself, and from behind, Rubio heard Varren give a grunt of irritation as he followed the psyker over the bole of a fallen trunk. 'Damn this place,' he went on. 'I should have stayed behind with Ison.'

Rubio said nothing. Varren's complaints were part of his nature, but they had become more noticeable since he returned to battle duty after

reviving from his sus-an coma. He suspected that Varren's wounds were
not as healed as the other warrior insisted, and that his eagerness to
get back into the field had clouded the former World Eater's judgement – but to suggest that aloud would be to draw open an argument
that would benefit no one. Rubio decided instead to remain watchful
and keep his own counsel.

For his part, Vardas Ison's duty in the Walking City would be to
enforce the last few elements of their orders from Malcador, securing
the wrecked metropolis before moving on. Stranded as it was now
in the snowy highlands, much of the city's surviving populace were
already fleeing back towards warmer latitudes. When they left, Rubio
had seen long lines of the displaced snaking down the peaks from the
window of their shuttle. Even though they had expunged the threat,
the end result was still a victory for the invaders. The Walking City was
hobbled, and the shadow cast by Horus across Terra grew a little larger
in the hearts and minds of the common people.

Rubio and the others had arrived in the jungle two days ago, and
marched without halt from the moment their shuttle climbed away
into the sky. Now they were close to the coordinates that the psyker
had plucked from the mind of the smuggler Gallor had captured trying to escape, the very man that other survivors had identified as the
gaoler of the woman Jydasian. Rubio knew him on sight, having assembled a memory of his face from the partial recall of the witnesses. He
broke easily, and they had Varren to thank for that. The warrior had
shown the smuggler a blade and told the man what could be done
with it. That was all it took.

'Hold here.' Rubio hadn't spoken for a while and the words came out
coarsely. Gallor dutifully dropped into a crouch and Varren grimaced
as Rubio surveilled the camp through the eyepiece of a monocular
scanner.

The trees thinned a few hundred metres distant from the team's
concealment, opening into a cluster of shallow, connected craters over-
grown by hardy plant-life. A way beyond that, across the hollows in

the ground, there were vast corroded arches, the skeletal remnants of great ship hulls gnawed upon by time and acid deluges. Little of the original form of the ancient vessels could be determined, but they must have dated back to the ages when the seas covered this landscape. In among the old frames lay an encampment, just as the smuggler remembered it, a mess of cube-shaped container pods repurposed as shelter beneath a wide, undulating plastic shroud. Alongside, there were a pair of spider-like transit crawlers and a makeshift landing pad. On the pad, an interplanetary hauler shaped like a winged bolt shell sat on its tail thrusters, the craft's biconic nose glistening in the bitter rain. The smuggler knew that ship; inside, it smelled of lubricant and stale propellant.

'Plasma drives on it,' noted Gallor, studying the craft. 'They would carry it to the Inner Worlds and back.'

'Aye,' said Rubio. 'And it is of small enough tonnage that it could make it through the security web around Mercury.'

'I see movement.' Varren came closer and pointed. 'Look there.' He indicated a pair of figures in bulky environment suits, moving sluggishly near the edge of the great tent. It was impossible to determine any details about them, the faceplates set to the darkest possible polarisation.

'That's vacuum gear they're wearing,' Gallor added. 'But the air here is breathable.' He glanced back at Rubio. 'Protection from the rains?'

Rubio did not answer and instead let his senses probe further ahead. He thought of the smuggler and the other criminals they had interrogated back in the Walking City, expecting that he would sense the same colours of persona here – the chatter of undisciplined minds, the base focus of the rough, the cunning and the violent – but at first pass, there was nothing. He scowled, refocusing his psyche to push deeper, and at once a different pattern made itself apparent.

Another psyker.

Rubio's hands rose in a defensive kata, instinctively drawing on a well of telepathic force to defend himself. In the same moment, Gallor and Varren reacted as a piece of the wet jungle moved strangely and detached itself. They aimed their weapons into the shimmer of what could only be another Falsehood.

'Hold,' Rubio repeated. The new arrival radiated mild, superior amusement rather than malice, and it gave him pause. 'Show yourself,' he went on.

The cloak faded and presented the trio with another legionary, his armour the same storm-grey as theirs. The warrior approached and dropped into a crouch. Light flickered from the matrix of psionically attuned crystals around the back of his head. 'They do not know we are here,' he said.

'Who in Nuceria's dust are you?' demanded Varren.

'An ally.' Rubio did not recognise the other legionary's voice, but his battleplate and the Mark of the Sigillite upon it were authentic, scanned and confirmed by the optical sensors in his helmet. 'Why did you come?' he went on. 'I need no support.'

'Give me your name,' said Rubio.

'Yotun,' came the reply, but there was a noticeable pause before it, as if this Knight-Errant found it a poor fit. 'You are Koios, yes?'

'Rubio,' he corrected. He thought he heard the undertones of a Fenrisian accent in the other warrior's words, but the timbre of the voice through a helmet filter made it hard to be sure.

'Ah. Yes, of course.' Yotun looked away. 'I see now. You did not expect to find me here.'

'Doing what, exactly?' asked Gallor.

Yotun waved vaguely in the direction of the smuggler camp. 'Observing.'

'We've walked a long way to find this place.' Varren was clearly irritated by Yotun's relaxed demeanour. 'If you have anything useful to say, psyker, then do so. Otherwise we go in there and tear it apart.'

'What do you expect to find?' The question was aimed at Rubio.

'I'll know it when I see it,' he replied.

Yotun gave a low chuckle. 'I will help you, then. Lead on.'

✠ ✠ ✠

VARREN MOVED AWAY with Gallor to approach from the south, and Yotun fell in with Rubio. For a moment, he questioned the tactical value in splitting the group into psyker and non-psyker pairs, but the telepathic stillness from inside the encampment made it seem unlikely he would have to face a psionically empowered opponent.

Rubio was not expecting a hard fight, but bitter experience warned him not to be complacent. For now, the Knights-Errant had the element of surprise on their side, and they would employ it to maximum advantage.

All of them pulled up their Falsehoods and let the techno-cloaks blend their shapes into the dull green colours of the jungle. Motion was slow and methodical, for while the cloaks could render even the mass of a fully armoured Space Marine invisible, they could not disguise movement. A guard with a keen eye might see the warping of the vegetation and raise the alarm, if they went too quickly.

'When did you take Malcador's mark?' Yotun said quietly, breaking the silence.

'I was one of the earliest,' Rubio replied. 'After Garro.'

'Garro wasn't the first,' Yotun said, with a sniff. 'Not in a chronological sense.'

'You asked the question. Does that matter?'

Yotun shrugged. 'I've heard of you, Tylos Rubio. Guilliman's discommended son. The one who walked away from Calth and never looked back.'

'I've looked back,' Rubio amended. 'But it serves nothing.' Now halfway across the brush-snarled crater, the two of them had little cover. He picked out paths of egress in the event that someone started shooting, but they were poor. It would be better odds to storm forward, if it came to it, and battle through any incoming fire.

'Good,' Yotun said. 'The path you and I are on leads to the future. Look forward, cousin. Always forward.'

Rubio hesitated, watching one of the suited figures cross his path up ahead. 'You speak like you know me, and yet... I have no friends among the Sons of Russ.'

Yotun gave that low chuckle again. 'I am not a Wolf.' He tapped his armour. 'We are Knights all.'

Rubio turned back to glance at the other warrior. 'What is your real name?'

The amusement dropped out of the reply. 'Here and now, only Yotun. Looking back serves nothing – you said it yourself.'

'Aye.' The shambling, bulky human shape of the suited smuggler disappeared out of sight behind a cargo container, and Rubio swiftly moved forward, reaching the edge of the great tent that covered most of the encampment.

The two psykers slipped around piles of loose storage pods, venturing deeper within. His hand on the hilt of his gladius force sword, Rubio reached out once more with his ephemeral senses and tried again to gauge the emotions of the smuggler clan.

Death. The Stygian cold of corpses, the rot of a breath from a cracked tomb – these were the impressions that assailed him, and he reeled from the sudden effect.

'You feel that?' whispered Yotun, and by his tone Rubio knew that the other warrior was experiencing the same thing.

He nodded woodenly. 'Something is very wrong here.'

'Look up.' Yotun said gravely, and pointed. Rubio twisted around to get a better angle.

The plastic shroud over the camp had been secured to the rusted frames of the old ships by dozens of thick hawsers, but the surplus lengths of those cables had been left to hang towards the ground. Bodies were strung from the ends of them, and the grotesque counterweights swayed in the breeze. The dangling corpses were bloated and rancid with decay, and Rubio's blood ran cold when he saw the glint of tiny, iridescent insect bodies crawling over the pallid flesh of the dead.

He looked away, finding a great corroded section of hull metal that had likely been the conning tower of an ancient seagoing freighter. Inverted and half buried in the crater floor, it had been converted by the smugglers into a strongpoint of sorts, and harsh sodium lights burned in the hollows worn wide by age.

'In there.'

Yotun nodded, making the same tactical evaluation. 'Silent weapons only.'

'Aye.' Rubio drew his force sword, deliberately keeping the flow of psionic energy to it at a low ebb. Yotun had a blade of his own, but his was an axe with a wicked, half-moon head that shone with an inner light.

'*Rubio, respond.*' Varren's rough voice grated over the vox-channel.

'Go on,' he replied.

'*We have a number of the smugglers in sight. They're standing around. Doing nothing. They're not aware of us.*'

'Understood. Alert me if the situation changes.'

'*Watch yourself around the stranger,*' Varren warned. '*Just because he has the Sigillite's mark, it doesn't mean you have to trust him.*'

Rubio glanced at the impassive mask of Yotun's helmet, struck by the sense that behind it the other warrior was grinning at him. 'The thought had occurred,' he said, and cut the channel.

Moving in, they met no resistance, and spied no guards. That in itself was a warning, stoking Rubio's tension still higher. His grip tightened around the hilt of his gladius.

Picking their way through the corroded, upside-down passageways was difficult, and their bulk made it necessary for the armoured warriors to move in single file. Thus, Rubio was the first to come across what he would later describe as 'the laboratory'.

It had probably been a mess hall in the ancient days when the ship plied those long-evaporated oceans. The discoloured remains of benches and tables were bolted to the floor over their heads, but the inverted ceiling on which they walked had been laid out with half a dozen restraint chairs bristling with clamps and unpleasant-looking surgical tools on the end of angled gimbals. Holo-cowls – hood-like devices that could envelop a human head and project lifelike virtual imagery directly into the retina – drooped here and there, some still blinking with activity.

Rubio knew this kind of machinery. He dimly remembered it from an old past, a before-time that had been almost completely chemically erased from his mind. As a boy, when he had only been *human* instead of *transhuman*, machines like these had started him on the path to becoming a member of the Legiones Astartes. While other technology and invasive alterations had opened up his body to implant new and more powerful bioengineered organs, devices like *these* had implanted new knowledge in his mind. Through hypnogogic therapies, psycho-grammetric programming and re-education, the young Tylos Rubio had absorbed centuries of military knowledge, tactics, abstract train-ing and more. But such technology, if turned upon a being without the enhancements of a Space Marine, could have terrible, damaging effects.

Yotun fingered one of the cowls, then discarded it. 'I had not thought to ever see these again.' There was that accent again, with the hard edges of the Rout forcing through each utterance. 'Do you follow, Rubio? This is a chamber of agonies. Those brought here are robbed of their self.'

Just like Jydasian, thought Rubio, and then a cold and unpleasant conclusion came to him. The source of the dead, psychically barren atmosphere in this place was, paradoxically, coming from something alive. And if that was so, there was only one thing it could be.

'You feel that?' Yotun seemed to intuit his train of thought.

Rubio nodded, forcing himself to push out his telepathic senses against the heavy, negative weight of the null effect all around him. The dark void took on a hazy shape, coalescing a distance away beyond a hatch in the far wall. 'In there.'

Yotun gave a terse nod and approached the hatch. With quick, eco-nomical moves of his axe, he chopped off the hinges and left bright new metal visible in the dimness. Rubio stepped up and slid the great door off its mount, as quietly as he could. That ephemeral tomb-wind gusted out of the opening, and he followed Yotun inside.

The next room was a metal chamber that had once been a huge meat locker. Now it was filled with cube-shaped cages, piled atop one another in poor order. Most were empty, but several were occupied by emaciated figures in tattered rags. Each prisoner had the shaven pate and honour-tattoos of the Silent Sisterhood, and it angered Rubio to see them so poorly treated.

Yotun didn't wait, immediately moving from cage to cage, snapping off locks that kept them confined. Those he freed stumbled from their tiny prisons, not acknowledging the legionaries or each other, their faces blank and their eyes vacant.

All of them were speaking, some in mutters, others in crack-throated whispers. Rubio strained to listen, trying to pick out pieces of what seemed like whole words in among a murmuring, incoherent chorus. Unlike Jydasian, it was impossible at first pass to grasp what meaning there might be.

'Now we know why there was nothing to sense here,' said Yotun. 'Pariahs.' He said the word with open repulsion, and Rubio shared his antipathy.

'Indeed–' He faltered as he began to speak, glimpsing sudden, unexpected motion at the open hatchway behind them. Rubio pivoted, catching sight of a figure in a bulky environment suit. Silhouetted against the glow of biolumes in the other chamber, it was a thickset and ungainly form, and yet it reacted with speed. Skidding, half sliding away, the suited figure ran back towards the corridors beyond.

The warrior stormed after the smuggler and spun his gladius in his hand, bringing it up for a downward killing blow. His strike was true, piercing the suit's backpack, stabbing through the spine and out of the chest, impaling the smuggler before they could get away.

But something was wrong. The blade met little resistance as it cut, and the figure distorted as it fell, losing shape. The black-visored helmet struck the deck and cracked open – and from it burst a torrent of glistening, shrieking flies.

The suit deflated, becoming a sloughed skin, and the torrent of insects screamed away into the corridor. Striding in after him, Yotun came forward and kicked away the broken helmet. The blackened, corrupted form of a half-consumed skull was visible inside it. 'Another new horror for the reckoning,' he said, with a grimace.

Rubio heard answering screeches coming from all around, echoing down the passages of the ancient wreck, and a moment later Varren's voice was growling in his ear. '*Rubio! The smugglers are doing... something! Screaming! I see a dozen or more, they're coming your way!*'

He hesitated, weighing his options. This was clearly a manifestation event, and what passed for standing orders among the Knights-Errant called for such locations to be fully cleansed of all taint, even if that meant losing innocents into the bargain.

But Rubio was not about to let these captives perish, not when there were still so many questions that they might hold answers for. 'Varren, Gallor. Converge on this location – we're coming out with non-combatant rescues.' He shot Yotun a look. 'Get them to safety, yes?'

Yotun cocked his head. 'And what do you intend to do?'

Down the corridor, metal rang and clattered as the enemy came swarming towards them. 'I'll slow them down,' said Rubio, bringing his force sword up to battle ready.

VARREN SPRINTED AROUND the edge of the encampment with Gallor at his heels, both of them laying down fire towards anything that moved – but each shot ripped straight through the suited figures and kept on going, blasting harmlessly into the distant treeline. Buzzing black smoke coiled from the entry and exit wounds, and overhead the dangling bodies writhed and shook in grotesque sympathy.

He looked up and saw swollen bellies burst, revealing breeding masses of fat maggots and more newborn carrion flies streaming into the air. 'Curse this!' Varren scowled. 'By my life, I have never wanted a heavy flamer more than I do now!'

'Look there!' Gallor jabbed a finger towards a ragged hole in the side of the fallen conning tower, as a loose stream of gaunt walking wounded stumbled out into the light, with the stranger called Yotun herding them forward.

'Where's Rubio?' Varren demanded, his bolter rising, ready to believe the worst of this unfamiliar warrior.

Yotun used his axe to point back towards the wreck of the ancient ship. 'Buying us time to save these luckless souls,' he shot back. 'There are cargo crawlers on the eastern side of the encampment. Get the Sisters aboard and make for the trees.'

'But the spacecraft–' began Gallor.

Yotun cut him off. 'Poor choice.'

Varren's scowl deepened. 'You're giving us orders now?'

'I am *asking* for your help, cousin,' Yotun insisted, turning back towards the camp proper. 'I have something else to deal with.'

IT WAS HARD work fighting in the narrow corridors, but Rubio threw himself into it, turning his sword into a whirlwind of blades. The proximity of the pariahs dulled his ethereal abilities, but not those that grew from his hard-trained battle experience. Empowered by psionic force or not, his sword was still a formidable weapon, and it tore apart the freakish host-clusters of the mutant carrion flies. Each suited form that was ripped open exploded into another screaming swarm, impelled from the ragged remains of whatever unfortunate fool had become their living, walking breeding ground.

Some of the things inside the environment suits were not quite as far along that route of ghastly transformation, and their mutations were some steps past the bloated bodies of the flyblown. These ones resembled some hellish mixture of human form and insectoid, with mouths that had grown into chattering maws of mandibles, eyes into jewel-like compound orbs, skin puckered with brittle, sharp hairs and questing feelers.

They died as readily as any foe, however, and Rubio let himself settle into the pace of the fight, calling on his training to maintain focus and destroy anything that came to meet him. Still, the sheer numbers

of the enemy were pushing him back – but then he had never intended
to hold this position, only delay the inevitable.

Theoretical, said a voice in the back of his mind. *How long can one
warrior prevent an advance through a tactical choke point, given these limited engagement options?* The voice was a memory of a craggy-faced
instructor, lost to time and other wars. *Practical: until his sword breaks…
or his will does.*

'Neither will happen today,' Rubio spat. 'Varren! What is your status?'

'*We have the crawlers, and the captives are embarked,*' came the reply.
'*Disengage and get clear!*'

He sensed he had missed a step, but in the thick of the fight there
was little time to ask for a clarification. Rubio trusted Varren, and nodded to himself. 'Understood. Exfiltrating now!'

A pair of chattering mutants threw themselves at him as he spoke,
and Rubio cut one into chunks of fouled meat, punching the other
into a black smear across a bulkhead. Jerking backwards, he pulled
a krak grenade from his belt and thumbed the explosive to arm it.
Rubio hurled the device into the creatures as they scrambled over the
bodies of their kindred to reach him, and then sprinted away.

The grenade's concussive detonation made the rusted walls flex and
tremble, but he was out and free before part of the framework collapsed. Spotlights atop one of the many-legged crawlers stabbed out
and illuminated a path for him as the two vehicles scuttled away across
the clearing beyond the camp.

Rubio chanced a look over his shoulder and saw the same kind of
seething swarm that had fed upon the populace of the Walking City.
It writhed and howled, gathering mass in preparation for what would
be its next brutal attack. Now, as then, Rubio and the others were not
best equipped to deal with such a threat, but the Legions were made
to be weapons, and a weapon would always find a way.

He leapt high, grabbing a rung on one of the crawler's legs, hauling
himself up onto the vehicle's back, panting with effort. Looking back,
Rubio could see Gallor had squeezed himself into the command cab at

the rear, using the twin-stick controls to guide the machine away. Varren was driving the other crawler, and through vents in the iron hull Rubio could peer into the cargo bays beneath. He saw pale, blank-eyed faces looking up at him. Looking, but not seeing.

'Is Yotun with us?' He glanced over at Varren, and saw the other warrior shake his head.

'He went back.'

'For what?'

Any answer Varren might have given was drowned out in the thunderous roar of thrusters. The bullet-shaped ship on the landing pad spat white fire from its engine nozzles and rose off the ground. All at once, it was clear where Yotun had gone.

For a second, Rubio experienced disappointment, regretful that the unfamiliar Knight-Errant had decided to abandon them – but only for a second. Before it had even risen to the height of the acid-rainforest tree canopy, the cargo ship shuddered as the power of its thrusters faded, lift negated by mass. It groaned and began a tail-slide back down towards the pad and the encampment. The flames from the engine washed across the makeshift tents and incinerated them, boiling back up into a churn of fire that whipped towards the gargantuan swarm of carrion flies.

Rubio ducked, bringing up his arm to shield his face as the ship struck the ground and exploded, consumed in a second wave of fire that grew to smother the encampment and everything in it.

The crawlers were already deep into the trees, but the blast wave still buffeted them and threw plumes of burning fuel over Rubio's head in searing arcs. Gallor cursed as the spider-machine skidded out of control into a dense thicket.

'I believe that answers the question,' said Varren.

'Did… did he get out?' Gallor stared back at the wall of flames.

Rubio tried vainly to push out a telepathic call, but the deleterious presence of the pariahs made it impossible. At length, he released a sigh and signalled for the others to move on. 'Head back to the rendezvous point.'

'*We will honour Yotun's sacrifice along with all the others,*' said Gallor.

Honour it where? Rubio asked himself. The truth was, no Hall of Heroes existed for the Knights-Errant, no statues or memoria to recall their service and their passing. *Perhaps we need to build one ourselves,* he considered, as he climbed down into the cargo bay to ride out the rest of the journey.

Inside, the captives continued their muttering, and Rubio listened as the vehicle lurched on through the forest. Like repeating tones played at variant intervals, sometimes the words and half-sounds they would make came together in brief, sporadic synchrony. At times, he fancied they could be stanzas of poetry or shards of old, forgotten myths.

Then very clearly, he heard the broken chorus say the words that made his hearts seize in his chest.

'Horus. Come, Malcador. *Seek.*'

Rubio sprang to his feet. 'What did you say?' he snapped, looking wildly from one blank face to another. 'Answer me! Say it! Say it again...'

'Seek *peace,*' said the chorus, before it broke apart once more into unintelligible babble.

INTERVAL IV

No Flesh Shall Be Spared

[The warp; now]

'Hunda!'

The Bitterblood heard the whelp calling his name, and with irritable slowness, the old veteran allowed himself to come fully awake. His implanted auto-senses flickered into action, the visual, infrared, ultraviolet and terahertz-wave phases all overlapping into a single mass of input.

'Who speaks?' The question grated through the sour air of the arming chamber, issuing out of the vocoder module across the front of his armoured form. The barrel-chested Contemptor Dreadnought shifted on his support frame, making the iron girders creak. He flexed the thick fingers of his combat fists and turned an optic towards the legionary standing in the chamber's doorway. A line Death Guard, but his sigils were those of Captain Kalgaro's cohort, not of the First Company.

'It is I, Zurrieq...' The young warrior's reply seemed laboured, almost as if he were out of breath, as impossible as that was for a genhanced legionary.

'Raheb?' The Bitterblood generated a rough, saw-tooth noise that was as close as he could come to a chuckle. 'What are you doing here? It has been too long, young one!' The humour faded. 'Is something amiss?'

Zurrieq didn't answer, and instead he made sharp gestures to the serfs and mechano-menials who had been in the midst of performing a maintenance cycle on the venerable veteran's iron body. They took the hint and left quickly, leaving the two Death Guard warriors alone. 'Kalgaro told me to seek you out,' said the legionary, at length. 'We both agreed, if anyone aboard the *Terminus Est* can be asked to have an honest eye on this ship, it would be Hunda Skorvall.'

The Bitterblood laughed again. 'An honest eye on the ship... or its commander? I'll warrant you wish to know more about Typhon's intent than that of his vessel!'

'Aye, that is the truth.' Zurrieq halted, leaning heavily against a guard rail. 'For blade's sake, why is it so infernally hot in here?'

'What say you?' The veteran checked his aura-scan, but the ambient atmospheric readings came back within normal ranges.

Zurrieq was still speaking. 'You've been attached to Typhon's command since he took his splinter fleet and went on his sojourn... Kalgaro has his questions about what happened during the time the First Captain was away, and there are few we could trust to be...' He faltered briefly, as if losing his way. 'To be forthright. You are among that number.'

'I know little I could tell you,' the veteran admitted, shifting his heavy frame against the safety restraints that held him in place. 'Typhon had little use for me. I think he kept me down here because he knows I think he's an upstart. I knew him at the beginning, Raheb, just as I know you. Before you were uplifted to the Legion...'

He trailed off. Although all that remained of his flesh was interred in a plasteel coffin at the heart of the Contemptor's powerful cybernetic mechanism, the Bitterblood still remained more human than machine, and a pang of concern cut through him as he scanned Zurrieq's bio-signs. The young warrior's flesh was ruddy and filmed with oily sweat, and the veteran immediately recognised the signature effects of legionary internal implants operating over capacity. Even at a remove, he could tell that Zurrieq's preomnor, oolitic kidney and Larraman's organ were all engaged in fighting off something within him.

'Lad,' he said sharply, as Zurrieq's attention drifted away into the middle distance. 'Are you injured?' On a sub-channel vox-link, the Bitterblood was already transmitting a priority request for an Apothecary. 'What has sickened you?'

'I... I don't know.' Zurrieq pawed at his gauntlets, sluggishly pulling them free to let the metal gloves clatter to the deck. 'This fatigue... came upon me suddenly. As I moved down... down-ship to find you.' The legionary took a step and wavered, abruptly doubling over as if he had been struck in the gut.

'Ach.' The Bitterblood's concern overrode his decorum and he broke himself free of the safety locks, rising to advance on the other Death Guard. 'Raheb, look at me.'

'I...' Zurrieq tried to raise his head, but then a rolling shock of pain went through the warrior with such force that it silenced him. He went rigid, and gagged. A grotesque, liquid choking emitted from his open mouth, and suddenly Zurrieq was vomiting up a jet of viscous black bile, spewing it across the deck plates. He cried out in raw agony and sank to his knees before retching again, his hunched form quaking in uncontrolled spasms.

The veteran went to his side, the Contemptor stooping down to gather him up, and as he did the Bitterblood's sensors registered something writhing and moving in the dark pool of steaming ejecta. Tiny forms that resembled maggots were hatching as he watched, turning inside out to become silver-black flies with wet, flickering wings.

Zurrieq howled and drew into himself, his dense bones cracking against one another with the force of his palsy. Drawn back by the legionary's cries, two of the serfs stood mouths agape at the chamber entrance, and for a moment the veteran thought they were struck dumb by the sight of a nigh-invulnerable Death Guard in such agony.

But then the human menials began clawing at their exposed skin and screaming, before they too spat out their innards in streaming black floods.

'Contagion!' bellowed the Bitterblood, the word at once a digitised shout and a warning broadcast across the vox-net. 'Contagion here! Seal the decks!'

A trembling hand reached up and clawed at the veteran's armour. 'Help… me…' gasped Zurrieq, as his eyes turned milky.

All across the legionary's exposed flesh, hundreds of livid boils were rising to the surface of the skin, each one set in a cluster of three.

THE VALETUDINARIUM FELL silent as the primarch entered the compartment, and for a moment the only sound in the ship's medical bay was the huffing gasp of atmosphere processors and the low chime of life sensors.

Mortarion's searching gaze found Morarg, the Apothecary Crosius and the old war-dog Skorvall standing in a half-circle before a sealed chamber of plasteel and crystalflex. He marched to them, and the Dreadnought moved to block his way.

'Lord, no…' began the veteran, the tone of his vocoder surprisingly gentle.

'Step aside, Bitterblood,' Mortarion told him. 'I want to see.'

'It is a horror,' Skorvall said grimly. 'Blind me, but I wish I had not witnessed it.' The cyborg stepped back, and his machine form seemed to slump. 'I would not desire it for my worse rival.'

Annoyance flared in the primarch. *Old fool*, he thought to himself, *what sentiment is that?*

But then Mortarion looked into the sealed chamber where Zurrieq lay, and what he saw there was indeed a *horror*.

The Death Guard primarch had seen monsters and he had seen murders. The creatures stitched together from cruelty and corpses that the Overlords had made were the stuff of mortal nightmares. The wreckage of living things left behind in their battles, and then the wretched debris of ruined life Mortarion had met during the conflicts of the Great Crusade – all these sights were terrible enough to haunt the soul and curdle the spirit of a common man. Over time, he had become inured to such things. Indeed, he had often been *responsible* for them.

But this… It gave even his mighty will harsh pause.

What lay on the medicae bed was just barely recognisable as Raheb Zurrieq, but his body – stripped of his armour and skinsuit – was a grotesque parody of what it should have been. The lean and whipcord-strong form of the Death Guard had been corrupted into a livid, sickened mockery of itself. Flesh had become a grey, surreal mass of putrid matter, sloughing off the stricken warrior in stinking sheaves. Blackened nubs of bone protruded from great weeping wounds that dripped blue-yellow ichor. Thick, glutinous liquids pooled on the plas-teel deck, mixing and foaming. A cloud of silver-black motes danced around Zurrieq's corpse-like frame, the tiny flies alighting to eat at the raw edges of lesions or lay eggs that bloomed into writhing maggots.

Zurrieq resembled a corpse left to the rot of months in a wet, cloying wilderness, and yet impossibly he was still alive. His chest rose and fell in stutters, punctuated by coughing fits that spat green phlegm across the crystalflex barrier.

The young warrior had not been alone in there; Mortarion saw the dissolved remains of a pair of medicae servitors lying where they had fallen. The machine-slaves were quite dead, drowned in their own dis-eased blood.

'How… is he still alive?' The question slipped from Mortarion before he was aware of it.

'Unknown,' said Crosius. 'My lord, I have never seen the like of this. His secondary heart has already burst, and the majority of his organs have shut down.'

'His gene-seed?'

Crosius shook his head. 'I fear it is compromised beyond all hope of extraction. I am still struggling to grasp what I am looking at, but I believe it is a kind of chimeric disease vector.'

'Chimeric?' Morarg echoed the word. 'You mean like a mutant?'

Crosius actually smiled a little. He was transfixed, fascinated by the foul power of the contagion that had claimed the young warrior. 'Oh no, equerry. More than that. This viral clade is utterly protean and highly infectious. It is formless and all forms at once. It is not just one disease... It's *all* of them.'

'That's impossible,' grunted the Bitterblood, flexing his heavy fists. 'Why was I unaffected, then? I have flesh within my iron shell.' He banged twice on his chest-plate. 'I have not sickened.'

Morarg shot the primarch a look. 'Skorvall saw Raheb fall, my lord. And a dozen human crew along with him.'

'They perished in the time it took us to get him into the iso-chamber,' noted Crosius.

Morarg ignored the interruption and went on. 'I ordered full mag radiation scouring and decontamination protocols in all locations he visited. But there was nothing. No trace of the infection.'

'It is choosy,' Crosius offered, clearly toying with the idea. 'Perhaps it is intelligent.'

'Impossible,' scoffed the old Dreadnought. 'A virus is a mindless thing.'

'Is this something we brought from Ynyx?' demanded Mortarion. 'A weapon of last resort deployed against us?'

The Apothecary shook his head. 'I don't believe so. I see the hand of the warp in this.'

'You are so sure?' The Bitterblood made a grinding noise. 'How can you–?'

The Dreadnought's words were cut off as Zurrieq emitted a raw, bellowing scream that chilled every soul that heard it. Mortarion watched his warrior weeping black, bloody tears and deep in his heart, the Reaper of Men felt something unfamiliar and seldom experienced. *Pity.*

'He is in a great deal of agony,' said Crosius, breaking the sullen silence that followed. 'Enough to drive even the strongest of us insane.'

Mortarion barely registered the words. With a monumental effort, Zurrieq had managed to turn his head so his blighted gaze met that of his primarch. The cast of the legionary's face was a sorrowful entreaty begging for only one thing.

'Can you restore him?'

Crosius' lip curled. 'I do not know, my lord. I think it... unlikely.'

'Give me your knife,' said the primarch, holding out his hand to Morarg. The equerry did as he was told, his eyes narrowing.

Mortarion weighed the weapon, and then found his helmet hanging off the mag-plate at his thigh. Donning it, he activated an ultima-level environment seal in his armour with a blink-click command, and walked towards the airlock sealing the isolation chamber from the rest of the medical bay.

The Bitterblood raised one clawed hand. 'You will expose yourself to the contagion! Lord, you cannot!'

'Do not speak to me of what I cannot do, old friend. I do not fear this.' Mortarion entered the lock and let it cycle him through.

Inside the iso-chamber, a blood-boiling heat radiated from the stricken figure on the medicae platform. Zurrieq tried to raise a hand and failed, trembling with violent palsy. He mouthed a word, unable to speak it aloud.

Peace.

'Yes,' said Mortarion, holding up the knife. The blade was heavy, a bone-cutter, and it would do the required deed. He hesitated, turning the weapon in his fingers. 'I know what you wish.'

It took all of Zurrieq's will to manage a single nod.

Mortarion listened to his own rasping breath within the confines of his helmet. The sound was lonely and distant, heavy with the despair of what he knew he must do. 'You are my loyal son,' he told the legionary. 'You have served the Death Guard with honour. You need suffer no more. Rest now.'

With a swift motion, Mortarion buried the equerry's knife in Zurrieq's chest, cutting his primary heart in two. The killing blow was perfect. The stricken legionary sagged and became still.

'It is done,' intoned the Reaper of Men, eyeing the medicae auspex module floating overhead on suspensors. The device's chimes were silent now. 'Peace, my son–' he began.

Zurrieq bolted forward, half flinging himself off the platform, a ghastly howl escaping his froth-rimed mouth. His blind eyes were black with tainted blood, and the buzzing mass of flies around him became a cloud of frenzied, droning smoke.

Mortarion took a step back and watched, appalled, as Zurrieq moved like a jerky marionette, reaching up to pull the combat knife from his chest. The blade came out in a whisper of ichor, and the primarch saw that the metal was now corroded and brittle. The weapon clattered to the deck and broke into pieces as Zurrieq slumped back and writhed.

The auto-senses in Mortarion's armour swept over the legionary and returned nothing but negative life signs. *Zurrieq was dead...* And yet he was not, his body still moving, and those terrified eyes staring fixedly at his liege lord. *Begging him for an end he could not give.*

Mortarion drew back through the airlock and stood in silence for what seemed like hours, as the stringent decontamination process scoured every part of his armour. The primarch hesitated to look back. Whatever tormenting force now animated Zurrieq, it was not some ethereal intelligence that had co-opted his flesh, and Mortarion knew that with all his soul. The man back there in that chamber was the same one he had recruited from Barbarus many years before.

Dead, and yet undying.

[The planet Barbarus; before]

THE TOWNSHIP WAS called Heller's Cut, so Mortarion had learned on that first fateful night when he arrived, trailing after the souls he helped to liberate from Necare's capture. A small settlement in one of the valleys, it was little more than a cluster of domiciles around a low-ceilinged hall and communal storehouses. A wide disc of hard-wheat fields radiated out around it, providing harvest for the locals and food for their animals. There were perhaps two hundred lessers living within its domains, and they were terrified of him.

That first night – weeks ago now – had been fraught. So much happened so quickly, it had been difficult to assimilate it all. Still, he replayed and puzzled over the reactions of the people to the shock return of their kindred. So many of them wept with joy and showed each other affection of such purity that it made Mortarion's chest ache. He felt the echo of an emotion there that his young mind was unable to frame, a sentiment that he had never experienced, yet desperately wanted to.

But he hid that need out of old habit, for fear it would be seen as weakness. He buried it when he saw their faces turn towards him and the pale-skinned Calas, the outcast with the acid tongue and fast eyes.

An argument ensued. Some wanted to send the escapees back into Necare's clutches, for fear that the High Overlord would come to Heller's Cut and obliterate it in totality for daring to rebel against his culling. Others openly called for Mortarion and Calas to be put to death, despite the fact that they had been instrumental in the rescue. In the end, those they helped save brought forth a sort of accommodation, as meagre as it was.

They allowed the two of them shelter in a tumbledown stable at the edge of the village, gave them wood for a fire. And food, too, after a fashion. It was a grey stew from a communal cauldron, but to Mortarion it was better than anything he had consumed back up in his mountain bastion.

He stood for days at the door of the stables, an unmoving sentinel, waiting for his foster father to come after him. But Necare did not show his hooded face, and after a while, the settlement returned to a kind of equilibrium. In the weak light of the day, the hardy people would work the fields. As the night drew in, they would cluster together in the centre of the town to eat and to rest.

Calas told him that the odd, lilting sounds they made were called 'songs', and sometimes he would hear the lessers laughing. He had

encountered that before, of course, but the insane babble of golems or
the vicious sniggering of an Overlord were always troubling, unpleasant noises. He felt the ache again, and when he was alone he tried to
explore it, to map the dimensions of the strange sensation.

But all Mortarion found was a void inside himself, a space that he
did not know how to fill.

'I think we need to move on,' said Calas, drawing Mortarion back to the
present. He sat cross-legged in front of their firepit, poking at the yellow
flames. 'I've overheard some of them talking about us. A lot of the menfolk
think they'll avoid the Overlord's eventual revenge if you and I are gone.'

'No.'

'No what?' Calas shot him a look. 'Listen to me, Mortarion. There
are people who would gladly stake out our corpses on the hillside if
they thought it would grant them some protection from the culls. We
should go...' He paused. 'If we stick together, we can survive out there.'

Mortarion eyed the pale youth. 'Don't you want to stay with your
own kind?'

Calas' expression turned stony. '*My kind?* Do you know what my kind
did, in the village where I was born? They drowned my mother and
tried to do the same to me. All because she had been unlucky enough
to have an Overlord take a shine to her face.' He lost himself in the
flames for a moment. 'I'm an outsider like you.'

'You are not like me.' Mortarion turned to face him. 'I am just a killer.
You can make magick. I saw you do it, in the pass.'

Calas sneered and spat into the flames. 'You're mistaken. I have
some... skills, that's all. Things that soft minds don't understand.'

Mortarion considered pressing the point, then chose not to. For now,
other things were of greater import. 'Where can we go? If not here,
where? At least these people have shown us a degree of gratitude.'

'You seek kindness from them,' Calas retorted, making it a statement
rather than a question. 'We can't earn that. To them, I am a half-breed
and you are an Overlord's pet death-dealer.'

A group of solemn-faced harvesters trooped dejectedly past the stables on their way into the fields, all of them carrying flails and sickles as they set out to do the day's work. Their conversations became muted when they noticed Mortarion watching them, only picking up once more when they thought they were out of earshot.

'No,' Mortarion said again, as a moment of clarity came to him. 'This is not a matter of what I seek, Calas. It's about what these people need.' He pointed. 'Look at them. They grasp at every tiny spark of life, desperate and afraid in all their thoughts and deeds. Their existence is nothing but fear and dread.'

He knew that life just as well as the lessers did. For all the difference in their circumstances, Mortarion realised it was something that they all shared.

'That's the way things are,' replied the pale youth. 'The way things have always been.'

'That is going to change.' Mortarion pushed open the stable door and started after the harvesters.

'Where are you going?' Calas called after him, but he ignored the words.

Each day Mortarion had stood and waited for his foster-father's revenge to unfold, he had listened to the voices of the villagers and grown to understand their fears. Despite the grey and hopeless cast to their lot, many of the Barbaruns still tried to kindle a fire in their hearts. He admired their great endurance, and he understood their simmering resentment. This was a world forever turning on an axis of injustice, with the Overlords playing their petty games of hate and victimising the humans over and over again.

But these people lacked the impetus to do something about it. They were isolated and alone. They had no guidance. They had no hope.

The balance was wrong. It had to stop. The cruelty of Necare and all the other parasites would end.

And I will do it.

The idea swelled inside him as Mortarion walked into the fields, amid dozens of shocked gazes and silenced voices from the townsfolk.

It would take time. He would need an army. But it could be done.

Mortarion halted at the edge of a full-grown field of crops and watched the men there pause in their work, as they chopped at the tough hardwheat stalks with their hand-blades. Casting around, he spotted the broken works of what had been a heavy sickle cutter. Usually the great cart-like farming implement would be hauled by a burden beast, but the wheels were damaged and the device was inoperative. Undaunted, Mortarion went to the machine and opened it up, reaching inside its workings to dismount a tool that better suited his height and grasp.

His strong hands emerged with a great scythe gripped in them, the shaft and the dense crescent blade too heavy for any of the lessers to lift, let alone wield. He let it swing at the air a few times. It felt *right*.

Then, without waiting to be asked, Mortarion stepped into the field and began to cut. With each swipe of the scythe, he took down five times as much crop as any of the others, and it wasn't long before they were moving in his wake, gathering up the quicker harvest.

As THE DAY wore on, the work went quickly and evenly, so much so that the locals had to struggle to match Mortarion's pace.

He heard rough laughter cut the air. Good humoured, it was a faint ghost of warmth in the cold of the valley.

'Is this your plan?' Mortarion glanced back and found Calas by his side. To his surprise, the pale youth had followed him out and was doing his part to gather up the sheaves of hardwheat, albeit reluctantly. 'You think swinging a cutter will make them like you?'

He paused to take a deep breath. The sallow sun was setting, and off towards the edge of the fields, a faint mist of chem-haze gathered where the long shadows fell.

'I will earn their respect,' said Mortarion. 'You would do well to do the same, Calas.'

Far across the fields, a horn hooted. It was the signal to end the work of the day and return to the village proper.

The pale youth glanced in that direction, then smirked and nodded towards the scythe. 'You don't need to *earn* anything, Reaper. You could *take* it. Not a soul back there could match you in a straight challenge.'

Mortarion shook his head slowly, eyeing the encroaching edges of the mist. He reached up to push a length of black hair from his eyes. 'Fear is a weapon I only use on my enemies.'

Calas' smirk grew towards a sneer, but before he could say more, a distant crunch of breaking wood and the sharp cry of a child echoed through the air.

Mortarion's grip stiffened around the scythe and he pivoted towards the source of the sound. Off across the fields, a scatter of dust was moving on the wind, marking the place where one of the village's communal carts had tipped over. He saw several of the harvesters drop their gatherings and run towards the stricken vehicle. The child's cry came again, this time a thin scream of agony.

Someone shouted for help, and other men sprinted back towards the village. Then Mortarion's preternaturally sharp senses caught the odour of fresh blood. Without thinking, he jammed the shaft of the scythe upright into the brown-black earth and covered the distance to the stricken wagon in a few heartbeats.

The locals clustered around saw him coming and backed away, giving Mortarion room to see what was going on. Men had been dragging the heavy cart, laden with bales of hardwheat, back in the direction of the storehouses and a wheel had become fouled in a hidden gully. He saw how it had happened – the massive weight of the wagon broke the wheel as it shifted the wrong way, sending the whole thing off balance.

There was a child trapped beneath the wagon's frame, pinned into the gulley where the cart had caught her as it fell. A waif of a teenage girl, one of the younger villagers who had the duty of carrying bags of twine for securing the bales. Blood flowed freely from a gash on her head, and she was turning white with shock. The muddy ground beneath her was slowly giving in, and moment by moment the wagon pressed more of its weight upon her thin, bony body.

'We can't leave her out here!' hissed one of the harvesters.

'Sun's gone down now,' argued another. 'The mist rising with it. You know what that means.'

Mortarion knew. The people in the settlement kept pitch-blend torches burning all through the hours of darkness to fend off the fogs that encroached in the night. Things moved and skittered about in that fog, predatory things that he knew full well would take apart any human they came across. The lines of torches didn't extend out this far, though.

'Look at it!' snarled the second man, as the cold breeze picked up. 'We'll need twenty able souls to move that thing! By the time they get back here, the mist will be on us!' He swallowed hard. 'It'd be more a kindness if we–'

'Stand aside,' said Mortarion. The harvester was reaching for his cutting blade as he spoke, but even the gentlest of Mortarion's shoves threw him back into the mud on his behind. He stepped around the fallen man and crouched by the hub of the broken wheel, fingering the axle.

The child trapped beneath it blinked at him, petrified. *What does she see when she looks at me?* The question rose in Mortarion's thoughts. *Death itself, come to claim her?*

He silenced the doubts and set his feet in the muddy ground to square a stance. Then, Mortarion put both hands around the cart's axle and lifted its tremendous weight with a low grunt of effort. It rose out of the mire with a sucking gulp and he held it there.

For a moment, no one spoke. All the harvesters were shocked silent. It was Calas who finally shouted at them. 'Don't just stand there gawking, you fools! Pull her out!'

The girl coughed and fainted as they moved her, and he spied an ugly wound along her thigh, but Mortarion sensed that she would survive. As a pair of the harvesters carried her away as quickly as they could, he let the wagon down once more, without disturbing a single one of the bales piled upon it. He watched the men diminish towards the glow of the border torches being lit, aware of the night coming in all around. The wan light of the day drained away as swiftly as water would soak into earth.

The man that Mortarion had knocked down was back on his feet. 'We're going to have to leave the cart.' He seemed to have some degree of authority among the other harvesters, perhaps as a foreman or some-such. 'Everyone take as many bales as you can carry!' he ordered, and the other harvesters set about to follow his command.

'Leave it,' said Mortarion.

'We can't!' retorted the senior man. 'That's a day's work there, not that I'd expect you to understand...'

Mortarion looked around. The breeze was stiff and strong now, and buoyed along with it, the curls of the mist were moving more swiftly. He caught sight of Calas' face. His outcast companion was staring out at nothing, as if aware of something that only he could see. 'What is it?'

'They're here,' he whispered.

'Hurry up!' called the foreman, climbing atop the tilted wagon to supervise the others. He coughed and gasped as tendrils of mist wove overhead. 'The clouds will take our breath if we tarry!' He turned and aimed a finger a Mortarion. 'You! If you're so strong, then you can carry a dozen times as much–'

He never finished the sentence. Mortarion glimpsed the black, cloaked shape rise up from the stands of uncut wheat and flash through the air in silence, saw it come up behind the man and dive in for the kill.

There was the dull flash of distant torchlight off a wide, bronze short sword, and the foreman lost his head. A fountain of glittering blood sprayed across the harvesters and they scattered in fear.

Mortarion's thoughts raced – *how had he failed to hear the enemy approaching, had it been the matter with the girl that distracted him?* – even as another, more martial part of his mind saw the ghostly shapes forming in the depths of the fog bank. He regretted leaving the scythe behind, and scrambled to grab something like a weapon. His long fingers snatched up a fallen grain flail as new screams issued out on all sides.

Nearby, Calas reacted to the sight of one of the harvesters being jerked back out of the light and into the shadows. Mortarion heard the grinding crunch of bitten bone and the giggle of hungry golems.

'He came after us...' said Calas, gripping a cutter blade. He coughed as the mist began to thicken.

Mortarion tasted the faint tang of the toxic haze, but the poison meant little to him. 'No,' he said, eyes narrowing. 'This is not my foster father.'

Had Necare wished to strike at Heller's Cut, the High Overlord would have begun with rains of fire-spears and a horde of kill-beasts. He was never one for subtlety when things angered him. No, this was somebody else. Mortarion heard the whicker and hiss of the bronze sword. He knew the owner of that weapon well.

Desalem was another of the minor Overlord cadre, an overconfident schemer who long ago had planted his banner next to Necare's, a sly creature who feasted off the crumbs of power that fell from the High One's table and grasped at any opportunity to show how sycophantic he could be.

A rabble of Desalem's golem-soldiers boiled out of the gloom and set about whomever they found. Calas fought wildly, stabbing and cutting, and the few remaining harvesters who hadn't immediately run turned their work implements towards a desperate defence. A few fell, the golems diving on them to guzzle at opened wounds or drag them away. Mortarion ignored the carnage, taking a second to get in synchrony with the unfamiliar weight of the flail.

Finding the rhythm, he used the heavy blunt end to stave in skulls, and the chain-linked head to break arms and legs. He lost himself in the killing, and it was easy to do.

In the middle distance, Mortarion heard Desalem's high-pitched, grating laughter and it drew his attention from the immediate fight. His vision, far faster to night-adapt and keener than that of the others, let him pick out the spindly, cloaked shape of the minor Overlord. Desalem sailed through the fields of hardwheat as if floating, surrounded by a ring of his warriors. He appeared to be directing the actions of his golems with piercing shrieks of sound, in the way a shepherd would use a herd-hound.

Mortarion picked out other noises as well. The screams of villagers, off in the distance. Desalem's golems had attacked there too, and he could see them falling back now, carrying the bodies of those they had taken. Most of the abductees were still alive, thrashing and clawing at their abductors – but the moment they entered the mists, the humans stopped fighting and began clawing at their throats. The toxic air would soon suffocate them.

Calas too was gasping and wheezing now. 'The fog... Getting thicker.' He staggered away, following the surviving harvesters as they were forced to retreat back towards the relative safety of the settlement and the clearer air around it. 'Can't stay... here.'

Mortarion hesitated. Desalem's laughter echoed from deeper into the mists, mocking and baleful. 'He thinks they won't follow.' Mortarion said the words out loud. 'He thinks they can't.' With a grimace, he tossed the flail away and broke into a run once more, his powerful whipcord legs pumping as he sprinted towards the place where he had left the scythe.

The weapon was still there, the curve of the sickle blade a steel pennant frozen in motion. Mortarion snatched it up as he passed and pivoted towards the mass of the retreating golems without losing momentum.

He understood now why his foster father had not come for him in person. Necare was too clever for that, too underhanded. The High Overlord would be treating his foundling son's latest defiance in the same way he did with every aspect of Mortarion's growth – as a test.

As by what metric that test would be judged a failure or a success, Mortarion no longer cared.

Desalem was still braying his contemptuous laughter when Mortarion caught up with the Overlord in the thickening mist just beyond the edge of the crop fields, and butchered all but one of his warriors.

The human abductees were all dead now, choked into cold silence, but those who had taken them followed the same path into darkness at Mortarion's hand. The farm-machine scythe became a very different kind of tool as the shining, sharp edge cut down the babbling, stitched-together creatures.

Cords of intestine and steaming heaps of gore spattered over the sparse grasses of the moorland, as howls of agony were cut short. Mortarion made certain to disarm and near cripple one single golem, before using the flat of the scythe to batter Desalem into the mud.

The Overlord spat venom back at him, screaming curses at Mortarion for daring to strike one of his betters.

'You believe you can come here and kill with impunity,' Mortarion told him. 'You believe the mists protect you. That nothing human can touch you.' He gestured at the poisonous haze all around them. 'That changes tonight.'

Desalem's ratlike face screwed up in a moment of confusion, and that was when Mortarion killed him. The hooked tip of the scythe entered the Overlord's body at the throat and travelled down the length of his torso, allowing a stinking flow of mutant offal to burst out and soil the dark earth.

Mortarion turned to glare at the remaining survivor. 'You live because I want a messenger.' He leaned in and spoke slowly and clearly, so that there would be no misunderstanding. 'Tell Necare and the others to prepare. However long it takes, the reign of the Overlords on Barbarus will end. I shall come for them all.'

Then he turned away and walked back towards the flickering glow of the torches.

[The warp; now]

Dead, and yet undying.

The horror of it had driven Mortarion away, and even the stringent decontamination process had not been able to boil off the sick dread that washed back and forth in the primarch's thoughts.

What he had seen in the isolation chamber was something he had always believed was impossible.

He was humble – or perhaps, he had been humbled by hard experience – enough to know that there was much in the universe that he did not understand. Mortarion had witnessed many things in his time, terrors and delights alike so strange that no common mind could have beheld them and remained sane.

But throughout all his years as master of the Death Guard, there were a handful of unshakable truths that he held as inviolate and unchangeable. They were the pillars upon which his sense of self, and upon which the very soul of his Legion, were based.

The Death Guard never retreat. We always resist. We do not fear death. We are not weak.

But Zurrieq's horrifying decay and undeath put the lie to all of that. Never in all his life had Mortarion encountered a venom or weaponised malaise that the Death Guard had been unable to defy. His warrior sons drank poison like water, they breathed nerve gases and toxins as if they were the purest inhalation of air, and their unbreakable constitutions shrugged off any viral clade that either nature or twisted science could throw at them.

No Death Guard legionary had ever died in that fashion. No one, be they a Pale Son or Terran-born warrior, had ever shamed the XIV Legion by falling prey to something as paltry as a *sickness*.

Until Zurrieq. For that was what had claimed him, a contagion so incredibly virulent that it could burn through the fortress walls of his body and the soldiery of his bloodstream. Poor Zurrieq had been *invaded* – no, worse than that. He had been *conquered* from within by the chimeric phage that Crosius had spoken of.

A disease that could cripple the most indomitable of the Legiones Astartes? Before, Mortarion would have ridiculed the notion. But he had seen it with his own eyes, and the reality shook him. The strength of the Death Guard was to him an immutable law. To see it so thoroughly broken was an event he had no way to frame.

And if that were not enough, it seemed the power of this capricious virus reached into the realm of the unearthly as well. How else could one explain the undeath? By all known measures, Zurrieq should have been a corpse, and yet he lived still… if such a grotesque existence could still be called that.

Mortarion looked down at his gauntlets. He had silenced the beating of his son's heart as a mercy, to free him from this shame, only to watch the blade he used turn to rust and crumble. The decay, the living rot, the infestation, whatever it was, had transformed the legionary.

Into what, the primarch did not know.

ON ENTERING THE command deck of the *Terminus Est*, Mortarion's gaze was immediately drawn to Typhon. The First Captain was engaged in conversation with his officer Vioss and Mortarion's equerry. Morarg gave his master a warning look, and he had the immediate sense that the matter of Raheb Zurrieq's strange condition was only one of his problems.

'What now?' he demanded, cutting through the tense silence that had fallen.

'There's been a development,' said Typhon, his expression neutral. 'It seems our trial is upon us.'

Mortarion angrily waved him away and focused all his attention on Morarg. 'Speak, Caipha.'

The equerry's hands clasped one another. 'Lord Mortarion, the vox-operators have been following my orders to check in with the commanders of the other ships in our flotilla. The reports they have returned are… troubling.'

'It is happening out in the fleet,' added Vioss. 'Documented instances aboard the *Balefire*, *Indomitable Will*, *Lord of Hyrus* and several others.'

'How many?'

'Hundreds. And more with each passing hour,' said Vioss.

Morarg gave a solemn nod. 'The same malady that befell Zurrieq. The chimeric infection.'

'How can this be?' thundered Mortarion. 'There has been no phys-
ical contact between those ships and this one! How could it spread?'
He glared at Vioss, daring him to say that was not so, but the Grave
Warden nodded in agreement.

'No direct contact has occurred between any ships since we left Ynyx,
with the exception of the docking of *Greenheart* and the shuttle that
brought the lieutenant here from the *Endurance*.' Vioss anticipated Mortarion's next question before he uttered it. 'Captain Kalgaro's senior
Apothecary confirmed there have been no recorded outbreaks of the
chimera aboard your battle-barge, my lord.'

'Not *yet*,' muttered Typhon, drawing a hard glare from his commander.

'Our enemies could have secreted a weapon on our ships,' offered
Morarg, thinking out loud. 'Something that acted in a delayed fashion.'

'Your theory does not track. The craft that have declared contagion
outbreaks follow no pattern to that end,' said Vioss. 'Some are part of
the splinter fleet, newly arrived from another sector. Others are those
that travelled with the *Endurance* to Ynyx.'

Morarg glanced at Typhon. 'True. But if the perfidy of the Navigators
was as widespread as the First Captain suggests, this might be another
aspect of that conspiracy.'

'Who among my loyalist brethren could even conceive of such an
underhanded assault?' Mortarion scowled. 'Guilliman and Dorn don't
have it in them. The Wolf or the Khan are too proud...'

'Perhaps the Lord Corax?' Morarg took up the thread. 'Ach. Curse me
if this situation doesn't have the fingerprints of the Hydra all over it!'

'The Alpha Legion stand with us under the Warmaster's banner,'
insisted Vioss. 'What benefit would they gain from attacking an allied
Legion?'

Typhon gave a shake of the head, cutting off the line of argument. 'Forgive me, but this must be said. We cannot limit ourselves to thoughts
upon conventional lines, and place blame in ordinary means.' He took a
step towards his primarch. 'Do not forget where we are! Our ships travel
through the deeps of the immaterium, and that must not be forgotten.

The realities of our material universe are malleable in this realm.' He drifted off, examining the shutters across the command deck's exterior portals, running a hand over them. 'Here, all barriers are permeable.'

'The Geller fields keep the warp at bay,' insisted Morarg. 'It has no purchase within our ships!'

'And yet...' Typhon gave him a sideways look. 'All walls can fall, if enough pressure is applied. Every Death Guard knows that truth.'

'Then what would you have us do, captain?' Mortarion demanded.

'You already know my thoughts on this, lord.'

Mortarion swallowed his annoyance and turned away to find the *Terminus Est*'s communicatory pit, where hooded crew-serfs monitored the intermediate-range vox-systems that allowed the vessels of the fleet to converse with one another over short, sub-stellar distances. He stalked closer and they all bowed in unison.

'Look at me,' he growled, irritated by their diffidence. 'Open the vox-network to all our craft. Voice-signal, hololithic, datum line. All channels and general frequencies. I want every ship in the fleet to heed my words.'

A brassy armature folded down from the ceiling of the chamber and turned to present a scanning head to the primarch. Unfolding into a flower, at its centre was a thick glass lens, and the device emitted a fan of red laser light, scanning in his form and rendering it into a digital form for transmission.

The most senior of the vox-serfs gave a bow to cue him, and Mortarion drew in a slow breath. He disliked the performative aspect of speaking in such a manner. He had never been one for clever speeches and poetic oratory – that sort of thing he left to Horus, Lorgar or the Phoenician. Mortarion did not know how to speak in as theatrical a way as his siblings did. He could only give from the heart, be direct and unvarnished.

'My sons,' he intoned, and Mortarion heard the echo of his words resonating distantly through the decks of the *Terminus Est*. Silence fell in their wake, here and on every craft where the signal reached. 'We have been waylaid.' He resisted the impulse to glance towards Typhon, sensing the First Captain at the edges of his perception. 'An unidentified malaise of great potency and chimeric form is loose among our number. At this hour, there is no cure. This weapon poses a true threat, even to us. It cannot be allowed to spread unchecked. And for the moment, the face of our true enemy... the culprit behind this contagion... remains unclear.' He paused to let that sink in. 'All commanders, log my order: every ship in the fleet is to seal its airlocks, landing bays and launch tubes. Teleportariums are to be taken offline. A total lockdown protocol is now in effect, so that we may marshal our strength against this insidious assault and work to expunge it. Lines of communication will be opened between all senior Apothecaries on all ships. Pool your knowledge, my sons. Examine this contagion and bring me word of how to kill it.'

He raised one hand to make a throat-cutting gesture to end the transmission, but hesitated before the motion. The faint shade of the bone-deep dread he had experienced in the isolation chamber ghosted around him, and Mortarion wondered if his legionaries sensed some measure of it too. Was there fear in his voice? He could not leave his sons with such thoughts to dwell upon.

'Be sure. This... pestilence,' he began again, grasping for the right words. 'This... *Destroyer plague...* It will not end us. We shall face it and do as the Death Guard will. We will endure. We will advance. My father's Palace stands, awaiting the thunder of our boots. We will see the sun set on the Emperor's corrupt Imperium, my warriors. I swear that to you, on the black sands of lost Barbarus. We will break those walls and have our due. What is owed shall be called to full account.' Now the words came to him easily, even as Mortarion realised that he was echoing what Typhon had told him earlier. 'We are facing a great test. But the Legion will survive this poison.' He reached back in his thoughts for a familiar oath, rejecting the hollow ring that came with it. 'You are my unbroken blades. By your hand shall justice be delivered, and doom shall stalk the halls of Terra.'

'For Barbarus and the Legion,' snarled Typhon, his attestation repeated a heartbeat later by Vioss, Morarg and everyone else on the command deck.

Mortarion knew that the same response was sounding on all the ships of the fleet, but drew his hand across his throat and cut the signal.

Typhon continued to lead his crew in the salute, but Mortarion put a hand on his vambrace and pulled him away. 'Listen to me,' he hissed, low and menacing, quiet so that only the captain heard his words. 'I want your *specialists* to get us out of this madness. Find a way to return our ships to the material realm.'

'My lord, what you ask is not a simple task.' Typhon mirrored his low tones. 'There are many dangers to be considered. Passing through the warp's veil is not like using a doorway. It is a maze that must be traversed, a shifting labyrinth with walls made of smoke–'

'Spare me,' Mortarion said, cutting him off. 'You say this malaise comes from the warp, but you are reluctant to leave it?' He leaned in. 'What are you hiding from me, Typhon?'

The First Captain hesitated, as if he were surprised by the primarch's accusation. Then he turned to look back at the sealed shutters, and his lips thinned. 'You more than any living being know the true colour of my soul, Mortarion.'

'I do,' he agreed, 'that is why I am asking you the question.'

Typhon did not reply. Then out of nowhere, an alarm tocsin brayed into life. Mortarion released his grip on the First Captain and turned to Vioss, snapping out a command. 'Report!'

The Grave Warden peered at a gas-lens screen and his eyes widened. 'Scry-sensors are registering an energy surge on board the *Coldreign*.'

'Captain Tayge's ship,' noted Morarg. 'A light cruiser from the Reprover battle element.'

'Show me.' Mortarion gestured, and from a hidden hololith emitter in the floor came a cone of emerald light. The glow formed into a scanner view of the Death Guard fleet, zooming in through the motes of colour to make the shape of the warship in question. The *Coldreign* was under power, moving off its assigned position, making erratic turns as it extended away from the fleet. 'Hail them,' he added.

'No response, my lord,' said one of the vox-operators. 'All communication channels are dark.'

'Confirming...' Vioss gave a bleak nod. 'Yes. The *Coldreign*'s warp engines are in flux and their Geller fields are reconfiguring. They are preparing to translate back to normal space.'

'That would be a mistake,' said Typhon.

Mortarion gave him an angry look. 'You have someone on that ship? Can you not... *reach* them?'

Typhon shook his head. 'There is only fear and terror aboard that vessel now. A moment of weakness has doomed them.'

The warning chimes changed tone, becoming strident and grating. 'Energy surge increasing,' reported Vioss. 'They are attempting the jump.'

Mortarion stared into the hololith as an eerie shimmer passed over the length of the *Coldreign*'s image. But what he saw was not the expected effect, with the destroyer falling away into a rip in space-time; instead the arrow-prow of the three-kilometre-long ship gave a violent shudder, and it began to *twist*. Mortarion's jaw hardened as he watched the vessel distort. It was as if an invisible giant held the craft at bow and stern, inexorably crushing it, bending and distending the *Coldreign* into an unrecognisable mass of adamantium. Explosions flared all through the ruined hull, and strange torsions of metal grew out of the dying starship. It turned itself inside out, exposing crew decks and systems tiers, discharging atmosphere and debris into the empyrean.

And then, as a final brutality upon it, the *Coldreign* imploded, collapsing into a dark, craggy fist of wreckage.

'No life signs detected,' said Vioss, after a moment. 'Sensors show evidence of atemporal displacement, mass inversion and–'

'The ship is dead,' said Typhon, silencing the Grave Warden. 'We must be cautious if we do not wish to see more of our brothers follow it into oblivion.' He walked away, without sparing his primarch another look. 'I will return to the sanctorum, and find our path once more.'

Mortarion watched him depart, suddenly gripped by the ominous sense that he had become a stranger aboard the ships of his own fleet.

FOUR

Eclipse
Messengers
The Sleeper Awakens

IT WAS DEEP night over Terra's greatest peak when Rubio returned to the Imperial Palace, and his suspicions were aroused when the monitors of the Adeptus Custodes granted him direct entry into the inner reaches, without first stopping to board and search the shuttle he had commandeered.

It was not protocol, and it was not expected. Although the Knight-Errant's permissions were all in order and correct, even he as one of the Chosen was not immune to the ironclad security procedures that the primarch Rogal Dorn had instituted across the Terran capital. Few beings could pass as freely as he did now, and that could only mean one thing.

Despite travelling in vox silence on his suborbital flight back from the edge of the acid-rainforest, Rubio was *expected*. The Sigillite knew he was coming, and he had smoothed the way.

Leaning into the cramped cockpit, the warrior looked over the shoulder of the mute servitor-pilot and saw the play of text on the hololithic monitor screen before it. They were being directed to a tertiary flight platform on the eastern range of the Briar's Arcade. Rubio frowned, his suspicions confirmed. The landing pad was isolated and provided direct access to Malcador's sanctuary tower.

After touchdown, as the dying whine of the shuttle's engine echoed out across the Palace towards the Petitioner's City and beyond, Rubio strode off the little craft's drop-ramp and into the middle of a cluster of Chosen troopers in grey carapace armour. None of them spoke to him or offered a word of explanation, and he did not need them to act as guides. Still, the soldiers jogged to keep pace with the legionary as he crossed a connecting bridge, and passed through the membrane of the shimmering void shield cowl that surrounded the tower.

Malcador's private domain had its own layer of secondary protection beneath the mighty barriers of the Palace, and they were more than just technologies that could resist energy weapons or kinetic impact. Rubio sensed other forces at the edges of his perception, and glimpsed semi-invisible warding icons that had been secretly worked into the tower's decorative sculptures and elegant architecture. That the Sigillite had reservoirs of power unknown to all others had never been in doubt, but Rubio found himself wondering, now he was close at hand, what depths they plumbed.

The bridge led into an entrance hall, and as they passed inside, Rubio caught a glimpse of another figure in storm-dark power armour moving off in the other direction. He saw a sullen, heavily scarred face before it vanished into shadow. It was another Knight-Errant, that much was certain, but his aura and his aspect were unfamiliar to the psyker.

How many of us are there? Rubio wondered if he would ever know.

The troopers halted in front of a wide door, as silent as ever. It slid open on whispering electromagnetics to allow Rubio into a great reading room. Other doors ringed the chamber, amid shelves of mnemonic tablets, datum orbs, scrolls and heavy, ancient books. Oddly, many of the shelves had obvious gaps where items had recently been removed, and Rubio saw a human-form mechanoid in the process of selecting a series of black-clad tomes. One by one, the silver-skinned robot plucked them from their places and craned them into a hod-like carrier mounted on its back.

'I am relocating a few items from my collection,' said Malcador, in a lecturing tone. Rubio followed the sound of his voice, coming across to him from a long, upholstered bench. Flickering light illuminated the surroundings, cast by plasmatic flames burning in a black metal basket atop a staff. An imperious iron eagle peered out of the fires, and the staff stood as rigid as a spear that had been rammed into the ground. The Sigillite had a data-slate in his hand, and he switched it off with a flick of his wrist as he looked up, dropping it on a nearby table. 'I am sending them somewhere more secure.'

'There is a place on Terra more secure than the Imperial Palace?' Rubio looked closer at one of the shelves and his eyes narrowed as he realised he could not read the titles on the spines of the books. It was not that they were in a language he did not know, but rather that the words were blurry and malformed, shapes that only gave the impression of being letters.

'There isn't,' Malcador agreed, then pointed at the books. 'Don't stare too hard. The cantrips in place upon these works have a deleterious effect on those without the clearance to know them.' He smiled, and there was a little cruelty in it. 'A Librarian in the greatest library, and yet unable to read. What a tragedy.'

Its work done, the now fully loaded mechanoid sped away on wheels hidden in the soles of its feet, leaving the two of them alone. '*This knowledge is forbidden,*' said Rubio. 'Isn't that what tyrants always say? To stop the lesser orders from learning too much, lest they challenge their dominance.'

Beneath his hood, Malcador's smile turned brittle. 'When you have my perspective, one understands that some things were not meant to be known by commonplace minds.'

'Who decides where the line is drawn between the common and the uncommon?' Rubio felt the pressure of the Sigillite's most gentle telepathic probe upon his thoughts, and even that was almost overwhelming.

'One day, you will,' Malcador told him. He looked away, and for the first time Rubio noticed a velvet bag on the nearby table.

A few silver coins lay atop it, their surfaces covered with intricate designs. Rubio had the sudden compulsion to come closer and pick one up, but he ignored the impulse.

'What are you doing here, Rubio?' Malcador went on. The Sigillite undoubtedly knew the answer, but he wanted to hear the warrior say it.

Rubio took a breath and spoke about Malida Jydasian, explaining Garro's orders to him and of how that had led him and the others to the jungle camp. Rubio told Malcador what they had found there, the survivors they rescued and of Yotun's sacrifice.

The Sigillite sniffed at the use of the word. 'That one is a lot like you,' he said, interrupting the flow of Rubio's report. 'He is resilient.'

'He thought I was someone called Koios.'

'Did he?'

'I don't know that name.'

Malcador looked down at the coins. 'Not yet.' Rubio's jaw hardened as he grew weary of the Sigillite's elliptical manner, but before he could say more, the hooded man went on. 'So you've sent them to the White Mountain. The logical choice. I would have given that order, had you sought it.' He eyed him coldly. 'But you act on your own volition, and that does not excuse the deed.' Malcador leaned back, his face disappearing into the shadows of his hood. 'You are picking up Nathaniel's bad habits. I do not approve.'

Rubio did not allow himself to be intimidated by the Sigillite's immense psionic presence. 'I came back to the Imperial Palace for a reason, to explain my actions to you. But now I wonder if I have wasted my journey. Do you know what is at hand with the Silent Sisters who were abducted? Do you know, but consider us all too commonplace to share it?'

'No.' Malcador laughed softly, and it seemed genuine. 'In truth, Rubio, I actually *don't* know.' He sighed. 'It's almost refreshing.'

Rubio heard the door whisper open behind him and half turned, expecting to see the silver mechanoid returning to gather up more books. However, the figure that entered the chamber was someone else, and shockingly familiar to him. A man in robes similar to Malcador's, but rangy and long-limbed, with sandy skin and oval, perse-shaded eyes.

The new arrival gave Rubio a curious look, but there was no recognition in it, only a measure of fear at being so firmly scrutinised by a legionary. 'I brought... the amasec,' he said haltingly.

'Thank you, Ael.' Malcador beckoned him closer, and the man gave Rubio a wide berth, carrying a silver tray with an elaborate bottle and a pair of balloon glasses over to the table. 'We'll continue our conversation in a moment,' added the Sigillite.

Rubio glared at the man. There he stood, perfectly well and apparently unharmed, and yet days ago the legionary had watched this person torn asunder by animal panic, watched the same man throw himself to certain death from the Eagle's Highway. 'You are Wyntor,' he said slowly.

The man put down the tray and retreated, closer to Malcador. 'Yes. Forgive me, Ser Knight, but I do not know you.'

I saw you die. The words formed on Rubio's lips, but the Sigillite gave the slightest shake of the head and they were never uttered.

'You came here because you have something for me.' Malcador became terse. 'Let's have it, then. As these days pass and the Warmaster draws closer, time is the only commodity we cannot waste.'

Rubio removed a loop of recording wire from one of the pouches on his belt and passed it to Malcador. The Sigillite gave the spool a curious look, then connected it to the data-slate he had been using. After a moment, a recording began to play.

'*Horus,*' said the voices, their timbre breathy and disordered. '*Come, Malcador. Seek. Seek peace.*'

Wyntor visibly flinched at the mention of the Warmaster's name, but Malcador's expression remained impassive. He listened to the recording play out and loop back to its start twice over before finally detaching the spool.

'At last,' he muttered. 'I suspected a message would form eventually.

But the content...' Malcador gave a dry laugh and glanced at Wyntor. 'What do you make of that, Ael? Don't be afraid to say what you are thinking.'

'I would be cast a fool to give voice to my first hope,' the other man said ruefully. 'But all right, I'll say it.' He sighed. 'It almost sounds like... an offer of truce.'

'Seek peace,' echoed Malcador. 'I have to dig deep to remember the shape of such a thing.'

'If the message is from Horus Lupercal,' said Rubio, 'only one thing is certain. This is a trap of some sort.'

'Very possibly.' Malcador got up, reaching for the black iron staff. It slid soundlessly into his hand and he used it to pull himself to his full height. 'So of course I have to see it for myself.'

Rubio folded his arms across his chest. 'That isn't why I brought this datum to you. I came to-'

'Warn me, yes, thank you.' Malcador dismissed the idea with a wave of his hand. 'But instead you played the role this design always had for you. The cogs turn...' He made a circling motion with a finger. 'The clock chimes. The hour is almost upon us.' He sighed, closing his eyes for a moment and looking inward. 'I really did think we might have more time, but the signs are all there. The turncoats are moving. The vipers in our midst are stirring.'

'You should not leave the Imperial Palace,' insisted Rubio. 'Lord Dorn would have my head if I allowed it.'

'Rogal has enough to occupy his thoughts.' The Sigillite spoke to Wyntor. 'Ael, have my personal shuttle prepared for immediate departure. Brother Rubio and I are taking our leave.'

Wyntor blinked. 'What... destination shall I give them?'

'White Mountain,' Rubio answered, uttering the name as if someone else had spoken through him.

THE SUN HUNG above the horizon, but scant measure of its light could find the warriors in the chamber where they had gathered, deep within the peak of the old, forgotten fortress. It was a broad, resonant space – a naturally occurring cavern that had been widened by the use of stone-burners and other geoformer tools, the dead rock remade into platforms and sharp angles of a kind that would never occur without human intervention.

Throughout the space, computational devices and cogitator-servitors worked in clicking, whirring harmony, with spinning brassy mechanisms and pale faces alike lit by the pallid glow of great hololithic panels. The ghostly display panels hung in the cold, unmoving air like great animate tapestries, with waterfalls of text and numerals rolling endlessly from top to bottom.

Garro looked around, and each panel he settled upon gave him no more understanding than the last. He found the scientician, the woman Brell, stealing a glance in his direction, and once caught in the act she shied away.

At his side, Loken pointed towards a larger holographic display on the highest level of the gloomy chamber – a vast projection of the globe of Terra, turning slowly on a canted axis. Indicators resembling long gold needles pierced the surface of the simulated planet in dozens of different locations. 'There,' he said. 'All the recoveries so far.'

Varren and Gallor stood directly beneath the ghostly sphere. The former World Eaters legionary glared at the display as if he expected it to insult him, while the younger legionary looked on in fascination. They had not had much opportunity to speak since their arrival at the White Mountain with their cargo of newly rescued captives, and Varren's terse report had left Garro with more questions than answers.

Garro threw them a nod and halted before the hololith, taking in the scope of it. 'So many,' he breathed, and then his tone hardened. 'What if this circumstance were reversed? What if it were our brother legionaries returning from the rolls of the war dead, and the Sisterhood were the ones keeping it from us?'

'There would be fury in that, and no mistake,' growled Varren. 'But the Untouchables are not fools. They would tell us...'

'Or else kill those they found and disintegrate the remains,' noted Gallor.

Loken ignored the opening and gestured at the display again. 'You wanted to see where they came from, here is your answer. As I said before, there is no discernible pattern to the abduction and return of the pariahs. They are from dozens of different Witchseeker cadres, all of differing rank and age. The locations where they were last sighted and the ones where they were found have no apparent correlation.' As he said the words, differing indicators lit up and datum panels rose and fell. Each one briefly showed the face of a Silent Sister, along with personal details and a field report.

Garro saw Malida Jydasian's image float by, and he frowned. 'The questions return. Who did this, and why?'

'If I may?' Brell cleared her throat and ventured closer, skirting the group of legionaries at the edge of the glow cast by the floating globe. 'We have known since the first instance of the Warmaster's rebellion that there are those who support Horus Lupercal on Terra and the colonies of the Sol System. A network of spies and collaborators.'

'We keep killing them and they keep resurfacing,' said Varren, with a sniff. 'The roots of the weeds run deep. Of course, if the Sigillite and the Imperial Fist would let us off the chain once in a while, it would be a different story.'

'Carry on,' Loken said, nodding at her.

Brell took a deep breath. 'The war has been taxing for the loyalist forces and those of the insurrectionists. The Ruinstorm caused disarray on both sides of the schism. Confusion, destruction and–'

'You need not speak of that which we have lived through,' Garro said quietly. 'Your point, scientician?'

She looked directly at him, and he saw a curious emotion in her eyes. *Hope*, or so it seemed. 'Have you heard of a text called the *Lectitio Divinitatus*? It is a manuscript, authored by the turncoat primarch Lorgar Aurelian in better days, when he considered his duty to the Throne a sacred one.'

'I know what it is,' Garro said.

Secreted amongst his wargear, unseen and unknown by Garro's fellow Knights-Errant, was a battered booklet of cheap paper and red ink. He had first found a copy among the personal effects of his faithful housecarl Kaleb Arin, after the man had given his life to save that of his commander.

The words within it, and the illumination they provided, had ultimately led Nathaniel Garro into the presence of a Saint, and set him on the path that he walked now. The book spoke of the Emperor of Mankind, casting the father of the primarchs and sire of Garro's own former liege, Mortarion, as nothing less than a god made flesh. A deity, the first and only to truly deserve the name.

In those pages, Garro had found purpose again. But a part of the veteran warrior was afraid of where that would lead him. He wanted nothing more than to know an end to this destructive conflict. He would go to his grave if fate willed it, if only that insight was granted to him.

Brell was still talking, and Garro quieted his own thoughts. 'At first, we believed there was some form of mental conditioning at hand among the followers of this so-called "Imperial Cult",' she went on, 'but the reality is far more prosaic. The anxieties and misplaced fears of those who seek out these churches are calmed by the words of the book and the hope it provides. Hope for survival in a turbulent galaxy, from the Emperor's hand.'

'You don't need to accept gods and pray to some brass idol to believe in that,' scoffed Varren.

'Some do,' Loken noted.

'The Imperial Cult are a wild card,' said Brell, in a hectoring tone. 'They support the Emperor's leadership and the ideal of the Imperium, but they undermine His vision of a secular universe! And in this, they open themselves up to subversion by the enemy.'

'We suspected these clandestine churches were actually fronts for insurrectionist cells,' added Loken. 'And some were. But most are just... disciples.'

'Doesn't matter,' said Varren. 'They attract those mutant vermin just the same. Better off if we rid ourselves of them.'

Somewhere on one of the cogitator consoles, a signal bell rang to indicate the detection of an incoming aircraft, and Brell scuttled away into the shadows to address it, while Loken ignored Varren's comment and carried on.

'Whatever their motivation, these groups are being used as unwitting foci for the will of darker powers. And into this bedlam come these lost pariahs, their minds taken to the brink of madness and then reformed. Returning to us, each bearing a shard of a greater message.'

Gallor eyed him. 'Whose message, Loken? You speak with conviction, as if you already know that answer.'

'Horus,' he said, with a nod to himself. 'I know my primarch's ways. I hear the fragments of his voice in theirs.' Loken jutted his chin at the panels showing the faces of the recovered Sisters.

'You hear his voice?' Garro said warily.

'Don't you?' Loken met his gaze, and for a troubling instant, Garro saw a shadow of the wild-eyed, tormented creature he had found in the ashes of Isstvan. He saw Cerberus, the broken soul that had almost consumed the former Luna Wolf. 'Horus speaks here. I know it.'

'Clearly you have an ear for this,' said Gallor. 'So enlighten us. What is he saying?'

Loken frowned, realising he had overstepped. 'Brell has yet to calculate a fully cogent syntax.'

'I did not ask you that,' Gallor went on. 'What does your instinct tell you?'

Garro watched the conflict play out over the other legionary's scarred face, as Loken found his way to a reply. 'I looked my gene-father in the eye on the *Vengeful Spirit* and he threw back any hope of reconciliation. But this message... It has all the shape of an entreaty upon it.'

'A bid for peace?' Gallor was incredulous. 'After everything the Warmaster has done? After all he has unleashed upon the universe? How could he be so *arrogant*?'

'He is Horus Lupercal,' Loken shot back. 'He defies definition, as both my general and my enemy.'

'It is a lie,' said Garro, and without conscious thought his hand dropped to the hilt of *Libertas*, resting there. 'You know that. The War-master places a final ploy on the field of battle, a last tactic to distract us before he launches his invasion. That is what we see before us.'

'Perhaps...' Loken nodded, then halted. 'But the question has to be uttered, Garro. And only I am fit to ask it! I am the only one in this room who was there at the start, before the fall at Davin tainted my primarch and the rot set in. No one here can hate him as much as I do – no one here can know the shame and rage that burns in me.' He jabbed a finger at the other warriors. 'You three share the same pain, of seeing your Legion's honour broken, of watching your brothers and your primarch turn against those we are oath-sworn to protect. That I do not seek to diminish...' He looked away. 'But my Legion was the *first*. My primarch, at the heart of it all. I will carry that burden into eternity... And that is why I alone must ask the impossible. *What if it is not a lie?*'

'He's still out of his skull,' snarled Varren, glaring at Garro. 'We should have left him with the cinders and corpses at Isstvan!'

Garro's mind raced at the possibility Loken suggested, but he fought to keep his tone neutral. 'Garviel. It cannot be. No one dares to utter the words, but the truth is there before us. Terra is caught in the pincers of the enemy advance. Horus has the momentum and great forces at his command. We will be hard-pressed to repel him from this world, and he knows it. So why then would he contemplate a truce?'

'Because Horus knows, somewhere deep inside, that this war will lead to the ruin of everything.' Loken spoke with conviction. 'Even as lost as he is, some part of him sees that dark and endless tomor-row unfolding. And so do I.' He pointed at Garro. 'So do *you*. Keeler showed you, didn't she?'

'Who in Hades is Keeler?' said Varren.

Garro's breath caught in his throat. He felt a gossamer touch on his hand, as if the Saint were there with him in that moment, bringing time to a halt once again.

'A few days ago you told me you were willing to execute these messengers,' said Garro.

'You made me reconsider my position,' Loken went on. 'As infinitesimal as the chance may be, even if in a billion iterations of events, the cards still fall towards treachery and betrayal... After all the murdered souls and burned worlds, after everything lost and shattered by this conflict, after all the unspeakable horrors that have been unleashed upon us... Do we not owe the galaxy one last hope to end this before the veil of night falls forever?' Suddenly, all of Loken's energy departed, and as if the effort had left him spent, he seemed diminished. 'We have nothing... and everything... to lose.'

'He's right, of course,' said a familiar voice. Brell returned from the shadows, accompanied by another legionary in slate-coloured power armour and a hooded figure with a black iron staff. The staff tapped out the distance as the Sigillite and Tylos Rubio walked into the light, with the scientician trailing at their heels. 'If there is even the slightest possibility we can end this war, it must not be ignored.'

Garro noted that Rubio seemed ill at ease, doubtless feeling the muting effect of the White Mountain's psychic countermeasures – but Malcador showed no such discomfort. As he always did, the Sigillite walked into every room he entered as if he had the answers to every question and the insight to know every outcome.

'You came to see for yourself,' said Garro. 'I expected as much. You would never leave such a matter to the hands of others.'

Malcador glanced at the Knights-Errant and then to Brell. 'You will maintain a secure perimeter while I view the recoveries and their chorus. *Alone.*' Then he looked to Garro, raising an eyebrow at the warrior's insubordinate tone. 'Understand, Nathaniel. Some things are too important to delegate.'

'No.' Garro shook his head, glancing at Loken and then back to the Sigillite. 'I do not believe that is at the heart of this. You are entranced by enigmas, Lord Regent. They are the warp and weft of you. And to keep them safe, your circle of trust is so very small. How many terrible secrets do you know that you have never spoken of to any other? You confide in no one.'

A strange mix of annoyance and sorrow glittered briefly in the Sigillite's gaze. 'It is a burden,' he allowed.

'It is a trap!' snapped Garro.

Malcador's expression shifted, hardening. 'I know you do not think I am unaware of that possibility. I know you do not think me a fool.'

'No,' Garro replied. 'But for seven years the galaxy has known the most destructive conflict in human history, all because the ambitions of Horus Lupercal were *underestimated*. Now is not the time to repeat that grave error.' He took a step closer to the Sigillite, knowing he had passed beyond the bounds of defiance for what might be the last time. Still, he persisted. 'The Warmaster lays out a mystery for you, the perfect lure, and you come to look it in the eye. It is hubris of the highest order.'

'Watch your tone, Nathaniel.' Malcador's reply was icy.

Garro did not. 'When you venture into the holding levels beneath us, what will surround you? The Imperium's most powerful counter-psionic technology and hundreds of psychic blanks. You will be robbed of every gift you have, Sigillite. You will be vulnerable.'

'You think so?' Malcador said dryly. 'I am almost insulted.'

'I will go with him.' Rubio spoke without looking up. 'I am the logical choice.'

'Oh?' The Sigillite glared at the legionary. 'How so?'

'I've already heard some of the message. I am already inside the circle, as Garro put it. And while my psionic skills will be negated, I am still a warrior of the Legiones Astartes. If danger arises, I will meet it.'

'Would you?' Malcador's piercing gaze returned to bore into Garro. 'And would that be acceptable to you, battle-captain?' Each word was a chip of flint, hard and cutting.

'It will have to do,' allowed Garro.

'Good.' Malcador turned away. 'Now you have finished giving me orders, I will give you *yours.*' He strode off, back towards the shadows, his voice echoing. 'Under no circumstances am I to be disturbed, on pain of termination. No record will be kept of what transpires on the holding levels, and monitoring will be disengaged until I command otherwise.' He paused, allowing Rubio and Brell to fall in with him. 'Hold this place safe, no matter what the cost.' The Sigillite's final words followed him into the gloom.

'Safe from what?' muttered Varren.

On one of the cogitator consoles, a signal bell began to ring.

THE DEEPER THEY went, the more Rubio felt the ghostly pressure upon him. In the trials he had faced as a youth on Ultramar – a lifetime ago in the before, when he had still been wholly human – his mentors had put him to the test by releasing him at the bottom of a great silo filled with icy lake water. The challenge was to survive as long as possible in the grip of the black depths, to resist the urge to race for the surface. Rubio had done well, and passed the trial. But he had never forgotten the dreadful sense of density about him, the suffocating force bearing down and threatening to crush his body.

The telepathic negation of the White Mountain brought that memory back, flaring brightly in his thoughts. The silence crowding in on Rubio was oppressive, and he wondered if this was what life was like for those born without the psyker gene. He had suffered temporary telepathic negation before, of course, in battle and in the presence of other pariahs, but never at such a nullifying volume as he experienced now.

It took a conscious effort to stop his breathing from becoming laboured and heavy, and he cast a sideways look towards the Sigillite, wondering if Malcador ever experienced the like.

The hooded man slowed as they approached a huge circular hatch set in a stone wall. 'Ah. There we are,' he said.

There was a diamond-shaped observation portal built into the door, as tall as a human, made of thick armourglass. Through it, Rubio saw the blurry shapes of open-fronted cells, lit by floating glow-globes.

'One moment, please.' Brell went to an optical scanner built into the frame of the hatch and allowed it to take an image of her eyes. Next, she put her thumb to a blood-lock sampler and presently the hidden mechanism in the great door began to cycle open. Rimes of hoar frost around the hinges and the edge crackled and split as metal moved on metal. As the seal between the hatch and the frame parted, warmer air from within puffed out and brought with it the sound of overlapping voices, muttering across one another in nonsensical profusion.

'Wait here,' ordered Malcador, and Brell's body language made it abundantly clear that she was eager not to venture inside. She bowed and shot Rubio a look that he couldn't read.

Forcing himself to ignore the constant pressure in his thoughts, the warrior followed the Sigillite into the holding chamber, and the hatch dropped back into place behind him. On the far side, Brell moved to stand close to the glass, peering in at them.

The voices were a constant refrain. Each cell was occupied by a woman in a shapeless coverall, some standing, others slumped against the wall or lying upon sleeping pallets. All of them bore the signature shorn scalps of the Silent Sisterhood, although their cadre tattoos varied widely. Some had been here longer than others, as evidenced by the fuzz of hair beginning to grow back. Each one had a life-support cuff around one wrist, and from it a plastic tube snaked away to a pack of glutinous nutrient gel hanging from a rack. Eyeless medicae servitors ignored the two new arrivals, wandering the edges of the chamber, pausing here and there to check on the status of the recoveries.

Rubio approached the closest of the pariah Sisters, wincing at the potency of her null effect. She stared blankly into the middle distance, apparently unaware of his presence. Every few moments, she uttered a word that was meaningless in isolation.

'Hearing one voice at a time will not suffice,' said Malcador. 'All of them must come together.'

'Perhaps there is... is a trigger.' He blinked. Rubio's thoughts were becoming sluggish, moving like ponderous icebergs through a thick sea. He set his jaw and concentrated.

'Just listen.' The Sigillite closed his eyes.

Rubio was conscious of his own hearts beating, the trip-hammer double-thud sounding through his bloodstream. He held his breath, forcing himself to find a moment of stillness. Time thickened as the minutes passed.

The tones spoken by the women were gibberish, a constant babble of noise that irritated him with its incoherence. His hands tightened into fists. He felt impotent and powerless to comprehend.

Until without warning the words began to take shape. Slowly at first, then more clearly as the piecemeal elements came into a kind of crude synchronisation. It was the aural equivalent of an optical illusion, a sound that appeared to be one thing suddenly reframed by his mind into something very different.

'His hand. Darkness. This place.'

It was not one voice that uttered the words, but all of them. Rubio gasped as the shape of the speech took form. He was on the brink of understanding it, so close to grasping the whole from the shattered pieces.

'Horus,' came the refrain. 'Lupercal.'

'REPORT!' BARKED GARRO, as Gallor raced to the security console.

The younger legionary grimaced. 'Scry-sensors on the ridgeline report detection of two large airborne objects, descending from altitude. They have ignored all automated vox signals warning them to divert from restricted airspace.'

'Show us!' said Varren.

Gallor stabbed a control key and the giant hololithic globe winked out, to be replaced by a simulated window projecting a live visual feed from scanners atop the grey peaks. A pair of smooth-flanked craft dropped out of the low cloud, falling fast on clusters of retro-jets mounted on stubby winglets along their bulbous flanks.

'Aeronefs,' said Garro. 'Cargo leviathans by the look of them. They have no business here.'

'Heat-sweep reveals massive thermal blooms within their hulls,' Gallor went on.

'Weapons?' growled Varren.

Gallor shook his head. 'Humans. Hundreds of them, packed within.'

Loken marched over to the security console and snapped out a command to the servitor working there. 'Bring fire control to this panel. Reveal and activate the defensive macro-cannon turrets.'

'There!' Varren pointed at the display pane. The images of the huge airships showed great black pennants unfolding along the flanks of the two craft, catching in the wind as they descended. 'They've shown their colours.'

Garro heard Loken stifle a growl of anger. Daubed crudely on the pennants was the symbol of a glaring, slitted eye upon an arrow stabbing downward.

'Horus' mark,' Gallor sneered. 'I doubt they'll be open to parlay, then.'

'How did they find us here? Isn't the location of this facility supposed to be a closely guarded secret?' said Varren.

'Not any more,' noted Gallor.

'Target those vessels and fire,' Loken snapped. 'Full salvo!'

The order should have been Garro's to give, but he said nothing. Had that symbol been the skull-and-star of the Death Guard, he might have reacted with the same vehemence.

The stone floor vibrated with the thunder of titanic guns as the weapons spat death from their hidden redoubts in the crags and crevasses of the White Mountain. Sprays of counter-fire from rocket pods bolted to the airframes of the cargo haulers blasted into the air, leaving corkscrew trails of yellow smoke behind them, and the rudimentary warheads clattered artlessly across the mountainside. The noise and fury of them was spent heedlessly, while the macro-shells from the fortress' weaponry hit their targets with pinpoint precision.

Both of the aeronefs were fatally holed, their backs breaking as their superstructures crumpled and split – but they were close to the ground, low enough that they could spill their cargo onto the grey ice fields even as they crash-landed.

Garro watched through the eyes of the sensors as countless specks – each one a person – ejected themselves from the dying craft and turned towards their objective.

In the squalid, grinding secrecy of the Silent War that Malcador had dragged them into, the enemy was always of this stripe – the misguided and the coerced, the brainwashed and the fanatical. But they had hidden their numbers, skittering away into the shadows while the Knights-Errant culled those too slow to escape. Garro suspected that the Warmaster's sympathisers had armies out there somewhere, and now he knew he had been right. Here was the fodder for the cannons, the first waves of the dismissed and disposable to be thrown at Terra's bastions, existing only to clog their pathways and tire their guns.

Horus was not here, not yet. But the shadow he cast fell far, and what hid beneath it was stirring.

'There's too many to target with the cannons,' said Gallor. 'What is the command, battle-captain?'

Garro allowed *Libertas* to slip free of its scabbard. 'We go to meet them,' he said.

THE DEEP RUMBLE of the cannons through the rock sent trickles of dust down from the ceiling, and Rubio instinctively grasped the hilt of his sword.

Malcador shook his head. 'Be still,' he admonished, and the Sigillite took a step forward, leading with his staff. He planted it firmly on the stone floor and leaned towards the nearest of the muttering Sisters, close enough that he could have laid a gentle kiss upon her cheek. Illuminated by the crackle of the unquenchable plasma flames in the iron basket atop the staff, the great psyker's aspect took on a fearsome cast.

'Oath,' said the chorus. '*Father.*'

'I am here,' Malcador said to the air. 'Speak your piece.'

Rubio's blood became ice when, at last, the group-voice became fully coherent. The fragmentary sound-elements merged in a sing-song cadence that disturbed him with its atonal patterns.

'These words are from Horus Lupercal, first among equals.' From the babbling disorder came structure, as if a shapeless froth of foam had randomly conformed into a perfect cube. *'He knows you would come, Malcador. He knows what you would seek.'*

'You hear that, yes?' The Sigillite raised a bony finger.

'Mark my soul, I do,' Rubio said softly. The chorus disquieted the legionary in a way he could not articulate. They were just voices, just words – but each one seemed to pluck at his sense of reality, peeling back another layer of it with each gasping utterance.

'This schism has broken so much. So many oaths sundered. Taboos broken. Worlds burned. Names lost.'

'Names…' Rubio was unable to stop himself from repeating the word. Yotun, the mysterious Knight-Errant he had met in the jungle, had reacted oddly when speaking his name, and he had called Rubio by a different title. Koios. What did it mean? The question shouted at him, trapped in the walls of his skull, unable to escape.

'If only time might turn back, what choice would he have made?' The chorus' questions echoed off the stone walls. *'Would his father have chosen differently? Or is it that he has known this age would unfold, and allowed it to happen?'*

'Fate shows us the path,' Malcador said, looking from face to face among the whispering horde. 'We choose if we walk it. Tell me what you want!'

'The Emperor once said, "I seek peace for a turbulent universe." You wish that too, Sigillite.'

In his mind, that turbulence was filling every iota of Tylos Rubio's being. Malcador seemed unaware of it, indifferent and callous to the suffering of the legionary.

But that was like him; the Regent of Terra ruled the Throneworld in the Emperor's stead with cold disdain for the people, not just of this planet, but all planets. They were pieces in his great game. He hated them. Hated everything.

Yes. Rubio understood that now. A wet gasp escaped his lips. Deep within him, something was rising. It had been buried deep, so deep that the legionary had never known of its existence. But now a puzzle made of memory began to reassemble itself. The shape of a lost thought, each piece unlocking as a long-awaited pattern of words reached his consciousness.

'*Horus strives for that ideal,*' wailed the chorus.

'That is what he was made for!' Malcador shouted back. 'It is the reason we are here.' His hands clenched tightly around the length of the black iron staff. 'For Terra's sake...' The Sigillite let out a peal of bitter laughter, and in this isolated place, where none would know it, he briefly allowed himself to be vulnerable.

Rubio saw Malcador's true age etched upon him, and a face filled with lifetimes of loss, terrible choices and hidden regrets.

In this moment, he was only a man, stripped of his incredible powers, weak and breakable like all the rest of humankind. He would never say it aloud, but there was a part of Malcador that dared to hope there could still be peace, a long-faded idealist who had once possessed the courage to reach for trust and faith.

But Rubio could only hate him. The disdain leaked from old memory, from a vision of the Sigillite's true self. He deserved no pity. He was a cancer on the world, playing his games while the Emperor toiled ceaselessly to hold back the tide of Chaos.

'Is that really what you ask for now?' Malcador was saying, ignorant of the turmoil in Rubio's thoughts. 'A ceasefire? How can you–?'

'*Not by the design of his father,*' said the voices, hardening into hissing and droning tones, breaking any possible thread of hope with savage insistence. '*Not a galaxy ceded to the unworthy, ruled by the weakest.*'

'No...' The Sigillite drew a hand across his face. 'After all this? What have you done, Lupercal? Was Garro right? Did you build this complex

riddle just to spite me?' His voice rose as he spoke until he was bellowing. 'Are you so grand and yet so small? So petty? Answer!'

'*Come, Malcador.*' The chorus whispered. '*Your time is at an end. Horus
will grant you the Emperor's peace.*'

'What...?' Something so uncommon to the Sigillite that it was almost
alien to him, twisted across his expression: *fear*. 'No. You cannot touch
me here. It is not possible.' He turned at a metallic sound slicing through
the rise and fall of the refrain.

And there was Rubio, slowly drawing his inert force sword from its
scabbard. 'You will to lead us all to ruin.' His eyes had lost focus, and
his voice was distant and unreal. 'I remember now. I remember what
I was shown.'

'*Through his hand,*' said the chorus, '*reaching to you.*'

As it rose in a killer's grip, the lethal, fractal-edged blade of Rubio's
sword was dead crystal, haloed with a dull shimmer by the light of
the glow-globes.

The final words of the message cemented the deed. Rubio was released
to complete the act, answering to a directive that had lain unseen in
his mind for seven long years, now unfolding into its terrible fullness.
'*Across the darkness. To this place.*'

The sword flashed backward in a reversed stab, the tip of the blade
breaking through the armourglass of the observation window. On the
far side of it, Teledion Brell, transfixed by the shock of what she was
seeing, did not escape as the weapon cleaved her breast bone in two
and burst from her thin shoulders. When it drew back, her ruined body
crumbled to a heap upon the stones.

The scientician's blood rolled off the massive blade, pitter-pattering
against the ground as Rubio brought it up and into an executioner's
stance. 'I remember now,' he repeated, his gaze lost and dead as the
chorus finally fell silent. 'It has been a long time coming.'

INTERVAL V

Undying

[The warp; now]

THERE WAS A compartment within the hull spaces of the war-barge *Greenheart* that none but the primarch himself could unlock. The entire chamber was an isolated module, so that if need arose, Mortarion could have it completely ejected into space. In addition, there were a series of powerful graviton charges mounted in the framework, each one equipped with enough destructive potential to crush a Rhino personnel carrier into wreckage when triggered.

These were the logical, practical safeguards he had put in place. Then there were the more esoteric precautions – the strange icons and psychogrammetric wards etched into the plasteel walls by laser beam, their shapes and forms copied from the pages of the daemonology lore Mortarion had gathered in his quest to better know this unfathomable power.

He entered *Greenheart* from the *Terminus Est*'s landing bay and made certain that the crew aboard the command shuttle knew not to disturb him. Sealing all hatches behind him, Mortarion made his way to the shadow compartment. His final order was to command the warriors of the Deathshroud to stand guard outside. He sensed their reluctance to obey, but did not comment on it. They would do as he told them.

What would happen next was something the primarch wished no others to witness. Removing one great gauntlet, he pressed his hand to a bio-reader and let it scan his genetic print. Dense phase-iron locks on the heavy hatch opened once his identity had been affirmed, and he passed inside and then locked it.

The prisoner was waiting where Mortarion had left it, held inside a great tank of reinforced armourglass, which itself was set behind a barrier of heavy, electro-charged mesh. Robotic autoguns dithered at the cardinal points of the compartment, briefly scanning the primarch to determine his identity, before snapping back to track the prisoner. They moved where it – where *he* – moved, following the sluggish and fish-belly-white creature as it shambled endlessly around the perimeter of the confinement.

Mortarion smelled decay and foetor in the air, and he saw where the glass tank was soiled and discoloured. Toxic mucus stained the deck where the prisoner's bloated feet passed. The materials that comprised the compartment had been newly fabricated when assembled a few solar months earlier, but now they exhibited decades, if not centuries, of rot and ruin.

'Ah,' gurgled the captive, pausing to make an exaggerated bow. '*What great honour is this? My commander graces me with his presence.*' Hands of pallid corpse-flesh spread in a gesture of obedience across a grotesquely obese humanoid form clad in scraps of corroded, distorted battle armour. '*How may I serve you, Lord of Death?*'

'Did you *ever* truly serve me, Life-Eater?' Mortarion did not address the creature by the name of the warrior it had once been. Ignatius Grulgor was the captain of the Death Guard's Second Great Company, but that was before the betrayal at Isstvan and the mass murder that had taken place as a world was consumed and sacrificed. The legionary that had been Grulgor died aboard the starship *Eisenstein* during that engagement – or perhaps it was more accurate to say he had died there for the *first* time.

What returned in his place was something else, a mutated and death-less flesh-vessel for the power that writhed and bloomed in the foetid insanity of the immaterium. It named itself the Eater of Lives, and after a fashion Mortarion had been able to snare the thing, holding it in his thrall while keeping its existence a secret from his Legion.

He looked upon the creature now, searching its bloated bulk for some aspect of the man it once was. Some of Grulgor was still there, he noted, in the arrogant swagger with which the beast held itself, and the snarling mockery of the words that drooled from its cankerous lips.

'The man I knew was always more interested in glory, not service,' Mortarion went on, and that earned him an irritable hiss from the creature. 'I do not imagine that has altered.'

The foul and corpulent form bowed its head, the single glistening horn in the middle of its brow catching the dull light of overhead lumens as it made an attempt to appear contrite. *'So much about me has changed since then. Rebirth gives one a new perspective on a great many things.'*

It was bigger than a line legionary, closer to the mass of a Dread-nought. Great clumps of doughy, reeking wattles hung in folds over leaking, pus-filled boils, upon a body that supported a skull-like aspect. The Eater's bloodshot, rheumy eyes fixed upon Mortarion as an unnat-urally long tongue emerged to lick at the air.

'You need only ask,' it went on, and the creature took in a wheezing breath, pleasuring in the act. *'I am ready to be your weapon, Lord Mortarion. I feel the song of the warp out beyond these walls. It fills me, energises me. Please, let me kill for you. Let me feast.'*

'You want that, don't you? For me to let you free. To put myself in your debt.' He shook his head.

'No...' The Grulgor-thing's bow deepened, a wounded tone entering its words. *'You own me. I do not deny it.'* A crooked hand gestured at the corroding wards on the walls. *'I serve you now, just as I did when*

I was Second Captain. I am your loyal soldier.' It showed a mouth of broken, blackened teeth in a cadaverous smile. *'If you did not want me to do so, then why am I here?'* It leaned close to the armourglass wall, foul breath misting the grimy partition. *'Why are you here, now?'*

'I am here because I have a choice to make,' said Mortarion, the words welling up from somewhere deep within him. 'And as much as I hate what you are, you may have insight I can use.'

The Grulgor-thing chuckled. *'I am so pleased I can help you at long last, my master. And fear not, for I already know the questions that gnaw at you.'* It waved a fleshy limb at the air, disturbing the cloud of black flies that hummed around its head. *'The warp whispers to you in the moments of silence, doesn't it? In those quiet times when you sequester yourself away to think, to ponder on events unfolding... or read from the books you think you should destroy.'*

Mortarion became very still. The Reaper of Men had spoken to no one of the troubling thoughts that plagued him during his meditations, and the dark semi-dreams that came upon him in his infrequent moments of reverie.

'You frame those whispers as something to hate and to fear.' The prisoner shook its head, ichor dripping from its jowls. *'No, my lord. They are the voices of opportunity, opening themselves up to you. They are the way to ultimate strength.'*

'What strength?' Mortarion shot back. 'Even now, my unstoppable warriors are falling to a *sickness!'* He spat out the word, insulted to his core by the very idea. 'The warp is a cancer!'

'Yes,' agreed the Eater. *'But that is its victory. The Gift is the bloom of life out of death. It metastasises from the old, bringing ceaseless undeath from the cage of poor, fallible flesh.'* It took another wheezing breath. *'The living death cannot die. It is the ultimate, enduring forever. What does not live will never be killed.'*

'You speak in riddles.' Mortarion's hand fell to the hilt of the *Lantern.* 'Perhaps I should put your claim to the test. I could erase you with sunfire in a moment.'

'*Do so,*' said the prisoner, baring a wattled, frog-like throat. '*But in time, my corpse will gather anew, my essence undimmed. This is the Grandfather's Gift. We all will know it, in due course.*'

Grandfather. It was not the first time Mortarion had heard that title invoked. It appeared again and again in the pages of the forbidden lore that he had been gathering. *A power,* he believed it to be, *one entity among others that existed beyond the real, a thing that could never die.* It would have been a lie to say that the primarch was not intrigued by the possibility.

'*Endurance eternal,*' said the Grulgor-thing, as if it were reading his thoughts. '*There is such greatness in it. The power to resist any enemy. To return against every foe again and again, until they are ashes and we are victorious. Is that not at the core of the Death Guard's character?*' It paused. '*It is not for all, of course. Many are too rigid in mind to see the possibilities. Too limited.*' The creature showed its teeth once more. '*And for those cowards, there will be a lingering end.*'

Unbidden, the Eater's words brought to mind a memory of another of Mortarion's most stalwart warriors – Battle-Captain Nathaniel Garro of the Seventh Great Company. Once, the noble Garro had been a trusted warrior among the forces of the Reaper of Men, an unflinching weapon in his arsenal; but the Death Guard's journey to the Warmaster's side had seen the battle-captain break faith with his liege lord and turn against his brothers.

Mortarion had hate for Garro, that much was certain. He felt the warrior's betrayal keenly, enough that he had taken it out on the remnants of the errant captain's company by chastising them for their commander's deeds. But that hate was marbled with regret, as he studied the thing that had been Ignatius Grulgor. He imagined some alternate skein of events, where it was Garro who fought by his side towards Terra's gates, and where these dalliances with the denizens of the immaterium were unneeded.

'*Look to the future,*' said the creature. '*Change always seems grotesque until you are the changed. And you will be, my lord. You will be.*'

'Enough,' Mortarion snarled. 'You say you wish to serve me? Then give me your oath, daemon. Pledge to obey my commands.'

'And you will let me loose?' The Grulgor-thing was almost childlike in its eagerness.

'I shall.'

It bowed low, scraping its jaundiced face across the deck. *'I humbly give all my loyalty to the Death Guard. I always have. I always will. Before the Grandfather, I so swear.'*

A sickly resonance trembled in the air at the instant of the invocation, but then it was gone again. Mortarion grimaced and turned his back on the armourglass cell, walking towards the heavy hatch.

'Wait... Wait!' The creature screamed at him. *'I affirmed the oath! Now let me out!'* It banged its leprous fists on the barrier, making the deck tremble. The wards in the walls blazed blue-white and the Eater hissed in pain as they forced it to shrink away.

'I will use you when I need you,' said Mortarion, without looking back. 'This has gone on too long. I have allowed myself to be led, and the inertia of old alliances and past deeds to direct events. No more.' He shook his head, and reached for the locking mechanisms. 'Typhon will obey me. I will make him return us from this dread realm, or I will take his head.'

As the hatch slid open, the daemon that wore Grulgor's warped face exploded into vile, gurgling amusement. *'You won't,'* it brayed. *'Still you cannot see, Lord Mortarion! Typhus is beyond your grasp! He has already accepted the Mark!'*

Mortarion hesitated on the threshold and shot a look at the prisoner. 'What did you call him?'

'Go ask for yourself, Death Lord,' chuckled the fiend, settling down on its haunches to pick at the oozing scabs across its flesh.

Mortarion let the hatch slam shut, and for a long moment he considered reaching for the ejection controls on the compartment's outer wall. But to cast this thing into the warp would not punish it, he noted.

'Ready weapons,' he told his Deathshroud. 'It is time to call matters to account.'

As his bodyguards snapped into combat stances, Mortarion reached for the bio-reader, placing his palm on it once more to lock the compartment. The heavy bolts slammed shut, and a spasm went through his fingers.

The primarch's eyes narrowed and he turned over his hand to study the bare, pale flesh of his long digits.

There, half hidden by a crease in his skin, were a cluster of tiny crimson welts in a perfect triangle, like the marks a biting insect would leave behind.

[The planet Barbarus; before]

THE CONVOY OF troops and crawlers finally crested the low hill and there before it were the outer walls of Safehold. Armsmen on the battlements saw the vehicles and the lines of soldiers as they made their approach, and called out to spread the word. The Reaper of Men had returned from the Southern Campaign, at long last.

Eight solars ago, Safehold had not existed. Back then, the rough granite tor around which it was built had been the home to a bandit camp – a group of renegades who called themselves the Sullen. The Reaper had beaten their leader in single combat and convinced him to join the Overlord War, and part of the agreement was the ceding of the lands to Mortarion's rebellion. The city – the first truly *free* city on Barbarus – took root there, and now it was a symbol for all those who fought. Safehold was, as its name suggested, a place of refuge and defiance against the domination of the Overlords. It was a place where humans could walk without fear, knowing that the high stone walls, the impregnable iron gates and the guns of the warriors on the battlements would hold back any punitive raids.

And truth be told, the vicious cullings of years past were growing rarer. The Overlords still attacked the lessers, and they still played their cruel games, but the war was sapping their power. Slowly, inexorably, the tide was turning all across Barbarus. For the first time in living memory, there was *hope*, or something like it.

The gates retracted into the walls as the first of the steam-crawlers approached the city, and the armsmen found themselves joined up on the battlements by civilians eager to see the return of the Reaper of Men. They looked out in expectant silence as the grey-painted vehicles rumbled closer. Lines of battle-weary warriors walked alongside the machines, clad in dented metal armour of the same slate shade, their guns and cudgels hoisted over their shoulders. Faces, many sporting new scars, turned up to scan the battlements. They searched for loved ones and friends, those for whom they had gone to war.

A hatch atop the lead crawler opened as the vehicle slowed, and a towering figure, gaunt and unsmiling, climbed out. Everyone saw him pull the common farmer's scythe from where he carried it over his back. He raised it high and shouted out a single word.

'Victory!'

Safehold erupted in shouts and cheers. They called out Mortarion's name as he leapt off the crawler and took the first steps through the gate. He nodded to all those who looked him in the eye, as if to affirm what until now they had only dared to dream. *We are winning.*

His troopers entered the city at his heels, and every one of them was greeted like the hero they were. For a moment, he almost allowed himself to bask in the energy of it. Mortarion could sense the shape of the emotion, that thing that others knew as joy, but as always it remained beyond his grasp.

There was much to be grateful for, that was true. But he could only truly hold the form of darker sentiments in his heart. Mortarion saw those in the crowd looking for the warriors who would never be coming back, the brave sons and daughters of Barbarus who had spent their blood to liberate the settlements and valleys far away in the mist-wreathed southlands.

He remembered Kwell the Gunhand and her reavers, who had brought down the airship of the Overlord Anvolian at the cost of their own lives; the great axe champion Sellos Mokyr, whose orphaned son still marched with Mortarion this day; and of course, Hesan Feign, the last of the Sullen. It was a pity the former bandit had perished beyond sight of his old hideout, but the Reaper of Men had ordered Feign's ashes brought back with the returning troops, so that they might be scattered here.

Mortarion had no such attachment to places. He had long ago decided that when the day came, wherever he fell would be as good a grave as any.

A woman in a scout's uniform pushed through the crowd towards him, and she offered a metal drinking canteen to the Reaper of Men. 'You look like you could use this,' she said.

He accepted it with a grateful nod. As the cold, decontaminated water passed his lips, Mortarion studied the woman and caught on a barb of memory. Her eyes were familiar to him. She was twenty solars old, he estimated, hard in the face but still a beauty. 'I know you,' he offered.

'You saved my life once,' said the woman. 'Forgive me, a canteen of the pure is not much of a repayment, for that or all the other things you have done.'

'It's enough.' He placed her now. 'A wagon fell in the fields outside Heller's Cut. That was you it trapped.' Off her nod, he went on. 'It is a long ride from there to Safehold.'

'Yes. But I wanted to fight, and here is where the war is.'

'The war is everywhere,' he said, and made to hand her back the canteen.

'Keep it.' She shook her head and walked away.

'Things change so swiftly,' said a voice from behind him, and Mortarion waited to allow one of his lieutenants to catch up before moving on.

'You think so?'

'I know so. We're living proof.' Hunda Skorvall was a hulk of a man, one of the heavyset breed from the Broken Moors, and a superlative close-quarters fighter.

Amongst the elite of the Reaper of Men's army, he was granted the mark of the skull and sun to show his rank and standing. The sigil was tattooed upon the thick, pale muscle of his bicep. The glaring skull signified the shadow of death that both loomed over the soldiers and marched as their ally, while the six-pointed star was said to represent the light of the new dawn freedom would bring to Barbarus. Those so marked as Skorvall was were Mortarion's Death Guard, his unbroken blades in the war against the Overlords.

Mortarion eyed Skorvall's right arm. The limb ended just above the wrist, the stump hidden behind a greasy, bloodstained bandage. The injury was only a week old, a trophy from the closing stages of a fight against a dozen kill-beasts. One of them had bitten off Skorvall's hand and swallowed it, but the warrior had still managed to rip out the monster's throat and drown it in its own blood.

'What in the name of all that is cold…?' Another familiar figure came to them through the throng, his broad face switching from a manic grin to a worried frown and then back again. 'Hunda, did you leave something behind out there?'

'No jokes, Dural,' Skorvall shot back, cradling his injured arm. 'I am not in the mood.'

'A kill-beast tried to make a meal of him,' Mortarion said levelly. 'I believe he is so unpalatable that it choked to death.'

'Now you mock me too?' Skorvall's expression fell.

'Ah, I understand why it died,' said the new arrival. 'You have bitter blood, Hunda. I've always said so.'

Mortarion clapped Skorvall on the back. 'That's a good name for you. You'll have to keep it.'

'Don't worry.' Dural Rask – another of the Death Guard cohort – let his grin return. 'The alliance we secured with the Forge Tyrant tech-nomads is yielding a rich harvest. Their mechsmiths can make you a new hand, better than the old one, you'll see!' He turned to look up at Mortarion, and continued. 'But to the question! Is it true, Reaper? I mean, we saw the fires on the horizon days back but we could not be sure…'

'It is true.' Mortarion gave a shallow nod. 'The struggle for the South

is over, my friend. The settlements down there are free now. I personally staked out the last of Necare's cohorts on the bare earth, and let
the lamprey worms feast on it.'

'Glorious,' whispered Rask. 'And there is word from Sune and Murnau. Their missions in the Western Sink bring similar news.'

'Indeed?' Mortarion nodded to himself. 'Good.'

'Good,' echoed Skorvall, eyeing him. 'Mark me, but you almost looked
as if you might smile just then.'

Mortarion's dour expression remained unchanged. 'Impossible. I
hear what the men say. They believe that if the Reaper of Men ever
smiles, the sky will crack open and shatter. So you understand my grave
responsibility, yes?' He paused, then glanced at Rask. 'Have you had
contact with Typhon's forces?' Months ago, his second-in-command
and trusted friend had gone into the foothills to chase down a minor
Overlord, but no messengers had returned.

'Our scouts report signs of his army to the east.' Rask said briskly.
'But he has made no attempt to signal us.' Then the warrior changed
tack, and his grin grew wider. 'That's a matter for another time! With
your return, and these victories, this is the tipping point. Today, here
and now. The extinction of the Overlords is inevitable!'

Mortarion scowled. 'We are not there yet, Dural. There are still more
battles to be fought.' As he said the words, he pushed down the urge to
turn and look away to the northern peaks, to where his foster father's
dark citadel still stood, wreathed in the most toxic of mists and heavily
protected – such that no Death Guard had ever been able to approach
it. 'And we have lost many along the way,' he concluded.

Skorvall gave a low grunt of agreement. 'Aye. But there are none
who would fault the cost, not any more. All those who chose to obey
the Overlords rather than join us have seen the folly of their ways.'

There had been humans – *lessers* in spirit as well as character – who
thought their lives better served under the Overlord yoke. Some were
broken souls who could not comprehend of anything else, and their
loss was to be expected. But others, the worst of them, were willing

slaves happy to trade in the lives of their own kind. The Death Guard gave them no mercy.

If any were left, Mortarion imagined they had been subsumed into the fleshworks of the Overlords by now, cut into new golem-soldiers for their armies.

'We are stronger than we have ever been,' Rask was saying. 'You trained the Death Guard, Reaper! You made us invincible. And in turn, the Death Guard have spread the war-maker skills to every human settlement. We are all fighters now. Every town is a fortress. Every harvester a soldier!'

'I'll drink to that,' said Skorvall, throwing a glance at the water canteen Mortarion still held. 'Provided you have something stronger, of course.'

Rask let out a bark of laughter and beckoned them towards a barracks-house. 'Come with me, I have just the thing.'

He led them to a room at the rear of the low, thatch-roofed building and as they entered, the smells of fermented sugars and heavy yeast assailed Mortarion's sharp senses. 'What have we here?'

Rask walked over to a complex mechanism of rattling pipes, open flames and bubbling flasks. 'The thing that most know about the Forge Tyrants is how good they are at making weapons. But they have another skill, one less obvious.' He turned a spigot on the contraption and it emitted a measure of smoky fluid into a metal cup, which he handed to Mortarion. 'They brew spirits like you won't *believe*.' He filled more cups, one for himself and one for Skorvall, then raised his in salute. 'A tribute,' said the Death Guard. 'To this victory and the next.'

Mortarion took down the drink and frowned at the taste. Skorvall and Rask seemed to savour theirs, but to his strengthened constitution it seemed like weak tisane. At length, he shook his head. 'You give me mother's milk, Dural? It has less kick than the water I drank a moment ago. Is this a libation suitable for our best warriors?'

'I thought it was smooth,' began Skorvall, but Mortarion waved him to silence.

'No,' said the Reaper of Men. He ran his long-fingered hands over the mechanical distilling rig, back along its length until he found a copper tank filled with unfiltered, still-raw fluids. 'This would be better.' Mortarion refilled the cups with that more powerful essence and made his own salute. '*Now* we drink.'

Rask eyed the murky contents of his drinking vessel. 'Reaper... This is half-toxic! A man might be killed by a draught of it!'

'If we are not strong, we will not win,' intoned Mortarion. 'If we cannot defy poison and darkness and pain, we cannot stand against death.' He stared into the depths of his own cup. 'My bastard of a foster father taught me one valuable lesson that I have never forgotten, and it is this – *everything is a test*. Life is a challenge that must be endured. Those who are not testing themselves every day are those who are already dying. So drink.'

'Against death,' said Skorvall, after a moment, and drank deep.

'Against death,' repeated Rask, taking a breath before he did the same.

Mortarion joined them, and he revelled in the rolling, fiery sting of the raw fluid as it coursed down his throat and spread across his chest. It made him feel alive, invigorated, as only battle could.

Skorvall and Rask both gasped in pain and took on hard colour as they struggled to follow his example. The bigger man crushed his cup in a moment of shock, while his comrade stood stock-still.

Finally, Rask let out a crack-throated howl of effort. 'Blood and fire, I felt that!' He wiped a film of sweat from his brow. 'Another measure and I'd welcome a golem's knife in my belly...'

'Then it served its purpose,' said Mortarion, the crooked twist of an almost-smile on his lips. 'I promise you we'll share the cups again when the war is over.'

'Aye!' Skorvall barked. 'We will drink from Necare's skull!' The hulking warrior let out a thunderous gale of laughter, but the sound was blotted out by something else – the keening wail of a war-siren.

'Attackers!' spat Rask, wrenching a roto-barrel pistol from his belt holster. 'Who dares strike here? They've picked the worst day for it!'

Mortarion threw his empty cup aside and stormed back out into the daylight, just as the heavy thrumming of rotor blades filled the air, dragging behind a great black shadow that carved across the feeble glow of the sun.

His scythe was already in his hands as he glared up at the airship, a twin to the one that Kwell's warband had turned into fire at the climax of the Battle of the Thorn Garden. Gunners on the battlements were frantically cranking their weapons up and around to target the low-flying craft, which had emerged from the cloudy sky with little warning.

Fast-ropes fell from the black windows of open hatches along the bottom of the craft, and Mortarion tensed for the fight to come. The energy of pre-battle crackled through his nerves, and whatever fatigue he had felt from the long march back to Safehold was gone in the blink of an eye.

But then figures were swarming down the ropes, figures in battered grey armour of familiar shape, and the fight he had half hoped for melted away. Death Guard warriors landed all around the square before the barracks-houses, each of them unhooking and giving Mortarion the salute of a mailed fist against their chest.

'Look-see,' said Rask, his momentum fading as he pointed towards the flank of the airship. Daubed on the side of the craft was the mark of Skull and Sun, covering the Overlord runes that had previously identified its owner. 'Ah. The cloud breaks.'

The last armoured man to descend wore a battered helmet that sported a single horn protruding from the brow, and equine-hair pennants hanging from his shoulder pauldrons. Detaching from the rope, Typhon twisted off his helm and his bearded face split in a savage smile as he laid eyes on Mortarion.

'I knew it would be you,' he said. 'When my long-sights spied the column returning to Safehold, I knew you were back.'

'You always do like to make an entrance,' Skorvall said coldly, making no attempt to hide his scorn. 'Count yourself lucky you were not burned out of the air!'

Typhon's smile turned crooked and wry. 'You don't like my prize?' He waved in the direction of the airship. 'I packed it with every barrel of food, medicine and pure water I could loot from Volcral's storehouses. I'm sure it can be put to good use here.'

'We don't need the Overlords to feed us any more,' hissed Skorvall, but Mortarion cut him off before he could go on.

'The people will take any bounty they can get,' he said firmly, shifting his scythe to plant it in the dirt. Mortarion's gaze raked over his second-in-command. No longer the skinny, waspish youth he had fought beside in the mists of the mountain pass, Typhon had grown into the cunning warrior he was always destined to be. He had proven himself a dozen times over during the first years of the war, enough that Mortarion had granted him his own cadre of Death Guard to lead.

'It is good to see you, brother.' Typhon came forward and clasped Mortarion's wrist in the old manner of greeting, their vambraces clanking together.

'It is,' Mortarion agreed, and found that he meant it.

Some – Hunda Skorvall among them – had never taken to Typhon, even with all his victories and wounds suffered in the name of the cause. Both Calas and Mortarion were outsiders, different from their Barbarun brothers in arms in measures of physical form and origins, but while Mortarion's towering stature and lean aspect had come to be accepted as part of who he was, Typhon's whipcord nature had never truly been acknowledged by his peers. The true stories of Mortarion's origin were known to very few, and spoken of in half-myth by others. Typhon, on the other hand, was visibly a half-breed, and despite Mortarion's best efforts, his comrade still suffered from that prejudice.

In the beginning, it had been the two of them who first rallied the lessers to fight for their future, it had been their shared example that gave the people of Barbarus the impetus to take up arms against the Overlords. But those days seemed long ago now, and the ease Mortarion felt at seeing his old friend again was darkened by a faint aura of doubt. Had something changed between them while they had been apart, fighting their separate battles?

No. He refused to consider that, and crushed the misgiving before it could fully form.

'You have defeated the Overlord Volcral's forces, then?' said Rask.

'More than defeated, Dural,' Typhon replied. 'Exterminated. There's not a black manse that still stands across the foothills, from here to the horizon.' He glanced at Mortarion. 'My men destroyed the great bridge across the Stonefall Rift as Volcral desperately tried to summon support from Necare. It didn't come. And you know what that means?'

Mortarion considered that fact. 'It means that the High Overlord abandoned one of his closest allies to be put to the sword. He chooses to consolidate his own defences rather than come to the aid of another.'

'Aye, that's my reading of it.' Typhon glanced up briefly as the airship drifted away, towards the fields where it could make a soft landing. 'Necare goes to ground where he knows we cannot follow. He's nothing if not predictable.'

'Coward!' snarled Skorvall. 'Hiding behind the tox-clouds and playing with those dark magicks – afraid to show that blighted excuse for a face!'

Typhon gave a weary nod. 'True enough. We won, but every battle fought now is of the same stripe. They send the golems and the kill-beasts, and sometimes Necare's minor cousins will even walk the battlefield themselves. But they never stand and fight. Every time, they try to draw us into the deep mists, to choke us with the poison of the high reaches. For all our victories, we are trapped fighting a defensive conflict.' He looked back at Mortarion. 'Now you have liberated the south, we have to consider anew how to reach our final triumph. Or else, we will soon reach a stalemate.'

'I imagine you have a suggestion,' Mortarion said, without weight.

'I do.' Typhon's smile returned. 'You will not like it.'

But Mortarion was not about to let him voice it, not yet. He held up a hand to silence Typhon. 'You are not alone in these thoughts.' He looked to Rask. 'Dural. I think it is time.'

'My lord…?' Rask's eyes narrowed. 'Are you sure? I mean… There is still so much that needs to be done…' His voice dropped to a conspiratorial whisper. 'We are not ready.'

'I'll be the judge of that,' he told the other warrior. Mortarion shot Skorvall a look. 'Bitterblood, listen to me. Find the healer's hall and have them assess that wound of yours. We'll do as Rask said, get you a machine hand that will punch twice as hard. Go!' Skorvall muttered under his breath, but he saluted the order and wandered away. Mortarion turned back to Rask, seeing the intrigued expression spread over Typhon's face from the corner of his eye. 'You'll take us to the works, Dural. I want to see what you have been making while we were away.'

Rask glanced at Typhon, then gave a salute of his own. 'Of course. It's this way.'

He walked on, and Typhon fell into step with Mortarion a few paces behind. 'I suspected you had given some project to our Master of Ordnance before we left Safehold, but at the time I didn't press you on it,' began the other Death Guard. 'Care to illuminate me?'

'I prefer to show rather than tell,' Mortarion replied, as they made their way towards the black granite tor on the edge of the settlement.

TYPHON SMELLED SULPHUR, acid and the hot rusty tang of burning metal. The odours assailed him as they passed through the narrow slot that gave entry to the interior of the tor, and he drank it in. Ashen on his tongue, it tasted like *warfare* and he enjoyed the memories of battle that it stirred in him.

So it was said, the Sullen had spent generations carving out the interior of the tor to create a safehold of their own, and there the bandit clan had built a culture that could weather the predations of the Overlords and the brutality of Barbarus' harsh winters. But their way of life was never going to last: either Necare and his minions would have eventually brought their most powerful magicks to bear on obliterating this stone bastion, or the Sullen would have killed each other through internecine fighting. Fortunate for the bandits then, that fate had brought

Mortarion to their gate. He claimed them all by trial of combat and made the Sullen a part of the Death Guard. Their home inside the tor, though... that he had given to someone else.

Rask led them deeper into the spiralling, high-ceilinged caverns that filled the tor's interior. Spaces that had once been set aside for Sullen clanner domiciles were now great workshops, where blacksmiths and metalworkers beat out sheets of salvaged battleplate into new shapes, and built armaments from scraps and ingots of tooled iron.

The tor belonged to the Forge Tyrants now, and they had made it their own. Here, the weapons of the Death Guard were made – the tools of the war constructed, repaired and improved upon.

Typhon's guns and blades were all cut by the tech-nomads, tailored to his reach and his fighting style. It was a benefit of rank and status as one of Mortarion's elite. But as he walked on after Rask, he saw killing machines of new design and form that drew his attention.

Mortarion nodded, noticing his interest. 'The smiths have been hard at work. I granted their artisans first choice of the mineral stocks from the Overlord mines we have captured, and all battlefield salvage rights. It is not just our blades they are keeping sharp, my friend.'

'I see that.' They passed work benches upon which lay weighty swords bristling with spiked guards, great lightning halberds fitted with electro-chemical batteries, and dragon-guns capable of projecting streams of ignited fuel and virulent acids. Typhon saw multi-barrelled ballistic slug-throwers fed by great ammunition hoppers, and rotary blades heavy with barbed chains and flail attachments. He feigned a look to appear impressed by it all, but inwardly he found little among the work of the Forge Tyrants to affect him.

Mortarion does so like his tools, Typhon thought to himself, glancing at the war-beaten battle scythe the Death Guard commander carried over his shrouded shoulders. It was his way, Typhon reflected, to reach for something physical with which to oppose the threats around him. Mortarion was not at ease unless there was a weapon within a hand's reach.

Does he know that about himself? The question passed through Typhon's mind, but without an answer it drifted away again.

There were other kinds of weapons, of course, other kinds of tools. More and more, Typhon had allowed himself to consider these things, to look at factors that others would have decried out of hand. The numinous and the unreal, these things could be turned to the business of making war as easily as blade or bullet, if one only understood how to wield them.

And if he could make Mortarion see those things as he was learning to see them… then, perhaps, the war with the Overlords could be ended in weeks. *Days*, even.

'In here.' Rask brought them to a smaller cavern off one of the larger spaces, and there stood a pair of heavyset warriors in full armour, each cradling a bell-mouthed shot cannon. They saw Mortarion and wordlessly stepped aside, drawing open a thick leather curtain cordoning off the hollow in the rock.

'More toys for us to marvel at?' Typhon slipped a little, allowing his disregard to show. He covered it quickly with a smirk. 'You've been keeping the Forge Tyrants busy.'

The chamber was dominated by a series of steel racks each taller and broader than a man, each covered by a great oilcloth. Tech-nomad smiths paused in their work at benches across the far wall, but Mortarion nodded to them and they went back to it. Yellow flares of sparks shot up from grinding wheels passing over armour plates, and there was the fizz and crackle of braising torches.

Mortarion halted in front of one of the shrouded racks. *'They never stand and fight,'* he began, repeating Typhon's earlier words. 'This is so. Our enemy hits us and fades away. The Death Guard can defend any settlement we place under our care. When we catch Overlord convoys in the valleys, we butcher them. There is nowhere on Barbarus where the air is clear, that they can walk unopposed.'

'But we can't kill them all,' added Typhon. He began to wonder where Mortarion was taking the conversation. 'Anyone who follows them too deep into the haze dies there. Necare and his animals don't need to lift a finger. Our human weakness ends us for them.' The last words sounded bitterer than he had intended them to. *There must be another way*, he wanted to say, the words forming on his lips.

'There is another way.' Mortarion silenced him with his reply, and for a brief moment Typhon thought he heard a buzzing cadence in his ears.

Rask reached up and pulled down the heavy cloth covering the nearest rack, to reveal beneath it a set of armour the like of which Typhon had never seen before. Over an under-suit made out of the tanned skin of lamprey worms, the battleplate sported lines of hawsers arranged in bunches like muscles, which in turn were protected by panels of steel daubed with the signature grey livery of the Death Guard. The device of the skull and sun was the only iconography upon it, visible on one shoulder pauldron.

'What do you think?' said Mortarion. 'This represents many months of effort from the best tech-nomad artisans on the planet.'

Typhon reached out, toying with the fingers of an empty gauntlet. The chainmail glove was more flexible than he had expected, and lighter with it. 'Fine workmanship.' There was a beaked helmet hanging slack at the neck of the suit, and he examined it. A band of cast armourglass would cover the eyes of the wearer, and the sharp snout of the headgear seemed to be fitted with layers of dense filter material. Pipes spun out of resin-treated paper looped back to a container on the armour's back, nestled between the shoulder blades.

'There's an air bladder in there, and a pump that works off the action of the wearer's movements,' Rask explained. 'With the helm affixed, it is completely sealed and no toxins can affect the wearer.' He paused, and licked his lips. 'Well. That's the idea, anyway.'

'I assume you've tested the suits in the mist,' said Typhon, still staring into the dead eyes of the mask. 'How far?'

Rask looked away. 'Not far enough,' he admitted. 'Some of the volunteers, they didn't survive. We had to drag them back down by their tethers.'

'That was the last iteration,' Mortarion insisted, moving to the largest of the racks. He uncovered the suit resting on it, and Typhon could tell by its dimensions that it had been tailor-made for the Reaper of Men. 'These versions have been improved. Rask's duties in Safehold were not only to defend it while we were at battle. He supervised the construction of this armour.'

'I see.' Typhon considered his own battleplate in comparison. What would it be like to wear something like these new suits, something so enclosed and all-encompassing? He wondered if it would overwhelm him. 'I admit I prefer to fight with more freedom available to me.'

'Unless you can learn to breathe poison, you'll never fight Necare,' Mortarion snapped, and Typhon stopped himself from rising to the bait. 'This is what will end the war for us.' Mortarion gestured around. 'In just a few years we have built a savage fighting force out of a population of frightened, cowed lessers. We have the best weapons, thanks to our metalsmiths and gun makers. But the point of the sword must be close to cut meat. *This...*' He placed his long-fingered hand on the breastplate of the battleplate. 'This will get us close.'

'Do you have enough of this armour to outfit an army?' ventured Typhon, but he already knew the answer. The equipment in this cavern was likely all they had, and Rask's silence confirmed the suspicion.

'I will take the best warriors we have,' said Mortarion. 'You among them, my friend. An elite unit that will cast a shroud of death across the Overlords. We'll end this in a single night of fire and slit throats.' He showed his teeth with those last words, lost in anticipation of the moment.

Typhon's steady gaze bored into Rask, who would not return it. 'Dural does not want to admit his doubts, but I hear them as loudly as if he shouts.' He glanced at Mortarion. 'This is a daring plan, Reaper. But it is a great risk. You rely on untested, experimental technology, in a pivotal battle against a foe that we know full well has powers beyond the material.' He stepped away from the armour racks. 'I am your brother in battle, and I would be remiss if I did not speak truthfully to you.

What you propose could lead to your death up there on the mountain, and that of all our best fighters.'

'I am no stranger to risk.' Mortarion folded his arms across his chest. 'I took a grave one on the day we first met. I know you recall that moment. That time has come again.' He shook his head. 'What other option is there?'

Typhon wanted to smile, but he hid it. *Perfect*, he thought, *he comes to the question without the need to lead him there.* 'I have an alternative. I brought it back to Safehold aboard the airship. Something with more potential than a handful of armoured suits.'

'What do you mean?' said Rask.

'I prefer to show rather than tell,' he replied, and this time Typhon's smile was revealed in its feral totality.

FIVE

Resurrection
The Fate of the Sigillite
Silver

FIRE AND DEATH whirled around Loken, keening in a song that he knew all too well. And yet it still felt wrong to be fighting here.

Since finding a purpose with the Knights-Errant, he had been called upon to shed blood on Terra's soil – many times – but in each instance it had been a skirmish, a minor engagement over in moments. This...

This felt like *the war*.

Although the birthplace of man was not the world where he was born, Loken had been raised like many sons and daughters of the Imperium to hold this planet in higher regard, to consider it as almost sacrosanct. In other times and places, that honouring might have been called 'holy', but there was little room for such things in the Emperor's secular dominions. Still, Terra – Old Earth, Gaia, Adem, Tellus or whatever ancient name by which you wished to know it – held a place above all others as the cradle of humanity. Untouched by battle since the Emperor's great Unification, it was meant to be the image in which the Imperium was to be forged.

A war here, like this, amid the screaming thunder of guns and the clash of blades, was an offence to that ideal.

The fallen aeronefs blazed where they crashed into the snowy land-scape, throwing up walls of acrid smoke that covered the approach of their passengers. Running into the lasguns of Malcador's Chosen at the outer markers, the horde did not slow, overwhelming the defend-ers and butchering them when their weapons ran hot and shut down.

There were hundreds, perhaps thousands of them. Humans of course, and of questionable levels of skill, but they made up for their lack of ability by sheer force of numbers. Some were career soldiers, perhaps mercenaries or even law officers, and they knew their way around weap-ons. Most were the ragged and the destitute, an army stolen from the hidden populations of the junkhunter tribes and tech-nomadics that lived outside the city-hives of Terra. Loken wondered who had walked among them, and what oratory and tricks had been used to turn them to the Warmaster's banner.

He wondered if it was warp sorcery that had done this. Or was it just the clever application of pressure to the desperation of those who thought they were maligned and forgotten? For all the glory that the Emperor brought from the stars, it must have shone dull and distant for these motley dregs. Loken considered how they might see the Great Dream of the Imperium. Not as the crusade to bring humanity to great-ness, but as a wasteful effort led by elites who did not know their plight, and did not care to.

He killed them all the same, though, and without pity. For even as the warrior strove to understand what drove them into the traitor's grasp, Loken did not forgive it.

His sword cut down a man in the carapace armour of the Imperial Army, the force of the blow slamming the bleeding corpse back at his cohorts, staggering them. Loken lost no momentum, extending his sweep and beheading the others. They fell into the slush around his boots, blood diluted by snowmelt into rose-coloured pools blooming at the foot of the White Mountain.

Lasers flashed and bolt shells roared, stitching a deadly web of light and tracer across the ice and stone. The makeshift turncoat army came in screaming Horus' name as a battle cry, funnelled into close order by sharp-edged hillocks of bare granite. Beams shot from pillboxes at the perimeter of the great grey peak lanced out, but the bulk of the killing was being done by the Knights-Errant.

Off to Loken's right, Varren was cackling and enjoying the brutality of the engagement more than was seemly. True to his previous statements, he had gone to the White Mountain's armoury and torn an anti-personnel flame projector off the pintle mount of a hover tank. He stood in the middle of a perfect circle of blackened corpses, pivoting to incinerate anyone who strayed within range of the flamer's hissing nozzles. Whipping tails of brilliant promethium fire looped out and savaged the bodies of the attackers, the weapon growling as it worked.

To the left, Gallor was nothing but cold, martial focus, moving and firing with textbook exactitude. As he deftly sidestepped the clumsy attacks of his foes, he put mass-reactive rounds into the midst of enemy packs, ensuring that those not killed instantly by impact or overpressure from the hits were felled by fragmentation from the fat bullet heads.

And of course, Garro was at the very tip of the spear. His sword caught sunlight as it wove patterns of murder through the air, culling without pause or mercy. Like Gallor's, the battle-captain's fighting style was simple, direct and deadly. Loken guessed it was a Death Guard trait, in keeping with the obdurate, hard-edged manner of their combat tactics. Garro's swordsmanship lacked the flair and showy grandstanding of Legion bladesmen such as those of the White Scars, Luna Wolves or the Sons of Fulgrim. But it was effective, as those who tried to fight him learned to their cost.

Loken's own sword resonated in his gauntlet as he twisted to meet a new attacker, this one huge by human standards but still a head shorter than the Space Marine. A chem-charged mutant of some kind, the man's face was a mass of scarification that turned his flesh into a distorted image of the Eye of Horus. His mouth of teeth, all filed to points, formed the arrow point of the sigil. Like the Warmaster he followed, the brute carried a heavy mace with a spiked head.

Against men, this one would have been fast and fearsome, but against Legion speed and Legion reflexes, he was moving in half-time. Loken caught the mace head and wrenched the weapon from his enemy's grip, but the haft was attached by chains to the brute's wrist so the motion took his hand off with it. The look in the big man's eyes told the legionary that he had likely never lost a fight before this day, and only now did he understand he was not invincible, no matter what those who spread Horus' influence might have told him.

Loken ended it quickly, cutting him down, his sword going to mid-breast before he pulled it. The brute's nerves misfired and he staggered into his killer, broken pieces of his crude armour falling away to reveal a torn body beneath. Loken snarled and shoved the dying fool away, and his gaze caught the tone of the flesh. It was covered with count-less crimson weals, like the bites of venomous insects, each leaking pus and shivering as if something crawled beneath the blistering. Sickened, Loken reeled back, and realised that his momentary distraction had allowed a new enemy to approach without being seen.

This figure was the biggest yet, larger than the brute, matching the stature of any legionary of the line. Loken couldn't make out much more beyond that. The enemy was hunched forward, all detail of him lost beneath a heavy, rough-hewn cloak that seemed to suck in the day-light and smother it. This one conjured the gothic arrangement of the Death-that-Walks, the skeletal form in hood and robes from antiquity that remained a fixture of so many human cultures. Black dust puffed up in each step he took, as the figure advanced towards Garro.

The battle-captain was busy dispatching a brace of mech-augmented gunmen, weathering a fusillade of bullets from the muzzles of a dozen auto-stubbers. He did not see it coming.

Loken shouted a warning and exploded into motion, ploughing through enemy ranks with his sword, drawing his bolter to firing position as he ran. Garro heard the cry and finished his work on the gunman, turning to see.

The thing beneath the cloak rose to its full height and provided

Loken with an ample target. He let rip with a pair of bolt shells, but the attacker's shape instantly blurred and reshaped. Loken had the sudden impression of the solid, real cloak becoming smoky and vaporous.

Garro fired too, and the black mass denatured. It blew apart with the shrieking, ear-splitting buzz of a million insect wings, becoming a stifling swarm of glistening carrion-eater bugs.

Now it was revealed in full, Loken looked upon a blackened, distorted figure that was some grotesque amalgam of a legionary's battleplate and the slick, shiny body of a giant mutant beetle. One arm was the claw of an arthropod, clacking madly – and where there should have been a face there was only a clump of iridescent eyes above a maw of twitching, spiked mandibles. It had a weapon in its more-human hand, a short stabbing blade that was rust-brown and crumbling.

'*My captain,*' said the creature, the words carried not by its voice, but in the orchestrated humming of the swarm surrounding it. '*I said I would return.*'

Shock burned across Garro's face. He *knew* this thing, knew it like a brother. 'Solun!'

Loken saw the monstrous insect-thing nod. '*I told you. You cannot kill decay.*'

'I will take that bet!' roared Varren. The former World Eaters legionary had heard Loken's warning and come to lend his might as well, brandishing his heavy flamer as he stormed into engagement range. Reflexively, Loken and Garro fell to the flanks to allow Varren an unimpeded field of fire, but the creature the battle-captain had called 'Solun' did not make any moves to evade.

Varren snarled and thumbed the flamer's firing stud, spraying a thick rope of white-hot inferno into the swarm-cloak, directly at the warped figure within it. Huge clumps of the carrion flies were reduced to sizzling cinders as they dived in to form a protective mantle before their master, but the flamer chewed them up and engulfed the insect-thing.

It became a living torch, the clinging fire sloughing off sheaves of chitinous material as it sprinted into the middle of the arc of attack. Roaring through the pain, the enemy waded through the flames, clearly in agony and yet undaunted by it. Varren's feral smile slipped off his scarred, bearded face like viscera dripping from a butcher knife as he saw the thing coming and knew it would not stop.

The blackened, half-destroyed creature came into arm's reach and batted away the nozzle of the flamer with its human hand, even as the pincer-claw shot out and snapped shut around Varren's neck. The Knight-Errant struggled and fought back, unleashing the full brutality of his Legion. The fight was a rapid melee of shattering blows and unstoppable counter-strikes.

Loken beat back another surge of rebels, momentarily losing sight of Varren's struggle, dispatching the humans as fast as he could in order to swing back and find a shot to put into the insect-thing. The distraction cost him greatly.

He was moving when he heard the stone-break snap of fortified bone shattering. Garro roared Varren's name and came thundering in with his sword held high, but the other warrior was already going slack, his neck at a horrid angle and dark blood gushing from his mouth.

Varren stepped back, stumbling into Garro's path as if he were dazed and trying to get his bearings, but the legionary's body was working on the last sparks of nerve impulses sent from a dying brain. He slumped, dropping the flame weapon, and crashed to his knees. Loken thought he saw something like a flash of surprise in Varren's fading gaze, before the glimmer of life was gone forever.

From all around them, the monstrous swarm of flies dived at the warrior's still-warm corpse, to feast upon his blood before it could cool.

THE SIGILLITE BACKED away, grasping the worn metal of his staff, and a small mutter of callous amusement escaped his lips.

'Ah, of course. Clever. Very clever.' He bowed his head to an unseen audience. 'You've done what none bar your father could do, Lupercal. You have outplayed me.' He gave a theatrical sigh. 'I suppose I only

have myself to blame. I have stretched myself so thin in recent days…
It was just a matter of time before you put something past me.'

The Warmaster didn't hear him, of course, but it seemed right to
make the statement. Malcador felt a perverse sense of enjoyment at
being right in his suspicions, with the final revelation that *yes*, this
entire charade had been one more among the dozens of intricate assas-
sination attempts against him, directed by Horus' keen and callous
intellect.

That little shard of *hope* that he had held on to – the faintest sliver
of faith that there might still be a way to end the war – turned to bitter dust.

Tylos Rubio advanced on him. There was nothing but antipathy in
the legionary's eyes, a raw and potent hatred of the kind that Malcador
had only ever seen in zealots and converts. Rubio's glistening sword
was aimed at Malcador's chest, the wicked edge ready to bury itself in
flesh and cleave him in twain.

But Rubio's murderous intent was not that of a cold-hearted assas-
sin. It was there in his gaze, it was the killing urge of the righteous
crusader. He wanted to execute the Sigillite because Malcador deserved
to die, and there was truth to that view.

But how had it been done? he wondered. Was there a telepathic cantrip
of such incredible subtlety at play here that even the Sigillite could not
have sensed it, despite all the times he had read Rubio's thoughts? He
dismissed that idea as soon as he conceived of it.

No. The Ruinous Powers did not have the keenness of skill to create
such a thing; and even if they had, in this place any psionic or sorcerous alteration of the Ultramarine's mind would be undone. No, this
was something far simpler… and ironically, more complex.

Rubio's hatred was truthful, old and long buried, but only now
returned to the surface. Perhaps the architects of this act had found
something real from the warrior's past life and made that the foundation of the rage he now felt towards Malcador.

How would I have done it? He pondered the question. *I would have searched out and twisted some long-forgotten emotion into a dark and hateful mirror of its former self. A childhood memory of trauma, or of a parent's love. Weaponised it. Yes. Then honed it and then left it to fester for years.*

Malcador's cold smile widened. He had done things like that and worse still from time to time, in the wars before this one. But in his arrogance, the Sigillite now saw that the lessons he had taught Horus were not the ones he thought he had. 'The boy always was a quick study,' he muttered.

There was a kind of clockwork perfection to the ideal of this, that Malcador would die in the bowels of some bleak and stony labyrinth at the hand of someone he thought he could control. It was a delicious irony that the Sigillite imagined the Warmaster was only too aware of.

He intends to laugh at me when it is done, thought Malcador. *He will not grant me the honour of a face-to-face death by his hand.* And that might be just and right, he reflected. The Sigillite was a liar and a plotter, a master of assassins. He was a schemer and a poisoner, so what right did he have to expect an honourable ending? There would be no heroic last stand for him, no mythic clash to be recalled across the ages in song and story. There would be no one to witness this.

He was to die in shadows, surrounded by the maddened and the broken. Horus wanted Malcador to perish in the deepest, most distant *silence*.

With his immense mental powers subdued, Malcador was only a very old man, the duration of his ill-lived life extended against nature and fate by juvenat tech and body modifications. But Rubio, rendered telepathically inert by the psi-negating aura of the White Mountain's technologies, combined with the dozens of pariahs crowded all around them, was still a monstrous killing engine.

The captive Sisters in the cages said nothing, but Malcador could hear the faint rush of them breathing in unison. Their presence was a heavy psychic fog on the horizon of his preternatural senses, a wall of gloom that shut out everything else.

The novelty of being temporarily rendered mind-mute was quickly fading. He became aware of his heart thudding in his chest, the constriction of the bio-augment collar around his neck and the low crackle of the plasmatic flame in the iron basket atop his staff. Each sensation took on a depth and colour beyond the norm, as if his mind were seeing new ranges to them now that his more ephemeral senses were lost to him.

'If I ask, will you tell me why you wish me to die?' At last, he spoke directly to his executioner in waiting.

'I know what you are,' said Rubio. 'I think I have always known. I saw it a long time ago... But only now do I remember.'

'Horus did this to you.' Malcador made the attempt to dissuade him, but he was cursory about it, going through the motions. The programming would not be easy to disrupt. He glanced at one of the Silent Sisters. *If Horus' agents could break them, they could remake a legionary.* 'You know that.'

Rubio shook his head. 'This is not about him. This is about you.' The sword in his hand shifted. 'Once, long ago, I saw what you were going to do to the galaxy. How you were going to change it. I glimpsed the plans you have that even the Emperor doesn't know of.'

Malcador froze, briefly perturbed by the certainty of the warrior's assertion. *Was that possible?* Then he shook off the thought. *No.* There were some places where even the most powerful psyker in the universe could not look.

'I know what you want to do after Horus is defeated. I remember. That truth has been hiding in my mind for a long time. So it is better you die here. Better you are forgotten.'

'Are you truly ready to kill me, Tylos?' Malcador said quietly.

'I believe...' Rubio began, his brow furrowing as he chased down the mercurial thought. 'I believe I have always been ready to do that.'

The legionary came at him in a blur, and Malcador was barely able to swing the staff around quickly enough to defend himself. Touching a hidden control caused the grumbling ornamental flames atop it to rise to become a shrieking fireball that jetted out through the frosty air. Normally, the Sigillite would have been able to telekinetically guide the churning plasma in any direction, but here the superheated gas struck the target off-beam.

Rubio shielded his face with his arm and the flames rolled over his slate-coloured battle armour, slagging the upper layers of ceramite where they touched. Grey became soot-black and waves of spent heat vibrated in the air, but the legionary did not lose a step.

His sword slashed right-to-left and struck the haft of the black iron staff with incredible force, knocking it out of Malcador's grip with enough power to shock him back into a half-stumble.

Every fighting reflex in the Sigillite was honed towards the instant use of his immense psionic talents, but now those instincts were like pulling the trigger on a useless, breech-jammed pistol. He raised one hand in a warding motion, the other clutching a fistful of robes at his chest.

'*Stop!*' bellowed Malcador, summoning all the raw force of personality he could draw on. 'I am the Regent of Terra and you will obey me!'

Rubio had already reoriented his sword, to commit to a downward executioner's blow. 'I am here to do this,' said the legionary, nodding to himself. 'The message. My recruitment. My entire life. All leading to *now.*'

'You have no right to judge me.' The words slipped out, surprising Malcador even as he uttered them. He couldn't stop himself. 'I regret nothing I have done. Nothing!'

'That is a lie,' said Rubio. 'I remember your face when you let Wyntor fall to his death. You regretted that… And I know there is more.'

There is. The Sigillite wanted to say, but the sword was already diving towards his chest, aimed to slice through his heart.

The tip of the blade met an invisible barrier a hand's span above Malcador's chest, causing a sudden flare of blue-white radiation as the force of the blow was instantly reversed in full, and redirected back at its origin point. Rubio was hit by the hammer of his own attack and slammed back, his boots cutting scores in the stone as he tried to resist it.

Malcador rose of his own accord and without support, dropping all pretences. As he moved, his robe fell open to reveal the metal icon hanging on a chain from his augment collar. Forged in the shape of the Sigillite's mark, the device glowed with an inner fire, and he reached up to trace a pattern on its surface.

His sly, hooded gaze met that of the legionary. 'Did you really think it would be that simple to end me?'

AN ASHEN PULSE of raw despair passed through Garro's chest. The emotion felt like his hearts momentarily seizing, as he watched Macer Varren fall.

For an instant, the sense of desolation was utter and perfect. *How many more would have to die before this war was at an end?* The question tolled like a dolorous bell. The World Eater had not been a Legion-brother to Garro – he had been at best a respected ally – but still the acerbic gladiator's end was offensive to the Knight-Errant.

Varren's killing was only one more in the unfolding battle, and Garro knew that at this very second there were other legionaries across the galaxy engaged in other conflicts, dying in the same moment on dozens of worlds. And that was the great scope of the transgression. That was the monumental, dishonourable horror of it. The Legiones Astartes, the demigod transhumans bred to unite mankind and bring order out of anarchy, had been reduced to *this*.

The rage in Garro expressed itself in a thundering roar from the depths of his chest, and he attacked Varren's killer with all his fury. The creature – this so-called *Lord of Flies* – reacted with shock and fought back, blocking the fall of *Libertas* with a clumsy parry and making the attempt to stab Garro with its rusted plague knife.

Garro snared the creature's wrist and broke it, the jabbing underhand blow becoming weak and useless, the corrupted blade slumping. With the pommel of his sword, Garro directed a salvo of bullet-quick hits into the face of the thing, smashing its spidery jaws and reducing its ugly aspect to a ruin of blackened, broken chitin. Each piece of skull and flesh that broke off it disintegrated into a myriad of motile flecks that buzzed angrily away, drawn up and back to fill any gaping wounds and clot the flow of inky, syrupy ichor.

Heedless to the rest of the skirmish going on at the foot of the White Mountain, Garro's attention was now solely fixed on the creature before him. Gallor, Loken and Malcador's Chosen armsmen could deal with the turncoats from the crashed aeronefs – but this thing would be his alone to destroy.

'I killed you on Luna,' Garro spat, advancing on the Lord of Flies as it scrambled to put distance between them. 'I threw your desiccated corpse into the sun! How can you be here? How can you live still?'

'The Octed Path carries this one to glory.' The droning swarm-voice sounded in Garro's bones. *'And the Grandfather is so very generous with his Gifts.'*

'If I must destroy you again, I will!' Garro roared back. 'And if need be, I will do so every time you return from whatever foul origin spawned you!'

'Then your war will be longer than you can comprehend, animal.' The creature gathered itself and turned its pulped mess of a face in his direction. *'The pestilence existed before your meat-kind dragged themselves from the ooze. It will be here when the last stars darken.'* Even as he closed the gap between them, Garro could see the Lord of Flies' terrible wounds knitting themselves closed, the destruction wrought over it rebuilding at a speed that the accelerated constitution of a legionary could not match.

Garro took a breath of the cold air, blood-specked snow crunching beneath the heel of his augmetic leg as he fell into a fighting stance. 'Solun Decius was a good lad. Whatever poison you are, you robbed him of his potential. For that alone, you deserve a thousand deaths.'

'Decius?' The creature broke into gales of obscene, cackling laughter. It jabbed its claw-hand at its chest. *'This vessel isn't that flesh, you moribund fool. You pitched him into a star, remember?'* The Lord of Flies' ugly aspect blurred and shifted, the particles of it drawing back

to reveal a human face beneath, the core over which the wretched thing had built itself.

'*Remember, Nathaniel?*' This time, the voice was a familiar one, emerging from the lips of a pallid corpse.

'Meric...' Surprise seized Garro's breath. 'No...!'

'*I found his body where you left it,*' buzzed the swarm. '*It fits me well.*' The flies massed around Meric Voyen's head, writhing and glittering. '*What did you expect, captain? You executed your own man. Your friend. The Grandfather took pity on him, gave him to me.*'

'You soulless wretch.' Garro's cold disgust hung in the air. 'How dare you defile his memory? I will make you pay for that.'

'*Staunch your own guilt first, Death Guard!*' the Lord of Flies spat back.

And the worst of it was, Garro could not. In the aftermath of his escape to Terra aboard the starship *Eisenstein*, bearing a warning of Horus' treachery, many of Garro's loyal brothers had suffered. Solun Decius had fallen to ruin and transformation, but Meric Voyen's fate had been to be broken in spirit by the horrors he witnessed.

Poor, pure-of-heart Meric, hoping against all odds that he might turn his skills as a Legion Apothecary towards curing the plague of undeath that was poised to infect their wayward comrades. Voyen had recovered the corpse of the Lord of Flies after Garro had first killed it on the surface of Terra's moon, believing it might hold the answer to a cure. But all it brought him was infection and a certain end. His hope became his ruin.

Garro would never forget the act he had been forced to commit. With this sword in his hand and with great sorrow in his heart. 'I granted Meric the Emperor's Peace,' he whispered. 'The contagion was already in him. It was that or allow my battle-brother to be consumed.'

The Lord of Flies spread its arms. '*Your failure is complete, then. You didn't save him, Garro. You doomed Voyen to become my vessel.*' The squirming horde of crawling things marched over the dead man's face, filling his mouth and nostrils, hardening again into a monstrous aspect. *'But I do grow bored with him. I think next I will take host in you. Yes. That will be fitting.'*

'You may make the attempt!' Garro snarled, but the creature paid him no heed.

Raising its head to the sky, the monster let out a piercing screech that seemed to vibrate down through the air and into the frost-rimed ground beneath Garro's feet. Blackened snow and grey earth churned with unnatural force, and everywhere the slush and ice broke apart as thousands of fat, corpse-white maggots erupted from below. Each was as big as a man's arm and their slime-slick, throbbing bodies ended in eyeless lamprey maws filled with yellowed needle-fangs. For an instant, they joined in the chorus – and then the grotesque, smothering tide thrashed blindly towards the Knights-Errant and the survivors of the Chosen.

HE WAS AN old man, heavy with the weight of centuries, to the degree that it was impossible for most observers to begin to guess at the Sigillite's age.

Malcador was a rarity, a human that had passed beyond a horizon of being to a point where concepts like 'mortality' became unwieldy and inapplicable.

But there was no decrepitude in him, at least not in this moment. While his spindly, robe-wrapped form seemed waif-like and unthreatening before the mass of a fully armoured Space Marine, there was no diminishment at hand.

'I do not die with ease,' he told the former Ultramarine. 'I've learned that lesson the hard way.' Malcador looked away, thinking again of the being who had set this in motion.

Was it Horus... or someone else?

'Are you so desperate that this is the only endgame you can play?' Malcador wasn't speaking to Rubio, or to himself. He addressed the question to the air. 'A sordid murder attempt hidden from all eyes. A wizened old warlock run through, speared on a sword as if he were a piece of overcooked meat...' The Sigillite laughed. 'So many foolish

assumptions, bred from a mind that lacks the experience of its betters, yes? Because your masters must have known.' His smile faded and
he looked down at his long, bony fingers. 'One cannot exist beyond a
certain threshold of psychic power without being forever changed by
it. Look at me. Look at my years. Every molecule of my being, soaked
in the aura of the empyrean for so long. I fell beyond the scope of
humanity long ago. So how could you hope to kill me as you would
a man, even after robbing me of my gifts? How?'

Lost in the wilds of his fury, Rubio attacked him again and again,
each time clashing his gladius against the impregnable force wall emitted by the microscopic conversion field generator in Malcador's icon.
Every blistering sword blow was reversed with a brilliant flash of light
in its wake, and the Sigillite took them as easily as he would have a
fall of raindrops.

The power of the device – a miracle of technology from before the
Age of Strife – often made Malcador speculate on what wonders that
lost era had contained. In a small way, it pained him to use the generator in so crude a manner as this. It had been made for greater things,
but those possibilities were dust and forgotten.

Rubio put all his effort into a final attack that reflected against him
with such power that it knocked the sword from his grip. The weapon
clattered against the stone floor and Malcador saw his opening.

'Now then,' he said, 'we'll get to the heart of this.' The Sigillite moved
quickly, pressing the icon to Rubio's chest-plate before the warrior
could react. White light flared from the device, and he shrank back as
Rubio was wreathed in an aurora of jagged lightning. Gravity multi-
plied and forced the legionary to his knees, holding him there under
a hundredfold of his own weight.

'He's tried to kill me so often, it has gone beyond tiresome.' Malcador gave a grunt as he stooped to reach for Rubio's sword, getting his
hands around the massive grip. 'But each time I have to step into the
trap. To know, do you see? To know if I am worthy of surviving it.'
With effort, Malcador hauled the weapon off the floor. The sword was

almost as tall as he was. 'And this time? Well. Damn him if he didn't bait the snare with *hope*. Clever bastard.'

The Sigillite lifted Rubio's sword until the tip of it rested on the legionary's neck ring. He would only need to put his weight behind it to send the weapon through Rubio's throat and finish him.

The legionary could not speak, but Malcador reacted as if he had.

'Do you think this is what he wanted, Tylos? Even if you fail, and I stand here, your sword in my hand, he still scores a victory. I die and you are killed because of it. I survive and I kill you. One death or two, he still gains. Because he knows your value as much as mine.'

Malcador steeled himself and got better purchase on the blade's hilt. Then, rather than end the Knight-Errant, he pulled it away and walked to the cells where the Silent Sisters waited in their blank-gazed torpor.

THE POWER OF the restricting field meant that Rubio could not even move his eyes, forcing him to only look ahead. But at the edges of his vision he saw the movement of the cell doors opening at Malcador's command, and he saw the first of the bodies fall. He heard the song of the blade he knew so well hissing through stale air and human flesh. There were no cries, of course, but the gush and spatter of slit throats had a sound all of their own.

As each Sister was dispatched, the telepathic fog abated by degrees, but it meant nothing to Rubio. The glowing device affixed to his chest was negating all energy-conduction in his armour, from the flex-metal power musculature of his arms and legs to the psi-attuned crystals of his psychic hood. He could do nothing but wait and witness, trapped in the amber of reborn rage.

At length, Malcador moved back into his field of sight. His terracotta robes were spattered with splashes of crimson, his hands red with murder. The Sigillite let Rubio's gladius drop and he came face-to-face with him.

'Now then,' he said, as colour returned to the old man's cheeks. 'Why don't we see how this all began, yes?'

No, Rubio wanted to say, but that reaction was built upon fear. Old, primal terror from his childhood, the dark and shapeless shadow of a forgotten terror experienced by the unfinished mind of a babe in a crib. Something buried so deep it was never to be remembered, but not so lost that a keen and hateful soul could not dredge it up and weaponise it.

Malcador cupped Rubio's twitching face in his blood-slicked hands and *pushed–*

–All the way back to Calth.

This was the place. A blasted wilderness of seared grassland beneath a dying star, kilometres outside the lines of defence set up upon the railhead that led to Numinus City. Rough cones of old rock forming shallow canyons. The fading winds of a thinning atmosphere.

Rubio and the others were out there on a reconnaissance sortie. The 21st Company had fallen back to this zone, bloodied and shocked by the brutal treachery of the Sons of Lorgar, and now the Ultramarines dealt with the horror of that sedition by returning to what they knew best – their tactics.

The orders from Captain Gaius were clear. Lone legionaries spread out in a finger-five deployment, each covering a sweep zone, searching for any sign of the Word Bearers or the hordes of insane auxilia they had brought with them.

It gave Brother Rubio and the others something to occupy their minds, something other than the question of why the XVII Legion had chosen to break their oaths.

The first shots of the rebellion fell here and he did not know it. But he would, in time. All the galaxy would learn the truth.

Their use forbidden by the Edict of Nikaea, Rubio felt lost without his psionic abilities, and in reflecting on that his distraction cost him dearly.

'There you are.'

In this memory he did not remember, Rubio whirled, bringing up his bolter to fire. Behind him, a figure in armour the colour of congealed blood, his face revealed in the weak light as if it were a parchment covered with lines of arcane symbols. The words defeated understanding, squirming out from under his comprehension.

'This is the one?' *said the Word Bearer, as if conversing with someone only he could perceive.* 'It doesn't look like anything to me.'

Rubio attempted to pull the trigger of his bolter, but no part of him could move. His eye was drawn to a glow in the off-hand of the traitor legionary, a mote of eldritch warp fire held there by the cage of his fingers in ritual pattern.

He knew the Word Bearer then.

Erebus, *said another voice, coming at him from outside the memory.* Of course.

'You don't seem special, Ultramarine,' *Erebus was saying, coming closer, removing his gauntlets so he could touch the flesh of Rubio's face with his bare fingers.* 'But I have learned not to question them. What the Octed knows of your path and where you will end up is all that matters.' *He leaned in, and unspeakable pain exploded across all of Rubio's sensorium.* 'What do you have that I can use, I wonder? Let me see.'

In real time, it took only seconds, but in the non-space of the mind an eternity unfolded. Imagine a bathysphere descending into the abyssal deeps of a fathomless ocean; thus was Erebus as he fell into Rubio's memories, searching back and back to the most primal of them, seeking the ur-fear formed in his mind before he had known true sentience.

Then, with the skill of cruelty's artisan, Erebus stitched that primitive terror to its red twin, to raw fury. He gave it Malcador's face as the root, and sealed it within a shell of words. Waiting for the day.

'Such pride and arrogance in your breed, Rubio,' *said Erebus, as he withdrew, the deed done.* 'It will amuse me to think of you as no better than a servitor, waiting for the right trigger command.' *He showed a mouthful of teeth.* 'That will amuse me a great deal.'

And then he was gone and the moment had never happened, swallowing itself, becoming nothing. Hiding.

Hiding until–

'WE CAN'T HAVE that.'

Malcador's fingers slipped through the matter of Rubio's flesh until he was touching the substrata of his raw psyche. Now it had blossomed, it

was easy to see where Erebus had hidden the trigger for the hate-bomb
that had lain inert for years in Rubio's mind.

The Sigillite had a grudging admiration for the ploy. It showed a
subtlety on the Word Bearer's part that he had not thought Lorgar's
lackey to be capable of. But then again, he imagined it was more the
voices that had whispered to him from the void behind such a tactic
than Erebus himself.

He kept Rubio suspended in negative time as he gauged the depth
and intricacy of the mnemonic implant. It wove around elements of
the Codicier's core self, his super-ego and the surface layers of Ultramarines hypnogogic programming. All were pieces of Tylos Rubio that
could not be easily excised without collapsing the whole.

The simplest solution would be to euthanise, of course, but then that
would upset the balance of the project on Titan. And although Malcador had built a degree of redundancy into the scheme, if the choice
came down to it, he didn't want to lose this particular one. Up on
the Eagle's Highway, when Malcador had halted him, the Sigillite had
seen into Rubio's heart. That kind of purity and devotion was impossible to fabricate.

So, with the greatest care, Malcador retraced Erebus' path and undid
his works.

RUBIO CHOKED AND his tripartite lungs quaked inside his ribcage as
they sucked in a gale of cold air.

He blinked furiously, trying to get his bearings. He was on his knees,
in the holding chamber within the White Mountain. He tasted blood
and the acid tang of spent ectoplasm.

'Steady, lad,' said Malcador, standing a few metres away. He held
himself up on his staff, the crackling flames in the iron basket atop it
giving his face a hard cast. 'You lost a step there, I think.'

'Aye...' Rubio felt wrung out and cold, but he shook off the sensation and rose. Before him, he saw the silhouette of his sword lying
in a spill of crimson. And beyond it, a line of dead bodies. The lost

pariah Sisters, all executed. He knew immediately that it had been by his weapon. 'What happened?'

'You don't remember?' Malcador sucked in a breath through his teeth. 'Psi-shock, perhaps. Such effects can obliterate short-term memory chains.'

Rubio looked back towards the hatchway and found it hanging open, stained with human vitae. The scientician Brell lay off to one side, unmoving. 'The last thing I recall is the door opening...' He trailed off. Beyond that point, Rubio's eidetic memory was a seamless negative space. He tried to grasp at the threads of it, but there was nothing there.

'It was the trap we knew it would be.' Malcador became solemn. 'The Sisters attacked us. It appears they were mentally programmed in some fashion. You took the sword to them.' He gave a nod. 'Rubio, you saved my life.'

'Yes?' He frowned, lost in the moment. 'I don't recall it.' Rubio's face clouded as he gathered up his sword and cleaned off the blade. There was something else missing, something he couldn't find a shape for. His only way to define it was by the void it left behind, and that was insufficient.

'Horus engineered this event to destroy us both,' continued the Sigillite. 'That was his intent. Kill me, and take you off the board into the bargain.'

'Why would I matter?' The question fell from him, unbidden. The hollow sensation in Rubio's mind made him feel bleak and distant.

Malcador approached and looked up at him. 'Because you have so much yet to do, my friend.'

The Sigillite offered Rubio something, and he took it: a silver disc, the same as the ones he had seen on the table in Malcador's private quarters. Turning it over, Rubio revealed a name etched there in High Gothic script.

'*Koios*,' he read aloud. The same name Yotun had addressed him with. 'I don't understand. What does this mean?'

'Make your peace with it.' Malcador's face faded into the depths of his hood. 'Soon that will be who you are.'

INTERVAL VI

Lords of Death

[The planet Barbarus; before]

MORTARION INDULGED HIS comrade, and followed him in silence back through the streets of Safehold, out to the barren field where the captured airship floated just above the churned earth. Tethers held the craft down against the stiff breeze that pulled at its bullet-like shape, and a steady caravan of people passed them in procession back towards the township, each one carrying a bale of cargo or a barrel of water recovered from the airship's belly compartment.

The people will eat well tonight, thought the Reaper of Men, gauging the bounty that Typhon's forces had brought back with them. He would allow it, just for this day, as a celebration for the victories of the Death Guard. But tomorrow, the supplies would be locked in the city's communal stores and regular rationing would return. Resources were precious on Barbarus, and those who did not consider that reality would die as readily as those culled by the Overlords.

He wondered if Typhon had an ulterior motive with this generosity. *Did he hope that it might make the people better disposed towards him?*

Mortarion doubted it. Despite all the battles his old friend had won, the intolerance towards the half-breed's nature could never be completely erased. Too many looked in Typhon's dark eyes and saw only the bastard child of a human woman and an Overlord. Mortarion had won loyalty despite his inhuman qualities and the dark past of his origins, and some might have said his was the higher mountain to climb. But for Typhon, his blood would forever be his burden.

'What is it?' Typhon sensed Mortarion watching and turned back to look at him as they approached the drop-ramp leading up into the airship.

'Only those who have fought beside you know what dedication you have to our war,' Mortarion told him. 'I will never forget it.'

Typhon halted. 'We are all united in our hate for the Overlords,' he said, after a moment. 'When they're dead, we'll have to find something else to kill. What do you think that will be?'

'I look forward to the day when I have the luxury of that question.' He gestured at the airship. 'What have you brought me to see?'

'Clear the cargo bay!' Typhon didn't answer him, and instead he jogged up the ramp, repeating the order to all within earshot. 'You heard me! Get out!'

Civilians scuttled frantically out of his way, almost falling over themselves to avoid Mortarion, some dragging barrels, others dropping their loads in fright. A handful of Typhon's hatchet-faced warriors strode off their guard posts and followed the citizens down the ramp. As Mortarion ducked his head to enter the low-ceilinged cargo compartment, he felt the airship's deck sway gently in the wind, and cast his gaze around. There were still many containers to be removed, but by far the largest was a metal crate made of steel panels, easily the size of a steam-crawler.

Typhon pulled a handle set into the wall and with a crunch of cogwheels, the cargo bay's clamshell doors slammed shut, leaving them alone. Mortarion suddenly became aware of a thick, greasy stillness in the air, and it made him ill at ease. 'I await your answer,' he told Typhon, a twitch moving through his fingers. He dismissed the urge to reach for the shaft of his scythe, to seek solace in the weapon's heft.

'You and Rask have the right idea with those armours of yours,' Typhon began, walking across to the metal crate. Something inside it made a noise, like the scrape of a talon over rusted iron. 'But you're going about it the wrong way. A handful of men, even with the best of weapons, won't be enough. You know how lethal the high crags are. A single pinprick hole in that plate and all flesh within would suffer an agonising end.'

'You have an alternative?' Mortarion scowled as he said the words, becoming more unsettled by the moment. 'A way to survive up there?'

'The Overlords live in those toxic reaches,' Typhon replied. 'They alter their golems and their helots to endure it. Imagine if we could do the same.' He reached for a heavy padlock secured to the front of the crate, and Mortarion saw a brief glitter of twisted light around the device. The padlock fell to the deck. With his other hand, Typhon touched his throat. 'You would not need seven warriors in ponderous, heavy armour suits. You could send a whole army up there, throw them screaming and furious through the thickest clouds. The final fortresses of our enemies would be overwhelmed.'

A cold surge of fury washed over Mortarion. He had often overlooked Typhon's more unpalatable statements and his unorthodox actions, partly out of a sense of loyalty and partly because the warrior fought hard and brought him victories. But what he suggested now was close to spitting on everything that Mortarion held sacrosanct. 'The Overlords warp their underlings with dark power. They change them with magicks!'

'What you call magick is only a talent they conceal from us,' replied Typhon. 'It is one we too could learn to command.'

'To what end?' Was Typhon testing him with these words? He could not be certain. 'You have seen what becomes of those turned into the golem-soldiers. Nothing of their will remains. They become mindless!'

Typhon nodded. 'Aye. But if some were willing to volunteer for such a transformation… If you asked it of them, Reaper of Men… Would it not be worth the sacrifice?'

His words brought Mortarion up short. *It is so*, he told himself. *There are those whose loyalty is such that they would do such a thing, if I offered it.*

He thought of Dural Rask, who had followed him from the earliest days of the war and treated him as if he were a fate-sent saviour. He thought of fierce Kahgor Lothsul, warriors like Morgax Murnau and Taragth Sune, even bookish Caipha Morarg and Hunda Skorvall – all of them would agree to give themselves up, body and soul, if they believed it would end this conflict forever. 'You would have us become the enemy in order to defeat it…' he muttered, grasping the full import of that dire possibility.

'We can learn their ways.' Typhon twisted a switch on the flank of the metal crate and the steel panels along its side snapped open, folding back to reveal a cage within. 'We can pull the secrets we need from this.'

Inside the cage, suspended from hawsers, was a deathly figure in soiled black robes. It looked up and revealed a bruised face of milk-pale skin streaked with watery yellow blood. Eyes alight with the deepest, most Stygian terror found Mortarion's and the mouth behind a barbed gag worked in panicked gulps. Unintelligible wails escaped the creature and it flailed feebly against its restraints.

'*Volcral.*' Mortarion made a curse of the minor Overlord's name. As a youth, he had witnessed this fiend harvest lessers to make into intricate sculptures of dripping meat and broken bone, for no better reason than to entertain itself. It was absolutely terrified of him, and it had all right to be. Mortarion pointed at the prisoner. 'Why is this cur still drawing breath? You told me you had defeated Volcral's army!'

'And I have,' said Typhon. 'I took their master as my prize. I made it watch as we built a pyre for the bodies of its minions.'

Volcral slumped against the floor of the cage, and Mortarion saw the reality of the creature's utter defeat in its expression. Typhon had broken it.

He sucked in a breath. 'The mission I gave you is unfinished. Kill the Overlord. Do it now.'

'You always told me never to waste a resource,' countered Typhon. 'Allow yourself a moment to think beyond your rage, my friend. Think of what we can learn from this creature. We *know* that their means and methods work against us. They are not unproven like the Forge Tyrant armour! We can take that power for ourselves, Mortarion! And not just immunity to the mists, but more.' He moved closer, his voice dropping to an urgent growl. 'You know better than all of us what forces Necare can call upon. Balefire from beneath the earth. Murder-mists and storms that tear at a man's mind. Imagine if we could turn that power against him.'

For a heartbeat, he did as Typhon asked, and considered his words. The temptation, the unbridled possibility of it, was difficult to ignore. But as he looked inward, all he could see was the piece of himself that would blacken and wither if he were to align to the same path as his foster father.

Mortarion flinched, as a droning buzz sounded close to his ear. He shook off the moment and glared at his old friend. 'I have considered it, and I am unswayed. Heed me, Typhon. I will not give this command again.' He turned his back on the cage. 'If Volcral does not die by your hand, here and now, then you will suffer in his stead. And know this, from today until eternity. By my oath, the Death Guard will never take that path. *Never!*'

Fuelled by anger, conflicted and sickened within, Mortarion stormed across the cargo bay and wrenched open the hatch, vanishing into the light outside.

Typhon watched the shaft of weak daylight creep across the floor of the compartment, and at length he released a slow exhalation.

'Ah well,' he said to the air. 'It seems I was premature.'

Volcral whimpered behind its gag as Typhon twisted the control wheel on the cage, and the bars unlocked. It shook violently, dislodging the tattered hood and revealing the naked shape of its head and shoulders. Only vaguely humanoid in nature, Volcral's skull was a distended egg shape, seemingly too large for the bird-like neck it sat upon. The creature tugged weakly at its tethers, unable to back away.

Typhon paused, glancing back over his shoulder to be sure that they were alone in the cargo bay. 'Just you and I now.' He reached up and pulled down the gag, exposing Volcral's swollen lips. 'Any final words?'

'He doesn't know, does he?' The creature blurted out the question, desperate to stall for time. 'That's why you silenced me. You were afraid of what I would tell him!'

'He is beginning to suspect, I think.' Typhon considered the possibility. 'Your words would only have confused the matter.'

Volcral tried one last time to put on the air of arrogant superiority that was the creature's usual bearing. 'I smell it on you, half-breed. The curdled stink of lesser meat fouling and diluting the strength of Overlord potential!'

'Strength?' Typhon took Volcral by the throat and applied a small amount of pressure. 'Your kind are so brittle when one sees you up close. Stripped of your powers and your cantrips, you're nothing.' His hand slipped up and around to cup the back of Volcral's head, and he pulled it near, until they were brow-to-brow. 'I *will* know the source of your power. But perhaps not today.'

'Yes.' Volcral gave a manic chuckle. 'It is already in you. The Octed. The Grandsire's boon, coursing through your blood. I can sense it.'

Typhon stepped back, dismayed by the abrupt certainty in the creature's words. 'We are not the same.'

'Agreed,' it said. 'Not yet. *Not today.* But the future is the herald of greater things.' Volcral lowered its hissing voice. 'I could show you.'

'You could.' Typhon turned the thought over, thinking of the dreams that sometimes came to him, in those rare moments when his mind was at rest.

A garden of rot, dying and blooming, again and again. As a child the mechanisms of decay had always fascinated him, and now, looking into the fathomless eyes of this twisted being, that old interest was rekindling.

'All you need do is spare me,' Volcral was saying. 'You want to destroy Necare? I will aid you. Spare me and I will give you knowledge. I will open such doors to you, and when the High Overlord is dead...' The creature nodded towards the hatch that Mortarion had passed through. 'Your Reaper of Men could be set aside. Barbarus and worlds beyond could be yours to rule.'

Typhon's head snapped up. 'He is flawed. But Mortarion is my friend. I will not kill him.'

Volcral saw the mistake it had made and hastily attempted to reframe its words. 'I did not mean that—'

'Yes, you did.' A bright blur of steel came from nowhere as Typhon let the battle knife in his wrist harness fall into his hand. He swept it up and across the line of the Overlord's neck, the lethally sharp blade beheading Volcral even as it took another breath.

Eyes blinking, jaw working in the few seconds before brain-death, the creature's head dropped to the deck and rolled to Typhon's feet. Volcral's body collapsed in a welter of acrid blood, and instantly began to decompose.

The warrior crouched down and watched it happen from close at hand, the spreading rot capturing every iota of his attention.

THE DEFENDERS FOUGHT with the desperation of the truly lost. Once, Mortarion had thought that the golem-soldiers had no capacity for human emotion, and that things like fear and anxiety were cut from their patchwork forms just as they were dissected and remade. But he had killed enough of the pathetic creatures to know that was not so. The golems would never remember who or what they had been before the flesh-smiths had performed their works upon them, but they did remember *terror*. Perhaps, at the end, that was all these derisible wretches had left.

He had no pity for them, however. A moment of inattention, a single breath of anything approaching compassion for the Overlord's soldiers, would be a grave mistake. The golems swarmed around Mortarion and the rest of the Death Guard, striking at them through the thick mist with blades and shot, screaming wildly. It was kill or be killed, as it had been from the first day of the war.

His exhalations thundering inside the confines of his heavy helmet, Mortarion gave his scythe freedom to spin in flashing arcs of metal, the crescent-moon blade at the weapon's length coated with soiled blood and raw viscera. A path of corpses disappeared into the haze behind him, and one would have been able to follow it down from the toxic foothills to the clearer air of the valley. The landscape was littered with his slaughter and that of his elite warriors. The remnants of a massive pack of kill-beasts lay opened and steaming around a granite gorge nearby, the remains of a clever ambush that had almost turned back the Death Guard battle squad.

Mortarion had pushed them through it, through sheer force of will and murderous endurance. Flanked by Typhon, Rask and Lothsul on his right, with Murnau, Haznir, Ahrax and the Bitterblood to the left, his warriors formed the tip of an unbreakable spear that rose up and up, inexorably advancing towards the last stronghold of the enemy.

Below, where men could breathe the air without assistance, the greater forces of the Death Guard army led by Sune and Morarg were butchering the last of Necare's raider bands, putting every golem and patched-together monstrosity to the sword. They could not follow where Mortarion and the others were going, but they would play their part in the final battle.

For months, Mortarion had been scheming and planning, fighting along the mountain range of lethal peaks known as the Spine in fast, brutal sorties that obliterated the High Overlord's defensive network. Every link in Necare's logistic chain had been methodically shattered. His fleshworks were burned and the chattel barns razed. Outlying fortress-citadels were demolished with chemical bombs, and the network of caverns and interlinking tunnels that threaded through the Spine were sealed up.

All the other Overlords lay dead. Target by target, they had been cut down, many of them by Mortarion's own hand. Each time he had killed one of those fiends, without fail their expression had been the same – shock and bewilderment, as if they could not comprehend how the lessers they had preyed upon for countless generations were now rising up to eradicate them.

Mortarion was the harbinger of this shift in the fortunes of blighted Barbarus. His leadership and his utter inflexibility in the face of the Overlords' injustice had become the beacon that all others followed.

You are the lantern that showed us the way, Rask had once said, in a fanciful moment. *And by that light, we'll burn this world clean.*

Only one obstacle remained to that ideal. High above them in the most deadly crags, visible through fleeting gaps in the poisonous clouds, was Necare's black manse. The most forbidding of all the Overlord bastions, it bristled with weapons and shimmered behind air warped by dark sorcery. Somewhere up there, Mortarion's foster father was watching them fight his golems, silently daring his foundling son to come to his gate and make challenge.

'Soon,' Mortarion grunted, pulling his gaze back to the horde before him. A gaggle of chattering freaks with blades for hands surged towards him and he planted himself in the mud, goading them with a beckoning gesture. The scythe became a whirlwind of motion, breaking on the backswing, slashing on the fore, leaving nothing but the stillness of death in its wake.

Through the bloodstained visor slit in his helm, he saw Haznir step close, the heavyset warrior snapping open the barrel of his thunder-gun to effect a rapid combat reload. Haznir was from one of the liberated zones at the equator, and he had once been a trawlerman catching the giant crustaceans that roamed the bottoms of Barbarus' shallow, oily seas. The coil of razor netting over the shoulder of his armour was a remnant of those days, turned to new use as a weapon in the great battle.

Like the others, Haznir moved in his sealed armour with the agility and confidence of the most highly trained fighters. Each of them bore an icon or a secondary weapon that made their identity clear, but it had been by Mortarion's order that they all carried a variant of his war-scythe. With heavy, metal-shod boot steps, they continued to advance up the slope, the air-packs on their backs labouring and venting as the clockwork mechanisms within worked to keep them alive. Filtering systems scrubbed the toxic mists as much as possible, extracting every last gasp of breathable air. Mortarion's training for his elite warriors included months of forced exposure to the killing clouds at lower altitudes, enough to strengthen their resistance and build stamina. But all their previous missions had been among the mid-ranges. How long they would survive in the higher reaches remained unknown.

The gear they wore was the newest iteration from the Forge Tyrants in Safehold, and the shape and form of it had become a symbol of the war's final phase. Mortarion was wearing his armour when they entered the ruins of Heller's Cut two days ago, having retaken the township. The civilians and the camp followers that came behind his army like a wave had broken and pooled there, reclaiming the place in the name of liberty. They had cheered his name, the sound bouncing off the low clouds.

Heller's Cut had little tactical value in the scheme of things, but securing it had a personal resonance for Mortarion that was undeniable. In a very real sense, the small farming settlement had been the site of his return to the human race, and the end of his servitude to Necare and the foul kindred of the Overlords.

He remembered the moment as if it had been yesterday, his perfect recall bringing back the sense of revelation he had felt on walking into that valley; the taste of air free of poison for the first time in his living memory; the sound of human voices in laughter and song; the odours of cooking meat, sweat and stale beer. Necare had always told Mortarion that the lessers in the valleys were nothing more than fragile prey. But on that day, Mortarion had learned who his own kind really were. He felt strangely beholden to these people, compelled by a motivation that he couldn't explain, a compulsion that seemed *bred* into him. He was a warrior, and he was here to protect the humans. He might doubt anything else, but never that.

Returning to Heller's Cut also signified something else – an encroaching sense of finality. The war was in its final phase now, and everyone knew it. Either Necare's castle would be stormed and the myth of the High Overlord's immortality destroyed forever, or the battle would stagnate into an unending impasse.

The latter choice was untenable. Mortarion was not willing to suffer his foster father to live.

It had to end, *and soon*. There were disturbing rumours that had reached him in the last few days, brought by fast-rider messengers up from Safehold. People in the southern settlements spoke of peculiar lights in the night sky, up above the thick cloud mantle, and one particularly troubling account reported the sighting of a strange flying machine, like a great metal hawk. Typhon had dismissed these as the words of fools and drunkards, but Mortarion was less inclined to do so. If these were signs that Necare might still have hidden assets elsewhere on Barbarus, then it made the killing of the High Overlord all the more urgent.

Haznir's gun roared and more golems went down in sprays of arterial crimson and black, noxious matter. Calm fell briefly in the space between assaults, and he saluted his commander, tapping the smoking barrel of the weapon to the brow of his helmet. 'They keep coming,' he said, with a breathy gasp, 'and we will keep ending them.'

The Bitterblood gave a rough chuckle, his growl muffled by the bulk of his filter mask. 'Better conserve your shots, fishwife.'

'No matter if I run dry.' Haznir shrugged, and reversed his grip on his gun. 'It makes a fine club too, Skorvall.'

'Look sharp,' Mortarion grated, silencing them both. This was not a time for levity. This march was a precursor to their gravest of battles, and it would not do for his men to let their focus slip, even for an instant.

'Reaper,' called Typhon. He had gone ahead with Lothsul and Rask, and the mists parted to reveal his armoured form at the mouth of a familiar mountain pass. 'Look here. We have come full circle!'

Mortarion strode across to his comrade's side, and for a moment he couldn't place the location. Then he realised the reason why. The last time he had been here, there had been a fortress tower standing on this very spot. Now there was only a heap of blackened and blasted stones, lying where they had fallen beneath some great destructive force.

'What is this?' said Lothsul, his low and urgent voice carrying. 'There's the rusted-out wreck of a steam-crawler in the pass, looks like it was abandoned years ago.'

'It was,' said Typhon.

Mortarion stooped and picked at a piece of the broken masonry. 'This was my home. *My prison.*' He stirred the black debris, the old ashes of burned books, and uncovered broken fragments of stained glassaic, slate and brick. The fingers of his gauntlet clicked on something made from metal and he dug it out.

It was a makeshift dagger, a corroded piece of brass that had been repurposed into a knife. Mortarion held it up and examined it, remembering where he had first seen it.

On a dark and threatening night, in the hand of a desperate youth who would have died rather than surrender to the Overlords. He stood up and called out. 'Calas! I have something that belongs to you.'

Typhon turned in his direction and Mortarion tossed him the old weapon. The other warrior caught it easily and stood quietly, turning it over. With his face hidden behind his beaked helmet, it was impossible to gauge the reaction the relic brought to him. After a long moment, Typhon put the crude blade in a gear pouch on his belt and brushed black dust from his armoured fingers. 'That might have meant something, if I were one to put stock in omens and portents.'

'It means we are on the right path,' Mortarion insisted.

'Full circle, just as he said.' Lothsul nodded to himself. His words came with effort, and he went on. 'Not far now.'

But Mortarion was not listening to him any more. On the wind, he heard a faint, grating sound that seemed to come from a place deep in the coldest reaches of his childhood memory. A harsh cadence of razor laughter, a sound like serrated edges dragging over one another, or the wings of corpse-eater insects droning in dull synchrony.

He looked up and a jolt of new adrenaline shocked through his body.

Mortarion saw the spiked balls of fire describing their high, narrow arcs through the air a split second before the keening scream of their descent reached his ears. Dozens of flaming comets were falling from the high crags above, hurled from the slings of the steam-trebuchets that lined the battlements of Necare's distant castle.

'Scatter!' he roared, bursting into motion, sprinting away from the ruins of his former domicile. Suddenly it was all too clear how Mortarion's former fortress had been demolished so completely. He imagined that bombarding it had been one of Necare's first acts after his rebellion, all those years ago.

The first salvo of fireballs hit the ground and turned the earth into a hellscape. Burning liquid pitch-blend spattered over everything, lighting streaks of flame in all directions. And impossibly, there seemed to be things *inside* the explosive payloads. Mortarion beheld a human-like figure stagger out of the cracked, disintegrating remnants of a fireball, as if emerging from a burning shell. It too was aflame, clawing madly towards the nearest target.

That target was Haznir, and the burning man fell upon him, jabbing and tearing at his armour with blackened, sizzling claws. The Bitterblood's machine-hand jerked as he fired his blunderbuss and blasted the thing off his comrade, but the damage was done. Haznir rolled over clumsily in the mud, swatting at himself in a vain attempt to douse the fires on his gear. Puffs of air escaped his armour where the talons had punctured the metal.

Mortarion killed two more of the burning figures in quick succession. His war-scythe sang through smoke and haze, and whatever dark science animated the attackers was immediately dispelled with each kill, their bodies flashing into ashy flakes as they died.

'Another barrage!' shouted Ahrax, and they were his last words. As if guided there by an unseen hand, a new fireball crashed down upon him, turning the warrior, armour and all, into a blackened streak across the muddy ground.

More hooked trails of smoke blazed down from up above, and now

Mortarion was absolutely certain he could hear the mockery of his foster-father in every tortured screech of seared air.

He rocked forward off his position and called out. 'Typhon! Skorvall! With me!' He pointed his scythe into the mists, at the winding path that led towards the high crags. 'We must be swift and take the pace. They cannot kill what they cannot hit!' In his mind's eye, Mortarion was already planning their advance. Whatever means Necare was using to target the trebuchets, there was still a delay in the firing of them. If the Death Guard could move fast, they might be able to stay ahead of the bombardment...

But then he saw Typhon standing before him, and the look in his old friend's eyes told him what would be said next.

'No,' his second countered. 'Brother, we have to fall back!'

The suggestion of retreat ignited a towering rage in Mortarion. '*Never!*' he bellowed, storming away from the next cascade of hits. 'Not now, not when we are so close!'

'I am the arrogant fool, not you!' Typhon shot back. 'Don't lose sight now, Mortarion! Necare *wants* you to be angry – he wants you to react instead of think!' The other warrior jabbed a finger at the carnage around them. 'Ahrax is gone! Haznir will suffocate before we can get him off this blasted mountain! We will be dead before we can reach our objective!'

Belatedly, Mortarion realised that his breaths were coming hard and rough, and he looked down to see that his own armour was peppered with impact damage, the undersuit beneath it marked with tears from shrapnel hits.

'*No,*' he spat, even as the red rumble of another fiery rain bore down on the squad. Mortarion saw a fireball hurtling directly towards him, the roar of it ringing in his ears. He swung his mighty war-scythe around in a shrieking arc, the blade at the head of the heavy shaft connecting with the infernal bolide mass a split second before it would have struck him.

The creature inside the flaming shell died in the impact with a

bubbling scream, but Mortarion did not hear it. Momentarily deaf-
ened by the thunderous detonation of the fireball, he was torn from the
ground where he stood and thrown like a child's doll, across the black
earth and far down the slope of the mountain pass. Mortarion's hood
was torn open and his helmet wrenched from his head by the force of
the blast, a shock that would have broken the neck of any other man.

He crashed down amid a spray of cracked stone slick with ash-
coloured lichen, skidding to a halt and recovering in a rapid twist of
motion. Robbed of his war mask, the stench of the poison haze filled
his lungs and he fought down a gag reflex. He had not taken an unfiltered breath of the air of this place since leaving it on that fateful night,
and the raw toxins made his gorge rise.

Shaking off the moment, he saw Typhon come staggering towards
him. Following close at hand was the Bitterblood, who worked with
Rask to carry the wheezing form of Haznir between them. Lothsul and
the other survivors came in their wake. Each man was injured, each
one's armour damaged and ragged.

'We can go no further,' Typhon gasped, as he came closer. 'If we pull
back, we can regroup, return with more men...'

Mortarion could not countenance a reply, unwilling to speak lest his
fury be unleashed by the act. He turned his back on his warriors and
trudged away, never meeting their gazes as he put his face towards the
clearer skies of the valley below.

A brooding, seething rage radiated from every atom of his being, a
fury stoked higher and higher by the warring voices in his heart that
left Mortarion torn between the need for revenge and the compulsion of duty.

In that moment, a piece of him *hated* Typhon and the others, hated
the lessers and all they were as much as he detested the Overlords. He
despised them for their weaknesses, for being unable to fight until he
had shown them how, for their frail human bodies that fell apart at
the first touch of the toxic mists.

Why could they not be the same as he was? He was cursed with ability, stronger and faster than any man who walked on Barbarus, quicker and keener of mind than any one of their doleful numbers. The others dragged him down, made him slow. Kept him from the one thing he wanted above all else – the death of Necare.

But that rage and frustration pulled against an urge that he could not express, could not fathom. *I am not like them*, he told himself. *I am no freak of nature, no Overlord experiment grown out of control.* Mortarion knew, as surely as night knew the day, that there was a reason to his existence. If there was a fate that had shaped him, then that purpose could only be one thing.

I am a weapon for the war. It was the only truth that fitted his reality. *But what war, if not this one?*

He walked on, haunted by the possibility and the image of Necare watching him from on high. The Overlord's laughter followed them down into the lowlands, biting the air and echoing at their backs with every leaden footstep they took.

WHEN THEY REACHED the site of the battle they had left behind at the foot of the mountain, there was only the silence of the enemy dead, and a single scout who sat waiting atop a blasted granite tor.

She stood as they approached, and Mortarion watched the passage of emotions across her face. He knew her; it was the woman who had brought him water on his return to Safehold years before, once the child whose life he had saved in a rain-soaked field of hardwheat.

She gave the salute of a mailed fist. 'Mortarion. I was ordered to wait for you. I have a message from Caipha Morarg.'

He looked around, scanning the bodies of the dead golems. They were shredded, torn remnants that appeared to have been blown apart by fusillades of pinpoint fire, from weapons far more powerful and precise than those wielded by the Death Guard. 'Speak it,' he said.

The scout pointed towards the horizon, and the distant glitter of torchlight where the ruins of Heller's Cut still stood. 'Our forces returned to the settlement to regroup after...' She paused, trying to find the words.

'After the Hawk came.' The scout pointed up at the sky. 'In a single swooping pass, it finished them for us. And then there was a voice, and...' She trailed off again, her gaze distant.

'The Hawk,' repeated Rask. 'You mean the flying machine that was observed in the outlands?'

The scout nodded. 'I can't tell you. Words... are not enough. You need to see it for yourself,' she told them. Her eyes were wide and there was a strange flutter in her voice. 'Then you'll understand.'

THE CRAFT THE scout called 'the Hawk' sat on the ruins of the crop fields out past the tumbledown walls of the blasted township, and it was like nothing Calas Typhon had ever seen before.

He knew machines – steam-powered war engines with great piston-legs or rattling tracks had been common enough among the battle order of the Overlords – but never anything like this. The low and eternally lethal skies of Barbarus made any attempt to achieve aerial superiority a foolish endeavour doomed to failure, and so conflicts were always fought down in the mud, where opponents could look one another in the face.

Even as the Hawk sat at rest, silent and still in the middle of a circle of burned grasses, it appeared to be flying. Sleek lines of bright, polished gunmetal and shimmering gold glistened in the weak daylight. The fuselage resembled something carved by a masterful artisan, the bullet-shaped main hull blending smoothly into wide, swept-forward wings and ventral lifting surfaces. Dense lines of ornate engraving covered every part of the Hawk's visible exterior, and as they approached, Typhon picked out what appeared to be writing in the old Gothic style along the wings.

Haltingly, he read the words aloud. '*Ave... Imper... Ator.*'

'Yes,' said Mortarion, walking at his side. His old friend was one of the few men learned enough to recognise the symbols for what they meant, and his tone made it clear how wary he was because of them.

Close by, Murnau faltered in his pace, his face a map of fascination as he beheld the golden vessel. He started towards the craft in interest, then caught himself and looked back to his commander. For his part Mortarion said nothing, and kept walking.

Still, Typhon slowed his march to take in as much as he could about the Hawk. He saw that a few bolder souls had dared to venture from the ruined settlement to take a closer look, but they were held back by a line of Death Guard regulars serving as a cordon. Typhon's fellow warriors were clearly supposed to be watching the vessel for any sign of subterfuge, but it was clear that many of them were as captivated as the civilians and camp followers. The elegant, teardrop weapons cupolas visible on the Hawk's fuselage made it clear that the craft needed no one to protect it, and Typhon briefly dwelled on the dark thought of what would happen to those men if the vessel chose to open fire. He remembered the obliterated remains of the golems and frowned.

The scout walked a few paces behind him, muttering to herself, but Typhon ignored her. Instead, he applied himself to considering a tactical analysis of the craft. There appeared to be only one way aboard, through a hatch that opened like a yawning mouth at the vessel's arrowhead prow. An odd heat-haze shimmer surrounded the Hawk, and upon the ramp leading up to the hatch, Typhon caught a flash of movement. A human figure in golden armour with a high, conical helm and carrying a great halberd moved on the threshold, then vanished inside.

Something seemed off, and it took Typhon a moment to understand the reason why. He had misjudged the scale of the figure in gold. Rather than the height of a normal man, the wielder of the spear would have to be at least as tall as Mortarion. He shot a sideways glance at the Reaper, and Typhon saw that he too had noticed the giant in the sky-craft.

At the perimeter of the township proper, they were greeted by other troopers and auxiliaries who took away poor, dying Haznir to give him aid – as pointless as that was. It was a marvel that Typhon's comrade in arms had lived long enough to reach the valley floor, a testament to Death Guard resilience. But Haznir was a dead man walking, as all who looked upon him knew. At least he would perish among kins-men, if that counted for anything.

The matter seemed secondary, however, as did all else but the presence of the new arrival. Those the morose returning fighters met in Heller's Cut should have been asking them about the failed assault on Necare's citadel. Instead, everyone was animated with stories about the arrival of the Hawk and a man they were calling the Newcomer.

One of them was Raphim, an armsman from a warband that Typhon had once trained, who fell in step as they marched on. 'This is turn-ing into a day for wonders,' said the younger warrior. 'When the Hawk came, we feared it was some new Overlord weapon. But not so! First the Newcomer aided us in ending the battle on the plains and then he brought us both supplies and medicines...' He spoke quickly, like an excited child. 'He has sciences unknown to us. New ways of healing. And food, he brought food!' Raphim pointed towards the follower camp. Typhon was aware that many of the non-combatants had been suffering from malnutrition in these last days of the conflict, holding on to the hope that once Necare was dead liberation would bring succour to all.

'Such generosity,' growled Mortarion. 'And what does this stranger want in return?'

'He talked about salvation. He said there are people like us out beyond the clouds... On countless other worlds. All united in a great empire.' Raphim shook his head as if he could scarcely process the idea of it. 'He said he will give us whatever we need to take back our world, even remake it if we so desire...'

Typhon watched the progression of Mortarion's ill mood, growing darker with every word that fell from Raphim's lips.

'An outsider bearing gifts drops from the clouds on the eve of our most testing battle,' said the Reaper, ice forming on the words. 'Am I the only one who distrusts this with every living fibre of his being?' By the end of the sentence, Mortarion was almost snarling. Raphim recoiled, lost for a reply.

'Where is this Newcomer?' said Typhon. His own curiosity was rising, but he kept it hidden. The younger Death Guard pointed towards the town's dilapidated lodge hall, visible through the mass of a whispering crowd that had gathered around it. Whoever this stranger was, they all wanted to catch a glimpse of him.

Mortarion grunted and set off towards the lodge, scattering those not quick enough to get out of his way. Typhon and the others followed, and Rask lowered his voice so that his words would not carry. 'I know that look, Calas. The Reaper of Men is angry enough to cut stone with those eyes.'

'Can you blame him? This was meant to be a day of deliverance for Barbarus. Mortarion has fought since the moment he freed me to liberate this world, but we have been driven back in failure only to find this?' He nodded towards the lodge. 'A man from the sky who chooses this exact moment to overshadow all that the Reaper has done for our people.'

'Can't be an Overlord trick,' said Rask. 'Those bastards don't have the patience for anything other than open cruelty.' He paused. 'There is the possibility this stranger may be what he appears... Never forget, the stories say that the Reaper himself fell from the skies as a foundling.'

'The thought did occur to me,' Typhon admitted.

Ahead of them, Mortarion put out his fist and slammed open the doors of the lodge, and his warriors hurried to follow him inside.

All within fell silent at the arrival of the Reaper. Seated at a table near the intact edge of the lodge, Typhon saw leaders from the civilian support cadre, along with the senior Death Guard warriors Mortarion had left in charge in his stead. And with them was...

A stranger...

For the briefest moment, the man that Raphim had called the Newcomer raked his gaze over Typhon, and it lingered there. He found himself frozen in place, such was the potency of the gaze. Dark eyes that were clear and fathomless, yet ancient with it, held him in check. The warrior suddenly felt as if he were transparent. He held his breath and there was a tension in the muscles of his legs – an instinctive compulsion to *kneel* – that he had to consciously fight off.

Those eyes were framed in a patrician face with bronzed skin like hard leather, and sable hair hung down to the Newcomer's shoulders. Then that gaze moved on, and found the Reaper of Men. A peculiar, conflicted aspect passed over the stranger's expression. There was sorrow in it, but also warmth. Anticipation, but also reluctance.

The stranger rose slowly as Mortarion came to a halt in the middle of the room, and Typhon saw a broad, muscled frame supporting heavy golden armour that was just as ornate as the scrollwork on the sky-craft outside. Upon it, designs of brazen lightning bolts and the stark motif of a two-headed eagle glittered in the dimness, and despite the obvious weight of the man's battleplate, he moved easily. His motions were fluid and graceful, but there was a coiled power there.

This Newcomer appeared, in every way that Typhon might have reckoned it, to be the polar opposite of any Barbarun-born. All of them were gaunt and pale, even the biggest of their kind like Skorvall, their physical aspect a legacy of generations amid the life-sapping toxicity of their home world. And yet, there was one with whom the stranger did share similarity.

Typhon glanced towards Mortarion, and he saw it. Subtle, and not immediately visible to the eye, but definitely tangible. There was a resemblance in the line of the jaw, in the way the Reaper carried himself. Something ephemeral but all too real connected Mortarion to this stranger, and Rask's comment about the Reaper's shrouded origins sounded in Typhon's thoughts once more.

If Mortarion shared this insight, he showed no outward sign of it. 'Who are you?' he demanded. 'What do you want on my world?'

'I am… a friend,' said the stranger, his voice calm and resonant. Now he was on his feet, Typhon noted the presence of a huge, wide-bladed sword that rested in a scabbard at his hip. The weapon was easily the height of a lesser, chased through with jewels and precious metals, but its mass and obvious balance made it clear the blade was not just for show. 'I have come to Barbarus in search of noble souls,' the stranger added. 'In search of *you*.'

'In the name of your... empire?'

'Indeed.' The Newcomer nodded, and Typhon shifted slightly.

Something about this stranger made Typhon want to keep him at a distance, and the Death Guard moved so that Mortarion and Rask were between them. For his part, Rask looked on dumbfounded, his hands clasped into fists.

'You have been orphaned from the Imperium for far too long, this world and thousands more,' continued the stranger. 'Our lost kindred. It is time to return to the fold. And I promise you, glory and prosperity await. It will be the dawning of a new age.'

Typhon found it hard to look away from the stranger. His words were mesmeric, and they seemed to echo through to him alone. A powerful, magnetic aura surrounded the Newcomer, and it became clear why so many of the Barbaruns had been quick to welcome him into their midst. He couldn't explain how, but Typhon had the very real sense that he was only seeing a fragment of the stranger's true aspect. There was far more beneath, and he was afraid to look deeper.

'We don't want your glory, outsider,' retorted Mortarion. The antagonism crackling away below the surface of his words rose. 'Nor your charity, or your Imperium.'

'Are you certain of that?' The figure in gold armour cocked his head. 'Our technology can turn your marshlands into verdant fields. Strip the poison from your air. We can heal those you would consider beyond help... Just as my servitors are doing now, with your friend Haznir.' He nodded towards the walls, and Typhon wondered how the stranger could know Haznir's name, let alone that he had been fatally wounded.

'Barbarus has endured alone for centuries beneath the talons of our oppressors!' The Reaper let his anger flare. 'Where were you then?'

'It is my great regret that it took me this long to find you... Mortarion.' The stranger gave a rueful smile. 'This never gets any easier.' Then the smile faded. 'Trust me when I say, I can give you understanding of your own origins. I can help you defeat the Overlords and purge the last of their ruinous taint from this world.'

'I have no interest in where I was *birthed*, it matters nothing to me,' Mortarion said, seething with cold fury. 'Barbarus is where I was *born*, it is where I was made *whole*.' He gestured to his warriors. 'The Death Guard are the only kindred I have ever known. My unbroken blades. And by our hand alone shall justice be delivered to the Overlords.' He turned away. 'You're not needed here. Go back to your pretty bird and fly away.'

'With respect,' said the stranger, 'I would contest your assertion. Your comrades here have told me much of the war you have fought. And while there are a great many victories to be lauded at the Death Guard's banner, the High Overlord still lives. You and your elite have been unable to reach the tower where he abides, is that not so?'

Mortarion's grip tightened on the shaft of his war-scythe. 'Necare's fate is sealed. He will perish soon enough.'

'By your hand?' The Newcomer asked the question without weight.

'It will be so!'

'If you are certain of the outcome, then I would put to you a challenge.' Spreading his hands, the stranger took in the room. 'You lead these people, Mortarion, and if you truly wish for Barbarus to be left undisturbed, I will respect your wishes.' His level gaze settled on the Reaper of Men once more. 'But only if you prove worthy to make that decision. If you alone defeat Necare, the Imperium of Man will withdraw from this system and never return.'

'And if he does not?' Typhon was almost shocked by the sound of his own voice.

'Then this world rejoins the great tapestry of humankind, and Mortarion and his Death Guard swear allegiance to me.' The stranger let his words sink in. 'Will you accept?'

'Aye,' growled the Reaper, and he strode out of the lodge and into the thin rain that had begun to fall.

Typhon raced after him, catching his friend as he marched away across the muddy square. 'Brother!' he snapped. 'There must be another way... You cannot go up there alone.'

'I will take fresh armour from the Forge Tyrants,' Mortarion told him. 'With no one else to slow me down, I can climb to Necare's citadel before night falls. I know the pass better than he realises. I can do this.'

Typhon grabbed Mortarion's arm and pulled him to a halt, earning a savage glare for his temerity. 'Why? Why are you allowing this stranger to goad you into this? What is he to you?'

'I am *worthy*.' The Reaper shook off his grip and glowered at him. 'I will prove it once and for all. Be ready,' he replied. 'When I return, everything will change.'

Typhon stood in the downpour as Mortarion walked on, and amid the hissing of the rain he felt a distant, droning pressure in his thoughts that seemed to come from nowhere. He called out, but the words tasted odd in his mouth, as though someone else were speaking them for him. 'Take care, Reaper. Do not stray from the path.'

SIX

Final Gambit
The Naming of Names
Origin

GARRO SWEPT HIS sword around in a shining arc of wicked steel, slashing open the writhing maggot creatures as they burst from the ground. Fanged maws dripped acidic venom, and those among Malcador's Chosen who moved too slowly found themselves falling to savage, burning bites from the blind monstrosities.

The legionary drew back, casting about the battle zone, catching sight of Helig Gallor in the far distance, engaged in a fierce firefight against high odds. All around, the sky was smoky with the swarms of carrion flies, and their worm-like kindred were quickly overrunning everything on the ground. The remaining traitors, ragged and bloody in their corrupted war-plate, moved in hectic, frenzied surges. So far, none of them had been able to reach the gates at the foot of the White Mountain, but it would only need one to make it through the gauntlet.

Vox communications were useless, smothered by unknown jamming, thwarting any call for reinforcements. The same blanket of nullification prevented Garro from signalling Rubio and the Sigillite.

This will end on the enemy's terms, Garro thought sourly. *They have the numbers, and this fortress was built for concealment, not strength.*

But the horror here had only just begun. Where the dead had fallen, Garro saw the maggots boring into the still-warm corpses and his lip curled in disgust. At first, he thought the vile creatures were making a meal of the dead, but then one of the bodies shook like a victim of palsy and began to move again. The head of a fallen Guardsman lolled forward as he dragged himself up. His jaw wide open, a thick maggot-head emerged through his mouth and probed at the air.

Others of the fallen twitched and reanimated. Sickened, Garro turned, hoping he would not see what he knew had to come next.

He was not granted that respite. Macer Varren's broken body was already on its feet, and beneath the flesh of the dead World Eaters legionary, fat serpentine shapes pulsed and shifted as they consumed him from the inside out. Before Garro could utter a warning, the shambling nondead broke into a chaotic, pell-mell sprint, virtually hurling itself at the nearest of the defenders – Garviel Loken.

Engaged in a firefight, Loken did not see the dead man hurtling towards him until he was unable to evade the attack.

Garro spun *Libertas* in his hand, shifting his weight to break into a run, ready to aid the younger legionary, but then a dark mass conglomerated out of the corner of his eye, a black buzzing cloak upon the shoulders of a mutant.

'*Do you turn your back on me, captain?*' droned the Lord of Flies. '*You have yet to pay for your debt.*' The rusted blade of the plague knife plunged for Garro's throat, and he parried it, razor-sharp flecks of splintered metal breaking off at the impact and splitting the air.

For now, Loken was on his own.

HIS ATTACKER HAD no weapons in his hands, and that was what saved Loken in the first seconds of the attack. Had there been blades, the matter would have ended differently.

The maddened, shambling thing that had been Macer Varren held its mouth open in a silent scream. The legionary's head lay cocked at a terrible angle, the bones of his neck ground to fragments in the claws of the creature that had killed him. A wild torrent of punches rained down on Loken, each one hitting with force enough to stagger him. Reflexively, he tried to disengage, but the dead man would not relent and kept up the blows, robbing Loken of the ability to do anything but react.

He kept his guard up, unable to find the space for a sword-strike, instead flashing back to the rote training drilled into him through countless hours in duelling cages and fighting rings. Loken weathered the hits, holding on for the moment when his opponent tired or hesitated – but Varren, or whatever was left of him, did not.

It was only when Loken's attacker suddenly changed tactics that he was able to snatch a heartbeat to act. Varren's blood-caked gauntlets went from punches to clawing and clutching, the metal fingers grabbing at any exposed seam of Loken's battle armour, twisting and tearing as he tried to rip it open.

Locked in a violent embrace, their faces barely a hand's span apart, Loken stared into the dead man's dimmed gaze and saw a mindless animal snarling back at him. Bloated serpentine things slithered in the crop of Varren's reanimated flesh, driving the body forward on violent impulse. It was a dishonour for a warrior to be used like this, becoming a vessel for raw insanity.

That thought had barely taken shape in Loken's mind before he recalled the shadow of another soul lost to unspeakable rage – his own.

'Varren?' He shouted the World Eater's name. '*Macer!*' Loken struggled, wrestling with the other warrior. 'Are you still in there, cousin?'

Once, Loken had fallen into the pit of madness and lost himself there. He felt a strange, powerful jolt of empathy for the former World Eaters legionary. And with it, the shame at being forced to witness this degradation.

Varren's gauntlets snatched at Loken's chest-plate, snagging on his ammunition bandolier, then found his throat and began to squeeze.

STEEL AND CHITIN sparked from one another as Garro and the Lord of Flies set to their melee. It was difficult for *Libertas* to find purchase on the creature's armoured hide, and the blade skipped off the curved shell of bony matter, gouging out black chips but losing the angle to make a deeper cut.

Garro fought to deflect his foe's plague-ridden dagger, knocking it aside time and again. He knew that it would only take the slightest nick of the polluted weapon's edge to foul his bloodstream with the profane chimeric infection lurking upon it. The Lord of Flies buzzed and cackled, enjoying the play of the fight, goading him.

'What do you want here, fiend?' Garro shouted. 'Why do you plague me, again and again?'

'I am a harbinger of the Octed,' it replied. *'But in truth? It gives me pleasure to torment you, Death Guard.'* The creature's giant claw-hand clacked together in a constant metronomic rhythm as it tried, almost of its own accord, to grasp Garro's sword and turn it out of his grip. *'He is close,'* droned the swarm-voice. *'Very close now.'*

Garro did not answer, but he instinctively knew who the creature was referring to. *Mortarion, the Reaper of Men.*

The primarch of the Death Guard and Garro's turncoat brethren would be at the forefront of Horus' invasion of Terra; it was an inevitability. The XIV Legion were the inexorable hammer, falling hard in every war they had ever fought, and this one would be no different.

'He has already accepted the Mark,' said the creature. *'There is still time, Nathaniel. You can return to your Legion. You can rejoin us.'*

'My Legion is *dead*,' Garro spat back, jamming his sword in to lock against the claw, his other hand holding off the dagger.

'Death means nothing to those blessed by the Grandfather. You have seen that with your own eyes. You see it before you now.' The mutant's foul breath curdled in the cold. *'Straight-Arrow Garro. Always apart, even when you were a battle-captain. But when the Legion emerges reborn, all those old divisions will be swept away forever. Terran and Barbarun, Dusk Raider and Death Guard, traitor and loyalist. Those terms will mean nothing. We will all be united under the Mark. The three. The seven. The whole.'* The creature struggled to disengage, but Garro held firm. *'We will never know weakness. We will never die.'*

'All things must die,' said Garro, and as he uttered the words, it was as if a great weight detached from his soul. 'That is how we measure what we are. What we do.' He gritted his teeth. 'The struggle only matters if we are *mortal.*'

Humming laughter surrounded him, the foetid, hissing glee of the Lord of Flies crawling over Garro's exposed skin. *'I will grant the mercy of killing you myself, Nathaniel. It will be a gift. For if not I, it will be his hand that claims you... and that would be an eternity of pain.'*

The claw pressed forward, slow and relentless, pushing *Libertas* back against Garro's exposed neck.

'I HAVE... SEEN that... darkness.' Loken forced out the words, each syllable an effort. 'I have been in the place beyond death.'

Varren's hands trembled as they closed ever tighter, and the squirming forms beneath his skin seemed to go into a kind of frenzy. Congealing blood oozed from the dead man's nostrils and wept in black rivulets from the corners of his eyes.

'There is no disgrace in the fear... The fear of that void.' Loken dug into memories he wished never to face again, letting the truth of his words be strengthened by the recollection. On Isstvan III he had died – or as near as be damned – and in the madness of it, rose again as the broken soul called Cerberus.

Macer Varren had been there. He had seen Loken at his worst, his lowest ebb, when he was fit only to be put down like some crazed wild animal.

'Do... you... remember?' he choked.

A scream – deep and primal, more the roar of a fatally wounded predator than a human – tore itself free of Varren's scarred lips in a bloody froth, and he released Loken in a jerking spasm of motion. Before the Knight-Errant could stop it from happening, Varren ripped Loken's bandolier off his armour, pulling a handful of krak grenades from it.

Bellowing, raging, biting and thrashing at himself, Varren staggered away. He clutched the rattling grenades to his chest in a strangely protective manner, even as the fat maggots eating him alive sensed the danger and burst forth. Slick with legionary blood, the eyeless things emerged from his skin and keened like sirens.

The arming pins from the grenades all came free at once, and Varren fell to his knees, fighting to complete his last act as a warrior of the Imperium of Man.

Loken raised his arm to shield his face and sank low as the ripple detonation blasted a crater in the frost-rimed ground, marking the World Eaters' sacrifice with a storm of fire.

'Submit.'

The command beat at Garro, coming from all directions at once. He hardened his heart against the droning voice.

'Accept the Mark,' it shrieked. *'Take the Cups. One last time, drink deep and know true power.'*

He stiffened, strengthening his stance as best he could, but Garro's augmetic leg was starting to vibrate as the servos were overtaxed. If the metal failed him, the Lord of Flies would impale him on his own sword, and the end Garro so desperately sought would be lost.

No. I will not accept that. I will not fall here!

'If you refuse, you will perish in agony undreamt of,' it told him. *'When you fled like a coward, every warrior you left behind in the Seventh Great Company was punished for your transgression. Reviled and hated, they were. Your castigation will be the same, magnified a thousandfold!'*

'Damn you,' Garro snarled, recalling the faces of those legionaries. He knew that not every one of them would have been swift to fall to Horus' rebellion, and to know that those resolute sons had suffered in his stead cut him to the core. 'And damn Mortarion for walking a path that I will never follow!'

'So be it.' The Lord of Flies shrouded the sky with its swarm-cloak, moving in for the kill. *'Die knowing your defiance means nothing. Your shambling corpse will be fodder for the cannons–'*

'Garro!' He heard the cry from Loken, and from the corner of his eye he saw a blur of bright metal as the other Knight-Errant hurled his blade into the air, sending it across the distance between them.

'Defiance is everything,' Garro retorted, and in a savage burst of motion, he used his full reserves of will to force away the creature's dagger-hand. His hyper-boosted inhuman reflexes enabled Garro to snatch the thrown sword from the air before it fell beyond his grasp, and the momentum of the motion transferred into a narrow, fast swing.

The pace of the fight, briefly locked in steel, now opened wide and to Garro's advantage. *Libertas* flicked up and Loken's blade came down over it, to form a cross with the Lord of Flies trapped between its axes.

The creature tried once more to stab him, but Garro did not hesitate, and closed the swords as if they were a set of shears. The head of the freakish beast was thrown into the air on a jet of oily vitae, and into the screaming mass of its attendant swarm.

And yet, it did not die. The decapitated body stumbled away, the great claw clutching at nothing, the plague dagger jabbing at empty air in mad repetition of the body's last actions.

'End it,' snarled Garro, as Loken and Gallor came around to flank him, their bolters rising to the ready. The other Knights-Errant opened fire on full automatic setting, committing an overkill salvo of mass-reactive rounds into the thing. The corpus of insects and filth that made up its form were obliterated, along with the corrupted remnants of whatever remained of poor Meric Voyen.

The roaring boom of gunfire echoed for long seconds over the tainted wilderness, drowning out the panicked howls of the surviving attackers and the endless buzzing of the constant swarm. Garro speared Loken's sword into the ground and left it for him, marching to the great blackened smear on the snow where gobbets of torn, despoiled flesh lay strewn about.

Seared, weeping maggots and colonies of crawling things slithered away as he approached. They congregated around the remains, and the swarm's metal-grinder scream grew in pitch as it came down in a mass.

For a moment, Garro thought the insects were eating what was left; but then the fleshy rags swelled and burst open with new, sudden growth. The killing ground became a garden of diseased meat, sinew and budding bone, pieces of it slipping together like the parts of a puzzle made from butcher block offal. Questing strands of sinew found one another and pulled tight.

'It's forming again,' he shouted, fatigue and disgust warring with his resignation and his anger.

'I won't have that,' said Malcador. The Sigillite emerged through the smoke and haze to stand beside Garro, walking awkwardly with his staff in motion, as if it were pulling him forward.

Behind him, Garro saw Gallor and Loken greeting Rubio as he walked from the great gate at the White Mountain's base. The Librarian seemed haunted, but his comrade's bearing was not of the greatest import at this moment.

Garro looked back, and saw that the reassembly of the creature was taking true shape, amassing a torso, an arm and the beginnings of a head.

Malcador gave him a sideways look. 'I would advise you to shield your eyes.' He stepped one pace ahead of the Knight-Errant and lowered his staff so that the burning basket atop it pointed towards what was left of the enemy.

It happened without sound – or perhaps it was a side-effect, an inversion of the laws of nature created by the colossal discharge of such arcane elemental forces.

The light of a miniature star burned in the basket atop Malcador's staff, emerging in a blinding stellar radius around the sculpted golden aquila at its centre. The overpressure made the scars on Garro's face ache like they were freshly cut. Then the noiseless wave of absolute energy burst outward, washing across the wastelands and destroying whatever it touched.

The swarm, the lamprey-maggots and their half-resurrected master became brief charcoal sketches against the whiteness, and whatever twisted spirits inhabited them were thrown back into the warp. The lackeys who had swallowed the propaganda of Horus' agents and the Alpha Legion's corruptors were atomised in the same nuclear fire, and what remained of the crashed aeronefs boiled into plasmatic vapour along with them.

At length, the light died and the stabbing pain in Garro's vision gradually abated. Despite the nictating membranes in his genhanced eyes, he ruefully accepted that he should have heeded Malcador's warning. Blinking away the purple smears of after-image on his retinas, he looked out and saw the landscape denuded of ice and snow. Before him now was a barren zone, the liquefied granite like heaps of molten black wax, sizzling and settling as rain began to fall from the sky.

'I didn't kill it,' Malcador told him, with a weary sigh. 'I've learned that you can't eradicate them, not really. Not in the sense that a warrior would understand.'

Garro jutted his chin at the black iron staff. 'Give me a weapon like that and I will try, as many times as I need to.'

'It's more of a tool than a weapon,' said the Sigillite, before he caught himself and fell silent, showing a thin smile. He started again. 'We are finished here, and we should court no further delay. You and the others will return with me to the Imperial Palace.' Malcador turned back towards the mountain. 'With luck, the rest of the incursions will have been put down by the time we land.'

'The rest of them?' Garro looked back at the cooling, crackling stone.

'Do try to keep up, Nathaniel.'

Garro scowled and fell in step with the Sigillite. He nodded towards the gate. 'I take it you found the answers you needed?'

For the first time, Garro noticed the dried blood marring the front of Malcador's robes. He could smell the faint odour of it, his olfactory senses picking out the particular scent of human vitae.

'Don't concern yourself,' replied the Sigillite. 'The matter is concluded.'

'And the Sisters?'

'Their battle is ended. The Warmaster has played his last shrouded pieces before committing to the endgame, at the cost of their lives. We're walking through his final gambit.'

Garro couldn't stop himself from looking up into the grey sky. 'He's on his way.'

'That has been true for seven hard years,' Malcador noted. 'Longer than that, even.'

Garro's gaze fell and found Rubio. The psyker turned away, but not so swiftly that he didn't see that haunted look again. 'What happened in there?'

'I told you not to concern yourself.' Malcador raised his voice to be heard over the rumble of thruster jets, as a slate-grey Thunderhawk descended from the White Mountain's landing bay to touch down beside them.

Garro kept watching Rubio. 'I know a grave wound when I see it.'

'He's more resilient than you give him credit for,' said the Sigillite, as the aircraft's drop-ramp fell open. 'You all are. That's why you were chosen.'

THE FLIGHT PASSED in the blurry, time-shifted state of the catalepsean phase, as Rubio allowed his brain implant to enter the half-woke state that was a legionary's closest approximation of sleep. Eternally conscious, it was in this demi-aware mode that he rested and gathered himself.

Partly, Rubio entered the trance because his body was fatigued and he had learned through bitter experience to snatch rest wherever he could; but he also dropped away from his fellow Knights-Errant so he could look inward and probe the gap in his memory.

The void was seamless and perfect, so firmly threaded into the weave of his experiences that it appeared as if it had always been there. Already, Rubio found himself subconsciously accepting the new pattern of memories, and he had the unpleasant feeling that in days from now, he would not see anything amiss at all.

Malcador's bright telepathic presence hovered on the edges of his preternatural sense, a far sun in an inconstant sky. He had no means to prove that the Sigillite had done something to him back at the White Mountain... But in a strange way, that absence of evidence *was* the proof. Only a near-sublime psyche as powerful as Malcador's could have re-sculpted a consciousness and left virtually no trace.

Rubio thought about the missing moments and wondered what else the Sigillite might have taken – or left behind.

His sense of time shifted, returning to normal synchrony, and Rubio absorbed the conversations going on around him, as multiple voices overlapped across the vox-channels.

The war-to-come had touched places other than the White Mountain. Reports of insurrectionist supporters, fifth columnists and sapper attacks filled the communications net. Some of the flashpoints were low-scale affairs left to the Imperial Army, the Adeptus Arbites or local city watches to deal with – riots that metastasised out of so-called peaceful demonstrations against the strictures put in place by Lord Dorn's edicts of defence, and the like. But others had the character of carefully planned sabotage and covert strikes. There had been armed assaults on the starports of the Nihon archipelago, running battles on the Atalantic Scarp, terrorist bombings in half a dozen hive cities. And amid these conventional attacks, there were reports of the uncanny and the impossible.

Every one spoke of *the flies*. Swarms appearing where none should have been possible.

Months of searching for and neutralising such things had given Rubio an ear for these phenomena. The tone of voice of common men confronted by unreal terrors had a particular cadence that he had learned to listen for.

These sort of engagements were where the Knights-Errant were dispatched, but now more than ever Rubio was coming to the belief that their numbers and their weapons were not enough to stem the tide. The Thunderhawk landed hard on one of the Palace's upper pads and Rubio chose to be the last to disembark, prizing his silence. As he exited the ship with the crew-servitors trailing behind him, he took in the scene. Other ships of similar tonnage, along with bristling gunships and Aquila-class shuttles, were crowded on the pad, each besieged by a gang of minor mech-adepts busily patching damage or preparing the craft to go back out into the field. Armsmen in the carapace gear of the Chosen patrolled the edges of the great platform, facing out over the capped mountain, the elegant towers, and far below, the shanty-city of the common-folk.

But what held Rubio's attention was the number of figures in storm-shade legionary battleplate, standing to attention as the Sigillite moved among them.

In all the time since that fateful day on Calth – *the memory made him wince, for some reason* – Rubio had never seen more than four Knights-Errant in the same place, at the same time. Along with himself, Loken, Garro and Gallor, there were eleven of them.

He had always suspected that there were more than he knew, of course, and in the past he had glimpsed warriors whose gait did not match those he was familiar with. He thought of the one he had seen leaving Malcador's chambers, and searched the unknowns, looking for commonality.

A familiar face passed beneath his gaze. Vardas Ison gave him a solemn nod that communicated a whole series of intentions, and he returned it. Nearby, another Knight-Errant unhooded, and Rubio saw the motion of carved charms about his neck-ring. Those were this warrior's sole keepsake, just as Rubio's was the Ultima-emblazoned gladius he had been allowed to retain from his parent Legion. The charms were a talisman favoured by the so-called Rune Priests of Lord Russ' feral Rout, and if that were not enough, the ashy-rust colour of the warrior's ragged hair all but confirmed his origin as a child of Fenris.

The former Space Wolf grinned at him as he stepped off the Thunderhawk's ramp. 'Brother Rubio. Well met.'

'Yotun?'

He nodded. 'Or is it Koios now?'

Rubio didn't answer the question. 'The lander... You crashed it into the traitor encampment. And lived.'

Yotun's grin widened. 'It'll take more than that to finish me.'

'Clearly.' Rubio thought about the silver coin Malcador had given him. 'Who did you used to be, brother?'

'Does it matter?' Yotun nodded towards Malcador. The Sigillite was in hushed conversation with his adjutant, the tall, slight man called Wyntor.

'I suppose not.' Rubio watched Wyntor carefully. The thin human's eyes darted nervously from side to side when Malcador's attention was not upon him.

Rubio had seen that agitation in him before – or at least, he had seen it in someone who looked like Ael Wyntor, spoke like him. The mystery of the man sent Rubio's musings back to the gloom that troubled his own thoughts.

'The shadow attacks have been put down,' announced Malcador, pitching his voice so all of them could hear it. 'We were ready, and we were in place when Horus' lackeys triggered them. But these will not be the last. I have no doubt that other weapons and other poison lies in wait.' He took a breath, and nodded to himself. 'But know this. These attacks are the tolls of a bell that sounds the beginning of the end. The plans and preparations that the insurrectionists have made are about to blossom. There will be fires and there will be death. There will be confusion and panic in the streets – this and worse, before the Warmaster's ships blacken that sky.' Malcador pointed a bony finger into the air, walking back through the group. As he did, Rubio saw Wyntor take the opportunity to slip away while his master was otherwise occupied.

'And what would you have us do about it?' The question came from another of those warriors unknown to Rubio, but the pallid cast to his features and the sable of his half-shorn mane suggested that this one was of Lord Corax's Legion.

'Nothing, Brother Ogen. Nothing at all.' Malcador paused, resting on his staff, taking in their faces. 'You should use this moment to rearm, repair your armour and replenish what is depleted. This is the calm before the storm, and it will never come again.'

'Calm?' Garro made no effort to keep the irritation from his voice.

'Cities are aflame across the planet. The people are dying. The war is already here.'

Malcador did not answer. Instead, the reply came from a dark-eyed warrior who stood in the shadows beneath the wing of a shuttle. 'This is not the war, Death Guard. These are just the ripples ahead of the wave, lapping at the shoreline. You should look up. The flood tide will be so great and so vast, you may mistake it for the sky.'

Rubio briefly considered the dark-eyed one through the lens of his psychic sight, and frowned in confusion. The shape of the warrior's soul was off-kilter, a form that seemed to be sculpted from shards rather than born into a whole. He drew the other Knight-Errant's attention and instinctively withdrew, but not before he glimpsed the image of a silver coin and a word etched upon its surface, fading as it was said aloud.

Ianius.

GARRO'S EXPRESSION TURNED stony and he walked away. The endless, grinding weariness of this maddening half-war constantly dragged on his focus, forever threatening to pull him from the true path laid out before him.

He took a long, deep breath. Now was not the time to become subsumed into another of Malcador's labyrinthine schemes. What he required was the clarity of his faith, and the strength that knowledge would bring.

The Sigillite continued to converse with the dark-eyed Knight-Errant and the others, but Garro's thoughts were elsewhere. He moved to Gallor's side, where the other warrior sat atop an arming crate, and spoke quietly so that only he would hear his words. 'Brother, I have need of you.'

'I am familiar with that tone of voice.' Gallor gave him a sideways glance. 'I heard it every time you tasked the Seventh Company to do something... defiant.'

Garro smiled, despite himself. 'True. And we did defy the odds with such zeal.'

'Aye, captain. Those days are another life to me now.'

The smile faded. 'To us both.'

Gallor looked away. Since returning to Terra, Garro's former rank of battle-captain had been reduced to little more than an honorific, and while he did hold the status of the Sigillite's Agentia Primus, the unspoken rule was that no Knight-Errant truly outranked another. If Garro gave Gallor a command, he could not enforce it except by invoking Malcador's proxy.

But that point became moot when the other Death Guard nodded slowly. 'I do not forget. Tell me what you need, captain.'

'You will find what remains of the Seventy, our brothers who escaped treachery aboard the *Eisenstein*.'

'Less now,' Gallor noted. 'And not all may be on Terra. They were not chosen as we were.'

'Gather who you can. Our last battle is almost upon us, Helig.'

Gallor gave a grim nod, and glanced in Malcador's direction as the Sigillite excused himself, leaving the assembled Knights-Errant to attend to their preparations.

Garro shook his head, answering the unspoken question. 'This is not a matter for the Regent to be concerned with. I ask you to do this, not as your former captain, not as a Knight-Errant. I ask as one Death Guard to another.'

The other warrior stood up. 'Then it will be done.' Gallor walked away without looking back.

Gathering the battered material of his combat cloak around him, Garro made for the gaping maw of a null-grav drop tube on the far side of the landing pad, deliberately avoiding the rest of the Knights-Errant. However, there was no way around Rubio, who stood waiting at the edge of the platform as if he had expected him.

'You are looking for something,' said the psyker, and Garro felt the gentle pressure of a telepathic probe.

He gave Rubio a warning glance. 'Keep your own counsel, Tylos.'

'There is much about you I have never understood, Nathaniel. The hidden places in your thoughts.' Rubio folded his arms across his chest. 'And questions unresolved. It seems those are falling like rain in these hours.'

Unbidden, the memory of a dead soldier's votive charm – a golden aquila upon a chain – rose in Garro's mind. *Was that Rubio's doing, or something else?* He hardened his resolve. 'I have never challenged you, Codicier. Do me the same honour.'

'How can I challenge what you believe in?' Rubio replied. '*The Emperor Protects*, yes? How can such a statement be assailed by any one of us?'

Garro pushed past him, and stepped onto the elevator platform. He left a warning in his wake. 'Look to yourself, brother. Soon, there will be no respite to do so.'

But Rubio could not end the conversation without one final push into Garro's surface thoughts, snatching his intentions from the ether. 'You are going to the deep dungeon tiers... Who do you hope to find there?'

Garro said nothing, and let the darkness take him down and away.

AEL WYNTOR'S HANDS were shaking so much that he almost dropped the cypher key, and it took a physical effort for the adjutant to slow his racing breathing to the point where his mind had clarity.

He laughed bitterly at that as he padded across the central atrium of the Sigillite's chambers, skipping from one ornamental rug to another as he tried to fox the sensing globes drifting up in the eves.

Clarity. The mere suggestion that he had something like that was ridiculous. If anything, Wyntor's thoughts were thickening, gaining a fog of confusion that became more opaque with each passing moment.

'If only they knew, if only I could say,' he muttered to himself. He glanced in the direction of the great arched window visible through the open door to the bedroom, and a blunt, suicidal impulse juddered through his body. A barrage of harsh, invasive thoughts struck him.

Wyntor imagined suffocating in the red silk sheets of that bed, releasing control of himself and thrashing wildly until he asphyxiated–

–Smashing a hole in the glassaic window with a chair and diving out of it–

–Stabbing himself in the heart with one of the antique knives in the dining room–

–Tasting the metal of a lasgun's muzzle on his tongue before squeezing the trigger stud–

–Swallowing the ink from Malcador's study in volume enough to be poisoned by it–

–Hurling himself off the edge of the Eagle's Highway–

He screamed and slapped his own face, the sounds rebounding off the carved walls. Wyntor gulped and hugged himself, fearful that his outburst might have set off some kind of alarm. But there was no siren, so he moved on, shaking his head, struggling to return to his previous train of thought.

'What would the people say if they knew what I know?' he asked the silent air. 'What if they could see the truth behind the insurrection?' Wyntor felt the tears coming. 'Why did *I* have to be told? Why did he have to tell me?'

He took a shuddering breath, and there was the scent of rich amasec on the air. A rare vintage. He had shared a glass of it with Malcador the night before.

No. That was not correct. Not last night. Months ago. Or was it years?

Wyntor clasped his face, the stolen cypher key pressing into his thin flesh. This was not how it was supposed to happen.

In his ideal, perfect version of this plan, the Sigillite would still be away at the White Mountain, gone for another day at least. Wyntor would have more time. But things had become complex. He had underestimated how long it would take him to get the key, to fabricate the permissions and get into Malcador's inner sanctum without being detected.

The memories of years of serving the Sigillite – *or was it months?* – gave him all the tools he needed. It was only the application that he had misjudged.

Then, what now? He skidded to a halt in front of the doors to the grand study. The sensor grid would let him in here without comment, but still he hesitated.

'I can still run. Flee and flight, yes...' The idea formed, but then it broke beneath another jagged bolt of reality. 'No. No. They'll find me before I make it to a flyer. So I need to know.' He steeled himself and entered the study. 'I needed to know. I won't go back.'

Malcador invited him into this chamber only rarely, and at first it had been something Wyntor enjoyed. At first, he had enjoyed *all* of their conversations. The Sigillite was learned, diverting company, and his vast collection of art and literature was compelling to Wyntor's questing mind.

They would talk, they would play regicide, and they would engage over amasec and speak of things that could not be discussed elsewhere. *At first.*

But looking backward from here, Wyntor now understood it had been an elegant, gilded trap, no different from any of Malcador's other schemes.

'Why am I surprised by that?' he said to himself, navigating around the great hololithic tables and reading lenses, between the paintings that floated on suspensors like mystic portals that had been cut loose to drift where they wanted. 'Why did I think he would treat me any differently?'

A cloying, overpowering sense of the inevitable seeped into Wyntor's every action, clinging to him as if it were the stench of fire smoke.

–Burning himself alive in the kitchen–

–Dousing his body in amasec and striking the tip of a lho-stick–

His hands still trembling, he found the place where the hidden door lay and pressed the cypher key to the stone column. For a moment, nothing happened and Wyntor felt a blind panic forming, but then the column groaned and retracted, revealing a passageway behind it. Cold, dry air wafted out, bringing with it the stringent odour of cleaning chemicals.

He ventured in, the cold of the metal flooring leaching the warmth through the soles of his thin leather shoes.

Past the point of no return, Wyntor was sick with dread as he advanced. He did not want to be here. He did not want any of this. But there was no way to travel back to that day in the gardens, to the moment when they had first spoken.

The offer of the game and a glass of Venusian wine. *If only he could take that back.*

Another bitter laugh. 'He would never have let me say no.' Wyntor's voice echoed off the narrow walls. Up ahead, the corridor widened into a laboratory space filled with automata and medicae devices from the lost Age of Technology. Spidery brass things and white ceramic constructs worked quietly and diligently at knots of decayed, foetal flesh afloat in sterile chambers.

The dry, chill atmosphere of the room, the hard, directionless white light of it, the whispering machines, all these elements conjured an abject terror in Wyntor that was like nothing he had ever experienced before. It was primal and inchoate, and inescapable, as if woven into his very being. He stumbled into the wall and vomited explosively.

I have never been in this room before. Why am I so afraid of it?

He had barely finished retching before a servitor machine detached from a wall socket and approached, stooping to clean up the mess.

Dizzy and terrified, Wyntor forced himself to press on. Soon Malcador would be done tending to his Knights-Errant and his Chosen, and then he might return here. The truth was in this room, Wyntor took that as an unbreakable article of faith. Why else had the Sigillite kept everything else but *this* from him?

Malcador had confessed so many terrible things and revealed so many awful truths to Wyntor that the adjutant feared the secrets he had been told had unseated his reason.

'A lesser man might have gone mad to know them,' he said, between gasps. 'I think perhaps I have.'

Malcador had unburdened his soul to Wyntor, over and over forcing the man to share the worst of him. It was so ordinary a thing to do. At once, it made Wyntor pity the Sigillite and hate him in equal measure.

In the middle of the chamber, he came upon a stasis capsule, and inside was the body of a naked male humanoid.

But not a human, no.

It had been old before the suspension field had captured it in a bubble of null-time, holding the corpse on the edge of decay by disrupting the forces of nature. Thousands of filament-thin probes penetrated the pale flesh of the body, and clear glass rods held it up as if it were floating in hazy water.

The body in the capsule was unnaturally tall, but not like that of someone born in low-grav, someone like Wyntor. Not like someone who had been bio-altered, but a form born that way.

Its aspect was all stiff angles and arrow-sharp eyes that were long since clouded by death. Elongated ears that had no soft curves to them, strange thin lobes that tapered to points. The body had elegance and grace in it, if viewed from one angle. Harsh, unkind and alien features when seen from another.

But the most disturbing fact about it was that the body had Wyntor's face.

'Ah.' In a single exhalation, Malcador gave up a lifetime of regret and frustration. 'You shouldn't have done this.'

Shuddering as he began to weep, Wyntor could barely form the words to speak as he turned and found the Sigillite standing in the corridor behind him. His favourite trick, to make it seem as if he were every-where and nowhere at once.

Wyntor sputtered out a question. 'Are... a-are you actually h-here?'

'Does it matter?' Malcador rolled back his hood, and Wyntor saw that his robes no longer had dried blood on them. 'This is the worst end-ing. It's rare you ever come this far.' He sighed again. 'I'm sorry. This is not what I want.'

'But that is?' Wyntor screamed the question, waving wildly at the body in the capsule.

'A xenos specimen.' Malcador's tone became that of a lecturer. 'Ael-dari. I found him in the webway, in the under-spaces beneath what you would think of as the Imperial Palace now. That was a long time ago. He was still alive then, but his essence – his *soul*, if you will – was blighted and fading.' The Sigillite showed a brittle smile. 'But you know me, dear friend. I'm never one to waste a resource.'

'Why does it look like me?' shouted Wyntor.

Malcador made a turning motion with his fingers. 'You have it backward.'

'No.' The sound Wyntor made was very small and very fragile. '*No.*'

The Sigillite studied him gravely. 'Fate mocks us, I think. Because you chose this moment, *this exact day* to break. Not a week ago, not tomorrow when it would not matter, but *today*.' He made a bitter grunting sound. 'If things were different, I could explain it all to you. Carefully. Delicately. But Horus' clock has robbed me of any grace in this.' Malcador shook his head. 'This must be how Dorn feels every minute of every day. Stressed to the limit before a wall forever on the verge of splintering...'

'Why is it me?' Wyntor insisted, only half understanding.

'Do you remember where you were born, Ael?' Malcador's tone hardened. 'Do you recall the names of your parents? Your siblings? The place where you grew up?'

'Of course!' The question was ridiculous. 'I...' He reached for the memory and found only sand. Nothing but the shape of what should have been there. An empty vessel that should have contained a man's past. 'I don't... Why don't I...?'

'Those things do not exist. That is why you never dwell on them or speak of them. Your mind has been conditioned not to think too hard about a history you never had.' The Sigillite nodded towards the dead alien. 'It took a long time to understand the structure of their genetic material, but adaptation was possible. He was dying when I discovered him, you understand? But even in those moments I realised what kind of being I had found. A kindred spirit. Something nigh-immortal, with an intellect I could actually spar with.' He sighed. 'So few can match me. Can you blame me for wanting someone to talk to? A confidante to keep me sane?'

'How can I be part of that?' Wyntor retorted. 'I am human!' His stomach churned at the thought of xenos blood coursing through his veins.

'Not completely,' said the Sigillite. 'Where he ends and you begin… The line is blurred.'

'Why have you done this? What is the point of this foolish charade?' Wyntor's mood rebounded towards giddy anger. 'I am sick of your needlessly complex games!'

'There are no lies in this place. We have no time for them.' Malcador leaned in. 'I made you so I would have a voice that was not an echo of my own. Stripped the alien from that corpse, merged it with something more akin to man. And you've been that for a long time, Ael. A good friend. Haven't we been good friends?'

Wyntor screamed. 'I don't want to hear your voice any more! Why did you keep telling me things? All the secrets and horrible truths about this war and all the ones to come afterwards, why confess them to me? I don't want the burden!' He beat at his chest. 'I can't contain them!'

'I know,' said Malcador. 'And that is why you killed yourself so many times. Hundreds of you, seeking death rather than live with what I told them. Another secret I kept.'

'H-hundreds?' Wyntor trembled, unable to believe what he was hearing.

'I regret it.' The Sigillite said the words like he meant them. 'But my need was greater than yours. Even I cannot carry my duty alone. So you helped me, my friend. You gave the keeper of Terra's secrets a place where he could put aside his mask, even for a brief time, and *confide.*' He bowed his head. 'I know the toll is great. But you have my deepest gratitude.'

'Each time, what did you do?' Wyntor glared at the capsule. 'Make another? Slice off a piece and grow me in a vat?'

'In a way,' admitted Malcador. 'But each iteration fades faster than the one before it. You are a copy of a copy of a copy. Degrading. The stability quotient is past the point of no return, down to mere days.'

Wyntor seized on those words. 'Am I the last? I am the last!' As soon as he said it, he knew he was right. 'That's why you are here, because you can't make any more!'

'Wait,' said Malcador, and he glanced over his shoulder, down the narrow corridor. 'I'll be there soon. Just wait, and I'll take this away from you. Give you back some peace.'

'I don't want that.' Wyntor advanced on the Sigillite, and now he saw that Malcador cast no shadow on the floor from the harsh lights above.

An imago, then. A projection of his reality.

He knew he had only moments until the illusion became the fact. Casting around, Wyntor found a metal stool near a cogitator console and hauled it off the ground, wielding it like a club.

'Stop!' Malcador's voice became a thunderous roar, but Wyntor had already committed to the act.

He battered the capsule with savage, mad fury, shattering the crystalflex walls. A gush of glutinous preservative fluids rolled out across the metal decking, and brought the body of the long-dead Aeldari out with it. As the air touched the alien corpse's skin, it instantly decayed, becoming a grey, pulpy mess.

Wyntor attacked the remains, stamping the flesh matter beneath his shoes. 'This is not me! This is not me!' He stumbled and collapsed in the pool of thick sludge, falling on jagged curves of broken crystalflex. Instinctively, he grabbed the largest shard and held it to his throat. 'I won't be used by you any more!'

'That choice is not yours.' Another iteration of Malcador stormed into the chamber, even as the one Wyntor was conversing with faded like a mirage.

This Sigillite was hard-eyed and there was blood on his robes. The shadow he cast fell across Wyntor and made the air in the laboratory turn polar-cold.

He tried to move the makeshift crystalflex dagger, but his body was frozen in place. 'Let me die.' Wyntor forced out the words through his rigid jaw. 'You have no right. How much... more? How many more... secrets do you have... to admit?'

'An infinity of them,' said Malcador, one hand on his iron staff as he lowered himself into a crouch. 'But I no longer require a confessor.'

He reached out and took the glassy fragment from Wyntor's hand and threw it away. 'You are needed for something else.'

The Sigillite laid his long fingers over the planes of Wyntor's face and closed his eyes. Ethereal light glowed beneath his flesh and seeped out, illuminating Wyntor's skull from within.

The adjutant began to scream.

INTERVAL VII

The Fall

[The warp; now]

THE FOULNESS OF the warp-plague was everywhere Mortarion looked.

He caught glimpses of the disease-ridden as he walked the shadowed corridors of the *Terminus Est*. Through the portal in a sealed hatch, he saw dead servitors collapsed before hundreds of human corpses stacked like cordwood, the helot crew consumed by the chimeric virus and the organic parts of the machine-slaves killed in the same fashion. But worse still were the warriors of his Legion, who rather than meet his gaze, shied away from their primarch's approach in shame at their infection.

It was as if the infernal contagion could be transmitted at the speed of thought, and no barrier nor counter-agent could halt it. Mortarion flexed his left hand, ironclad once more in his battle gauntlet, and chewed on the grim revelation of the triad blisters that had appeared on his own skin.

If this unreal disease could take purchase in *his* body, if it could get its microscopic claws into the raging furnace of a demigod's physiology, then what hope could his sons have to defeat it? Mortarion's sense

of self had always been strong, and if he reached inside, he could feel
the battle being fought in his bloodstream. It sickened him to admit
he too was *tainted*.

The Reaper of Men threw a sideways glance at the nearest of his face-
less Deathshroud warriors. Forever hidden behind the skull aspect of
their battle masks, no part of their physical form was visible, and there
was no way to know if any of them had been touched by this insidious Destroyer.

But Mortarion knew. His eye was keen, and he could see the signs – a
single dragged footstep, a momentary lag in motion. Like all the Death
Guard, his praetorians would perish in fire and fury before they failed
him. To openly show their master any faltering of strength would be
a betrayal.

The closer they came to the warship's sanctorum, the more loathsome things became. Here, the sickness seemed to be growing not
just to pollute flesh, but to contaminate the structure of the *Terminus Est* herself. The venerable battleship was centuries old, but it had
never been decayed or decrepit. Now Mortarion saw patches of crawling rust moving over walls that days earlier had been bright spreads
of polished plasteel.

A droning susurrus filled the air as clouds of tiny flies blackened the
illumination of the ship's lumoglobes. They writhed in smoke-like
knots, beyond reach and endlessly in motion. Colonies of the things
clustered around stoic Death Guard sentinels in fully sealed armour,
clogging the vents of their helms.

Down branching corridors that were shadowed and dim, the primarch saw those among his sons who were less fortunate. Here and
there, medicae and Legion Apothecaries toiled over the forms of warriors who sat slumped against the walls. One of them turned to look
in his direction, and he saw eyes turned a sour yellow by blindness, a
pale face raw with weeping sores.

Is this tragedy being repeated on every ship in my fleet? He believed it so,
and Mortarion's thoughts strayed to Raheb Zurrieq, and of the merciful

release that the disease had refused to grant him. *This is the fate that awaits us, if we cannot escape the madness of this realm.*

Mortarion's tortured imaginings envisioned the alternative – a timeless nowhere of unrelenting pain and agony. Throughout history, ships had gone missing in the warp, lost and consigned to cruel destiny. Was this what happened to them? It was not a fate that he would wish on his greatest enemy. The nothingness and the horrible inertia of it was worse than any death.

Give me a foe to fight or a target to attack, and I will turn the fate of worlds, Mortarion had once said to his father. *There is no battle that the Death Guard fear.*

But those words were lies. He knew fear, true and real. Here was a battle against a foe they could not see, could not grasp, and could not put to the sword. This was a fight that turned the Pale Sons against themselves. *Unwinnable.*

Unless...

Reaching the great doorway to the Navigator's sanctorum, Mortarion unlimbered *Silence* and let the massive scythe swing to the ready. 'Heed me,' he told the seven Deathshroud. 'First Captain Typhon will do as he is ordered or he will be put down. No hesitation in this.'

The warriors did not speak, but as one they saluted with a mailed fist against their chest-plates. Mortarion wrenched open the hatch with one arm and marched inside, setting his jaw as a stale exhalation of corrupted air and degeneration washed over him. He tasted the peculiar sweetness of corpse-flesh and the rough soil of death. It was unaccountably familiar to him; it was the air of old Barbarus, captured and recreated in this sealed sphere.

'Typhon!' he shouted, his voice rebounding off the blackened, crumbling interior. Like the rest of the ship, the sanctorum chamber was rotting from the inside out. 'This ends here. Take us back, or defy me and die.'

'Don't you see the truth, Reaper?' Typhon's words rumbled back at him from somewhere in the gloom. 'We cannot die in this place. Here,

we are as eternal and enduring as we were always meant to be.' A piece
of the shadows detached and moved towards him. 'It took me a while
to come to the understanding myself. But I have it now. I think perhaps I always did. I just needed to find the way.'

Typhon emerged into a shaft of sickly light and he resembled a phantom version of his former self. Pallid and deathly white, far more than
even the common pallor of a Barbarun, he was akin to a corpse. His
beard was matted and greasy, his eyes alive with malice but sunken
into dark hollows. The First Captain's battleplate was filthy with blood
and muck, as if he had crawled through the sewers of a slaughterhouse.

'What have you done?' breathed Mortarion. 'If there is any of the
comradeship still in you that we once shared, tell me why you have
trapped us here.'

'I regret I had to lie to you,' Typhon admitted. 'But it is better this
way. The Navigators *were* plotting, that was true, but not as I led you
to believe. Killing them ended a threat before it was fully formed, and
allowed me to bring you here. To see the Grandfather's bounty first
hand.'

That name again. Mortarion stiffened. 'You have made a pact with
something inhuman.'

'So have you.' Typhon showed yellowed teeth in a feral smile. 'I know
you have been courting the knowledge that your father forbade.' He
waved a hand. 'The whispers in the dusk, they talk to one another,
did you not know? You are walking the same path as I, only I am far
ahead of you.' The warrior chuckled. 'But in fairness, I was set on that
road from the day I took my first breath. Born to it, you might say.'

Typhon had never made a secret of his origins. The bastard child was
marked by the blood of his progenitor just as Mortarion was marked
by his. That darkness had always been made to serve the Death Guard
Legion – or so his commander had always believed. Here and now, the
light of events put the lie to that. Perhaps the reality was that Typhon
had always been leading them towards this point, to the door beyond
which lay the daemonic forces that Mortarion had glimpsed.

'What happened to you out there when you left my side?' he asked. 'What changed?'

'I awoke,' said Typhon, briefly losing himself in a memory. 'On a world called Zaramund. At the touch of an old woman's hand.' Then he nodded. 'You will too, this day. It is time for the Death Guard to accept the Mark.'

'No.' The tone of his old friend's words stoked Mortarion's cold anger into a seething, icy inferno. 'Return us to real space! Do it now!'

'I won't,' came the reply. 'Not in this life.'

And that was answer enough. With a snarl, Mortarion exploded into motion and drew the *Lantern*, laying a column of searing white fire over the other warrior. Typhon shrieked, but as the beam faded, he was still standing. Ash crisped and crumbled the upper layers of his skin, and scorched his armour, but the beam gun's effect was attenuated by some invisible means.

Without hesitation, Mortarion shifted tactics and brought up *Silence* in a singing arc of steel, slashing the blade through the stale air.

Typhon skidded away across the ichor-slick decking and narrowly avoided a strike that would have cut off his arm. He gave no obvious command, but without warning a dozen other hazy forms burst from the shadows of the chamber and set forth to attack the Death-shroud. They were members of the First Captain's 'specialist' detail, the fighters he called his Grave Wardens, and not one of them moved to engage their primarch. That duel, it seemed, was only for Mortarion and his old friend.

Eldritch fire sprayed and plasteel tore as the two groups of bodyguards clashed, and between them the primarch and his captain stalked each other, trading testing blows that quickly escalated in tempo and lethality.

Despite the years they had known one another, Mortarion and Typhon had never fought, not even in the sparring pits. It had always seemed like a test that did not need to be proven, a question never answered.

But as the clash unfolded, Mortarion found a single, unpalatable truth rising to the surface of his thoughts. *I do not know this man at all.*

Their blades sparked off one another as Typhon attempted to get inside his primarch's reach and knock him back. It was a bold tactic and from any other, Mortarion would have thought it a futile one. But Typhon knew him as no man did. The two of them had battled alongside each other across the bleak ranges of Barbarus in years of pitiless war, learning as they went, taming a world along the way. And then in the missions of the Great Crusade, the First Captain had always been there. His strong right arm. His confidante and trusted comrade.

Their weapons locked and the two of them struggled to a standstill. Despite his sickly appearance, Typhon appeared to draw upon a reserve of strength and stamina beyond that of any ordinary legionary.

Mortarion met his gaze and saw a stranger behind those familiar eyes. Everything he believed he knew about Typhon crumbled in that moment. The same changes that had consumed Grulgor were at work here, he realised. The man who was truly Calas Typhon – who had been a scared half-breed youth, a reckless rebel, then a trusted commander in his army of liberation – no longer existed.

The Reaper of Men let the last iota of brotherhood between them gutter out and fade like a dying candle, and hardened his spirit. 'If you are what keeps us here,' he hissed, 'then that binding will be severed.'

With a mighty surge of effort, Mortarion slammed *Silence* into Typhon's weapon and broke it in two, the bifurcated pieces spinning away. The First Captain staggered backward, but the primarch pressed the attack, leaning into the momentum.

Inexorable, unstoppable, the crescent blade of the great war-scythe tore into Typhon's chest armour and through it in a scream of ruptured ceramite. The curve of the razor edge dug inward and upward through the meat of his body, the yawning passage of its cut finding both of his hearts, and slicing them open. Black blood gushed in a torrent from the fatal, gaping wound, and Typhon sagged lifelessly, supported on the end of the blade like a hooked fish.

Forgive me, old friend.

The thought gathered in Mortarion's mind, about to be spoken aloud – but then Typhon's head snapped up and his jaundiced eyes glared back at the primarch, lit with a baleful fire. 'Did you think it would be that easy?' Noxious yellow froth drooled from his mouth as he spoke, pitting the floor and sizzling where it landed. 'I told you. We cannot die here. You cannot kill me, *old friend.*'

Typhon's arm blurred, coming at him with impossible speed. Mortarion shifted to block the attack, a dagger diving at his neck, and managed only to deflect it. The metal knife found a gap in the spaces between his armour plates and cut through the heavy undersuit beneath as if it were nothing. The Reaper felt the tip of the blade bite into his flesh, and the pain of it was incredible.

Shocked by the force of it, he staggered back, losing his grip on *Silence*, reaching up to wrench the dagger from where it lay.

He pulled at the weapon, riding waves of agony as it slowly drew out of his body. He knew this knife; the dagger was a piece of old brass, a makeshift thing that once had been lost and forgotten in the blood-soaked mud of Barbarus. It sizzled in his grip, oozing plague-matter corruption from within, corroding the metal palm of his gauntlet. He discarded it, looking back to see Typhon reach down and pull *Silence* from his belly.

'I have something that belongs to you,' said the First Captain, and he threw the war-scythe back. Mortarion caught it, disgust twisting his face as he watched loops of distended intestine and cankered organs hang loosely from the cut it had made in the other warrior. 'The mortal cannot end the immortal,' Typhon went on. 'And you will forever be the lesser if you do not embrace rebirth.' He pointed at Mortarion's hand, where the triad of livid boils had appeared. A fierce jag of pain lanced through the Reaper's arm, searing his nerves. 'It will take more than you to kill me,' he added, baring his teeth.

Mortarion straightened. 'Yes. I suspected that might be so.' This was the moment, then. He had only one more card left to play. 'It is clear to me now, to destroy the thing that you are becoming requires a weapon of singular origin.' He reached for the bandolier across his chest and recovered a slim metal rod attached there, depressing a button at one end before hurling the thing at Typhon.

It landed at the First Captain's feet, emitting a high-pitched whine – but it was no explosive device.

'A beacon?' As Typhon said the words, a concussion made of emerald light and twisted energy blossomed between the two warriors, dragging a huge and corpulent form into the chamber through a portal of matter-transfer.

The Eater of Life materialised in the sanctorum with a thunderous crash of displaced air, the fractured links of the chains that had bound it tinkling as they fell to the deck. It tipped back its foul head as it took in its new surroundings, and then roared with laughter.

'Grulgor...' sneered Typhon. 'Well met, brother.'

'*Not quite,*' gurgled the creature, eyeing him up and down.

'Daemon!' Mortarion called. 'You begged to kill for me, so I give you freedom to do so. You are oath-sworn to my command, and it is this – destroy Typhon!'

'*Is that what you wish?*' The Eater's giant podgy arm shot out with uncanny speed and clasped the First Captain before he could draw back, shaking him violently. Mutated talon-fingers clasped around Typhon's throat and began to contract.

Mortarion watched, grim-faced, as the daemon spawn strangled his comrade, ignoring every blow that Typhon rained down upon it. Finally, Typhon began to choke and splutter, as oily matter spurted from his gagging mouth and the monstrous tear in his body.

'*I fulfil my oath,*' snarled the creature, leering into the face of his victim.

Then the timbre and cadence of Typhon's dying exhalations changed. The death-rattle shifted, becoming a hate-filled, spiteful sound. The First Captain was *laughing* – and the Grulgor-thing joined in with him.

The claws released and Typhon staggered back, spitting out broken stumps of teeth and gobs of black mucus.

Mortarion started forward. *Another betrayal?* His thoughts roared against the prospect. *Impossible!*

The Eater of Life bowed to the primarch, giggling obscenely as it spoke to him. *'I regret to tell you, Lord Mortarion… My oath to the Plague God, the King of Decay and the Regent Most Vile comes before any pact I make with mortals. Nurgle's rotting reign holds sway over all, do you see?'*

Mortarion tried to utter the name the daemon spoke, but it turned to bile in his mouth and he was forced to swallow the demand he wanted to make.

Nurgle. The word had appeared here and there in the unhallowed texts he had discovered, and each time it was the icon of the greatest degeneration, the foulest corruption.

The Eater shifted its great bulk to face Typhon. *'What of you? Are you ready to take the final step, to submit to the embrace?'*

'Yes,' grated the First Captain, giving Mortarion a savage sneer. 'Make the sacrifice.'

'Calas Typhon dies today,' said the creature, and it spread its arms wide, tipping back its neck to expose the wide, pestilent mass of its goitre-bloated throat. The pallid flesh throbbed and moved, as if something trapped beneath it was trying to get out.

Mortarion broke into a sprint, swinging *Silence* high as he stormed in to stop whatever would come next, but Typhon threw a wall of invisible force towards him and the air thickened to slurry, each step taking the effort of a hundred men.

Typhon dived at the daemon's throat and tore it open with his bare hands, ripping it away as if he were skinning an animal kill. Through the gash he made came a detonation of black, screaming motes – a hurricane swarm of shining flies that blasted outward and engulfed the First Captain, hitting him with enough force to knock him off his feet.

Acting on instinct, Mortarion slammed *Silence* into the deck and used it to hook himself there as the howling gale of insects swept over and around him. He felt thousands of tiny razor-sharp mandibles biting into every inch of his exposed skin, and the burn of acidic venom in his blood. Turning his face away, the primarch glimpsed coiled clouds of the swarm breaking apart and diving upon the survivors of his Death-shroud and Typhon's Grave Wardens, attacking both sides alike. The flies feasted on them, eating in through the soft tissues of their bodies and the jelly of their eyes. Even those sealed tight inside their battle-plate could not escape, as the warp-tainted insects seemed to be able to pass through the tiniest of apertures in search of meat to chew upon.

Then, like the outrush of a retreating tide, the screaming swarm left the desiccated bodies of the fallen behind and imploded back towards the centre of the chamber. At the eye of this pestilent storm stood Mortarion and his former brother in battle.

Whatever animating essence had been Ignatius Grulgor boiled out of the daemon flesh as it died. The flies ignored the dissolving, putrid mass that had been the Eater of Lives, content to let the daemon discorporate and crumble. Instead, they whirled around Typhon in a stream of dark blurs before suddenly diving *into* him. The swarm bored up through the great wound Mortarion's scythe had left in the First Captain, and they plunged down his open mouth. He welcomed them, taking everything they gave.

Aghast, Mortarion could do nothing as Typhon's body twitched, writhed and distended to accommodate the transformation eating him from the inside out. His back swelled amid the crackle of fracturing bone and ceramite, and dense flutes of fissured horn burst out, each one spitting clouds of flies as smoke would belch from a chimney. He shuddered, sloughing off lumps of dead, grey flesh to reveal the new bloom of rotting muscle beneath. Where his battle armour ended and the putrid meat of him began was impossible to see.

Finally, with a repellent crunch of breaking cartilage, the nub of a twisted horn grew from the First Captain's swollen face. He glanced up, wheezing and shuddering, and with each indrawn breath and exhalation Mortarion could hear the droning of the flies inside him. He had become a hive for the things, a living nest for the Destroyer plague.

'Calas...' Mortarion whispered in the deathly silence that followed. 'What have you done?'

'Know my name,' came the seething reply. *'I am the Herald of what we shall be, Mortarion.'* He drew himself up, flexing his arms and testing the play in his mutated new form. *'I. Am. **Typhus.**'*

The utterance seemed to resonate through the air and strike something deep in Mortarion's spirit. There was a dark and bottomless pit of sorrow in the soul of the Reaper of Men, a hole in his being that had been in him from the day he first opened his eyes, among the bloody carnage of a spent battle across Barbarus' foothills. He had ignored it, buried it, denied its existence – and for a while, when he had found purpose in the creation of his Death Guard and again in the Great Crusade, the pit had scabbed over.

But it had never left him, and the act of witnessing the other warrior's change ripped away all pretence at concealing it. The yawning void of his greatest despair hollowed him out as he saw the truth. His Legion was going to fall to this ruin and decay, and nothing he could do would stop it.

'This is always how it was going to end,' said Typhus, his words the wind from a sepulchre. *'The fate you refused to accept ghosted with you at every step. The questions in your mind, laid there when we were just foolish youths and fearless rebels. Planted like seeds to bloom into doubt.'* He flexed his skeletal hands, offering one in a macabre parody of friendship. *'Your dalliances with daemonology. Your chaining of the Life-Eater...'* He nodded at the frothing pool of feculent slime that was all that now remained of the creature. *'All preordained by the eye of the Grandfather. To bring us to this moment, and remake me. To remake **all** of us.'*

'You led me here...' The grief and misery of the primarch's own admission burned worse than any venom, cut deeper than any blade.

'Yes,' said Typhus. *'But the last step must be yours. **Submit, Mortarion. Surrender.** Or you will doom the Death Guard to an eternity of weakness and suffering.'*

✠ ✠ ✠

[The planet Barbarus; before]

EACH STEP TOOK more out of him than the last, but still Mortarion pressed on, climbing over the chem-slicked slate of the high crags.

Every breath was a labour, taking in a lungful of toxic air and squeezing the last fractions of breathable elements from it. The primitive air-tank on his back had run dry hours earlier, and he had sloughed off the kit, leaving it on the blasted hillside where a fresh salvo of fireballs had tried and failed to destroy him.

With his war-scythe at his side, Mortarion continued his advance, pulling himself up – step by brutal step – ever closer to the dark, menacing towers of the final citadel.

The outer plates of his armour were already corroding, as the acid haze around him burned through the sheen of the metal and weakened its structure. Cured leather straps dissolved and he felt a section of his vambrace detach and fall into the poisonous mud. Mortarion ignored it and walked on. His thoughts contracted to a single point, to the act of putting one foot in front of the other.

Mortarion did not allow his mind to embrace any other notion. Anything else would sap his will. He held on to the old, familiar rage that he had known since his childhood. He dug deep to find every last fraction of the hate he held for the one who tormented him. And there was something else, too – the impulse to prove himself in a final confrontation. The inevitability of it was becoming manifest.

Today would be the end. After years of fighting, the war for Barbarus would conclude on this forsaken mountain peak with a single death. It would be his enemy, or it would be him.

The Reaper of Men's fingers tightened around the haft of his weapon as he struggled for breath. In the secret places of his soul, places Mortarion allowed no others to know of, this act was enshrined as his greatest desire. But in truth, there were other needs he hid away, and in the silence of the thick fog they threatened to emerge.

The stranger in the lodge hall, the Newcomer. There was a familiarity about the bronze-skinned man that he could not escape. Mortarion did not know how, but he instinctively felt he *knew* him.

He was unwilling to explore that emotion, in dread of what he might find if he looked too deeply upon it. Mortarion's origins were an enigma, and if this stranger was somehow *connected* to him, the possibility of learning the facts behind his greatest mystery could be within his grasp.

But what good would that knowledge serve? The question whispered to him. *How would that make me a better man?* He glanced up again at the citadel. *How can it help me in this fight, here and now?*

Mortarion shook off the traitorous thoughts, silencing them. Who he was and where he had come from was unimportant. What mattered in this moment were his deeds, not his past.

He was close now. The shadow cast by the last stronghold of the Over-lords loomed large above him, glimpsed in pieces through the veil of the venomous clouds. He could sense his foster father up there on the battlements, glaring down at him as he approached.

One last test, he told himself, *and then this will be over.*

The ground at his feet levelled out and he found himself at the foot of towering gates forged from black iron, set in a tower that vanished into the orange-black mist.

His body trembled from the ill-effects of the murderous toxins in the air, but still he managed to take a deep breath. Never before had he been able to rise this far, to the gates of his foster father's castle, but the rage that drove Mortarion on sustained him like fire.

'Necare!' He bellowed the name of the High Overlord in a crack-throated snarl, the sound echoing across the peaks. 'Answer me and face your final justice!'

The words left his lips, but the energy it took to utter them was gargantuan. Mortarion's chest was afire, his body seething with sweat as it tried to fight off the punishing toxicity of the haze. His muscles were beset by tremors, making it difficult to remain steady, and his scythe shook in his hands.

A true and chilling fear settled upon him as Mortarion experienced something he had never known before. He heard the wheezing of his own breath, tasted the metallic tang of blood in his mouth, and knew that he was staring into the abyss of his own mortality.

With that revelation there came a callous moment of understanding, as the universe showed him a pitiless truth. *The final battle need not be one of swords and fire. It must only be a war of will. The inexorable entropy of all things ranged against the bitter rage of life, forever screaming into the darkness.*

'You disappoint me,' said a voice. Mortarion twisted and Necare was suddenly *there*, craning over him, a horrifying spectre of bony shapes sheathed in burial-black robes.

Mortarion tried to swing his war-scythe into an attack posture, but the trembling in his arms was beyond his control and he lost all purchase on the weapon. It fell into the churned earth and began to crumble like rotting wormwood.

'You were never going to be worthy,' said the Overlord, stalking towards him. The poison in the air seemed to thicken and gather around the creature as it came closer, reaching out in wispy tendrils to smother Mortarion.

He was choking. The air was as heavy as lead, and it tore him up inside. Never before had the Reaper of Men felt as fragile as he did now. He staggered back a step, a rain of rotting fragments falling from his armour as the hoses about his breather mask disintegrated.

A deep and endless pit was opening inside him, a terrible well of absolute misery that dragged Mortarion's spirit into its inescapable grasp.

I have failed my people. If it had been in him, he might have wept.

'I warned you. Your life is forfeit.' Necare made no effort to attack. The Overlord simply stood and watched, allowing Mortarion's own hubris to destroy him. He watched as his foundling son lost balance and stumbled to his knees, bringing his death closer with each breath he took.

'Do you understand?' said a sombre voice, following him down to the ground. *'Defiance alone is not enough.'* The words echoed in a droning chorus, striking him like physical blows. It was not Necare who had spoken, but something else. An intelligence reaching out to address him, something vast and decrepit, ancient and undying. *'To defeat death, you must become–'*

The words were drowned out by a howl of golden flames that cut through the air over Mortarion, and he saw the mist itself atomised in the wake of a great, broad-bladed sword made of glistening metal. *Burning brighter than truth.*

As a grey, bloodless nothingness crept in from the edges of his vision, he saw the stranger in his shimmering battleplate rushing across the blackened mud. The killing fog did nothing to slow him, and the Newcomer brought his weapon up on a lethal backswing that struck Necare across the thorax. Lightning flashed from the sword's shining edge and the High Overlord of Barbarus was ended with a single blow. His severed torso never fell to the ground, instead discorporating into thick feathers of soiled ash that were borne away on the wind.

Mortarion slumped and felt his body seize. The Newcomer filled his vision, and upon this stranger's face was such compassion that he had never known. 'Be still,' said the stranger. 'You will not perish this day... my son.'

Mortarion struggled to speak, but the words he tried to utter were stolen from him – stolen away just as his long dreamed-of victory had been. As he lost consciousness and plunged towards despair, the words echoed after him.

I will always hate you.

[The warp; now]

SORROW ENGULFED HIM.

The cruel circularity of events fell upon Mortarion as he stalked through the corridors of the *Terminus Est*, the hollowness within his soul as punishing as the foul air of Barbarus had once been in his lungs. Then, he had stood on the edge of despair's abyssal reaches and barely pulled back from the bottomless gloom of desolation. Now, he was in free fall, lost to it.

His brother in battle, Typhon–

No, call him what he is now.

Typhus.

–The warrior who had once been his closest friend and ally was changed forever. Or perhaps it was more truthful to say that everything false about the First Captain had been stripped away and revealed the core of him. The nondead monster Typhus, reborn through unity with the powers of the warp, was what his old comrade was always destined to be.

Unwilling to listen to more of the creature's words, Mortarion left it behind, clinging desperately to what fragmentary pieces of reason he could still grasp. The shattering reality of his situation was inescapable. Willing or not, aware or not, Mortarion was to blame for bringing his sons to this place, and for exposing them to the insidious power that Typhus had been courting for his entire life.

Like Ignatius Grulgor before him becoming the Eater of Life, Calas Typhon would now forever be the undying Typhus, the Herald of the Destroyer Plague. Suspended by dark sorcery in the place between the decay of disease and new bloom of life, he was the embodiment of the Death Guard ideal: indestructible and ever-enduring. But what a grave price he had paid to achieve that status.

And not just him. Mortarion cast around, seeing the shambling, changed things that his legionaries were becoming. Every Death Guard he saw was caught in the throes of the same loathsome transformation. Their bodies were riots of mutation and metastasising plague vectors. Vile buboes and rivers of pus ran from dissolving, reforming flesh, as meat and bone became indistinguishable from rusting, corroded metal and crumbling ceramite. Bloated faces grew buds of insectile eyes, pseudopods reformed from fingers and arms, all of it happening in a sewer-stink fog of noxious, infectious exhalation.

Some of his men lay dazed and disturbed by the changes upon them, fighting their own bodies in battles Mortarion could only glimpse. Others had gone mad with the pain of the transformation, their reason broken and lost. Worst were those who seemed at ease with it, as if – like Typhus – they had been waiting for this moment to come to pass.

How long had they been in this unreal domain? Days or weeks? Months or years? The passage of time within the warp was as malleable as everything else about it. If they broke free, *where* would they find themselves? *When* would they be? The Death Guard might return to reality in some lost era of the distant past, revert into a future age millennia hence, or find that only a heartbeat had elapsed. *If we can return at all.*

No matter how much he might have wished otherwise, the primarch was on the same path as his sons. All too keenly, Mortarion felt the raging conflict within his blood, sensing the chimeric infection as it surged back and forth against the defences of his resolve. If his body was a fortress, then it was under siege by an enemy of unparalleled power. The poison would overwhelm him in an instant if he were to allow it, and there was a seductive nihilism to that possibility. All it would take would be for Mortarion to will it, and the line would be crossed.

He was beyond the point of no return. Only one choice remained. He could embrace the despair or fight on towards... *what?*

An eternity of weakness and suffering. Typhus' words pressed down on him. He could only see a battle without end. A war with only victims, not victors.

'I have failed my sons.' He gave voice to the thought without realising it, and the Reaper's utterance echoed back at him from the flaking plasteel walls of the warship's landing bay.

Guided only by his instinct, Mortarion had returned to where *Greenheart* had docked. His shuttle, once battle-ready and primed for war, now resembled a wreck exhumed from some quaggy marshland morass. It, like everything in the grasp of this septic reach of the immaterium, was beset by decay.

Out past the rusting dock cradle where *Greenheart*'s creaking space-frame lay suspended, were main doors sealing off the bay from space. The heavy barriers had sagged under their own weight and cracked open, allowing some fraction of the mind-twisting aurorae beyond to cast feverish light into the chamber. In any other circumstance, Mortarion would have expected the bay to suffer explosive decompression, but then this was *the warp*. And he was learning that nothing in this place mirrored the laws of the universe he had been born into.

The wild glow of the empyrean beckoned him. Out there was the source of his torment, he reasoned. Out there was where the forces corrupting his Legion had gathered. Out there was the end point.

Mortarion pulled back the hood over his pallid face and cast it away, staring that madness in the eye, gathering his strength to step through and confront the truth.

His boots rang with strange echoes as he advanced. The hull of the *Terminus Est* ranged away from him on all sides, the metal shifting and altering, growing like weeds. The other craft in the fleet hung about him as tarnished ornaments, tethered to a screaming sky of raw, inchoate force. Writhing colours made of delusion and impossible horizons folded way into infinity, but there was one unchanging constant.

Mortarion saw the sketch of what might be a god's face, upon it the form of three glaring eyes in a forbidding triad. He was gripped by the truth that it had been waiting an eternity for this moment to come.

Unbidden, the Reaper of Men's black and total despair took physical form around him, in a cloak as dark and hollow as the void between stars. The war in his blood seethed, burning him from within.

And here, Mortarion's hate and misery, every last iota of his rage and his melancholy, took shape in the single demand he bellowed into the warp. It was a cry of pure frustration, a spear hurled towards cruel fate and everyone who had ever condescended to name themselves as his 'father'.

'What do you want from me?'

When the answer came, the buzzing timbre and the distant, papery touch of the voice on his flesh was familiar to him. *'Defiance alone is not enough.'*

Mortarion's hearts seized in his chest. He recalled the first time he believed death was upon him, up on the blighted crags of Barbarus, and the moment his deepest despair had first showed itself. He failed that day, betrayed his promise to his kindred and his world. He had fallen while another stepped in to take the glory that had rightly been his, and the shame of it had never dimmed.

Then, the unfinished words were left incomplete, but now they were spoken in full – and the truth the Reaper of Men did not wish to face was made undeniable. *'To defeat death, you must become it. To endure beyond all, you must submit. If you wish to be granted deliverance from your agony, you must surrender your soul.'*

'I remember...'

Do I? Is anything in this place real?

The two parts of Mortarion's spirit warred, decay against defiance, submission versus rebellion, the future battling the past.

The vast and terrible shape hove closer, taking on definition. The form of it was protean, a huge colony-creature of writhing viral clades given dimension and singularity. It reached out for him, a colossal, leprous claw with three talons spreading wide to envelop Mortarion's sight. Upon the degenerated skin of it was the triad sigil, repeated over and over in fractal profusion, the same as the cluster of boils that manifested the primarch's exposure to the chimera virus.

'My champion. I will give you all you wish,' sounded the voice. *'A dominion of your own that can be shaped to your will. You will be what you always wanted to be. All you need do is take the Mark. Take it and swear loyalty.'*

SEVEN

Revelations
Knights
Black Sky

THERE WERE CITIES beneath the Imperial Palace that few would ever see.

Some were made of labyrinthine passageways, arcades and atria that led into the heart of the Earth, towards prohibited zones where only the Adeptus Custodes, the Silent Sisters and the Emperor Himself could venture. Others were the overbuilt remains of the first living complexes constructed in this place, great forests of stone pillars carved by intelligent machine-artisans during the Reign of the Iron Men.

Garro's destination was elsewhere, however. He arrived in a cavernous space three hundred metres below the Palace proper, a yawning abyss that resembled the inside of a gigantic beehive. Each compartment along the inner surface of the void was a prison cell, and like the defences of the White Mountain, they were shrouded by devices of ancient and intricate design built to limit the powers of the unnatural and the unearthly.

Almost all the cells were empty, their adamantium doors hanging open in the moist, blood-warm air. Those few that were occupied held captives of a particular kind – men and women who were too valuable to be executed and too dangerous to be sent beyond the immediate reach of the Emperor of Man and the Regent of Terra.

Garro rode a servitor-skimmer past the sealed cells and wondered who he would find within if he chose one at random and opened it.

Each one of these chambers holds another of Malcador's secrets, he thought. *Or worse than that? Perhaps they are confinement for his mistakes.*

Presently, he alighted from the skimmer before a cell door on the seventh tier, much to the shock and surprise of the guards standing watch there.

'You... you're not supposed to come down here,' said one of them.

Garro paid the statement no heed and surveyed the pair. Both men were in the grey of the Chosen, and they had an encampment of sorts set up on the wide catwalk, exhibiting ample evidence that they had been there for a long time. On a small folding table, Garro saw what looked like a roughly made book of plas-paper, lying open to show pages of dense red text.

'Ser Knight...' the other man said hopefully. 'Are we relieved?'

Garro shook his head and advanced to the adamantium door, leaning forward so the sensor mounted within could read the Mark of the Sigillite etched into his armour.

'We're not told anything,' said the first soldier. 'How goes the war, my lord?'

The cell door unlocked and Garro gave the men a look before he stepped inside. 'When it gets here, you will know.'

'The Emperor Protects,' said the soldier, clinging to the words as if they were an inviolate shield.

The door clanked shut behind him, and Garro took in the space. The cell was larger than he had expected, and curiously decorated with an eye towards the homely. A heavy blanket bisected the chamber, and as he took a step into the room, it rose to allow a slight and unassuming figure – a pale-skinned blonde woman in a simple shift dress – to pass around.

'Nathaniel. Hello again.' Euphrati Keeler gave him a nod of welcome and she smiled warmly, genuinely pleased to see him there. The moment was so ordinary, it was incongruous.

Garro found the same emotion pulling at the corner of his frown. 'Saint,' he replied, bowing slightly.

Keeler made a rude noise. 'Don't call me that. It makes you sound like Kyril. He's always doting on me with that word. *What do you wish, Saint? How may I aid you, Saint?*' She sighed. 'He has a good heart but he can be trying sometimes.'

'Where is your iterator?' Garro looked around, seeing a sleeping pallet in one corner and ephemera about it that might have belonged to the old man. He felt a momentary flash of concern. The last time he had spoken with Kyril Sindermann, on the aertropolis platform Hesperides, he had sensed the weight of ages in him. 'Is he well?'

'Kyril comes to visit me on occasion, but he spends most of his days carrying the word to those who wish to hear it. He is my conduit to the galaxy beyond the walls of the fortress.'

Garro raised an eyebrow, wondering how it was possible for an elderly human with no training and no combat prowess to move freely through the most secure complex on Terra without raising some kind of notice.

The woman walked to a wine jug and poured cups for both of them. 'We have a lot of friends,' she said, answering the unspoken question. 'More than even Malcador knows, I think.'

'The Sigillite turns a blind eye to it?'

'What he doesn't understand, he doesn't see.' She handed Garro a cup and he took it. The drinking vessel was tiny in his hand, like a child's miniature in the palm of an adult. 'But let me assuage your concern, Nathaniel. Kyril is better than he was. Stronger.'

'Did you help with that?'

Keeler gave a slight shrug. 'I think he thrives on challenging times. As long as he has something of import to say, I believe he'll outlive all of us.'

'A pity he is not here,' said Garro, meaning it. 'I would have liked to see him again.'

'I'm sure you will.' Keeler took a careful sip of wine. 'But you came here for me.'

'Aye.'

She shook her head and reached out, placing a hand on his vambrace. That radiant smile of hers shimmered just out of sight. 'We've been here before, Nathaniel. Each time the question sounds loudly in your thoughts, you seek me out. But you should know by now... I can only tell you what you already know.'

He smiled. 'That may be so. But I enjoy our conversations.' Garro looked upon this slight and unassuming woman, and wondered by what quirk of fate she had become what she was now. Euphrati Keeler, once a remembrancer with the fleets of the Great Crusade, carrying her picter into the unknown in order to document humanity's campaign, to reunite all Terra's disparate children and beat back the encroaching tide of alien influence beyond. That ordinary identity, that unremarkable destiny, had been obliterated by the events put in motion by the Warmaster's insurrection.

Something greater than all of them – Horus, Garro, Keeler herself – had been unlocked in those early, turbulent days. The woman had been forever changed, becoming a conduit for a higher power. Euphrati Keeler the artist and commoner had become Euphrati Keeler, Saint and Hallowed Soul.

She returned his smile. 'We are a strange pair, you and I. Both of us reborn in the same transformative fire.'

'Both on the same path?'

Keeler cocked her head. 'It will be your hand that sees me set to freedom.' She had said those words to him once before. 'It will be your sword that holds fast my safety. But not today.' She let her hand drop and stepped away. 'You are too early. It is not time.'

He put down the untouched wine cup. 'The Warmaster is close. You must know that. His forces advance on Sol even as we speak.'

'Horus has *always* been close,' she countered. 'It's not a matter of crude distance. He's here, right now, in the walls of this place. In every hive city and settlement. Everywhere a slow knife glitters and the wings of black flies rasp.' Keeler gestured at the cell around them. 'Be thankful you don't have the eyes with which to see.'

'All the more reason to get you away from here.' Garro felt himself falling towards an old and familiar argument once more.

'Horus isn't the one you are concerned about,' said Keeler, cutting down his next words before he uttered them. 'It is your gene-sire who haunts you.'

'Aye.' It took Garro a moment to allow himself to admit it. Before the Saint, there was no point denying anything.

'Mortarion has changed.' The warmth and light in Keeler's face faded and she became solemn. 'In ways you cannot imagine.'

Garro thought of the warped creatures he had first seen on the *Eisenstein* and then several times since – his old rival Grulgor and the abhorrent Lord of Flies. 'Will I face my primarch again?' Garro was suddenly aware of the weight of his weapons, his sword and his Paragon bolter hanging heavy from his battleplate.

'What would you do if you did?' Her hand went to her mouth, as if she wanted to shroud the question from the world. 'Do you believe that you could stop Mortarion? Kill him? Redeem him?'

'I have to try. I am sworn to you, and if you ask it, I will turn away from any confrontation. But–'

'But you wish it,' she said, and he nodded. After a long moment, Keeler spoke again. 'You look to me, Nathaniel. You look to the words of the *Lectitio Divinitatus* and the God-Emperor Himself for guidance... But in truth, you have never needed to find it in any of those places.' She walked back towards the far end of the cell. 'You've always known what to do, my captain. Trust your instincts.'

'I–' Garro raised his hand, words forming on his lips, but before he could utter them, a tone sounded from the vox-bead in the neck ring of his armour.

'*Agentia Primus,*' said a mechanical voice, '*the Sigillite summons you to the Hall of the Ages with all due alacrity.*'

'Malcador will be annoyed if you disobey him again.' Keeler showed that radiant smile once more, as she ducked under the makeshift curtain. 'Don't worry, Nathaniel. We will see each other once more, before the end.'

LOKEN WAS AT the back of the group as the loose pack of Knights-Errant strode into the tall, brightly lit chamber. It resembled the cathedrals of antiquity, all high arches and fluted stone columns supporting a vaulted ceiling – but unlike those buildings, the Hall of the Ages had no walls.

In each arch, where a place of pious worship might have sported chancels and great stained-glass windows of devotional art, there were ever-moving panes of holographic imagery.

The three-dimensional projections showed renderings of events from the history of the Imperium. Loken saw the volcanic obliteration of Ixlund from the Wars of Reunification on one side, and across the way, the Fall of the Hadean Spire in all its gore-spattered glory. He resisted the temptation to stand awhile and watch the projections loop through their short moments of theatre. Each was scaled to true size, so that an observer could walk amid the instance, side by side with war engines and Thunder Warriors, to capture some sense of what it might have been like to be there.

He wondered if, after all this was over, some holo-artist would commemorate the insurrection in the same way. *Or will this era be so shameful that we forever turn our faces from it?*

The thought brought a chill to him, abetted by the cold breeze coming through the arches. The Hall of the Ages was high up on the eastern ranges of the Palace, high enough that a human would need a heat-cloak if they strayed too far from the invisible thermal fields in the middle of the chamber.

Loken's attention drifted from the gigantic hololiths to pass over the last few Knights-Errant gathering in the hall. Those he did not know drew his gaze once again, and he couldn't help but allow his martial nature to come to the fore. He analysed them automatically, as if they were potential enemies. Which ones moved with the telltale motion of a legionary with an augmetic limb? Which gravitated towards the comfort of the shadows? Which stood boldly in the centre of the chamber, eschewing the merest suggestion of concealment?

Once, to look upon a fellow Space Marine and consider how one might be called upon to kill him was a fanciful idea, a notion bordering on crass and discreditable. *How things have changed for the worst,* Loken thought grimly.

On the way here, it had been impossible to miss the surge in activity taking place throughout the Palace's domains. Troops of Chosen jogged past the Knights-Errant, bearing weapons and equipment towards strongpoints, and flyers darted around in the hazy sky. Snatching surreptitious looks where he could, Loken spotted the bright yellow of Imperial Fist colours down on the lower tiers, as heavy tanks and companies of Dorn's legionaries deployed to their battle stations. The silent, crackling energy of warfare-to-come threaded through the air, and if Loken was honest with himself, the dread he felt at knowing Horus' arrival was imminent was tempered by a fierce kind of excitement.

And perhaps there was relief, too. One way or another, the war was going to end on Terra's shores, and after long years of enduring this bloody, horrific revolt, Loken was ready for it to happen. In battle, there was always clarity.

He looked into the sky, past the ghostly shapes of the few remaining suborbital plates, sighting the pale disc of Luna. The moon had been turned into a hardened strongpoint, her defences augmented with combat flotillas, automated systems and defensive grids. Further out towards the ranges of the asteroid belt and afar, he imagined battle preparations already under way. Some stations and war platforms had already gone vox-silent, locking down and preparing for the worst of fates.

What did the long-range scry-sensors see out there? he wondered. *What great terrors has the Warmaster held in reserve, saving them to be unleashed on this day?*

'That question will be answered soon enough.' Rubio moved up to stand by his side.

'I didn't speak it aloud.' Loken shot him a hard glare.

'In here, your thoughts are as loud as gunshots,' replied the psyker. Then he gave Loken a long, measuring look. 'Have you ever wondered why that is?'

'Whatever you are implying, Rubio, spit it out. Now is not the time for prolixity.'

Rubio tapped his temple. 'I think there is a touch of the warp in you.'

'Did Tormageddon knock something loose in your head, psyker?' Loken snapped back. His traitorous brother had almost killed Rubio during their mission to the *Vengeful Spirit*. 'Don't insult me.'

'Far from it. Although I did have time to think on this whilst I rested in a healing coma.' The other Knight-Errant raised his hands in a conciliatory gesture. 'I am merely commenting on... Well, call it an unexplored possibility.'

'Let it remain that,' Loken replied firmly. 'And in the interim, stay out of my head.'

'The pair of you quarrel too much.' The comment shot at them from the depths of a hooded cloak over a suit of aged, clanking battle armour. The voice was all too familiar.

'Severian?' Loken's eyes widened as the hooded figure revealed his face, showing the craggy, scarred map of all his years to the open air. 'I did wonder what had become of you.'

'You're not to call me that any more,' said the veteran Luna Wolf. 'By Malcador's edict, the man called Severian no longer exists.'

Rubio gave a wary nod. 'Show us the coin.'

'What coin?' said Loken.

Reluctantly, the other warrior fished into a pocket of the cloak and his hand returned with a silver disc, not unlike the ones Loken had seen as tokens of the Davinite Lodges in the days before Horus' rebellion. 'Name me Iapto,' he said, his breath emerging in a white cloud of exhalation as he rolled the coin between his thick fingers. 'It will fit me eventually.'

'As you wish... *Iapto*,' Loken allowed.

The warrior whom he knew as Severian had also been part of the ill-fated pathfinding mission to the Warmaster's flagship, but he seemed different now – like all of them gathered here. Each of the Knights-Errant was a changed soul. Some, like Loken, had been broken and made anew by the events of the insurrection. Others, like Garro and Rubio, had been torn from their previous existences and thrust into roles they had never expected. And then there were those like Severian, the warrior they called 'the Wolf', who seemed to grow to fit whatever circumstance the war put upon them.

'He summoned you too, then,' said Iapto, looking around. 'Do you feel it, lad? This isn't like before.' He raised a hand, fingering the cold air as if it were a tangible thing. 'The last apocalypse forms beneath our feet. I see it. Don't you?' He looked towards Rubio, who gave a slow nod of agreement. 'We'll be at the end soon enough.'

'I am not ready to die just yet,' Loken replied, answering without questioning where the words came from.

'No,' agreed the older warrior, turning towards the entrance as Malcador entered the great hall. 'But you *are* ready to die.'

Loken followed Iapto's line of sight and saw the Sigillite walk doggedly across the baroque mosaic flooring of the chamber, ignoring the panoply of simulated history around him. Silence fell, save for the metal clacking of Malcador's staff as he came closer. The great psyker looked refreshed and renewed, a different man from the solemn and grim one that had travelled back with the Knights-Errant from the White Mountain. Trailing behind him came his tall, waif-like adjutant, and he too was changed, but not for the better. The nervous, wavering energy the man had shown only hours before was gone and now he seemed a hollow vessel, a fragile mimic of the person Loken had previously seen.

Rubio observed the same thing and muttered darkly under his breath. Loken caught a name – *Wyntor*. 'You know that one?' he whispered.

'I don't think I do.' Rubio's reply was distant and cautious.

'This has been a long time coming,' said Malcador, his voice carrying. 'But as true as that is, it has come too quickly. What you have heard… What you suspect. It is so. The Warmaster Horus Lupercal, the turn-coat allies at his banner and the Ruinous Powers he has made his pacts with… They will be here very soon. The invasion of Sol will rage, and the page will turn to the siege of Terra in short order.'

None of the Knights-Errant spoke, but they exchanged glances and the same implicit question. *Why are we here?*

Malcador looked from one face to another. 'Some of you were recalled in the middle of a mission. Some have been waiting, biding their time…' He paused, and showed a cold smile as another armoured fig-ure emerged from among the hololiths. 'Others have been following their own paths.'

The last arrival, the tenth Knight-Errant, resolved into Garro. The battle-tarnished gold of his cuirass caught the light of a low sun as he nodded to the Sigillite, then found Loken and gave him the same ges-ture of acknowledgement. But of Helig Gallor, the other former Death Guard, there was no sign.

Malcador went on. 'I have assembled you here for one reason. Each legionary in this hall is of greater purpose than you can know. Each of you are bound by fate to become titans. In the crucible of the most brutal war the galaxy has ever known, you were tempered. But the duty which lies ahead is of such scope it dwarfs that conflict.' He paused to let them take in his words. 'When we leave this place, it will be to undertake the last orders I shall ever give you.'

'We will lead the fight to the Arch-Traitor, then?' The question came from Yotun, who stood with his arms folded and a ready challenge in his manner. He gestured at his face. 'Blind the baleful eye?'

The Sigillite's cold smile returned. 'No. That work is destined for other hands. You, my friend, will never raise your axe against Horus Lupercal.' Loken stiffened at Malcador's words, and he sensed the consternation spreading through the other assembled Knights-Errant. 'Let me say it clearly, so there is no misunderstanding,' continued the Sigillite. 'You believe you are gathered to meet the spear-tip of the Warmaster's invasion. You are mistaken.'

Disbelief swirled in Loken's thoughts, and he could not remain silent any longer. 'If we are not to take up arms against Horus, then what worth are we?' He cast around, meeting Garro's troubled gaze and Rubio's hooded glance. 'Everything we have done, everything we have become since the first shot was fired in anger on Isstvan, all of that has led us to this moment!' Loken took a step towards Malcador, and he saw the Sigillite's aspect shift, becoming defensive. 'Now the most decisive battle of the rebellion is unfolding and you wish us to... stand down?'

'The lad is right,' said Iapto. 'If this is some sort of test of our obedience, Sigillite, it's a poor one.'

Fittingly, it was Garro who summed up the mood of the gathered warriors. 'What if your order is refused?'

'Then untold trillions of human lives are doomed to vassalage and degradation,' Malcador answered, but his piercing gaze remained on Loken, lancing into his soul. 'An eternity of darkness falls across all the stars. And horrors will be unleashed. Things of such terrible dimension that their predations would make the worst deeds of Horus Lupercal seem like the bite of a fly.'

His words echoed around the hall with enough power behind them that Loken could not immediately summon a reply.

Then finally, mercifully, the Sigillite broke his gaze. 'I will show you,' he said to them, his words hushed but their force undiminished. 'Look here, and see what fate will transpire if my word is denied this day.' Malcador raised his hand and every one of the hololiths about the Hall of the Ages crackled and writhed. 'What appears next is not an illusion. Rather, it is a window into one of a billion skeins of time where the deed is left undone. Look without flinching, and *you will see.*'

At the Sigillite's unspoken command, the hololithic fields grew and merged into a twisted, flickering dome that enveloped them, blotting out the pillars of the chamber and the ceiling high above. The lambent forms of the historical projections fused into one another, flowing like mercury as figures from long-forgotten wars and distant vistas were repurposed into new forms.

And suddenly they were standing on a ridgeline staring at the Imperial Palace many kilometres distant, through a battle haze of aerosolised blood and human ash. As Loken watched, the massive, majestic keep of the Terran capital cracked from within, as if it were the shell of a gargantuan egg.

From the jagged fissures in the donjons and shield walls came floods of black oil as a dreadful colossus was birthed within. Tentacle-like appendages as big as battle cruisers burst out into the tainted air, and the Palace collapsed in on itself, bursting with fire and dust as its towers and gardens were torn asunder.

Out of the tumbling mountain of wreckage emerged a cephalopod creature covered in rheumy eyes and clacking beaks. It reached for the sky and screamed a blood-chilling birth-cry.

The scene reformed.

Now the blackness of space was the arena, and drifting before them was Terra herself, the wounded globe lit by millions of corpse-pyres across its nightside. Off to the edge of the shimmering vision, Loken beheld a broken grey hemisphere amid a slick of thick dust and planetesimal masses. It was all that remained of Luna, ripped apart by incredible forces and remade into a lethal ring system of blasted rock.

Warships by the thousands fought in this death zone, trading fire from massed batteries of mega-lasers and salvoes of cyclonic torpedoes. Then the distant yellow disc of Sol flashed with a sickly shimmer and in a blink it grew to fill the black sky. The unstoppable wave of a supernova shock-front engulfed the remnants of the moon and the dying ember of the Throneworld, and in the last moment before the white-out filled his vision, Loken glimpsed a cackling daemonic face at the heart of the fire.

And now the images picked up speed, each one changing faster than the one before.

Loken saw what could only be the grand capital of Ultramar laid out before him, but the once majestic boulevards of Magna Macragge Civitas were drenched in rivers of crimson, and where the great banners of the XIII Legion had once flown there were only ragged flags made of flayed human skin.

Everything that lived on this world was a slave to the monsters prowling in hell-forged shadows, the few survivors chained for their pain and suffering, alive only so they could be continually despoiled and abused for the amusement of these immortal fiends.

Another transition, swift and disturbing with its velocity: the endless night of deep space, and ranged against that backdrop a flotilla of desperate refugee ships of all kinds, engines flaring as panicked crews attempted to escape.

Then the night moved, great jaws as wide as worlds opening. The blackness came alive with a million laughing maws that swelled to savage the ships, biting them in twain, swallowing them whole.

Loken reeled. The images were coming thick and fast now, testing his constitution with their dizzying motion. They whirled around him in a hurricane of dire possibility, and everywhere he looked, he saw a greater and more profane sight than the last.

The unmistakable forms of dead primarchs, crucified against the walls of a fortress-monastery or hanging, decayed and ruined, from a giant gibbet. A daemonic mecha-engine of immeasurable size, its cogs carved from continents, its gears made from the cores of savaged planets. And at the end, the galaxy itself subsumed into a seething, infinite ocean of tormented souls, as the hell-scape of the immaterium spilled into real space and transformed this dimension into a wasteland of madness.

Then Malcador slammed the tip of his staff into the floor and all was as it had been. The hololiths moved through their rote loops of history, and the mournful wind among the pillars was the only sound. None of the Knights-Errant spoke. None of them could find the words to parse the sights the Sigillite had shown them.

Loken knew the images were unreal, nothing more than synthetic creations of light and sound – *was that not so?* But he felt sick inside, chilled by a deep, inner cold that leached the heat of life from his soul. The things Malcador had shown them were too tangible to be a fabrication. Somehow, the Sigillite had imbued the hololiths with a reality that made them more than just captured photons and simulated reality.

'How… can you know these things will come to pass?' Garro broke the silence, speaking in wounded, unsteady tones.

'I *know*,' Malcador told him. 'I have been there, to those otherwhens, my soul barely tethered to the now. I have walked as a phantom in those dark and terrible tomorrows. And they will come to pass unless you follow my word.'

'What would you have us do?' said Yotun, at length.

Malcador nodded and reached into a pocket of his robes, his hand returning with a small drawstring bag made of dark velvet. 'The first step is to leave all you were behind. Each of you were severed from your parent Legions when you became my Chosen, my Knights-Errant. You gave up your birthright. Now you must accept the erasure of what is left.' He walked to Yotun and the warrior held up a silver coin, similar to the one that Severian – now Iapto – had shown. 'You have already taken your new name, child of Fenris. Now take the last step.'

Malcador nodded, and Yotun bowed his head. The warrior wore a handful of charms about his armour, carved things that only a Son of Russ could have called his own. With grave formality, he broke the cord that held them in place and threw them to the floor. 'I am *Yotun*,' he said. 'I am a Knight.'

Beside him, Rubio marched forward and dropped his gladius to the floor, the carved Ultima in the hilt catching the light. He looked down at the sword, and then to Loken's shock, he revealed a coin of his own. 'I am *Koios*,' intoned the Codicier, looking into the distance. 'And I am a Knight.'

The dark-eyed warrior who kept to the shadows was next to speak his new name, offering his silver to the air. 'I am *Ianius*.'

'*Iapto*,' said the old Wolf, with a resigned bow of his head.

Malcador walked to Vardas Ison and pressed a coin into his hand. 'Voice it,' he commanded.

'*Satre,*' replied the warrior, reading the word etched into the metal before sparing Loken a wary glance. His other hand opened and a tiny, jewelled object fell from his fingers, a faceted fleck of bright ruby set on gold pinions.

'I am *Ogen.*' The legionary with sable hair and pale skin was stone-faced as he discarded a string of onyx beads carved to resemble the skulls of avians.

Next, the Sigillite moved to a hooded Knight who had never shown his face, and rolled another coin from the bag into his waiting palm. 'Never had a true name before.' The taciturn warrior's words were icy. He looked up, studying Malcador. 'This will do. I am *Epithemius.*'

'*Khyron.*' The hatchet-eyed legionary carrying a staff, who had been watching them all like a hawk from the very start now broke his silence to utter that single word, and in that moment it was clear that he would not speak again.

Then Malcador was standing before Loken, and the Sigillite pressed a silver coin into his palm. It was unusually heavy for something so small.

He looked down. The name on the disc was *Crius,* and Loken almost said it aloud. The word pushed at his lips, but he forced himself not to voice it.

Then he saw that the velvet bag was empty as the Sigillite let it drop from his fingers.

Nine names, he thought. *Nine tokens.* But there were ten Knights-Errant standing in the hall.

Slowly, all eyes turned towards Nathaniel Garro.

AT THE FAR end of the Hall of the Ages, a rectangular section of white stone groaned and dust fell from it as it retracted into an alcove. Revealed behind was a passageway, one of the hundreds of undocumented conduits that threaded through the walls of the Imperial Palace, into the great building's hidden spaces known by the few aware of them as 'the Shrouds'.

Garro stood rigidly as the other Knights-Errant began, one by one, to walk by him and make for the shadowed entrance. As Loken crossed his line of sight, the younger legionary gave him a solemn nod, an affirmation of respect between the two veterans.

His jaw set, Garro locked eyes with the Sigillite as Malcador approached, and for the first time in a long while, the warrior did not know what would come next.

Was this his end unfolding? Keeler had told him it was not so, but could the Saint be mistaken? Garro's thoughts turned inward and he looked back over all the times he had disobeyed Malcador's edicts, tested his limits and pushed at the boundary of the Sigillite's tolerance. Perhaps today he had reached the line that could not be crossed.

'This is as far as you will go, Nathaniel,' said Malcador. 'The others… Their destiny lies elsewhere.'

And then he knew. 'You are taking them to see *Him*.'

Malcador gave a nod. 'You wondered why I gave you a list of names, back at the start of all this. I never told you the reason. Not all of it. I let you infer and fill in the gaps yourself.'

'Those men you sent us to find, to bring back.' Garro looked away, watching the figures in grey troop past him. 'Rubio. The Nemean. Loken…'

'And the others. Not all of them are here, of course. Not all of them were meant to be. But there was a greater design in it. Now that plan moves into its final phase.'

He looked back at the Sigillite. 'So why am *I* here?' A kernel of annoyance came into being in the vault of his chest. 'You bring me to this, only to deny me the next step?'

'What do you think will happen, Nathaniel?'

'It is in the heart of every true servant of the Imperium to stand before the… the Emperor, and know His will.' In his haste, Garro had almost said *God-Emperor*, but he caught himself in time. 'How could I not wish to be a part of that?'

'He will not turn His face to you,' Malcador said, without weight.

'Not here. Not today. Whatever hopes you have, my friend, that doorway does not lead to their realisation.' He nodded towards the open passage. 'I do not say this to you as a reprimand. I speak in honesty, as you have always done to me.' He smiled thinly. 'After your selfless and devoted service, I owe you no less.'

'Not that selfless,' Garro admitted. Many was the time he had pursued his own agenda under cover of following the Sigillite's opaque orders, venturing to places off the map in search of other followers of the *Lectitio Divinitatus*, and the Saint herself.

Malcador raised an eyebrow. 'Captain. You know what I am. What I am capable of. Do you really believe there was ever a moment where I did not know what you were doing?'

Garro scowled. 'You are mighty,' he admitted, 'but you are not omnipotent.'

'True. But I do know people, and I do know *you*. I didn't need telepathic mastery across the entire planet to see the path Nathaniel Garro followed. Knowing the kind of man you are, knowing what you believe in, that was enough.'

'I have been your puppet all along, then?'

'You were never that,' said Malcador, affronted by the suggestion. 'I have too much respect for you.'

The admission was unexpected. 'Indeed?'

The Sigillite gave a low sigh. 'I have learned through bitter experience that the river of fate can be navigated, even diverted, but never halted. The wise man learns the currents, turns them to his own ends. You, Nathaniel, are being carried down a stream where I cannot follow. There is a duty here, far from where Loken and the others will be taken. You must fulfil it.'

Keeler. Her name was there on the tip of his tongue, and Garro knew that Malcador had to be reading it from the surface of his thoughts.

The Sigillite drew himself up, his manner becoming formal. 'Battle-Captain Nathaniel Garro. I release you from the mantle of Agentia Primus and my command, but you will retain the rank and privileges you have earned. From this moment on, you are free to do what you wish. You may determine your own future.'

Garro took a moment to process the decree. 'I am... masterless?'

Malcador nodded. 'I grant that to you. Because I know you will be guided by something greater. Your moral spirit. Your noble soul.' He walked forward, until he stood at Garro's side. 'I cannot control everything. I cannot account for every variable and possibility in this maddening vortex of war. So I set vectors moving, you see? I encourage, I coerce and cajole. I set others free and hope they find their true path.' He gave him a last nod, and stepped through the doorway. 'Good luck, my friend.'

When Garro turned to look back across the empty hall, he saw that one figure in grey remained. 'Rubio,' he said, then corrected himself. '*Koios*.'

The other warrior offered his hand. 'We haven't always seen eye to eye, captain. But I wish you were coming with us. It has been my honour to serve in your company... brother.'

'Indeed, brother.' Garro accepted his hand and their gauntlets clanked together. 'I hope you will forgive me for what I did to bring you here.' He had always felt a stab of guilt for compelling Rubio to go against the Edict of Nikaea on Calth, and against the strictures of his fellow Ultramarines.

'Tylos Rubio of the Twenty-First Company would not absolve you,' he replied, after a few seconds of silence. 'But Koios will.' He released his grip and passed from the hall.

The white stone rumbled back into place and sealed the passageway shut, the entrance to the Shrouds vanishing seamlessly into the structure of the walls.

In the cold vantage of the hall, there was a moment when Garro experienced a sense of colossal distance, an abyssal feeling of isolation that dwarfed anything he had known before.

Without a primarch, without a brotherhood, one could say there was no legionary more truly alone than he was in this instant. Then the emotion faded and was put aside.

Garro strode away, one hand upon the hilt of *Libertas*, as he marched towards the battlements and the war yet to come.

'Your purpose does not lie on Terra,' Malcador told them.

Loken's mind was still reeling with the import of what had taken place in the Hall of the Ages, and he found himself struggling to keep up. Even in his darkest moments, he had dared to hope that there was a greater purpose in all the madness and destruction he had witnessed, but the former Luna Wolf could never have known it would take this form.

The secret passage brought them to another chamber, a spherical space bordered by inky shadows and lined with humming power cores and other complex tech-arrays, whose purpose he could only guess at. In the middle of the hollow, a shape of curves and sharp points was hidden beneath a great drop-cloth of black silk, the form of it more than three times the height of a line legionary. Servitors with sealed-blank faces moved around the chamber completing tasks, clicking at one another as they used echolocation to navigate. Whatever the purpose of this place, Malcador did not wish anyone to see it.

'I showed you the deep future, the tomorrow where humanity is lost,' the Sigillite continued. 'Soon I will take you to another world where the foundations of a defence against it have been prepared. You will be the masters of that place. The finest weapons and advanced technologies await you in the citadel. A cadre of recruits, selected from across the galaxy, ready to be moulded into a fighting force like no other. A vault of the blackest secrets and my most forbidden knowledge, all at hand for you to pore over and come to command.' He nodded to himself. 'I will take you to build a Legion. Not for this war. Not for any war that the common of mind can comprehend. You will be masters of a knightly order to fight the war that never ends, in the realms beyond the real and into the infernal.'

'How can this be done?' said Yotun. 'An entire Legion cannot be forged whole overnight! Even at the greatest pace, it would take generations... Centuries, even.'

'Correct. And you will have the time you need.' Malcador looked across the group, finding the dark-eyed warrior. 'Ianius, you will lead your brothers in this. And you alone will know when the moment is right to return.'

'I do not understand,' Loken said quietly, his voice carrying through the chamber. 'All of us have seen the unnatural horrors that breach from the immaterium. We've fought these things in their variegated forms, dispatched them as best we can. Yet you show us a future when that fight has failed and bid us to change it before it comes to pass.'

'You seem to understand it well enough from my perspective,' said the Sigillite.

'Answer me this,' Loken replied. 'If this tragedy is inevitable, if it is, as you suggest, a greater danger than the Warmaster's rebellion… how will one Legion be able to stop it?'

'Will it shake your faith in me if I admit to a failure?' The answer did not come from Malcador, but from the air around them. 'I hope not. We remain human in some way, yes? Imperfect even as we seek a way to perfect ourselves.'

Malcador bowed deeply to a presence that shaped behind Loken, and the legionary was immediately overcome with an urge to sink to one knee as the voice took form, and the form became a figure, and the figure became–

'Rise, my children,' said the Emperor of Mankind, an earnest, fatherly smile playing across His lips. 'Rise. I would not have my loyal warriors stare at the ground while I converse with them.' As He spoke, the servitors in the chamber stopped dead in their tracks and dropped to the floor; only Wyntor, the Sigillite's dull-eyed adjutant, remained as he was, gazing blankly into nothing.

In the past, Loken had been gifted with the rare opportunity to stand in the same room as some of the greatest primarchs ever to draw breath, and in those moments he had known what it was to walk among warlords, demigods and beings out of myth.

All that paled to nothing in the Emperor's dazzling presence. Loken could not bring himself to meet the great being's scrutiny, but he could sense it on him, measuring and knowing him in all his fullness.

He stole glimpses of a gallant aspect, something elegant and hard as carved teakwood but noble and forceful in motion. The Master of Mankind's golden armour was a treasure house of elaborately crafted workings, inset with gems and precious metals, yet it moved with him in sinuous, flowing action. There was no hint of encumbrance or affectation there. This was a being in total and absolute control of His nature.

Loken could find no other emotion but awe to think that, in some small fraction, the blood in his veins bore a measure of the Emperor's great power within it.

'I will confide a truth to you,' He told them, beckoning Malcador to his feet as He passed him by. 'In the time before the Great Crusade, my inner eye was opened to the menaces unnumbered out in the void. The xenos. The strains of lost humanity too far gone to rejoin us. The witchkin and the mutant.'

The air thickened and grew dim. As He spoke, the Emperor moved slowly from warrior to warrior, studying them in turn as a mentor might consider a student on the cusp of their greatest trial.

'To defeat those threats I brought your gene-sires into being, and the Legions along with them. But there are other forces that crave the destruction of our civilisation. Forces I believed were held in check.'

Loken could barely believe what he was hearing. If the Emperor Himself feared these daemons, then what chance did they have?

'The Legiones Astartes were made to wage war in this universe, not the non-space of the warp. My errant sons...' He hesitated, and there was a knife of regret in the brief silence. 'In their eagerness to unseat me, they have broken a seal, and allowed an enemy you were never meant to fight into our reality.'

The Emperor stared into the eyes of Ianius and time seemed to stop. The expression on His face was unreadable, and Loken tasted the acidic tang of psionic force in the atmosphere. Then the moment faded and He moved on, seeking out the warrior who was now Koios.

'Although my friend and I have disagreed on much over the centuries, Malcador has been right about more things than he has not.' The Emperor examined Loken's comrade with equal intensity, before giving the Sigillite a questioning look. Malcador inclined his head, but no words were spoken, and at length the Master of Mankind moved on. 'It was he who conceived of the need for a new kind of weapon. He who brought me the design for a Legion unlike those that came before it. It was Malcador who convinced me that the war beyond this war is coming.'

Then the Emperor was standing over Loken, and the warrior was robbed of his voice, of everything but the will to stand and accept whatever command his highest lord would give him.

'I speak of a conflict where the infernal must be battled in kind, fire against fire, like against like,' He intoned. 'I will have you forge your souls into swords, your minds into shields. *If that is to be your fate.*' The last words echoed through Loken's spirit, as if spoken only to him and no other.

An icy claw of doubt seized his heart and Loken looked down as the Emperor moved away. *This is wrong,* said a voice in his head. *I should not be here.*

This is not my fate.

When Loken let his gaze rise again, there was only the nine of them, the servitors, the Sigillite and his adjutant. He felt oddly bereft, as if he had lived his life in darkness and briefly glimpsed the sun, only to have deep night fall again.

Malcador gave Wyntor a command, and the robed man walked stiffly to the veiled shape below the drop-cloth. Gathering up armfuls of the black silk, Wyntor pulled the covering away and let it fall to the floor.

Revealed there was a tall arc of what appeared to be bone. The surface was detailed with alien iconography and iridescent hemispheres that took on a soft, radiant glow as Malcador approached it. The sight of the construct was one more shock among all the others, but still it gave Loken hard pause.

'What is that doing here?' he said, in a low voice.

'Serving a greater cause,' Malcador replied. 'Now you understand what is at stake. You have been judged and found worthy.' He glanced back at the assembled warriors. 'What was given to you is for you only. Consider it a gift... A final word of guidance from the Emperor Himself.'

Wyntor laid his long-fingered hands on the glowing orbs that protruded from the sides of the bone arch, and as he did so, raw power from the battery modules arrayed around the chamber bled into the structure along sputtering cables.

'He shouldn't be able to do that,' said Yotun. 'Only one of *them* could–'

'Wyntor has a purpose to fulfil, just as we do.' *Was that remorse, or something else Loken heard in the Sigillite's terse reply?* He could not be certain.

'Your servile is not human,' said Koios. 'He never was.'

A faint sapphire glow began to gather in the crook of the arch, and Malcador looked up at it, the cold colour casting his face with ghostly shades. 'Wyntor is what I... He is what he needed to be. As am I. As are you.'

Thunder cracked around the chamber and the glittering mote of light grew into a rippling, coruscating ring. As Wyntor moved his hands in a complex dance, making glyphs in the static-filled air, the energy effect stabilised into a portal. Through it, Loken could see the hazy image of a smoky, orange-hued landscape pelted by harsh chemical rains. The rich odour of raw methane seeped back through the gateway.

'Titan,' said Satre. 'And the fortress there–'

'Prepared, as I said.' Malcador took a step towards the shimmering threshold. 'It is too dangerous to make the journey by starship, and time is no longer our ally. Quickly now. Go through, and I will show you your destiny.'

The group advanced towards the portal, but Loken did not move. The Sigillite saw his hesitation and turned back to face him.

'Crius,' he began, but Loken raised a hand.

'No,' said the warrior, producing the silver coin. 'I had another name once before and it didn't take. I am Garviel Loken. I was born as such and death will know me as the same.'

Malcador's expression became stony. The Sigillite was not a man who was often refused. 'Consider carefully what you say next. The arc of your life will turn upon it.'

'I have never been more certain of anything,' he replied, and Loken meant every word. 'With respect, Lord Regent... I refuse you.' He tossed the silver coin into the air and Malcador drew it into his clawed grip with a telekinetic pull. 'Whatever destiny I have, it lies on Terra, not Titan.'

Conflicted emotions passed over the Sigillite's face. It would have been a simple matter for the great psyker to compel Loken to obey him and follow to the distant Saturnian moon – but what righteousness would there have been in such an act? At length the coin vanished into the folds of his robes. 'Eight... Eight will carry the day, then.' He looked up at the warrior, who now stood alone on the far side of the chamber. 'As you wish, Loken.' Malcador stood silently by as Koios, Yotun and the others vanished through the gateway, with Wyntor trailing at their heels.

When only the two of them remained, Malcador gave Loken a terse nod of farewell and turned away, towards the portal.

'Horus will destroy you,' the Sigillite said quietly, without looking back, 'and Cerberus will not save you.'

'We'll see,' Loken replied, as the thunder cracked about him once again.

GARRO'S GAZE RANGED over the walls of the Imperial Palace, past the grand plaza beneath the tower where he stood, down and down across the distance to the Acensor's Gate and the glowing lights of the Sprawl Magnifican beyond it. To the south and the Katabatic Slopes, he saw flights of grav-carriers moving slowly through the dusk, great chains beneath them carrying the beweaponed ingots of superheavy tanks out to their muster points. In the Western Districts, the battle-horns of the Adeptus Titanicus formed a distant, ululating chorus, echoing their defiance off the mountain peaks and over city blocks. Garro could pick them out, shapes as tall as hab-towers moving with ponderous pace.

Up above, it was an unusually clear sky, slowly gathering in a cobalt shade as the sun fell towards the horizon. The light had a strangely perfect quality to it that was almost palpable.

A smile, genuine and human, split Nathaniel Garro's face. If he dwelt on everything that had conspired to bring him to this point, he might have buckled beneath the weight of it – but none of that mattered now.

The past and the path he had walked was sand in the storm, torn away and gone. All that mattered was the next moment, and the next, and the next. His purpose was at hand; it beat in his chest like the double-pulse of his hearts. Cut loose and without fetters upon him, Garro was free to enact the object of his will. He was a weapon of fate now, a blade drawn that never again would be sheathed.

He saw ranks of legionaries in the plaza below, in battered power armour the colour of storms. There, at the fore, Helig Gallor led them in weapons drill, and a forest of swords and bolters were raised in salute as they signalled battle readiness. The Seventy – *in name and honour if not in number*, he thought – were prepared to meet the enemy, no matter whose colours they wore.

Garro drew *Libertas* and matched their salute, holding his sword high by the hilt, with the blade aimed downward.

'Do you accept your role in this, Nathaniel Garro?' He asked himself the question, whispering it, casting it away. 'Will you give your life for the God-Emperor and the Imperial Truth?' His voice rose. 'Do you promise to stand in defiance of those you once called brother?'

'It needs two of us to make that formal.' Another figure in grey armour walked to the edge of the battlements and cast a glance in his direction.

'Loken?' Garro's eyes widened in surprise. 'How are you still here–?'

'I am where I am meant to be,' he replied. 'What Malcador wanted… That was not my fate.'

'You refused him?'

'Do you think he'll carry a grudge?'

'I do not care.' Garro let out a laugh. 'I am glad you are here, Garviel. Our odds have just improved.' He saw that the other warrior now carried a second sword in addition to his own, a weapon with a familiar golden Ultima forged into the hilt. 'That is Rubio's blade...'

'Aye,' said Loken, with a wary shrug. 'Seemed foolish to leave it there to gather dust, don't you think?' He nodded at *Libertas*. 'Shall we finish this?'

Garro took a breath, and closed out the oath. 'Do you pledge to protect the Imperium to your dying moment?' Then he placed his hand on the weapon, and Loken did the same.

With one voice, they spoke the affirmation. 'On this matter, and by this weapon, I swear.'

As the winds took their oath of moment, the warriors turned their gazes upward. In the new night above them, from across the infinite and the blood-soaked fields of countless battles, distant, glittering pinpricks of brilliant light signalled the fire of vast weapons on the edge of interstellar space.

Out there a million jagged blades of shadow clashed in the darkness, and the promise of a glorious death beckoned.

CODA

'SWEAR YOUR LOYALTY to me.'

Bowed down upon one knee, Mortarion could not hold his gaze towards the black, blasted mud of Barbarus, and he looked up, into the shining eyes of the Newcomer. The stranger's words seemed to stop the passage of time. An aura of power, vast and barely contained, crackled about him.

He looked into Mortarion's eyes and saw into the murky depths of his soul, to the lost and forgotten places within that the Reaper of Men kept hidden even from himself.

Mortarion's jaw stiffened. He did not want to be an open book. He did not want to–

'Give your fealty to the Grandfather.'

Bowed down upon one knee, Mortarion could not hold his gaze towards the rusted, broken steel of the *Terminus Est*, and he looked up, into the menacing eyes of the great entity that swallowed the wild sky.

The god-thing's utterance made the strings of reality hum and resonate. A dark ether of corruption was falling like thick sleet, thickening
the space around him.

The entity that called itself the Grandfather filled Mortarion's lungs
with spores of living death and opened him up from within, teasing
apart sealed spaces to find the rich meat of his unseen fears and his
most secret hopes.

Mortarion's fists clenched. He could feel his soul stripped bare. There
was–

'YOU HAVE CHOSEN the only path you can,' said his father *said the
grandfather*. 'You are my son *you are my champion and I have waited so
very long for you* and this day's dawning has been long awaited.'

Time and moment, past and present, the structures of them crumbled
and turned into sand, smothering Mortarion in the elsewhen.

He was there on Barbarus and it was decades gone *and he was here
in the utter insanity of the immaterium*. Together and *separated*, divided
and *merging*.

His father, the Emperor of Mankind *his patron, the Lord of Decay Nurgle*
beckoned to him, offering Mortarion what he could not refuse. His
oath and his honour forbade him from taking any other path from
this moment forward.

He had sworn to bend the knee to the stranger at the lodge if he could
not defeat the High Overlord *and he had avowed to protect his gene-sons
and his Legion beyond all else*.

Mortarion struggled, frantically trying to grasp the truth *and the lies*,
desperate to separate *the ragged, deathly present* from the echoing, ashen
past. Which was his reality, or were all things true?

'What price is an oath given in madness?' He whispered the words
he howled them into the void.

'What do you want, my son?'

'What do you want, my champion?'

The voices merged into a single titanic reverberation, through his bones and physical form, into the bounds of his turbulent and unquiet psyche.

'I want... to *endure*.'

'THEN RISE,' SAID the stranger.

'Rise, Mortarion. There is a brotherhood awaiting you out in the stars, the like of which you cannot comprehend. And with it, a purpose that will illuminate the galaxy. A crusade, upon which your name will be etched into eternity.'

'THEN RISE,' THE Grandfather told him.

'Rise as a Prince Born of Death. Vengeance awaits you in the realm of men, and with it the blackest, most dire purpose. A slaughter, by which your name will be feared, until the last human soul fades to entropy.'

MORTARION SAID THE vow without reservation, then. 'I give myself to your banner. My blood and my bone, the unbroken force of my will and the power of my spirit. These are yours to command, if you grant me deliverance.'

His hand found the damaged, cracked blade of his war-scythe and he gripped it hard enough to cut metal and draw blood. 'By this I so swear.'

He looked down *and saw the transformation take hold of him.*

A force of immeasurable mutational power crashed through his physical form and overwhelmed the pitiful limits of flesh and blood.

Mortarion tore away, rising to his feet, changing with each heartbeat. From his spine burst pestilent, insectile wings that quivered and crackled with new change. His soul soaked in the corrupting energy, dying and living, reborn and obliterated.

The flesh across his gaunt features pulled tight, dragging his mouth into a rictus grin. The smile of Death itself.

He would endure.

'WELCOME HOME,' SAID *the voices.*

✠ ✠ ✠

[The Sol System; now]

THE WARP PUCKERED beneath the surface of reality before detonating into existence.

It was an ugly, catastrophic eruption that vomited raw madness and broken shards of tainted impossibility. Opening into a festering wound on the face of space-time, the tear in actuality defied the pathetic rules of what was and what could be. Freakish things that could not live outside of nightmares became solid for brief moments, the sheer force of the breach willing them into existence.

Around the rippling, shrieking edges of the tear, great coruscating tides of lethal radiation and charm-tainted particle storms turned the airless void into a blaze of soul-twisting pseudo-colours. And from their becalmed prison in the deeps of the immaterium, the flotilla of the Death Guard Legion found their escape.

Hundreds of rusting war hulks burst forth into the skies around the greatest bastion of the Emperor's Imperium, soiling the darkness with their presence as the rays of faraway Sol fell upon their blighted hulls. Daggers of corroding metal that had once been proud symbols of the XIV Legion poured out, and wove among one another as carrion flies would swarm about a hunk of bloody meat. Gargantuan battle-barges came with them, slow and ponderous, trailing streamers of decay and poisonous effluent.

At length, when the blighted fleet had passed through the portal in its entirety, the wound in space snapped shut. Slowly, the mass of nondead matter and diseased steel that was the Death Guard reborn turned their bows towards distant Terra.

That world was beheld in the eye of a gaunt and skeletal being, a towering hooded Reaper clasping a giant scythe in one clawed hand. He raised the other, to point towards the glittering ember, flexing the muscles and seething blood of his changed form in the action. The order was given in silence.

Lost there in the dire shadows of his fathomless hood, Mortarion allowed himself a smile.

ACKNOWLEDGEMENTS

First, and most specifically for their support and counsel during the writing of *The Buried Dagger*, my thanks go to Nick Kyme, Laurie Goulding, John French, Chris Wraight and Josh Reynolds.

Along with them, I raise the Cups to my other comrades in (literary) battle, with whom I have been honoured to march on the long road to Terra over the past decade – Dan Abnett, Alan Bligh, Ben Counter, Aaron Dembski-Bowden, Christian Dunn, Marc Gascoigne, Toby Longworth, Graham McNeill, Lindsey Priestley, Neil Roberts and Gav Thorpe.

And finally, a salute in the ancient and martial manner to all my readers. I want to thank every one of you for your support of my writing in the Horus Heresy saga over the past eleven years, and for your dedication and loyalty in allowing us at Black Library to craft this epic mythology. We couldn't have made this journey without you.

Here's to fellow travellers and absent friends.

ABOUT THE AUTHOR

James Swallow is the author of the Horus Heresy novels *Fear to Tread* and *Nemesis*, which both reached the *New York Times* bestseller lists. Also for the Horus Heresy, he has written *The Flight of the Eisenstein*, *The Buried Dagger* and a series of audio dramas featuring the character Nathaniel Garro, the prose versions of which have now been collected into the anthology *Garro*. For Warhammer 40,000, he is best known for his four Blood Angels novels, the audio drama *Heart of Rage,* and his two Sisters of Battle novels. His short fiction has appeared in *Legends of the Space Marines* and *Tales of Heresy*.

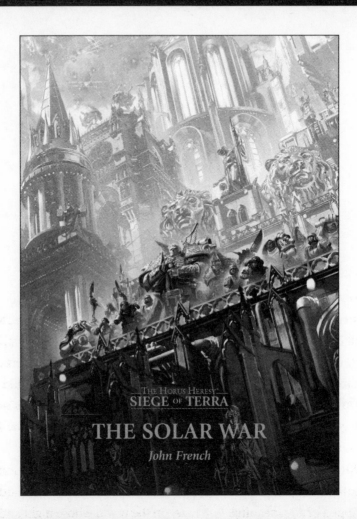

THE SOLAR WAR
by John French

After years of devastating war, Horus and his forces have arrived at Terra. But before they can set foot on the Throneworld, they must first break the defences of the Sol System.

An extract from
The Solar War
by John French

ON THE FIRST of Primus the sirens rang across Terra.

On the myriad worlds conquered and ruled by the Imperium of Man, they talked of year divisions, of time sliced into a thousand equal slivers. First division, second division, third, and so on, without variation or character, until the weight of counting reached a thousand, and one year tipped over into the next. On worlds of endless night or blinding days, a year was the same. In an empire spanning a galaxy, anything else would have been meaningless.

0000014.M31 was how surviving records would mark the first moment of that day, stamped and corrected for temporal accuracy, standardised and stripped of any meaning. But, here, on the world whose night and day and seasons had given mankind its concept of time, the old counting still meant something and so did the moment that one year died and another was born: the Feast of Two Faces, the Day of New Light, the Renewal – on and on went its names. But for longer than memory it had been the first of Primus, firstborn of the three hundred and sixty-five days that would follow, a day of hope and new beginnings.

The turning of that year began with snow on the northern battlements of the Imperial Palace, where three brother demigods watched the night skies above. It began with the dawn light and icy chill reaching into a tower-top chamber and stirring the painted cards dealt by a man who was older than any knew. It began with the sirens calling out, one at first, high on the Palace spires, before the cry was picked up by others, on and on across the turning globe. The sound echoed through the mountain-sized space ports and rasped from vox-horns in the deep strata of the Atlantean Hives.

On and on it went, stilling the hands of people as they ate and worked. They looked up. In caves beneath the earth, and hive vaults, and under the smog drifts, they looked up. Of those that could see the sky, a few thought they could make out new stars amongst the firmament and froze at the promise of each pinprick of light: a promise of fire and ash and an age of loss. And with the sound of sirens, fear spread, unnamed but still spoken.

'He is here,' they said.

Prison ship Aeacus, *Uranus high orbit*

'I understand you have a story...' she said. The wolf stood before her, the fur of its back silver beneath the moonlight. 'A particularly entertaining one. I'd like to remember it, for posterity.'

The wolf turned, its teeth a smile of sorrow.

'Which story?'

'Horus killing the Emperor.'

Mersadie Oliton woke from the memory-dream with sweat on her face. She breathed, and pulled the blanket over her from where it had slipped onto the floor. The air was cool and dank in the cell, scented with the tang of air that had been exhaled too much. She blinked for a second. Something was different. She reached out a hand and touched the metal wall. Moisture clung to the rivets and rust scabs. The thrum of the ship's engines had gone. Wherever they were, they were stationary in the void.

She let her hand drop and let out a breath. The tatters of the memory-dream still clung to her eyelids. She focused, trying to pull back the threads of the dream even as they slid into darkness.

'I must remember...' she said to herself.

'The prisoner will stand and face the wall.' The voice boomed out of the speaker set above the cell door.

She stood instinctively. She wore a grey jumpsuit, worn and faded. She put her hands on the wall, fingers splayed. The door unlocked with a clang, and footsteps sounded on the grated floor. The guard would be one just like the rest: crimson-clad and silver-masked, the humanity in its voice concealed by vox distortion. All the gaolers were the same, as constant as the ticking of a clock that never struck the hour.

Small spaces, locked doors, questions and suspicions – such had been her world for the seven years since she had come back to the Solar System. That was the price for what she had seen, for what she remembered. She had been a remembrancer, one of the thousands of artists, writers and scholars sent out to witness the Great Crusade as it brought the light of reason to a reunited humanity. That had been her purpose: to see, to remember. Like many clear purposes and shining futures, it had not worked out that way.

She heard the footsteps stop behind her, and knew the guard would be placing a bowl of water and a fresh jumpsuit on the floor.

'Where are we?' she asked, hearing the question come from her mouth before she could stop it.

Silence.

She waited. There would not be a punishment for her asking, no beatings, no withdrawal of food or humiliation – that was not how this imprisonment worked. The punishment was silence. She had no doubt that other, more visceral methods were used on other prisoners – she had heard the screams. But for her there had only been silence. Seven years of silence. They did not need to ask her questions, after all. They had taken the memory spools out of her skull, and those recordings would have told them everything they wanted and more.

BLACK LIBRARY

Including
Limited
and Special
Editions

Multiple
formats
available

MP3 AUDIOBOOKS | BOOKS | EBOOKS

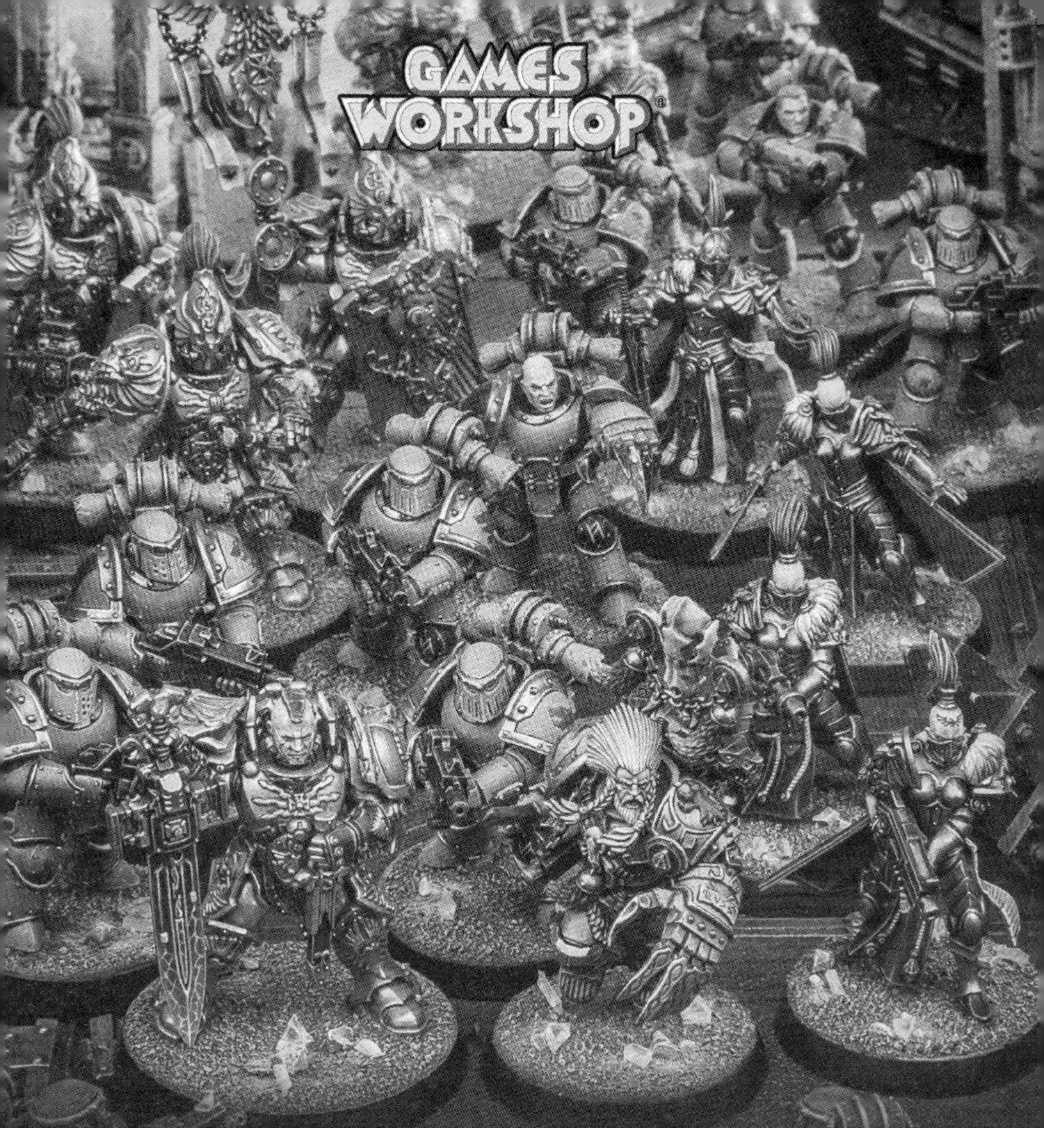
GAMES WORKSHOP®